LET'S
DANCE

Let's Dance

Typesetting and Cover Design by FormattingExperts.com

LET'S DANCE

BRIAN PICKERING

To
Linda and Rachel
who believed I could do it

ACKNOWLEDGEMENTS

My sincere thanks to Jeffrey Buchanan for his support and encouragement in writing this story. He was generous with his time and with his comments on early versions of the opening chapters. And Janet Pickering who gave time and effort to proof the manuscript and check for inconsistencies.

Any faults or errors remaining are entirely mine.

1

It wasn't the kind of thing you expected to find in the religion section of a school library. Thomas Frampton wasn't particularly religious. From the age of about ten or eleven, he'd picked up that people like him were predestined to suffer eternal torment cast down into perpetual damnation, or words to that effect. Over the following four years, he'd looked through whatever books he could find here or in the Weymouth Municipal Library to find out more about who he was attracted to, to try and make sense of how he felt without being scared by what might happen when he died. He even toyed with becoming a Catholic but had been intimidated by angry looking nuns at St Jude's. They weren't the romantic iconic types like the Carmelites, instead wearing navy-blue crimplene skirts to just below the knee, short veils and hand-knitted cardigans.

This part of the library was right at the end, away from the double doors at the entrance and the librarian's office. It was a narrow bay on the back wall, where he took refuge at free periods. Since the Boys' Grammar had gone co-ed two years ago and mixed not with the Girls' High School as they'd expected, but with a rough comprehensive on the outskirts of town, he'd found it paid to avoid the other lot. In turn, they would not be seen dead in a library. When they'd first become the jauntily named Jordan Hill Comprehensive in deference to the Roman site not far away, Tom had been quite excited. There would be more boys now, and he'd found that the ex-comprehensive ones seemed to be physically more mature and well-built. The skinnier, wan ex-grammar-school pupils and the brawnier new arrivals rarely mixed though.

Finding himself alone this period, Tom had strayed into the religious section as usual just on the off chance there might be something new and maybe a bit more enlightened now they had girls. But it was the same old stuff. He took down the *Illustrated Children's Bible* from its shelf about a third of the way up and sat cross-legged on his rolled-up blazer ready to flick idly through the pages. Someone had given his sister, Lottie, a copy for her confirmation, and Tom had liked looking at some of the pictures. He'd grown up, therefore, thinking that Jesus was fair-skinned, had long blonde hair and a goatee. The disciples looked like a rock band. The archangel Gabriel was a strapping blonde too, and Tom fantasised for a while that Gabriel might pop down sometime on a night-time visitation. His favourite though was Saul on the road to Damascus. He liked pictures of Roman gladiators and centurions anyway, though he never understood what appeared to be skirts hanging down over muscly legs. Saul was a particularly fine specimen of manhood. Lying on the ground having fallen from his horse, his rugged face turned up to Heaven and a strange light breaking through the clouds, his breastplate was particularly muscly and shiny. Tom believed that all Romans were fit with broad and well-defined chests, because that's what the breastplates looked like.

The book fell open unsurprisingly at Saul's dramatic conversion, when Tom noticed something from behind where the book had been on the shelf. This part of the school was all prefabricated sections, taped together it seemed, offering little insulation either from the heat in summer or the cold in winter, and with no soundproofing at all. Tom checked again the partition wall behind where he'd taken the book down. The adhesive tape had finally lost all stickiness and fallen away from the join. It must be a new crack between the partition panels, because where the tape had been was still pretty clean. There was light coming through from the other side, and if Tom stuck his head between the shelves to get close enough, blocking out the light from the expanse of windows in the library, he could just about make out the room beyond.

At first, it was just an empty and rather small room he thought. But then someone appeared. He was tall and the slit showed him from his thighs to a little way up his back only. As Tom peered, he realised it was Mr Woodcock, the P.E. teacher – he recognised the tracksuit bottoms. Tom didn't know what to do. He was transfixed and couldn't pull himself away, but he feared being caught, not least by an accusing eye looking back at him from the other side. Mr Woodcock was well-built. His name had caused much immature comment when he'd first arrived a few years ago. No one would dare say anything to his face though. He walked round, usually a good head taller than all the pupils, and wore a nascent sneer on his face which added to the perception of hard man. Tom caught himself speculating whether there was even partial truth in his surname.

He watched as Mr Woodcock began to undress, taking his t-shirt off first and rubbing it across his back to wipe the sweat off. For a while, Tom had wondered whether to sign up for extra sport just to be able to enjoy the teacher's physique. But common sense had prevailed when his closest friend, Paul Armstrong, had pointed out that Tom was no sportsman. He knew Mr Woodcock was relatively hairy. He'd been caught one P.E. lesson when the teacher had stretched up to demonstrate a shot at goal and the t-shirt had ridden up to reveal a few inches of flesh. He'd been looking at the pattern of dark hairs in the small of his teacher's back, fascinated by how they seemed to point down towards the crack between the bum cheeks, and wondering how far they might go over his buttocks.

"You're supposed to be looking at my outstretched hand holding the basketball, Frampton, not my backside!"

Tom was startled and flushed slightly. His classmates teased him as a "shirt lifter" for a few weeks after that until they latched onto someone else to taunt. But Tom had never forgotten the feeling of seeing that taut, slightly hairy back. He'd set off to Bournemouth City Library that weekend, searching for some explanation or at least comfort from their better-stocked and more liberal shelves. And he'd been quite relieved to see that adolescent crushes on a male P.E. teacher were a common rite of passage. He picked out one book with a broken spine and grubby finger marks on many of the pages which explained that this was perfectly natural since hormonal changes as a boy grows into puberty makes them more sensitive to the archetypal masculine physique. He would grow out of it, they said. Tom was still waiting.

He caught his breath when Mr Woodcock took down first his tracksuit bottoms and then his briefs. Tom felt he was sweating. He wondered if the teacher would turn round, perhaps, or even just a half-turn to show his body in profile. Instead, he bent over and picked up his towel and headed out of view. A few minutes later, Tom could hear the splash of water as presumably Mr Woodcock had got into the shower in the teachers' changing rooms. Although perched up painfully on his folded legs, Tom didn't feel any physical discomfort. He was too busy trying to think whether there was another room somewhere that might just provide a similar peephole onto the shower cubicle itself.

The water stopped and Mr Woodcock came back into view. He held the cheap and barely adequate towel round his waist not leaving much to the imagination. The teacher turned his back to the wall again and began to dry himself off, his buttocks glistening as water droplets slowly formed into rivulets running down onto his thighs, emphasising how firm and round his cheeks were. He stood once more and turned this time to face the wall. Tom gasped and clasped his hand over his mouth, hoping no one had heard. His eyes widened.

"The Bible!?" Tom jumped and snapped the book shut loudly. "You're not turning weird on me, are you?" Paul stood at the end of the bay, silhouetted against the sunshine from the windows opposite. Fully clothed, with the sun behind him, Paul had all the same curves and tautness as Mr Woodcock, just a younger version. Tom was relieved it was his friend and no one else, as he carefully replaced the *Illustrated Children's Bible* onto the shelf where it belonged, fussing a little with the other books to make sure the split between partition sections was hidden. "Here. Give us a hand, Paul," Tom was stuck. He hadn't appreciated that trying to kneel up with his legs crossed would numb his legs. He held out his left hand, expecting Paul to take it in his left, handshake style. Instead, Paul repositioned himself against the bookcase Tom had just been peering through and took hold of his friend's hand in his right. Hand in hand, like a couple might do, Tom thought. Back on his feet, though, Paul withdrew his hand immediately and stepped away from the confined space of the shelving bay.

Eddie Armstrong married Peggy Bennett a year before Paul was born. He'd worked at the ferry terminal but had had a serious accident when Paul was still a toddler. Falling between the quayside and a boat, his pelvis and thighs had been crushed. It had been touch-and-go for some months, but finally he was allowed home. He never worked again. Paul was only three, and apart from anything else, the accident had left him an only child. To start with, Nana Kathleen, Eddie's mother, had helped Peggy care for her son. Although she had enough to do with Paul, she didn't complain about looking after Eddie. 'Till death us do part,' she would often say. But from about six, Paul had been expected to do his share of caring for his father.

At that time, Peggy worked nights to try and bring some money in to top up Eddie's disability benefits. But then she'd changed to evenings, starting work at about five thirty, cleaning shops and other premises once they'd closed. So Paul had been in sole charge from when he'd got home from school till he'd taken himself to bed.

"Wow, that's harsh. That doesn't really sound very fair," Tom had said when they were about thirteen.

"Oh, I don't know," Paul had answered, "I've never known anything different. I'm used to it really."

Nana Irene, Peggy's mother, would sometimes pop in to check things were alright. Those were rare occasions now, though. Apparently, there was some kind of scandal about Reg, Irene's husband. No one ever mentioned it, and it wasn't until Nana Irene's funeral that Paul had found out he had a grandfather on that side at all.

"So," Tom put his fingers together with his elbows on the desk in front of him, "what was this scandal with old Reggie, then?"

"No idea!" said Paul.

"God, you're so unimaginative, Paul. Maybe he was a gangster, like the Kray Twins?"

"What, with a name like Reginald Bennett?"

The pair of them laughed. It was true, though, Paul wasn't really interested in what his grandfather had done. Since Nana Irene had never mentioned anything, he'd never thought to ask. Peggy had once tapped the side of her nose and nodded knowingly when her sister, Jessie, had come over and they were in the parlour having tea. But that was it.

Spending such a lot of time on his own making sure his father was alright, Paul had got used to his own company. He read anything he could get his hands on. He'd got through everything in the house before he left primary school. He'd then started working his way methodically through what the public library had to offer. At fifteen, he'd stumbled across *Lady Chatterley's Lover*, which he'd enjoyed, as well as *The Go-Between*. This he'd followed with *What Maisie Knew*, and thought about how the child in each had been exploited by unthinking parents. The poor child would be scarred for life, Paul thought. But they described a world that was alien to him. They were set in some other era and told of people he'd never met.

When he'd tried to take out *Maurice*, just because it was there on the shelf, the library assistant had stared at him sternly over her half-moon spectacles.

"How old are you?" she demanded.

"Fifteen. Why?"

"And why do you wish to read this smut?"

Paul didn't know what she meant.

"I've read everything else," said Paul, thinking the library should have a better range.

Still staring at him, the assistant backed away over to a colleague and whispered something to her without turning her back on him. The other librarian put down the books she'd been dealing with and looked back over her shoulder at Paul, eying him up suspiciously. He was beginning to feel decidedly uncomfortable as well as rather annoyed. Eventually, the library assistant came back over. Picking the book up by one corner and with a look of distaste on her face, she dropped it onto the returns trolley.

"Sorry," she said, "You'll have to pick something else."

"No problem," said Paul, "I'll go to a proper library."

The following Monday, Paul went to see the school librarian.

"Excuse me, Mrs Swale," Paul began politely, "Would you happen to have a copy of *Maurice*, please?"

"Of course," she replied. She'd known Paul for many years now and knew too that Miss Mobberley in the English Department spoke highly of his breadth of reading.

"May I borrow a copy, please?" Paul went on.

"Sadly, no," said Mrs Swale. "You'll have to read it in the library."

Like all he read, Paul would tell Tom what it was about. Tom was doing well with music, and it was an unspoken agreement. That way, Tom might find inspiration for songs. So Paul explained about *Tristan and Iseult* when they were sitting on the seawall looking out to sea. About forgetting to change the black sails to white, and Tristan believing Iseult to be dead. And *Young Werther* committing suicide because of his love for Lotte which she doesn't return even marrying someone else.

"Clearly not my sister, then," Tom joked. Then he added: "Does anyone live happily ever after?"

"Literature is made up of conflict," Paul laughed. "I suppose there's always *Maurice*, strangely enough."

A week or so later, Tom and Paul were in the public library together after school. Paul couldn't stay long. He needed to get back. But it was on the way, and Tom only wanted a classical score for schoolwork. At the checkout desk, Tom put the score of *Götterdämmerung* open on the page for date stamping while he found his library card in his blazer pocket. The same assistant librarian that had refused Paul the book the previous week came over to issue Tom's book.

"He's read it, you know," he said to her. Paul was horrified and mouthed 'Stop it!' to his friend.

The librarian looked at him blankly.

"That book. *Maurice*," he explained.

She started as she remembered. "Filth!" was all she said.

Tom started to pack the score in his bag.

"So, it's alright to inflict Nazi sympathisers like Wagner on students, but not a love story by one of our greatest novelists, is it?"

"I'd keep your views to yourself, young man," said the assistant. "Wagner is a great composer." The head librarian had looked up and was coming over. Paul pushed Tom towards the door and outside. They walked on for a few minutes in silence. Tom expected Paul to berate him for showing him up in public.

"Thanks for looking out for me," he said, much to his friend's surprise.

"That's OK," said Tom, beaming and striding out more confidently. He'd have slapped Paul on the shoulder, put his arm around him, and walked on like that for a few hundred yards like buddies do. But they weren't like that. "You watch my back, so I do the same for you." Paul liked the sound of that. After all, friends look out for each other, that's perfectly normal.

"When have I ever done that for you, though?" Paul looked puzzled.

"No one dares call me a queer or anything when you're around," he smiled at Paul, aware of the irony.

"Anytime," Paul smiled too, and they walked on, talking about nothing much.

The next day, Tom and Paul were summoned to the

Deputy Head's office. Mr Gapes looked at them disapprovingly. Mrs Swale, the librarian, was in the office with him.

"We've had a complaint, Frampton," he started.

"Sir?" said Tom.

"The public library has complained about your attitude."

"Attitude, Sir?" Tom didn't really know what Mr Gapes meant. Paul thought he did, though, and blushed slightly. He wondered how they'd known their names until he remembered that Tom had handed over his library ticket, of course.

"In future," Mr Gapes continued, "you will be more civil to the staff. You are to stay away from the library for the rest of this term, and write an apology, which I will vet before it is sent. Both of you."

"But, Sir," protested Tom. "Why is it acceptable for some aristocrat to spread her legs for the gardener…"

"That will do, Frampton. The matter is closed." Mr Gapes shuffled papers on his desk to indicate the meeting was now over.

"No, but seriously, Mr Gapes, there seems to be double standards here." Tom was genuinely upset.

"With respect, Sir, E. M. Forster is a very well-respected novelist, Sir," Paul added.

Everyone looked at Paul at the same time. No one had expected him to speak.

"The matter is closed, Armstrong…" Mr Gapes was saying.

"What's wrong with homosexuality, Sir?" Paul was quite serious.

"Enough, Armstrong! I will not have language like that when there are ladies present." Mr Gapes was becoming angry. Mrs Swale stood up and showed the two friends to the door.

"Thank you, Mr Frampton, Mr Armstrong. You can go now," she said, giving each a little nod.

"They've got a point," she said once she'd closed the door, turning to the Deputy Head.

"I beg your pardon, Mrs Swale?" said Mr Gapes, taking his glasses off to look at her. "We have a responsibility to protect young impressionable minds from such perversion. Thank you. You may go now." He pointed at the door with his glasses and looked back at his desk.

"Perish the thought we should educate them to think for themselves," she muttered as she left his office, closing the door behind her.

Tom had not developed the physique of his friend but was becoming a good-looking young man nevertheless. He'd deliberately avoided thinking about girlfriends and dates and that sort of thing, hoping with increasing desperation that he'd grow out of whatever phase this was and he'd be able to do the slow dance with a Kathleen Wyatt or a Zoe Griffin at the next summer dance. Today, though, something had changed. When Tom watched Mr Woodcock's towel drop, ever so slowly, revealing more and more of the hairy space below his navel, the hairs pointing suggestively towards his pelvis, he'd given up the fight. He was lost.

Paul was tall as well as broadening out. He was a decent sportsman, too, unlike Tom. He watched rugby with his father, when they'd managed to get a television upstairs for him. Over time, he was watching more for the players than the game. Not so much the big prop forwards, but the wirier types like the fly halves. His father liked rugby preferring it to football.

"Real men play rugby," he would say, "footballers are all soft pansies with their hugging and kissing on the pitch. Makes you sick just to see it."

Paul played rugby at school as well until one particular year. He enjoyed the physical contact, telling himself that as an only child he'd missed out on that kind of thing. As time went by, though, he became more unsettled. Putting his hand through a classmate's legs in the scrum, resting his face against his backside, and stretching up to take hold of his waistband near his navel was a little too close for comfort, especially if he could feel hair. It was even worse when the player in the row behind did the same to him. He would pray for the scrum to collapse quickly. And that no one's hand touched something it shouldn't. Worse still, felt something he was trying to hide.

It was even more tortuous in the changing rooms. If Mr Woodcock was supervising, he was contemptuous of them all and so kept himself to himself changing in the staff changing room this side of the library. But Mr Rutland, the weasel they called him, would insist on watching them shower naked and all together. Fortunately, the water was usually very cold. If there was no teacher around, though, anything might happen. Charlie Donaldson was already well-known across the school for the size of his penis; and Peter Tipler hit puberty a lot earlier than almost anyone else. He started shaving when about twelve, and his body hair sprouted thick and extensive, making it hard to miss. Paul would desperately try to get the bench in the corner, preferably hidden by someone's clothes hanging on the pegs, so that he wouldn't inadvertently catch sight of someone as they took trousers and underpants down. They all seemed to be far less self-conscious than he was, though his own body compared well with any of the rest of them.

One particularly disturbing day for Paul, Charlie, Peter and Dermot O'Donnelly were having a competition to see who had the biggest. Things got out of hand and, with some of the other boys egging them on, it had ended up with having to wipe down the floor, a bench and the wall hastily with paper towels before Mr Rutland arrived. Despite his best efforts, Paul caught a glimpse of Charlie trying to squeeze himself into an already stained jockstrap. Mr Rutland insisted they wore nothing under their rugby shorts, but both Charlie and Peter had started wearing jockstraps out of necessity they said.

Paul had tried to forget about the incident by the time they came back into the changing rooms after a messy game with scrum after scrum for almost half an hour. He was relieved to get showered and be changing before Donaldson and Tipler came back in talking loudly and hanging off one another's shoulder. They started to undress ready for the icy shower, but Peter thought it would be funny to flick his jockstrap at people like a sling. Charlie Donaldson joined in, of course, while Paul desperately tried to put his socks on over his cold, damp feet. Finally, he made it, even though his hair was still dripping, picked up his kit bag and slipped out. "See you guys!" he shouted over his shoulder, glad to get away at last.

At home, Paul generally did all the washing, though Peggy would iron everything on a Sunday. So, two days later, he was unpacking his kit bag to make sure his games stuff would be ready for the next week. It was vaguely musky and unpleasant, with the kit rolled up in a ball. He was horrified, though, when he unravelled everything to check he had shorts, socks and rugby shirt, and a jockstrap fell on the floor in his room. He automatically kicked it under his bed, looking round to check no one had seen and making a note to sort it out later. That evening, after he'd washed and changed his father, watched some television with him, and made him some Ovaltine, he finally made it into the quiet of his bedroom. His heart was thumping, and his throat was dry. He knelt down and waved his hand around under the bed to find the jockstrap. He had to lie flat on his stomach after a while before he actually spotted it. Slowly, he retrieved it and sat on the bed. He made himself undress, put on his pyjamas, and get into the bed before he picked it up again. He looked at it for a few minutes and rubbed the cloth between forefinger and thumb feeling the texture of some of the dried-on stains. Finally, wishing he'd thrown it in the bin with the leftovers, he lifted it to his face, closed his eyes and sniffed. After a minute or two, he was aware that he was aroused by the smell. He switched off his bedside lamp and lay on his back, his arms clamped by his side on top of the duvet, not daring to move. He was afraid to close his eyes in case he remembered the scene in the changing rooms. Eventually, he turned on his side, drew his legs up and tried to get some sleep. He came to with a jolt, thinking Peter Tipler was actually there in bed with him. He checked just to make sure, even though he knew. He turned on his other side, only to find the jockstrap again right in his face.

The next rugby practice, he decided the best plan would be to get there early and shove the unwashed jockstrap under one of the changing room benches. Unfortunately, Miss Mobberley stopped him to have a word about a planned trip to Stratford. By the time he got to the changing rooms, most of the others were there.

"Who'd want your sweaty old jockstrap, anyway, Tipler?" Charlie Donaldson was already naked and shaking himself around like some kind of rutting male.

"Better than your pissy old granddad's one," Peter shouted back.

"Probably one of the pervy fourth years pinched it," said another lad, who Paul couldn't quite see, "You know what a load of fairies they are this year."

"Or that bender, weasel!" Peter and Charlie burst out laughing. Paul decided he would say nothing and hid the jockstrap in a side pocket of his kit bag. He was distracted for the whole practice session, hoping no one would find it. Once practice was over, and he was dressed again and heading to the library, he made up his mind that he was going to drop out of rugby all together. The physical side was getting too much. The alpha male preening had taken it to the next level, with Peter Tipler holding Dermot O'Donnelly down while Charlie Donaldson sat on his face as he was walking out.

There was more to it than that, though. Paul knew that men could engage in sexual behaviour. He read about it somewhere. It was supposed to be a consequence of too few women in a community. Or, like in Ancient Greece, an accepted part of an older man mentoring a younger one. He'd read too that in the early days of ranchers in South America, there were dances which involved two men. Not a man and a woman as normal. So all of that was out of necessity, it seemed. He wasn't prepared though to realise that a man could actually be attracted sexually to another man. His friendship with Tom was just that, he thought. They were best friends, that was all. In some of his darker moments, he thought Tom was just being kind to him because Paul didn't have anyone else to talk to. What he realised now and what disturbed him so much was that he, Paul Armstrong, was one of those men. He tried not to think of anyone in particular when masturbating. He concentrated instead on the physical pleasure. But now he was faced with another possibility.

He'd explained away his discomfort around other boys like Peter Tipler and Charlie Donaldson as a natural part of growing up. Tipler in particular was much closer to being a full-grown man than anyone else. Surely, then, he told himself, it was perfectly understandable, a bit like having a crush on a male P.E. teacher. The awful thing was that he'd realised something far bigger. He was prepared to admit that the smell of the used jockstrap was sexually arousing like pheromones in their biology book. What he was struggling with was the fact that he was now fantasising about Tom in bed in the dark at night, both of them aroused. That frightened him.

When they came to reproduction in biology, he just accepted that animals did things to their mates, usually the male mounting the female from behind. He didn't question that at all. He'd assumed too that two dogs in the street would always be a male and a bitch. When it came to human reproduction, he was completely disgusted at first. Why would a woman want a man to do that to her? Although ashamed of the thought, he was also grateful for his father's accident so that he wouldn't have to listen to them the other side of the bedroom wall. It had taken time, but he'd finally stopped worrying about it and accepted that was nature's way, and so was perfectly normal. Now, though, he was having to confront once again the thought of two men together. He swung between distaste – he had started hearing comments that it was unnatural and punishable as a grave sin – to a genuine and purely practical concern that surely it would hurt. He lay in bed now though with the irrepressible feeling that he wanted to behave like this with Tom. He wished it were Tom's jockstrap he had hidden under the bookcase in his room.

"You alright, Paul?" Tom could see something was wrong.

Paul jumped. He'd been deep in his own thoughts and hadn't heard Tom approach from behind. "Nothing really. I was hoping Woodcock would be there so I could tell him I can't do rugby anymore."

"Why's that?" Tom asked. Then without thinking, "It's not because of all that sperm flying round the changing rooms, is it?"

"How do you know about that?" Paul had turned to look him briefly in the face, blushing slightly.

"OK, OK. Calm down. One of the third years, Tony Griffith's brother, was telling people at break last week."

"It was just Tipler, O'Donnelly and Donaldson..."

"He the one hung like a horse?"

Paul ignored him. "O'Donnelly got changed at some stage. But the other pair were being immature and decided to have a bit of a competition, that's all, see who could ejaculate furthest."

"Some competition, from what Tony's little brother said! Spunk flying everything, he said." Tom was clearly enjoying this. Pity, he thought, that this is not Oxford or Cambridge. Maybe I could sign up as the cox, he said to himself. "They're animals, those two!" Tom added, and they carried on walking to the library together in silence.

As the summer holidays approached, Tom started to feel more and more depressed. He'd miss Paul; they never met up over the summer; Paul would be looking after his bedridden father, of course. It would be six long weeks of nothing except maybe a surreptitious glance at a well-built sailor off the cross-Channel ferries. He didn't have the courage to get any closer, to follow one of them into the rather seedy public toilets near the ferry terminal. He was nearly sixteen now and almost an adult. Even so, he wasn't brave enough yet. He'd just keep obsessing about Paul for those six endless weeks.

Tom had an older sister, Lottie. There was six years between them. Then a brother, Jeremy, two years older than her. Jeremy and their father, Bob, were men's men. Both played cricket in the summer and rugby in the winter. There was always a lot of back slapping when Jeremy appeared and interminable talk about people Tom had never heard of. Though some of them, Tom had to admit, were fit.

Gwen, Tom's mother, had been very protective towards Tom since he'd been born. Lottie would tease him, gently. Like when Gwen bought him his first platform soled shoes.

"I'll teach you how to walk on high heels!" she joked.

"They're not high heels, stupid," he poked his sister in the shoulder, so she almost spilled her tea.

"You'll break your ankle if you're not careful!" Lottie was not being unkind. Fashion crazes like this were risky if you weren't used to them, she knew from experience.

"Platform soles? You bloody fairy!" Jeremy looked round his paper.

"Oh look! Fathead's awake." Tom was not afraid of his brother.

"That's enough, you lot, can we have breakfast without arguing please?" Gwen asked.

"And anyway," Tom whispered at Jeremy, "it's not me that puts his hand down other rugby players' shorts." Paul had told him about the scrum when he'd started playing rugby. Apparently, he was really embarrassed that boys were expected to touch one another like this. Tom had just changed the detail a little to annoy his brother.

When Jeremy realised what Tom meant, he was about to protest. But Gwen raised an eyebrow at him. She knew that Tom would be able to look after himself, though. He could already answer back with confidence and humour. She was relieved too that Paul Armstrong was around.

He was taller than Tom and would be physically able to protect him if it came to it. She knew Tom was likeable, but he had a sharp wit and she worried that it would land him in trouble someday. That and the rather flamboyant behaviour at times. She knew Paul was shy. She understood that it wasn't easy for him at home. So, she didn't mind that he never visited. It was Gwen too who had taken Tom to music lessons at the weekend. There was no point forcing him to go with Bob and Jeremy to a match, after all. She was delighted, therefore, that he showed a real talent for music. She knew enough about contemporary music to appreciate that performers tended to dress outlandishly. Some of the men even wore makeup. But she knew too that they attracted lots of girls. She was just happy that her youngest was not a sportsman.

Gwen had always worried about the younger of her sons. Bob just didn't understand him, especially because he felt so close to Jeremy. Gwen would dismiss any comments from her husband about Tom's lack of girlfriends. By the time Tom was 15, though, if she were honest with herself, she knew that Tom was struggling with something. Her only concern was that he should be happy. It saddened her too that he did not feel he could confide in his mother. She'd begun to wonder why he only ever spoke of his friend, Paul. However, she knew not to pry. It wasn't long before Tom just stopped talking about relationships when he was home. But that was growing up, she understood.

For his part, Tom was lonely at home. He didn't really care what his brother thought or said. But he wished his father would at least come and listen when he performed. Even just show some interest in what Tom was doing, instead of looking at him as if he were some kind of freak. Being by the sea, it was particularly hard for him over the summer anyway. A lot of men stripped down to their trunks on the beach. Although resigned to how he was, Tom still had a long way to go. He knew he was too young and inexperienced, but just didn't understand how he was supposed to get that experience. It was difficult to talk with Paul and see whether he felt the same dread of the long vacation. He seemed to be in a strange mood just then anyway. Tom even worried that he was starting to suspect that he had feelings for him. That year, it was different.

It was the last week or two of term, and already Tom was wishing the six weeks away. The next school year was all he had to look forward to. They'd finished their O Levels, so now there was nothing else but to wait for the results. Tom felt listless and often sprawled across the library tables drumming with his pen or pencil to the music he heard in his head. One of Paul's tech drawing exams finished really late, and Tom was waiting so that they might spend what little time they had left before the summer holidays finally swallowed them up. Paul came softly into the library. Despite his growing frame, he always trod quietly almost as if he had something to hide. Tom didn't hear him until he coughed in that strange, exaggerated way you would on stage. Tom jumped up in his seat only to see Paul, eyes turned down onto the library table, tracing with his finger generations' worth of graffiti.

"The thing is..." Paul began.

"Yeah?" Tom prompted. Then after what seemed like ages. "So, this thing then. What is it?"

Paul looked up and half-smiled and then looked out of the windows. For all the books he'd read, all the Shakespeare, and latterly Jane Austen, he couldn't find the words. He thought that somewhere it should talk about how to ask someone you secretly love something without letting them know that you really hope they'll say yes. At the same time, Tom had an initial moment of panic. He thought he knew every line on his friend's brow, every gesture, every shrug of those broad shoulders. But this seemed to be different. He was scared that Paul may have found out how Tom felt about him and was coming to tell him to leave him alone.

He looked at Paul's face and tried to catch his eye. He wanted to know what the thing was, but if Paul wasn't going to tell him to sod off, he just wanted to help his friend to be comfortable with him and relax. He knew he cared for Paul, it wasn't just lust or some teenage crush. His mind was racing, and he wondered if this might be some confidence that Paul needed to share and could only share with him. As for Paul himself, he was desperately trying to avoid betraying any sign that he might want to be anything more than a friend to Tom. Nevertheless, this was the first time that he might get to spend time with Tom outside school. He was so excited at the prospect. As if all the hidden feelings and visceral yearnings were not enough, he'd spent a sleepless night worried that Tom would not want to. He really had no idea what Tom did during the holidays.

"Well, the thing is..."

"You said that."

"You see. I have these relatives the other side of Winchester. And my uncle's just died. So..."

"Come on, Paul, spit it out. Don't tell me: they're all mass murderers who organise human sacrifice up by Winchester Hill Fort."

"No. Listen!" Paul was losing his nerve, though really, he was just nervous. "They've got this farm, see. And they need a bit of manual labour."

Tom couldn't really see where this was going. So, some country-bumkins in the next county along were in need, it seemed, of some big strapping Amish lads to build a barn and gather in the corn. What did that have to do with Tom?

"You see, Mum and Dad wanted me to go and help out. But the thing is..."

Tom couldn't bear the suspense any longer. "For God's sake, Paul, you're driving me nuts here. Spit it out. Be a man!" He regretted the last bit straight away. Paul laughed briefly despite himself.

"Look, you can say 'No' if you want to. Honestly, I won't mind."

"I think this is all like some post-exam traumatic dream... What can I say 'No' to?"

"Look, sorry, I shouldn't have mentioned it. Forget it..." and Paul was about to turn away and leave Tom in the library.

"What!? Jesus wept, Paul. You haven't mentioned anything yet. Say it. It can't be worse than all this suspense."

"The thing is... If I go and help, they don't want me going on my own..."

"Why not?" Tom interrupted, "are these relatives of yours really weirdoes?"

Paul still didn't look at him. "So, well," he went on, "I was wondering if maybe you'd like to come along and keep me company? Maybe." Paul took a deep breath. There, he'd said it. Tom couldn't believe what he'd just heard and hesitated just a bit too long. "See! You don't want to. It's okay, really. I'll see you next term." And Paul turned crestfallen to leave.

"For God's sake!" Tom shouted a bit too shrilly across the library, gathering all his stuff together hastily and making after Paul.

"Thank you, Mr Frampton," Mrs Swale's voice came over loud and clear from her office down the other end of the library. "Please remember, *you* may have finished *your* exams, but this is still a library!"

"Sorry, Mrs Swale. Just a bit of an emotional crisis here."

He caught up with Paul in the corridor. Being careful not to get too close even though he just wanted to hug his friend tight,

"Hey great! When do we leave? Have I got time to pack?" This was said as a bit of joke. Paul smiled broadly. His face began to hurt.

"Oh, there's a few weeks yet; the 21st of July," he said. "But really, you don't have to come, you know, if you've got better things to do."

"Fuck off, Paul. You're stuck with me, mate. And I'm a dab hand at feeding the chickens and collecting the eggs. You can swill out the pigs and stuff."

"It's not that kind of farm, stupid!" Paul wanted to put his arm round Tom's shoulder now, he was just so happy that he wouldn't have to spend time at his cousins on his own. Lucy, the younger of the two, made him feel uncomfortable and kept making lewd comments about bunking up in the barn and that sort of thing. There was more than that, though, and he knew it. But Paul didn't want to face the fact that he really wanted to spend time alone with Tom. He wanted to be near him. Just the two of them, miles from anywhere. Just to see what it felt like, and to see if his feelings for Tom were still so strong when there were no other distractions. At the same time, he was afraid he would lose control and do something he'd regret. He didn't want to think about any of that, though. He was so happy at the thought of being with Tom.

Three weeks later, Tom and Paul boarded the through train to Winchester, with an anxious Mrs Armstrong telling them not to fall asleep in case they missed their stop and ended up God knows where, even London. Tom imagined for a moment as the train slowly pulled out of Weymouth falling asleep and his head settling onto Paul's shoulder, whilst Paul in turn lay his head against Tom's. This was unlikely. For a start, it was early afternoon. And second, they sat opposite each other in a slightly grubby compartment. Sixteen now, Paul's legs were pretty long, and Tom struggled to find room to stretch out his own without their legs touching.

Whatever their private fears, very soon they were talking easily as the train crawled from one passenger-less station to another across the New Forest, not even noticing the ponies close by the railway track. Finally, they pulled into Winchester, crossed from the up platform through the dank underpass, and looked for the Petersfield bus they had to catch to get to Paul's cousins' place. It was getting on for five when they got off the bus and trudged up the dusty lane to the farm. About halfway along was a large sign saying "Welcome to Savage's Farm – Your fruity treat".

"My God," laughed Tom, "your relatives really are scary!"

Paul was puzzled until he noticed the sign too. "Fool!" he laughed, "that's my uncle's name."

"And that's supposed to make it alright?" Tom pretended to be worried.

Tom carried on making savage and wild-man jokes as they trudged all the way up the dusty lane.

They spent three and a half weeks all told on the farm just outside Bramdean. It was not all *Cider with Rosie* and lying around on hay ricks, sucking an ear of corn, and snoozing under a warm summer sun. Tom and Paul had to work hard picking various fruit and vegetable crops, which made their backs ache and left their throats dry. But the farm food was wholesome, plain but nourishing, and very welcome after a nine-hour day out in the fields. They fell into their painfully narrow single beds in the loft each night and talked and talked into well after darkness had fallen. When they finally fell silent, Tom would listen for Paul's breathing to steady, a sign that he'd fallen asleep, Tom thought. He would then imagine lying naked with his friend under the stars. Alone together. With no one to judge or criticise. No one to make inappropriate and prejudicial comments. Inevitably the fantasy meant so much to Tom that he would reach down under the bedclothes, trying to keep as quiet as he could as he masturbated. Hoping that Paul hadn't heard him, but also hoping he had and would join in.

A week or so into their visit, the four young people were making their way back to the farmhouse along the edge of one of the fields. Dust rose into the balmy air caught by the early evening sun. Jessie was kneading dough, ready to put it on the shelf above the range to rise. The upper part of the farm door was open, and she had a clear view of the fields leading up to the farm itself. She could just about make out the four figures at some distance walking back through the insects and pollen clouds, though she wasn't able to make out which figure was who. She carried on preparing supper and had the occasional look as they came slowly towards the house. She'd put a clean cloth on the table to hide years of stains, burn marks and the rings from the bottom of many mugs still damp as they were put down onto the wood. All the knocks and scars of real life. She moved over to the sink, fishing cutlery out of the water, drying them off and starting to lay the table. She looked up and out of the window, now able to recognise Paul leading the others walking back towards the farmhouse. Steve was behind him, but she couldn't see who the other two were to their left. Bits of the hedge on that side were hanging over them. More work, Jessie thought, Frank would have started trimming them by now.

When the sisters had spoken on the 'phone at the beginning of the summer, Peggy had been worried. She couldn't fault Paul for his devotion to his father. She was concerned, though, that he spent so much time on his own. Jessie's call had come at exactly the right time. With Frank just buried, she needed help to get in this year's harvest. For Peggy, she thought it was a great opportunity for a break for Paul. She and Eddie were a bit worried about sending him on his own, and so it was Peggy who'd suggested asking Tom. They'd never really met Tom, and although he'd got Paul into a few scrapes every now and then, he lived in one of the nicer houses up the hill. So, Peggy was sure he'd be well-mannered and would be good company for Paul.

"The other thing," she confided to her sister, "I'm worried that he's never brought a girl home."

"Well, with Eddie and all, perhaps he feels a bit awkward," Jessie replied.

"There is that. But sometimes I wonder if he uses Eddie as an excuse. No one ever comes round, and no one invites Paul anywhere. There's only ever Tom we hear anything about."

"Look on the positive side," said Jessie, "it could be worse."

"How do you mean?" asked Peggy.

"He could've been like old Reggie, the shirt lifter!"

They both sniggered suggestively.

"Yes, that's true. Paul's not like that, of course. Up till I got him that job in the newsagent, he played rugby! Nothing more manly than that."

Paul was growing into a fine young man, it was true. Handsome too. Jessie and Peggy agreed that it might do him good to have female company his own age like

Lucy. His cousin was not shy at all, and so the two sisters thought she might be able to teach him a few things about asking girls out and that sort of thing. Paul was smiling and laughing at whoever it was he was talking to. He kept looking over to his left as he smiled. As they came closer, Jessica guessed that Paul was looking his companion up and down each time he looked across. There was clearly some kind of animated conversation going on between the two of them. Occasionally, Paul would lean in closer, as if they were exchanging secrets between the two of them. Confidences that no one else should hear.

"Must be Lucy, I guess," Jessie said as she smiled to herself. She was happy to see the cousins getting on so well together. Hopefully, being with Lucy like this would give Paul some confidence around girls. As first cousins, of course, it was completely non-threatening for him. She turned to put more cutlery and some crockery on the table. When she turned back to the window, the four were almost at the house and the branches from the hedgerow no longer hid the two walking next to Paul and Steve. She was rather surprised as Paul's companion came into view. It wasn't Lucy after all. She was with her brother a short distance behind. It was Tom.

The conversation that evening over supper was animated and good-humoured between the young people. Jessie was enjoying the laughter in the house again. Since Frank had died, things had been rather gloomy. She still had to work out if she could keep the farm. And then there was Steve and Lucy. Steve already had a steady girlfriend, she suspected. He'd taken to getting off the bus from college a stop earlier and walking the rest of the way. Lucy was a worry, though. She was fun, no doubt, but Jessie was anxious about where that might take her. She enjoyed having Paul and his friend, Tom, there too. They seemed very close, and Paul was a lot more relaxed and open than she'd remembered him.

Paul felt so unsure about how he felt towards Tom. After the episode at rugby when he'd decided to give it up, he was struggling even more. He felt ashamed of being aroused, but then he knew he couldn't help it. Men didn't go with men, he thought, not that way. They could be friends, but that was all. Everybody knew that a man married a woman, they had children and settled down. That's what his parents had done, and presumably, their parents before them. It was normal. Coming away together like this was supposed to help. Watching Tom with his cousins and his auntie just made it more confusing. He was funny, and he was charming. Lucy had even thanked Paul for bringing Tom along. He thought she was starting to have feelings for him, and that Tom was encouraging her.

They'd got into a routine each morning after breakfast and before they went out in the fields to harvest the fruit or vegetables that day. All four of them, Lucy, Steve, Tom and Paul had to take off their t-shirts so that Jessie could smother them in sun cream. Lucy wore a camisole over her bra. Paul thought how difficult it must be to have three layers in the current heat. Jessie would work along the line smearing copious amounts of the sweet-smelling cream before they were dismissed, and she moved on to the next one. That morning, the 'phone rang just as she finished Tom.

"Here," she said, "You better do Paul."

And she handed him the bottle before going next door to answer. Lucy was packing the sandwiches in one bag for her and Steve and in another for Tom and Paul.

Tom shook the bottle, as he'd seen Jessie do, and squeezed a line across Paul's shoulders. He didn't react even though Tom knew the cream was cold. But when Tom began to rub the cream in, he could feel Paul's back tense. Tom tried to copy Jessie's movements as she'd applied the cream and not to linger anywhere in particular on Paul's back. Running out of cream just below the shoulder blades, he applied some more a little too enthusiastically and it ran down Paul's back towards the waistband of his shorts. Tom leaned forward to catch the trickle and rubbed it into Paul's lower back. Across the small of his friend's back as he rubbed, Tom could feel Paul's muscles relax and contract.

"You OK?" he asked.

"Yeah, fine... Finished yet?" There's was something about Paul's voice. Lucy looked up.

"Come on, slowcoach!" she flashed a smile at Tom.

"Alright! Alright!" he laughed. "This has to be done properly, you know."

Paul sensed he was smiling back at his cousin. He tried to relax. He was relieved when Tom snapped the stopper shut and announced "Perfect! All done." Paul kept his t-shirt in his hand hanging over the front of his shorts as he picked up the bag of sandwiches and they left the kitchen. Lucy and Steve set off towards the top fields. Walking side by side now, Paul handed the bag to Tom while he put his t-shirt back on. They went the other way towards the lower fields and the fruit frames.

He was quiet for most of the morning, concentrating on the blackcurrant harvest. All the time, he was trying to decide if there might be something between Tom and Lucy. By lunchtime, he decided he was being selfish. He should be happy for Tom.

"You've been quiet this morning," Tom said as he passed Paul his sandwiches.

"Sorry, Tom, I didn't sleep too well last night," Paul answered, his eyes on the greaseproof paper he was unfolding. Tom felt slightly uneasy.

"So anyway," Paul went on, "What do you think of country life, then?"

Tom took a bite from his sandwich and immediately spat it out again. Paul just looked at him.

"You OK?"

"Yes, sorry, it had sun cream on it!" Paul snorted, almost losing the bite he'd just taken too.

"It's really odd all this sun cream," Tom went on. "Lucy and her brother must be used to the sun if they're out in the fields all day. And we live by the sea. All that bracing, salty sea air!"

Paul laughed. "You know parents, though," he said, "always seeing problems for their kids where there aren't any."

They chatted more easily after that. By the time they were heading back to the farmhouse for supper, everything was back to normal. They were just friends, enjoying each other's company.

A few days later, during a particularly hot morning, Tom stopped picking and stood up to listen. He'd heard something in the distance. Wiping the back of his hand across his forehead, he told Paul to stop what he was doing.

"Listen. Can you hear water? Or am I imagining it?"

"You look as though you could do with some water... You've got a great dirty smear across your face."

Tom threw his glove at Paul.

"No, but you're right," Paul went on. He looked around as if he was trying to orientate himself to where they were exactly.

"Down there," he pointed with the secateurs he was holding, "there's a stream which broadens out into a pool at that point. Nice shady place to eat lunch, actually."

"Deal," said Tom. "And can you swim in the pool?"

"It's been a while, but I think so."

"Pity we don't have any swimming gear."

"You joking?" Paul smiled. "You're not shy, are you? No one would want to look at you, anyway." Tom threw the other glove at him.

"Let's finish up here, then we can go down and see what it looks like. I won't tell anyone if we go in naked, if you don't."

Paul had never suggested anything like this before and Tom wondered what this was about. In reality, Paul had decided that Tom was interested in a normal relationship, maybe even with his cousin, Lucy. So, he was trying hard to be just good friends. Skinny-dipping on a hot summer's day seemed the kind of thing that mates did.

Paul was first to take his clothes off and launch himself into the water. Tom was a lot more hesitant. He was surprised and pleased to think of Paul naked in the water, but still felt a little constrained. He edged himself gingerly into the water. Paul kept a discreet distance, his back turned towards him. When he finally heard Tom start to swim towards him, he turned and smiled. "That's better. Cool at last!" There was no splashing or attempting to duck one another under the water. Instead, they trod water looking at each other, smiling. As they drifted closer, Paul kept his eyes fixed on Tom's lips. Without thinking, he licked his own. Tom's heart beat faster. He'd always known he loved Paul but had wanted some sign that he loved him in return. Now, he was almost sure. For now, at least, Paul's resolve to be just friends was wavering. It was too much for him now and he was almost carried away by the moment. Tom closed his eyes, waiting.

"Is it really cold?" Lucy and Steve were stripping off and ready to jump in and join them.

"Oh," shouted Lucy, "watch out. Cold water makes everything shrink!"

Tom could have cried. Paul turned away and swam to the other bank. Tom couldn't work out whether he was angry or just wanting to enjoy as much of the cooling water as he could and while he could. Annoyed and frustrated, Tom was far too socially aware to show any signs to Steve or Lucy that they were intruding. He knew from dealing with his older brother and sister that it was best to play along and not take things too seriously. He tried to avoid the splashing and attempts to push his head under the water, whilst laughing along, waiting patiently for Lucy to grow tired and just relax into the cooling water.

Paul watched from the other bank. If only, he thought at first, if only they'd been on there own for just a bit longer. Now he wasn't sure again. Tom didn't seem to mind Lucy and Steve butting in. Especially not Lucy. He wondered if he'd misread the signs. He watched Tom's back as the three of them played around in the water. He wished Jessie had asked him to put cream on Tom's back the other day. So then he'd have an excuse to run his hand over Tom's bare skin. Slowly across each shoulder in turn, rubbing into the little indentations to make sure the cream spread evenly. Being careful to massage up the back of Tom's neck. He suddenly realised he'd been sulking on his own the other side of the pool. He swam across to the others who had stopped playing around now and were just enjoying the water. He tried to make a little conversation, just to be part of it all. He didn't look at Tom.

"That was really great today in the stream," Tom offered that night when they were finally in bed.

"Yeah, it was," said Paul, and before he could stop himself "until Dick and bloody Dora came and spoiled it."

It took a minute or two for Tom to process this. "Oh!" he said. He couldn't think of anything else to say. He agreed, of course, but wasn't sure that his resentment of Paul's cousins crashing in on their midday dip was the same as Paul's. He left it too long to try and find out. He could hear Paul's breathing change and knew he was now alone with his thoughts and dreams. He had missed his chance, he thought, and caught himself wondering how Paul might compare in the full-frontal stakes with Mr Woodcock. To be fair, it didn't really matter. Tom's mind was already made up. And he'd wait for as long as it took.

The morning they were leaving, Paul had to go to the top field to help Lucy and Steve with a broken cartwheel. Auntie Jessie asked Tom to strip their beds and put the bedding in the boiler. Tom didn't mind housework and was happy to do as asked. He flung the windows open to air the room, folded the blankets neatly, took off the pillowcases, having a long sniff at Paul's and prepared to pull back the sheets. He was relieved in a way to be dealing with the bedding just in case he'd had any tell-tale spillage himself during the balmy nights just an arm's length from Paul. He was surprised, though, and even laughed to himself to see Paul's bottom sheet.

"The crafty bugger!" he thought as he stripped Paul's sheets to find as many stains on his sheets as on his own. "Next year, I'll make a note to stay awake all night if necessary and catch him at it!" The thought put him in a good mood, and he enjoyed the smell of his friend as he wrapped the two bottom sheets together ready to take downstairs. He paused, though, Paul's musky scent still in his senses. Slowly he untangled them again. He held Paul's sheet up to the light. He could smell that familiar smell of teenage self-gratification. He could smell Paul. He thought for a moment. Their bags were still there, almost ready to set off.

The boiler was already steaming when he got to the laundry room this side of the barn. He carefully removed the lid so as not to scold himself and put the bedding into the water, using the wooden tongs to push everything down and make sure they were soaked in the bubbling soapy liquid. Last of all, and with one last caress to the face, he put the tangle of bottom sheets and pillowcases.

"I'm really sorry, Auntie Jessie," Tom began, holding up the sheet, "I must have caught it on the bedframe or the door handle. There's quite a tear, I'm truly sorry. Shall I buy a new one."

"Don't be silly," Jessie said as she glanced up to catch Tom quickly folding the sheet up again.

"It's only a sheet," she said, "Pop it in the sewing basket in the scullery. If I can't repair it, I can make it into dusters."

He tossed it into the basket as she'd asked, pushing it down amongst other bits of cloth already there.

"You look happy to be going home, young man," said Jessie when he went back into the kitchen.

"Not really," said Tom, "it's been lovely here. Thank you so much for having me."

"Thank you! You've both worked really hard."

"I'd love to come back," Tom ventured hesitantly.

"Well, if we're still here, the crops will still need harvesting."

And Tom thought nothing more about it. Jessie thought that maybe it was Lucy that was on Tom's mind.

After an early lunch, it was time to set off. Tom had had to repack, apparently. So, Paul was waiting patiently downstairs. He kissed his auntie on the cheek and thanked her again for having them. He held his hand up to his cousins. Tom was a lot more friendly in a way. He thanked Jessie and was going to shake her hand, but she hugged him close and said he'd always be welcome. He went to hug Steve, but he took a step back and held out a hand which Tom shook briefly, and even before he could decide with Lucy, she'd thrown herself around his neck and kissed him hard on both cheeks. Everyone laughed a little awkwardly, and Paul and Tom set off down the lane to the bus stop.

The bus crawled along the road stopping at all the villages. But Tom didn't mind so much this time. When they got to Winchester, the heavens opened, and they'd had to run to get out of the downpour under one of the bus shelters. Panting, they watched the rain relentlessly soak the road, the pavements, and anyone who was brave enough to walk out in it, before turning to look into each other's eyes. Paul seemed to be deep in thought. He was struggling with different emotions. With no other motive in mind, he turned to Tom, smiled and said:

"I wish we didn't have to go straight home."

"Me too," Tom agreed. "I loved spending time with you, Paul." Paul raised an eyebrow. You mean with Lucy, he thought.

"No, I mean it." Tom continued, "I really have. It's been..."

"The rain's stopping, look. We'd best try and make it to the station while we can. We don't want to miss the train."

Tom watched Paul go up the incline of the station approach, before sighing, picking up his rucksack and following his friend. He couldn't understand what was wrong. He hoped Paul was just tired. He longed to be alone with him at night in the dark, their beds almost touching. For now, he had a week or so to get through at home before he'd see him again.

Things on the farm settled back into the old routine. Jessie would gradually work through the mending basket, sitting outside in the late afternoon sun. Occasionally, she'd find some cloth which she'd embroidered many years before. She used to stitch all the time, hankies for presents and keepsakes, collars for the children's clothes when they were babies, even a tapestry once for the nursery. Now, there was no time except for mending. She was surprised one afternoon to discover the sheet in her sewing basket with a fairly large ragged square hole in the centre.

"How on earth did he manage that?" she thought as she held it up towards the light, the low afternoon sun streaming through it and onto her face. But just then, Lucy popped her head round the kitchen door.

"Hi Mum, I'm home if you want to get on with packing," she dumped her school things on the nearest chair and ran upstairs to change. When Jessie heard her coming down again, she came back inside, put the new dusters in a pile on the table and followed her daughter out to the packing shed. Steve and Lucy had got the last of the fruit in, but it needed packing quickly. The woman from the farm shop was coming in the morning to inspect the fruit and take what she needed.

"Are you going to pack any of that fruit or just eat it, young lady!" Jessie glared across the workbench. Lucy stopped eating the fruit and instead tossed it into the punnets. "And try not to bruise them, either."

Lucy looked over to her mother but decided not to say anything. They worked on in silence for a while.

"How did Frank die again?" Lucy asked suddenly.

Jessie stopped what she was doing, her wrists resting against the side of one of the boxes. She stared off into the distance.

"Your father," she corrected, "died out on the top field. He had a heart attack, as you know. Then he fell over the front of the tractor. It was hours before we found him. Why are you asking?"

"Oh, no reason," said Lucy, "just that people were talking about it at the bus stop."

"You don't want to listen to any of the tittle-tattle in Bramdean, Lucy, you know that."

"I guess," said Lucy.

They carried on putting the fruit into punnets. Every now and then, Jessie would take them and weigh them before packing in a larger cardboard tray.

"Did you love him?" Lucy asked. Jessie looked up at her.

"What a strange question. Of course I did." Jessie thought nothing of it.

"Paul's getting ever more dishy," Lucy carried on, "nice body too."

"He's your cousin, Lucy, leave him be." Jessie laughed, but she agreed. He was growing up to be a very good-looking young man. He'd break someone's heart one day, she thought.

"His mate, Tom, wasn't bad looking either." Lucy popped a few raspberries in her mouth before her mother could say anything. It was several minutes before she added, "Such a funny guy, too. Even old stick-in-the-mud, Steve, found him a good laugh towards the end. I miss having him around."

They finished up what they could and went back into the house. All this talk of Paul and Tom set Jessie thinking. She thought about the sheet and the rather odd hole in the middle. She imagined some silly game between the two of them ending in a massive tear. She wondered how Peggy had managed without Paul and why she'd never really mentioned Tom before. Frank blamed Eddie for Paul's shyness. He said it wasn't right for a growing lad to have to stay in and care for his dad. That was woman's work, he said. Jessie had a different view, but Frank wouldn't listen. She didn't speak to him for a fortnight. In the end, she'd relented, partly because he hadn't seemed to notice.

Jessie was peeling the potatoes at the sink when she remembered Lucy asking if she and Frank loved one another. They'd met in Weymouth. Frank Savage was on holiday with a group of farmhands. He'd started walking past Irene's shop deliberately to try and catch her eye. Eventually, he managed to get to speak to her and asked her to go to the funfair with him. She'd never been allowed to go before, and she'd never laughed so much. Frank was a perfect gentleman, even winning a teddy bear at the target shooting range which he'd ostentatiously presented to her. He'd come back at Christmas to see her, and the following Easter, he'd spoken to Irene to ask permission to marry her daughter. Jessie had been delighted, mainly at the thought of leaving Weymouth.

Married life as a farmer's wife had been hard, though. It took her a while to settle in and she missed the smell and the sound of the sea for many years. For a while, she kept writing to a girl she'd been very close to at school back in Weymouth. But when first Steve then Lucy had come along, she had a distraction and soon forgot about the coast. Letters with Peggy back home kept her in touch with what was going on down there. When they had their telephone installed, though, they ended up talking together each Sunday morning. There wasn't that much difference, Jessie decided, between Peggy and Eddie's relationship and her own marriage. She and Frank never went out together, except later when they had to go to the children's school. There always seemed to be something to do at the farm otherwise. Though Frank went out every Saturday for his evening with the lads. With the children, she didn't think anything of it. So, she supposed she loved him. She'd just got on with it really, that was her lot.

"You made your bed," Irene used to tell her and Peggy, "you lie in it."

Jessie thought about that supper when Lucy and the other young people had all been laughing and joking with each other. Tom was indeed a very funny young man. Lucy was right about Steve too. He was laughing as much as any of them. But it was Paul she remembered most clearly. He was a shy teenager. She knew Peggy was worried about it, though Jessie had always said he'd grow out of it. With Tom there, though, he was a different person. He was as animated and vocal as anyone. She remembered too that Tom was apparently dependent on Paul. He seemed to seek his approval, focusing most of the time on Paul's reactions. In his turn, Paul would calm him down if he became over-excited. They were a perfect match, Jessie realised.

She loved Paul, almost as much as she loved her own. It was no life for a child to be looking after his father. Unlike Frank, though, she admired him for it too. He'd never complained. At least as far as she knew. They didn't know what Peggy would have done without him. Now she was in a similar position herself. Without Steve and Lucy, she would not have managed the harvest this year. She wasn't sure what would happen now. It wasn't just the harvest itself. There was always a lot to do. She didn't want to have to depend on them like Peggy had done with Paul. She wanted them to have their own lives. Do what they wanted to do.

She smiled to herself thinking about what Lucy had said. She would be happy for Lucy and Tom to get together, now she came to think of it. She liked him, and it was obvious that he was caring. Judging by how he was with Paul, she felt that he would look after Lucy. She hoped too that Paul would find a girl just like Tom. For seeing Paul light up when Tom was around, having a nice young lady exactly like him would be perfect for her shy, withdrawn nephew. She'd enjoyed having all four of them together on the farm. It wasn't just the farm work. It was the company, the laughter. They were all so relaxed with one another. That made her happy. She concluded she hadn't loved Frank after all.

She dried her hands and walked over to the mantelpiece above the range. She took down the faded framed photo of Frank taken shortly after they were married. There was nothing remarkable about him. Perhaps she'd just got used to him, she thought. Automatically, she wiped the glass with her apron and set the photo back on the mantel. She hesitated, though. A little further along was an old-fashioned music box. She took it down, wound the key at the back and opened the lid. A tiny plastic ballerina pirouetted to the tinny music. Jessie smiled to herself. When she was little, Lucy loved to watch the dancer turn, mirrored against the inside of the lid. She didn't replace the box straight away though.

Jessie pulled a chair out from the table and sat for a moment with the old music box in front of her. Removing the insert layer, which was meant for small items of jewellery, she pulled a roll of letters from underneath. As she flattened them out, she recognised the writing and smiled to herself. Her old schoolfriend had written to her faithfully for a few years when she'd got married and moved to the farm. But it was just the really special letters that she'd kept. Her eyes staring into the middle distance, remembering something, she picked the top letter up and took it out of the envelope. It was the last letter. Jessie had not replied to the one before it, resolving to make do as best she could here, especially now that she had children. This made her feel sad. Scanning the letter briefly, she looked at the end. "Please, Jess, just let me know you're alright." It was signed simply 'O' with a single kiss.

For a good ten minutes, Jessie sat looking at the letter and then at the table in front of her. She regretted not replying to the last two letters. She wondered where her friend might be now and the type of life she had. Would she have married? Did she have children of her own? Jessie began to imagine what life might have been like had she not left Weymouth and her closest friend. She took a hankie from her apron pocket and blew her nose and dabbed her eyes. "No use crying over all that nonsense now," she said to herself. Putting the letters carefully back into the box, she replaced it on the mantelpiece and carried on preparing tea for Steve and Lucy.

Whilst Tom took music and persevered with French, mainly because he rather liked the French teaching assistant with his swarthy chin and Gallic good looks, Paul stayed with tech drawing and engineering. This meant they only met in English and the dreaded General Studies. The tech drawing made people underestimate Paul. However, and despite timetabling difficulties, Miss Mobberley insisted he be allowed to take English. He'd been awarded the highest marks in the county for English Literature O Level, and she wasn't prepared to miss out on that sort of ability. For years now, Paul had been reading as much as he could get hold of, anything from Austen and James to Graham Greene. He'd become sensitive in his interpretation of poetry and especially Shakespeare. Most of the stories, Paul had told Tom, derived from Shakespeare as far as he could see. Tom loved it when Paul, clearing his throat nervously, would finally start to get involved with whatever discussion was going on in class. He felt proud of his friend, basking in vicarious glory.

Their friendship continued as easy as it had always been. Tom relied on Paul as well as loved him. Paul was becoming more withdrawn, though. He'd kept with engineering subjects so he could be with the other boys and just keep his head down. He felt awkward and uncomfortable around girls. That meant he was less often with Tom, though. That was hard, though it helped. It made it easier that way for it to be a friendship even though deep down, he still loved Tom as much as ever.

"Hey, have you seen the new music teacher yet?" Simon

Jeffries had come up to Tom and Paul in the corridor. Tom said he hadn't.

"It's what this school needs, if you ask me. Rumour has it he's been seen with mascara and eyeshadow out in the clubs in Bournemouth. And," Simon leaned in closer for the last bit of news, "he wears platform soles!"

"Oh my God, really?" Tom's eyes widened. "Do you think Abbott will tell him he's not allowed to wear platform soles in school?"

Ed Aldridge turned out to be just as Simon had described. He also liked pupils to call him 'Ed', which Tom was really enthusiastic about. As a dreary grey Christmas spilled over into the New Year, Ed announced there'd be a summer musical production and invited pupils to audition in the main hall. Like all schools, the hall had a raised platform complete with curtains, some backdrops that could be replaced with scenery and an ancient lighting rig connected with spotlights along the length of the hall ceiling. Hopefuls would have to stand mid stage and sing a song of their own choosing while Ed, Miss Mobberley from the English department, and Mrs Gibbons, the part-time music teacher and piano player for school assemblies, sat in judgement at a set of tables about three yards back from the stage. There were many more girls auditioning than boys, yet it was difficult to find anyone who could hold a tune from either sex, let alone sing in harmony. Ed was beginning to despair.

"Come on, Paul," Tom pleaded, "Please. It's my big chance."

"It's a two-bit comp in the back of beyond in Dorset. It's not Broadway, Tom." Paul was not being unkind; he was just naturally shy and was not getting up on any stage for anyone.

"Please, Paul. I need... I want..." Tom struggled for words. "Just a bit of moral support, maybe?"

Tom and Paul were sitting side by side at the far end of the library. Tom would have put a cajoling hand on Paul's shoulder, but they didn't do that sort of thing. Instead, he had his hand on the back of Paul's chair and shook it like a child would who wants something from their parents. He bent his head slightly and tried to look into Paul's face. That did it. Paul snorted through an embarrassed smile and looked sideways at Tom.

"All right," he said, "but I'm not getting up on that fucking stage for anyone."

Tom almost skipped out of the library. He calmed down for Paul's sake, but was still obviously excited. He spent the evening trying to decide what he'd sing. Gwen thought he should do something timeless and classical. Burt Bacharach, perhaps. Lottie disagreed and thought Tom should do something from the charts. Tom was unsure. The next day, and with Paul at his side, he went to the school hall during the lunch break. Ed was looking fed up; Miss Mobberley was looking fondly at him; and Emily Gibbons was trying to keep a kindly, neutral expression on her face. A girl from upper sixth maths had just finished *Those were the days my friend*, without a single right note. Ed was beginning to wonder if this was such a good idea after all. There was the girl from the fifth form with a passable voice and, all three teachers agreed, a bit of stage presence. But time was ticking on and the possibilities were rapidly disappearing. Then Tom took to the stage.

"It's Tim, isn't it," said Ed through a yawn.

"Tom, Ed," he corrected. Paul looked surprised.

"OK, Tom, what's it to be."

"I'd like to sing two numbers, Ed, if that's alright."

Ed sighed. "OK, when you're ready," he said, and sat down with his arms folded across his chest. Tom cleared his throat and looked over to Paul who was standing awkwardly to the right of the stage, his hands in his pockets and trying to look invisible.

Tom coughed a little again and took a deep, audible breath. Jiggling his arms to relax himself a bit, scrunching his shoulders and putting his head first on one side then on the other, Tom finally threw his head back and opened his mouth to bellow "Well!" in the same way, but without the hoarse voice, that Lulu had with *You know you make me wanna shout* some ten or so years before. Miss Mobberley put her nail file down; Mrs Gibbons folded her cardigan across her bosom and sat back with a broad smile on her face. Even Paul was moving in time to the beat. Ed Aldridge was on his feet, swaying from foot to foot, and clapping loudly along to the old classic. Not his kind of sound, Ed thought, but this boy could sing. At last.

"Well, indeed," he said as he was about to sit down.

"There's my second song, Ed." Tom looked over to Paul and winked.

Ed looked up at Tom and shrugged a non-committal "OK, let's hear it then."

Despite bellowing out Lulu's hit just seconds before, Tom Frampton gently went into *The Girl from Ipanema*. He dared to look over to Paul as he sang the first few lyrics before turning back to face his audience full on. Miss Mobberley sat wide-eyed; Emily Gibbons tapped the *bossa nova* rhythm with her chubby fingers on the table. Ed looked on, amazed.

"You're before your time, mate," was all he could say when Tom finished. Paul was clapping enthusiastically despite himself.

"Ladies," Ed continued, "I think we have our lead."

"OK," Ed moved things on. Looking at Paul: "So, what do you sing?"

"Me?" Paul stuttered. "Oh, I don't, Sir, no."

"Paul does backstage," said Tom quickly. "Scenery, lighting, that sort of thing."

Ed looked at the spotlights strategically hung along the iron frame of the flat roof.

"Alright," he said, "get this lot to work properly and you're hired!"

It was a toss-up in the staff room between *Grease* and *The Rocky Horror Show*. Miss Mobberley wanted *Grease* and promised to mentor the fifth form girl personally for the part of *Sandy*. Surprisingly, Mr Woodcock championed the other, asking if the teachers would get to dress up. He got his way mainly because of the lack of decent singers. He looked suitably grotesque in fishnet tights when he came for all three performances, and Tom preferred to think back to his library 'performance' rather than him as a cross-dressing roadie. Tom Frampton from Lower Sixth Music carried the show, though. Four encores on the last night before Mr Abbott, the Headmaster, had called things to a close. Paul had found an entire set of coloured filters and although a bit nervous to begin with had played with all the lights throughout every rehearsal till he felt comfortable he knew what he was doing. The lighting was so good that you didn't even notice how good it was. And Tom and Paul got to spend most of their free time together.

"Lordie! Lordie! Why, Master Armstrong, I do declare..." Tom was camping it up with an exaggerated Texan drawl.

"Sssh, please! Not so loud. People might hear us." Paul looked around the canteen to see if anyone was looking at them. He liked to remain anonymous and avoid conflict or unpleasantness.

"What's the matter?" Tom leaned back in his chair and looked at Paul, laughing. "Worried your big butch macho mates from tech drawing will get funny ideas about you?"

"Don't be a prick!" Paul blushed slightly.

"Keep it down, you fucking queer," shouted Andy Gerard, putting his tray down to come and harass Tom. Paul stood up and folded his arm. The boy looked up at him. He swallowed nervously.

"Err, no. Sorry, man. I was shouting at someone through the window." Paul watched him go and then sat down again.

Tom let the front legs of his chair back on the floor and sat back at the table. "Hey, look. I'm sorry. I just haven't come down yet after the show last week."

Paul smiled at him, "Yeah, that's OK. You should be proud of yourself. You were absolutely amazing." Tom couldn't help but smile. "I mean, I knew you could sing, but that just took my breath away."

Tom looked at him, suddenly quite serious: "You know... hearing you say that means a lot to me."

"Fuck off!"

"No, really."

Paul looked down at his plate. He wanted to smile and laugh with Tom and make him feel special and happy. He was just a little afraid. He wondered if he'd overstepped the mark a bit already and whether Tom might think he was a bit strange. He wanted to slide his hand over to Tom's, look him in the eye, and tell him just how good he was. But blokes don't do that sort of thing, Paul thought. What would people think? It didn't feel right.

Instead, Paul went on: "There's one thing that's got to go, though."

Tom looked at him and raised an eyebrow. "And?"

"Thomas Lionel Frampton."

"OK, yes, that's my name. What about it?"

"You need a proper stage name. You're bigger than a summer season at some washed up southcoast theatre, and definitely something more than a wet Saturday matinée in Weymouth."

Tom looked thoughtful. Paul was right, of course, but he'd never really considered it until now.

"Look," Paul said, collecting his things, "I've got a lesson now. Let's go down to the seawall after school." Tom was all for that.

It was probably true: his name would be a drawback. Paul and Tom were sitting on the seawall looking out over the English Channel. This was a favourite place of theirs in the summer term at least, and they'd been coming after school since they were about 14 or 15. Paul's parents had not wanted them to be unsupervised before that.

"You can't be a headline act with a name like that!" Paul

laughed. "Who's ever heard of a pop star with a name like Frampton?"

"Well, actually," Tom started. He squinted at Paul's face, just checking he was being serious. Which he was. Paul had lots to offer but being up to date with the pop scene was not one of them. "You're probably right. I need something a bit snappier."

"And Lionel's an awful name – makes you think of that queer dancer bloke." Paul regretted saying it as soon as he had.

"Better than Reginald!" Tom laughed, digging Paul in the shoulder gently.

"Point taken. Paul Reginald Armstrong wouldn't sound too good on *Top of the Pops* either, I suppose."

"Well, Reginald..."

"You won't ever tell anyone about that, will you, Tom?"

"Of course not. Your secret's safe with me. That's what mates are for after all." Tom looked out to sea and went on: "You know *any* secret between us is safe with me. I'd take it to my grave."

They sat in silence for a while. Tom didn't know whether he'd gone a bit too far, and Paul looked away down the coast, wondering if he could see as far as Devon that way.

"Anyway," said Tom, with a mock punch to his friend's arm, the way real men do, "back to my stage name. So, what's it to be?"

"Keep the 'Tom'."

"Not Thomas?"

"Too biblical."

"Okay. But is that 'Thom' with an 'h'? Make it a bit more exotic."

"You are joking, aren't you? 'Thom' would just be ridiculous. No one would know how to pronounce it for one thing."

"Alright," said Tom. "So, we keep 'Tom'? How about Tom L Frampton?"

"Bit of a mouthful." Tom flinched slightly, but his friend continued, "Drop the 'L' and what about the 'Frampton'?"

"Something like 'Spark' – you know, something out there."

"What, like the Channel Islands?" Paul snorted "They'd think you're an electrician!"

"'Tinkle' then? Tom Tinkle. The alliteration makes it better."

"Sounds like something a little kid does in the toilet."

"Oh, God... this is hopeless. You got any bright ideas?"

"That's it!" Paul shouted and turned to his friend. He almost touched his shoulder, but his hand came to rest on the seawall again. "Tom Bright... Perfect!"

"Really?" Tom sounded doubtful.

"No. It's perfect. It sounds upbeat and positive. Makes me smile."

Tom awkwardly grasped Paul's arm and put his own round Paul's shoulder and rocked him back and forth in a matey, jokey sort of way. This uncharacteristic gesture made Paul feel uncomfortable, but he was glad to have found a stage name that Tom seemed to like. Tom had always ached to touch Paul, just to be close friends and not feel embarrassed. Other blokes did, so why couldn't he? But he could feel Paul stiffen and he let go quickly enough.

"Time we were heading back," said Paul. And Tom's heart sank.

They strolled along in silence for a while. Paul was

gazing out to sea, and Tom just looked at his shoes. He felt wretched and just wished he hadn't gone so far. But then:

"You will remember us, won't you," Paul was still looking out over the waves, "when you're big and famous?" Tom perked up immediately.

"I'll never forget you... forget this place and you guys!"

"Tom Bright... Tom Bright..."

"Alright, don't wear it out!" Tom chuckled.

"I can see it now: Tom Bright in neon at the Bournemouth Palais. Maybe I could do the lighting?"

"Stuff Bournemouth, mate. It's the West End. Or maybe Vegas. Would you come and see me in Vegas? I could get you a green card to work there too!" Tom was getting a bit carried away again and was trying to get Paul to turn and look him in the eye.

"Maybe not Vegas," Paul said, glancing at Tom then at the ground, "bit tacky. Maybe New York, though, or... San Francisco."

Tom stopped and gawped at the back of Paul's head. His hair was unfashionably short. But that just meant it emphasised how well-proportioned his head was against his broad shoulders and back. Paul looked round briefly. "Come on, slow coach! You've got packing to do."

"The selfish bastards!" Paul hissed when he met Tom one morning on the way into school.

"What's wrong, buddy?" asked Tom. He was actually quite worried, since Paul so rarely showed any emotion. Something must really be wrong.

"They've sold the fucking farm, the hillbillies!"

It took a few seconds to work out what his friend was talking about. Then the penny dropped.

"Will tell you all about it later!" and Paul was gone down the tech corridor.

Tom turned and slowly went down the arts corridor. He didn't know whether to laugh or cry. He was devastated on the one hand that this would mean no long hot summer's nights in the middle of the countryside just a hair's breadth away from Paul, no jumping into the cold stream in the all-together to cool off, no spreading sun cream across those beautiful shoulders and up his neck. But on the other hand, and he had to control his excitement here: he wanted to jump up and punch the air and shout. If Paul was annoyed with his relatives for selling up, then Paul wanted to spend the summer with him again. Even Regis Fournier, the handsome French assistant, couldn't distract him from that thought.

The spell was broken soon after though, as Vickie Freeman plonked herself down next to him whilst Regis droned on about something incomprehensible:

"The subjunctive is the mood for possibility, for dreams..." he was saying in that thick French accent that Tom found so appealing. He also liked watching his lips when he said 'mood'. He sat back and waited for Vickie to say something. She asked him to pass a message onto Paul. She said that she wanted to go out with him. For the whole lesson, he couldn't concentrate. It was stupid, he knew that, and he was torn between loyalty to his friend and wanting him to be happy, and his own hopes and dreams. It set his head in a spin. True, Paul was handsome in an understated way and maybe girls liked the shy, strong, intelligent type. But what if Tom had misinterpreted the signs all this time? Perhaps wanting to go back to Bramdean farm with him was no more than good company. Maybe the stains on the sheets were for a girl? Even Vickie Freeman?

"Vickie Freeman came and sat next to me in French today," said Tom in a casual way as he and Paul ate lunch together.

"Who?" said Paul.

"You know that girl in my French class with the long straight hair and split ends." He wished he'd not mentioned the last bit. "She hangs round with Janice Walker."

"OK, help me here. Who's Janice Walker?" Tom looked at his friend. Was he playing hard to get, or did he really not know who these girls were? "Anyway, look. She wants to know if you'll go out with her."

"Shit!"

"What's wrong?"

"I don't... I'm not into..." Paul blushed a deep red. Tom had never seen him this uncomfortable since they were about 11. Narrowing his eyes, he looked carefully at his profile. Paul put his head in his hands. Was Paul trying to tell him something? Neither of them said anything for quite a while. Tom was thinking.

"How about this," he began, unsure whether he should say it. "We make it a foursome." Paul stiffened slightly. "You take Vickie and I'll take that girl in the fifth form from *The Rocky Horror Show*."

Paul sat back. He was thinking about this now. But not just this particular occasion. Tom was popular with people, and since the musical, people had found him cool. Even if some of the Neanderthals had called him queer and poofta and that sort of stuff, but generally people liked him. For Paul, it was different. He wasn't 'normal' to some people, he was shy, he didn't fight, he could be an egghead especially about literature, and at the same time, he was a bit of a nerd when it came to technical things, especially lighting. Paul preferred to stay in the shadows and blend into the background. Maybe going on a date with a girl, though, would mean that people would treat him as just another lad. And they wouldn't think he was strange anymore.

Paul looked into his friend's face. This was so uncharacteristic, and his gaze was so intense, searching for something, wanting something, that it was Tom who looked away and bowed his head a little.

"Did you like that fifth form girl, then?"

Before he could think, Tom blurted: "Fuck me, no! Not my deal..." then, hurriedly, "I mean, if I'm going to ask someone... a girl out, I'm more likely to succeed with someone who's younger than me! That's the way it is with these things." And what the Hell would you know about it? He thought to himself. Paul considered what he'd said carefully.

"God, I don't know..."

"Look. *Murder on the Orient Express* is on in town. We could take them there. Buy them sweets and a drink. That'll do. They'll love it!"

"And where did you get all of this experience all of a sudden?"

"Trust me!" Tom didn't know why he'd said that. He shifted uneasily in his seat. He was thinking of the two girls sitting between him and Paul, and then when the lights went down, feeling for Paul's finger tips behind the seats. Romantically holding hands while the two girls slurped their Coca-Cola and munched popcorn and drooled over a 20-ft Sean Connery or Michael York on the silver screen. Come to think of it...

"Oh, God. I don't know. Shit!" Paul looked uneasy.

Paul was puzzled by Tom's suggestion they should take these girls out. He felt that maybe Tom was in fact moving on. Although they were still good friends, maybe it really was time to concentrate on just being a friend, Paul wondered. Since he'd always managed to hide his true feelings, he thought, it shouldn't be too difficult. Peggy noticed that his mood had changed that afternoon. She didn't have time to ask questions before she had to set off for work. When he asked the next day whether she minded him going out with two girls and Tom to the cinema the following Saturday, she decided that that must have had something to do with his mood. She felt relieved. That night, he lay awake till the small hours, trying to decide what he should do.

Two days later, Tom was completely nonplussed to see Paul shoulder his bag during morning break and go and ask Vickie Freeman out. She messed with her hair and went all coy. She said she'd have to ask at home, and she'd let Paul know tomorrow. With a weird and uncharacteristic swagger, Paul turned and came over to Tom.

"You alright, buddy? You look a bit green round the gills. You sick or something?"

Paul swallowed and took a deep breath. He didn't look at Tom.

"Your turn now. You have to ask that girl out too." No pressure, then, thought Tom. By lunchtime the next day, the four of them had arranged to go to the cinema.

"Erm, I wanted to ask a favour," Paul looked nervous.

"Fire away!" said Tom brightly.

"Well, the thing is..."

"Stop right there. I'm not going to have to drag this one out of you, am I?"

Paul laughed nervously.

"Look. I've no idea about clothes," Paul went on. Tom raised an eyebrow. "Can we meet in town on Saturday afternoon, and you can, you know, just give me a bit of a hand? You know, if you're not busy and..."

"Of course!" Tom was absolutely delighted. "So, you want to look a smooth, sophisticated, James Bond type?"

"Fuck off! I just don't want to look like some throwback from the sixties."

So they met on Saturday outside *Boots* at two. Paul was anxious to buy something from the first shop they went into, but Tom insisted they go to several different places and compare what was on sale. Finally, an hour later, Paul was ready to go home with a flowery shirt and some flares. Tom had wanted something more flamboyant, but they were loud enough, Paul said.

"I just want to blend in," he'd said tight-lipped and on edge.

"You'll look great," Tom reassured him. As they left each other having made plans for where to meet that evening, Tom felt a little guilty. But he knew Paul would indeed look amazing. So, he just concentrated on having a good time that evening and seeing Paul in tight, figure-hugging trousers.

Around seven, they converged in the centre of town and made their way to meet the girls before heading for the cinema. Paul noticed that his outfit toned with Tom's, the colours in the paisley subtly complementing the swirls in Paul's flowery shirt. No one held hands, and no one seemed to mind. Pauline Shooter, the fifth former Tom had asked, had her coat buttoned to up to her chin. Vickie clutched her bag as she came out of the door to meet them. Her hair had been smoothed and set into a bob and she wore an old-fashioned short dress with a Peter Pan collar and dropped waist, finished off with black patent leather shoes. Pauline, in her fashionable maxi dress, looked at her contemptuously. Paul couldn't take his eyes off Vickie's hair. It didn't seem to move however strong the breeze. Tom noticed his fascination and fell silent as they walked to the cinema. Pauline walked on her own, her arms folded tight across her chest.

Fortunately, the back row was full by the time they got in and *Pearl and Dean* had just started. So, they found their seats halfway down with some difficulty. Paul had a sneezing fit brought on by Vickie's hairspray. She leaned away from him to keep her hair straight and dress clean, which meant that Pauline had to lean too to keep out of her way. Once they'd all settled again, and Paul's reaction to the lacquer had settled, Tom idly put his arm across the back of Pauline's seat. He was still imaging Paul reaching across in his turn while the girls watched the film. A few minutes later, Pauline responded to the arm across the back of her seat and nestled into Tom's side. He stared at the back of her head in disbelief. He adjusted how he was sitting, which she took as an invitation to get closer. To Tom's increasing discomfort, Pauline even put a hand on his thigh and rubbed it gently. Tom froze and stared, wide-eyed, in Paul's direction, who suppressed a laugh and winked back at him. Vickie seemed to be focused on her drink and the popcorn he'd bought for her. So Paul could relax.

Vickie drank her Coca-Cola too quickly and had eaten all her popcorn by the time the interval started. In the second half, she started on a bag of wine gums she'd brought with her but didn't share. Three quarters of the way through the film, she felt queasy and said she needed the toilets. With lots of sighing and loud whispers from the people in the rows behind, Pauline managed to get Vickie out of their row, up the aisle and to the *Ladies*. Paul took advantage of the girls leaving to move and sit next to Tom. He rolled his eyes and smiled briefly at Tom, who was pleased to have him so close. He didn't move his arm. They were both growing teenagers now and struggled in the narrow gap between rows in the cinema. As Paul shifted down in his seat to make sure he wasn't leaning on Tom's arm, he couldn't avoid his leg pressing against Tom's. Neither moved. They tried to remain nonchalant.

About ten minutes later, Pauline stomped her way back down the aisle, peering along each row till she recognised Tom and Paul.

"Vickie's been sick and needs to go home." She told them in a loud stage whisper. Paul wanted to curl up and die. Tom thought it was funny. They made their excuses and a lot more discreetly this time, exited the row, and the auditorium. They walked Vickie home – she didn't live too far away – and when her mother opened the door, she took one look at her daughter and sighed.

"When will you learn, Victoria Freeman? Only have one treat at the cinema and share them!" She waved Vickie in and turned to the rest of them. "She does this every time. We tell her when she goes, then she fetches up home before the film's finished. Did she make it past the interval this time?"

Tom and Paul offered to walk Pauline home. But she was alright on her own, she said, and left them to themselves. Alone at last, they both seemed to relax.

"Same time next week, then?" Paul said. "Only just us two this time?"

Tom laughed. They walked back together along the seawall, discussing who they thought was the murderer, until Tom had to peel off and walk up the hill towards where he lived. As he walked the last bit home on his own, Paul thought back over the evening. It had been exhausting dating a girl, he thought. He'd laughed at Tom's reaction to Pauline getting up so close. But still he was unsure. After all, Tom seemed to get along very well with his cousin, Lucy. Perhaps he just didn't like Pauline. Maybe she was too young for him? It began to dawn on him that being just a friend with Tom was going to be upsetting and exhausting. He was determined to try, though, he didn't want to lose Tom all together. He just didn't know whether he was strong enough to share him.

Vickie did not appear in school the following week till Wednesday. She couldn't look at Paul or Tom. But Paul went and found her when she was on her own.

"Hey, are you OK?" he asked as gently as he could.

Vickie flushed red and went to turn away.

"I just wanted to make sure you're alright now. Please, don't be embarrassed. Really."

At last, Vickie looked up at his face. She tried a little smile.

"Thanks, Paul," she said, "I just get a bit nervous."

Paul smiled and tapped her gently on the arm as he turned and went back to Tom.

Pauline had not gone straight home, apparently, but had met up with her own friends in town. She'd been taken home unceremoniously by the police. That was it, then. Paul had tried dating and would leave it another year before he'd let Tom persuade him again. They'd established their credentials as datable material. Meanwhile, they had each other.

Ed Aldridge was asked to leave halfway through his second year. He'd been arrested for smoking dope at a party in Bournemouth, and Mr Abbott, the headmaster, thought it would be better if Ed agreed to leave. There would be no more school musicals. As a compromise, Regis Fournier suggested they do something around *Les Liaisons Dangereuses* that the French A-Level group were studying. Miss Mobberley and Mrs Gibbons suggested they could have a masked ball in the summer. But Tom was bitterly disappointed.

"Don't worry, Tom," Paul was trying to cheer his friend up, "when you get to drama school, there'll be plenty of opportunities to sing and act again. And anyway," Tom looked up half expecting something special to come next.

A date, just the two of them, maybe? "You're too good for round here!" Tom smiled; along with everything else, Paul was loyal – the complete package. He knew he'd never find anyone like him again. He didn't know how he'd manage college without him there each day.

"Paul?" he looked across at Paul. He'd had to start shaving sooner than Tom, and his jaw was covered in real stubble not just fluff. Wearing only a t-shirt today that was a little too small for him, as he raised his arms, and folded them behind his head, Tom could see his armpits had sprouted a lot of hair. Tom tried not to look, but he wanted to be closer and smell his friend's body. He tried to focus on something else but then could see a lot more body hair marching down towards his pelvis than he'd remembered, a bit like on Mr Woodcock's back and stomach. Paul glanced sideways at him.

"Will you miss me?" Tom asked out of nowhere.

Paul righted his chair abruptly, returning all four legs to the ground pretty noisily. Mrs Swale looked across.

"I don't want to think about it." Paul said. And Tom just sat there. Surely this told him what he'd longed to know for so very long?

"Well, Guildford's not that far from Bournemouth." Tom was moving closer to London to study, and Paul had been accepted on a technical lighting and stage management course closer to home. "And we'll have our grants and everything. So, we can meet up at weekends!" This seemed to set Paul's mind at rest, for now. But then he said:

"I don't want this year to end." The bell rang, and Paul picked up his things and set off for his last tech drawing lesson before their A Levels.

Once they'd finished their exams, they had more time together and began to plan work on the assembly hall to get it ready for the ball.

"I'm not wearing any fucking mask, you know," Paul sounded petulant. "Bloody stupid idea!"

"Me neither," said Tom. "Who's going to be fooled by masks anyway? Oh, except that oaf, Woodcock, of course. He'll doubtless turn up dressed as bloody Zorro."

"Apparently, lower sixth art have produced a fucking great banner we're supposed to string across the front of the stage."

"What are you doing with the lights?"

"The theatre's lending me a glitter ball. So once that's fixed, I need to get some moving spots to sweep the room and occasionally hit the ball."

"Sounds fancy."

"Not really. I'll need to light this banner they've done. So, we can't hang it too far back on the stage. Otherwise, none of the spots will reach it. They don't hang that low or swing that high. But we'll leave that till last."

"Alright. Show me where, then."

Paul and Tom made their way to the assembly hall. There were still exams on, but not that afternoon. So they were able to go up on stage and check out the lay-out. Paul said they weren't allowed to drop any of the rigging in case it fell and hurt someone. They'd have to use the stepladders to put the banner up. The week went achingly slowly while the tail-end of the exams finished.

"Come on Armstrong," Tom announced the day before the dance.

"What?" said Paul, looking at him as they sat together looking out across the Channel. They'd both been meeting as often as possible, just to chat and make plans for how they would be able to meet up next year.

"You need something special to wear to the dance," Tom looked Paul up and down.

"But I've got that stuff we bought to go to the cinema that time," he shuddered slightly at the thought of it.

"That's so last year, Paul, you've got to keep up with the times, if you're going to attract the girls!" He regretted saying it as soon as the words came out of his mouth. Neither of them spoke for some time. Tom was not looking forward to saying goodbye to Paul after the dance. He wasn't sure they'd meet up during the holidays, and he didn't want to think about packing and leaving for Guildford on his own. Of course, Gwen would take him and settle him in, but that wasn't what he was thinking about. He dreaded being away from Paul a whole term. Saying something stupid like that was just a joke to try and lighten his own mood.

"Alright," Paul agreed reluctantly, "but none of those tight trousers. I didn't know where to look!"

Tom dragged Paul into the local department store, and they searched through the men's fashions in the basement. Tom pulled shirt after shirt from the racks and held them up to Paul to have an impression of what they looked like. It didn't seem to matter what Paul thought. But Paul didn't mind. He liked the attention from Tom. He was finding it hard thinking of what would happen after the summer. Being just friends seemed to be difficult too. He thought he was managing quite well until Tom had mentioned dressing him up to 'attract the girls'. That wasn't what he wanted at all. Did Tom mean, though, that he was hoping to attract someone special at the dance? Paul stood obediently like a mannequin while Tom dashed around picking clothes. He refused to let Tom into the changing rooms with him, but he was patient enough to try on whatever Tom asked him to.

"What about you?" Paul asked finally.

"Oh, I'm alright," Tom said airily, "I'll find something that matches."

On the ground floor, as they made for the door, they had to go through the perfumery.

"And you need some aftershave," Tom dived down one of the aisles, knowing Paul would follow. The sales staff where a bit taken aback with two young men in shorts and t-shirt with bags from men's fashion downstairs and messing around with testers. Or rather, Tom was spraying Paul whenever he wasn't looking.

"Nothing too girlie!" Paul protested. So, Tom approached one of the cosmetics consultants. She found several fragrances and they cornered Paul, spraying up his arms until he was completely confused. Finally, the consultant had sprayed two men's fragrances on each of Tom's wrists and told Paul to see which he preferred. He was hesitant but leant forward slightly and took a sniff. Reluctantly, he chose one. Tom smelt it and agreed. The consultant then cleaned Paul's own wrist with cleansing wipes explaining that some fragrances smelled different on different people and sprayed a generous amount onto his skin. Tom and Paul almost knocked heads as they both leaned over to see what it smelled like. That was it. They both agreed, though for Paul it was more about pleasing Tom. Having something special to remind him of the friend he loved and didn't want to lose. So obediently, Paul bought a 100ml bottle of *Masculin II* and they were done.

"It's only just been launched," said the cosmetics consultant with a nasal twang to her voice as she put the aftershave in a small paper bag.

"Don't you want something, Tom?" Paul asked, pocketing his wallet.

"Nah, there's loads of stuff at home. I'll just decide on the night what suits my mood." He tweaked his eyebrows suggestively at Paul, who tutted, and they both headed for the door at last.

"You will wear it on Saturday, won't you?" Tom asked.

"Well, if it'll make you happy, then yes, OK."

"The aftershave as well?"

"The aftershave too."

Tom had fallen in love with the distinctive fragrance and couldn't wait to see other people's reaction to Paul wearing it. The fit, shy guy, with the beginnings of a beard and smelling like a real man, looking suave in his chocolate brown satin shirt and tight flares. He couldn't wait.

Eventually, Paul and Tom agreed they'd come in on the Saturday of the ball during the day and hang the banner. Taking advantage of their new freedom as 18 year olds now, Tom suggested they have a few drinks at the pub on the way in. Several *Carlsberg Special Brews* later and feeling merry, they took themselves off to the school. The caretaker had given them a key, provided, he'd be very insistent, they make sure it gets back into his office by Monday morning at 10.

The assembly hall was quite dark and shady that afternoon. They could barely see one another across the gloom. Tom went straight up on stage, and before he knew it, he was bathed in a single spot.

"Ladies and gentlemen," a disembodied voice began somewhere, "please be upstanding and welcome onstage the one and only... Tom Bright!"

Tom took a bow and waved to his imagined and adoring fans.

"You idiot!" he laughed. "I'd almost forgotten my new stage name!" Paul was grinning when he joined Tom on the stage with a rather rickety set of stepladders.

"I'm not sure I should've had that second *Special Brew*, you know." Tom looked at Paul.

"You OK?"

"Yeah, I'm fine. Would you mind going up the stepladder though? I'll hand you the banner and take the weight, and I'll steady the steps." Tom nodded and dragged the steps stage right and more down- than upstage.

"This about right?" he said. Paul came over dragging one end of the banner.

"Yeah, that should do." So, they started to hang the banner from some of the rigging, moving the steps along to a new point to tie the six sets of ties to keep the banner up. Tom could smell a mix of *Special Brew,* Paul's sweat, and the *Masculin II*. He felt really happy here alone in the shadows with Paul. He made himself focus on the here and now. He didn't want to think about tomorrow, or the summer. He loved Paul so much, he knew it was going to be desperate without him. He felt he needed to do something, to show Paul how he felt. Now, this evening, this was his last chance.

They'd almost finished with Tom up the step ladder stage left. The big rainbow banner stretched from one side of the stage to the other, lit for the moment by the single spot Paul had trained on Tom. The ladder wobbled disconcertingly, and Paul grabbed for it to steady it so that Tom wouldn't fall.

"Sorry, that was me," said Tom, "I think I'm the one that needs steadying."

Paul wrapped his arms around Tom's legs. He knew this smell, even under the alcohol and perfume. Tom's legs were hairier now than they had been that summer in Bramdean. And the sea air had bronzed them slightly. He liked their shape. Nothing over muscled, but a real man's legs now. Tom was growing up into a very attractive man. Paul didn't want to let him go. He began to breathe deeply and steadily. The smell was as he'd always known it, though now, he noticed, it was stronger and muskier. Paul ached inside. Whether it was the drink or the aftershave or his friend's scent, he didn't want to be apart from him. Even for just a term.

Tom was aware of Paul's breathing. It took him back to hot balmy summer nights. He remembered how he'd felt that first night when darkness had fallen, and he was just inches away from Paul. Nothing else mattered right now. He wondered if he could change his course from Guildford to Bournemouth. How would Paul react? He imagined turning up as a big surprise. The look on Paul's face. The beaming smile. The bright eyes and square jaw above a broad chest. Or was he just imaging it like that because he wanted Paul so much. After all, Paul had agreed to buy the clothes and the aftershave to attract the girls. Wasn't that what he'd said?

Tom could hear nothing but Paul's slow, steady breaths. He could feel Paul's strong arms around his thighs, his head close to his pelvis. He could smell nothing but Paul. He was excited. At the same time, he was worried. He only had shorts on and, for the first time ever, he'd worn a jock underneath, to see what it felt like. He desperately tried to concentrate on what he was doing. He could feel Paul swaying slightly, his strong arms firm around him, his beautiful face so very close. Paul coughed a little. He was starting to feel nauseous. But he had a job to do. He had to hold on to Tom, his legs, his shorts, his divine smell. As if their lives depended on it.

"All done!" Tom announced at last.

Paul loosened his grip. Another time maybe and with more confidence than the beer gave him – which if he were honest was beginning to turn on him and make him feel unwell – another time, he'd have held Tom's hand to steady him down the steps. Confused himself, Tom misjudged the final rung and landed heavily on his back foot, the step ladders crashing down towards centre stage. Paul ignored the ladders and grabbed Tom to steady him. He didn't want him to fall. He wanted to hold him and protect him. He didn't want him to leave.

But he didn't know what he wanted at that precise moment. The beer was already in his throat. He felt queasy, but he couldn't let Tom go.

And then it happened.

Neither of them really knew how or what they felt. As Paul held Tom as gently but as firmly as he could, his strong arms keeping his closest and dearest friend from falling and going away from him.

Tom didn't really know why he did it. He would go over and over it as he got older. Like so many times when they were growing up together. Before either of them knew what was going on, Tom leant forward in Paul's arms and kissed him awkwardly on the lips. Paul froze and backed away. The last thing Tom remembered was Paul downstage left, retching into the legs at that side of the stage.

2

There was a bit of a delay at Dover, fortunately nothing to do with the choreographer, José-Luis. He'd come off the ferry as a foot passenger with the big rucksack and its many compartments on his back as usual. The immigration officer had waved him through, but the customs official had insisted on rummaging through the rucksack. Once that was all sorted, he was left to repack. He promised himself he'd get something more practical, less conspicuous, and maybe even more fashionable rather than the large, square canvas box which always drew attention from customs officials. He wasn't a student anymore after all. He walked slowly up the slope from the ferry terminal to wait for the tour bus.

Even with unpacking and repacking all the pockets on the rucksack, José-Luis still had to wait a good 45 minutes for the bus to appear. The relief driver had managed to get a message to Tom at the airport to let them know what had happened. Usually coming from France would be straightforward. But the Conservative Party Conference in a few weeks' time at Bournemouth had meant heightened security. Saying that they were heading for Weymouth made it worse. The security officers seemed to have checked everything: all the seats, in the luggage spaces, even the engine. Of course, they'd found nothing.

The bus pulled off even before José-Luis had managed to get to a seat, sending him stumbling towards the back of the bus, doing his best to keep his balance. He slumped onto the back seat and tried to sleep. He wasn't sure how long it would take to get to Heathrow and meet up with the others. He was uneasy with both drivers whom he felt to be uncomfortable around men like him. Without Tom and the others, he felt particularly vulnerable. Being foreign as well, olive-skinned with a noticeable accent just made it more obvious. And he already sensed that there was a hostile climate in the country which was difficult to ignore.

Tom was glad for the message, especially knowing that José-Luis had walked straight through. Well almost. He was glad too that they'd got the message before they'd ventured out of the terminal building. There'd been a lot of photographers as usual when they'd got off the plane, and lots of questions about what the tour might include, about why it had taken this long for Tom Bright to come back to the UK. And the eternal question about whether there was anyone special in his life yet. The paparazzi had only ever managed pictures of him with some uncomfortably young girl stealing a kiss on the cheek. The press were beginning to ask why there was never any scandal in this direction. Not even the usual hush-hush deals about drug-fuelled promiscuity. Tom accepted it as part of the job, but it was still tiring, especially at these times after their flights. What he dreaded most was the hordes of teenage girls screaming outside when they were trying to get onto the coach. He hoped no one had found the name of the hotel in Weymouth, though admittedly there weren't that many options. For now, anyway, they could wait inside the terminal in the VIP lounge until they heard otherwise.

There were the usual collections of magazines in the lounge. Glossy pictures of perfect properties presumably housing perfect couples, whose children – a boy and a girl – were well-behaved with cut-glass accents, spending their weekends riding or playing rugger. Nothing as cheap as *Jackie* or the *New Musical Express* and *Smash Hits*, where he was used to appearing. But there was a copy of *The Face* that unexpectedly caught his eye. There was an issue of *Vogue* in front of it hiding the bottom of the face. And there was just something about the eyes which drew his attention. A sadness which strangely he identified with. Pulling the magazine out of the rack, he recognised his own face immediately. He couldn't remember that particular shot; he was wearing a cap he didn't know he owned which was his excuse. What he was struggling with was the look in the eyes. He was looking over his right shoulder directly into the camera lens, a single spotlight on a stand in front of him and out of shot to the right, so behind him from the camera's perspective. 'What on earth was I trying to hide?' he wondered. And without thinking, he turned to look over his shoulder, just to check if there was actually someone there. Watching him. Knowing more about him than he would wish to tell. He just never realised how uncomfortable he was with life.

Finally, Jason, the sound engineer, appeared in the doorway to the lounge.

"It's here!" he shouted, "and they're loading everything up now. Give them ten minutes or so. There's quite a few girls outside. Here," Jason handed him some shades, "you might want to wear these. Hide that rather scary glare!" Jason was smiling as he said it, but Tom found the throw-away comment disturbing.

They gathered up their hand luggage. Tom put *The Face* back on the rack. He still couldn't take his eyes from the picture. Finally, he turned away and hurried to catch up with the others. Otherwise, he'd have to run the gauntlet of the screaming girls alone. Somehow, he couldn't stop thinking about the cover of *The Face*, and that sad and worried gaze over his shoulder. The odd effect of the light shining across his chest, but him turning away from it and still visible. As he prepared to try and make his way through the excited teenagers, signing whatever they handed to him and unable to hear himself think above all the noise, he caught José-Luis's eyes glaring down at him from the coach. He looked serious. Pensive, almost. Then, coming out of his reverie, his stare softened, and he flashed a sympathetic smile at Tom battling his way through the crowd.

The tour bus edged slowly forward, the driver being careful not to run anyone over. There were occasions, though, when the banging on the windows was so insistent that he was afraid they'd break something. He'd grit his teeth and hope for the best. José-Luis knew to stay put while the coach moved off, camera flashes through the windows as they crawled forward. Tom didn't want anyone seeing them embrace, even though José-Luis was obviously foreign. As everyone knew, foreign men kissed each other all the time in the street. Even macho Spaniards and Italians. People in the UK just didn't go in for that sort of thing. Just before they picked up speed, there was a final determined thud on the side of the tour bus. Tom jumped. He turned to look over his shoulder to see where what had happened. The lights of the terminal lit his chest and the side of his face.

"Wow! Look at that!" Jason was sitting in a set of two double seats with a table between them. He and Greg, the musical director, had some beers for the journey to Weymouth.

"What?" Greg said, turning to see what Jason was looking at.

"That's the same pose on *The Face* in the VIP lounge. How weird is that!?"

Greg stood up, ready to move next to Jason on the double seat facing the direction the bus was travelling.

"Oh yes," he agreed, "I'd not seen that pose before."

"Montreal," a muffled voice came from behind them. "I got that strange Canadian guy to take some shots to see if we could use any of them." Julia was in the back looking at the newspaper she'd picked up in the lounge with extensive coverage of the Conservative Party Conference in Bournemouth. Hidden by the back of the seat, Jason mouthed 'Smart arse' and Greg laughed as he sat down.

"She's a know-all, that one," Greg said, taking a long swig of beer as he sat down, looking through the window at the shrubs between the road and the security fence.

"Too right," said Jason. "Why is she so waspish? She's turned into a right bitch."

"Hell hath no fury…" Greg winked knowingly at Jason, putting his finger in front of his mouth to tell Jason to keep it quiet.

"What?" Jason whispered, "you mean she fancies Tom?"

"Fancied. Barking up the wrong tree there, of course," Greg nodded, "but ever since then, she's been a bit prickly." Jason realised he knew what Greg meant.

"What do you think about that sort of thing?" Jason asked, "You know, shirt lifters?"

"Well, none of my business, really," said Greg. "It's show-biz, lovie!" he lisped, letting his hand flop from a limp wrist, and they both laughed. "No really," he went on, "Tom's a decent bloke. He can do what he likes with whoever he likes as far as I'm concerned. Just so long as they don't expect me to bat for the other side, like."

"What, a bit like the Mormons?" Jason pitched in.

"Prick!" Greg snorted. "No, but he is a nice bloke. A lot of popstars I've worked for are real arseholes."

"Bad choice of words there," Jason pointed out, sniggering like a school boy.

"Don't be a dick… Oh, anyway. No, really. Some of them stay in swanky hotels and travel first class and all that stuff. Then expect mere mortals like us to travel economy and slum it in some draughty B & B with candlewick bedspreads and shared bathrooms." Greg shuddered as he said it.

"Yeah, you've got a point there," Jason agreed. "Well, there's other fringe benefits to it, though."

"Such as?" Greg asked, looking sideways to Jason.

"Well, if he's not interested in girls," Jason took a swig from the can in his hand, gesturing back to the terminal, "More for us!"

"You sad bastard!" Greg laughed, and then, "You're right, though. And they all think you'll get them closer to Tom."

"I never thought of it like that," Jason said. "Not sure I feel too good about it either, now you come to mention it."

Greg pulled a coin out of his pocket. "Toss you for Julia," he said, struggling not to laugh.

"Yeah, be my guest, pal!" Jason laughed. "But anyway, Tom's always been straight with me."

"Now you're the one using unfortunate words," Greg laughed. "I'm liking this particular job, when it comes down to it. He surprises me every time he sings, you know. You should hear him without the backing music. It'd make the hair stand up on the back of your neck. Not sure about Weymouth, though. I'd only ever heard of it vaguely before. You ever been?"

"No," said Jason, "me neither. Is it all Kiss-m-Kwik hats and candyfloss?"

"Isn't that Blackpool?"

They started to talk about Weymouth and what the theatre was like there and where they would be going after that.

"A mate of mine over in Bournemouth reckons this is a real coup for Weymouth," Greg said.

"What? A bunch of fairies with maracas?" Jason couldn't help himself and laughed loudly.

"Yeah, yeah! Very clever," Greg rolled his eyes and gulped down some more beer. "Apparently, there's some whizz who does the lighting and stuff like that though."

"He a gay boy too?" Jason asked.

"God, you're obsessed, you are!" Greg said.

"Yeah, sorry. It's the beer talking. That's me done now with queers. So, this lighting chap. Why is he so good?"

"Well, my mate said he'd been in Bournemouth straight out of college, like. Right from the off, he was doing things with the lights they'd not seen before."

"Sound like a gem. So, why did he leave Bournemouth to go to some shitty little place like Weymouth?" Jason asked.

"Now, we don't know that..." Greg caught Jason's eye. "Alright, well, if you like *Val Doonican* and *The Black and White Minstrels*." They both laughed and clinked cans. "Apparently," Greg continued, "he's a bit of a quiet type. But knows all of Shakespeare off by heart."

"Yeah," said Jason, "that really does sound weird. Mind you, in my experience, all the guys who work backstage are bit strange."

"Bet they don't all know Shakespeare, though," Greg observed.

"True. So, wonder-boy is at Weymouth now, then?" said Jason.

"Yep. One less thing for Tom to worry about, I suppose." Greg took a long swig from his can and looked out of the window at the rain. A while later, when they'd used up all the things they had to say to one another, Greg moved back to the other side of the table and dozed off.

Eventually, the tour bus pulled out of Heathrow and onto the main road. Tom's face staring down at them from the billboards at the junction. José-Luis was surprised to see that look he'd come to know so well, the fashionably untidy hair, the smile and the perfect teeth, and that sadness about the eyes that had first attracted him to the singer. He saw a vulnerability in Tom which made him feel that he would be a good friend. He shared that same loneliness, José-Luis had felt, and that was really why he'd gone up to him and offered to show him how to play a cajón properly. That was a couple of months ago now in San Diego, shortly after he'd arrived from Colombia. He moved down the bus and sat next to Tom, who'd fallen into a troubled sleep as soon as they were on the peripheral road of the airport and safely out of reach of his adoring fans.

As the bus bounced over a sleeping policeman, Tom woke up with a start, his heart racing and clearly upset. Sitting next to him, José-Luis squeezed his hand gently.

"Hey, hey. It is OK. It was just a bad dream."

Tom looked at him for a few minutes before he realised where he was.

"Oh, thank God for that!"

"Do not worry, *guapo*, it is all OK now. Try and sleep some more. Or maybe share your dream and it will go away."

Tom sat up a bit and looked out into the drizzle as they drove towards the A40. He looked at José-Luis, brought his hand up to his lips, and kissed it gently.

"I'm so glad you're here," he said with relief.

José-Luis stroked his head and tried to shush him gently back to sleep.

"I had this horrible dream," Tom said peering out of the window.

José-Luis looked at him kindly. "I know," he said, "but it is over now. You are safe here with me."

"I was backstage somewhere. I didn't recognise where it was at first. There were hundreds of curtains and legs..."

"Legs?" José-Luis interrupted, "There were lots of people standing around?"

Tom looked at him for a moment before he understood. "No, no," he explained, "*legs* are the thin bits of curtain at the side of the stage. You know, to hide the wings? ... I mean the sides of the stage. And *flats* are the bits of scenery hanging at the back."

José-Luis nodded. "So, go on... I am sorry to interrupt you. I want to know."

"So, anyway, I was struggling to get through them all, the curtains and the legs and all this stuff just hanging down. I kept getting tangled up in them. I was trying to push them aside and see where I was. Then..." Tom trailed off. He looked away, pressing his face against the window, still squeezing José-Luis's hand tight. "And then... It was horrible. There was this rickety old step ladder lying on the floor and above it just two feet swaying slowly..."

"Oh *guapo*, that is awful. Do you know who it was?"

"No," Tom lied. He recognised the shoes and the bare legs, presumably leading up to a pair of shorts. He closed his eyes again and tried to push the memory and the fear away. Taking a few deep breaths, he opened his eyes again. Even though he was still groggy from his fitful sleep and the unpleasant dream, he could feel José-Luis was pretty upset beside him. "Hey, José-Luis, are you alright? I'm really sorry. I didn't mean to upset you. It was only a dream... Honest. You seem to be pretty disturbed. What is it?"

José-Luis looked past him out of the window, the rain getting heavier now. He was shaking a little, and he was about to start crying. Tom held his hand tight and slid his arm round José-Luis's shoulder pulling him in close.

"I know what that is like. That is all," José-Luis sobbed quietly.

"How do you mean?" Tom was puzzled.

"It is just," José-Luis was trying to dry his eyes with the sleeve of his sweater, "seeing the legs of someone just hanging there... It is not a good picture for me."

"I'm sorry. I don't understand." Tom stroked his hand gently, trying to sooth the sobs.

"It was like that for me but in real life," José-Luis sniffed, "It haunts me just to think about it."

"Oh, José-Luis, I'm so sorry." Tom took both hands now. "Was it someone you knew?" he asked.

"Donatello."

Tom drew his breath in sharply. He knew the name, and he knew he'd been killed. But José-Luis had never told him what had actually happened.

"I want to tell you, *guapo*, but it is terrible." José-Luis smiled weakly, lost in his thoughts, and the distress round his eyes increased. "We were so happy when the law changed. We did not have to hide no more, we thought, and so long as we were discreet and keep things in private between us, the law will protect us. But people do not change so easy. Even families turn on their own. Hound you. Betray you."

He looked out into the darkness again as if searching for something. Tom stroked his hand. "You don't have to tell me."

"No, I want to. It has been almost a year now. It will be the anniversary very soon. It's time.

"I was working in Bogotá, rehearsing a new show that had moved into Latin America from New York. It was very exciting. Meanwhile... I do not know whether I tell you that Donatello was a doctor? Anyway, he was working in the villages in the countryside near our town where we lived. He was caring for the children there, checking they were properly fed and vaccinating them. The Government was making big news out of these programs, telling other Governments in the region how well they treat even native people.

"My mother telephoned the theatre one day, and she say it was urgent. She have to talk to me straight away. I thought it was a relative or my father or someone else in my family. But when I got to the telephone, she tell to me I have to leave. She begged me to go as quickly as I can without going back home. I say but I have to talk to Donatello. And she say me he is dead."

Tom was in shock. "Oh, I..." But José-Luis interrupted.

"She say I must leave straight away. She say too not to read the newspapers, just go.

"There was something about the way she was talking to me. She told me that my father didn't know she was calling me, and I must not go to them or to my family. There is no place to hide in Colombia, she say, nor with my family, nor with Donatello's, nor with anybody. I have to leave.

"I panicked and took the next plane I could get a ticket on to Panama and then a ship takes me to Puerto Rico. From there, it is easy to get to the United States. I work in Mexican restaurants till I arrive to San Diego. The rest you know. We meet there. And I am so happy for that."

Tom was silent for a moment.

"I saw pictures in the news," José-Luis carried on, though Tom wished he wouldn't. "They hanged him from a tree still wearing his white coat. Not even that saved him. It was his brother who told them that he was evil and a pervert. That their children were at risk. His father had told his son to do it. To get rid of the shame of the family. I tried to find more information. Where he was buried. But nothing. I could not find anything else about it."

"I don't know what to say."

"There is nothing to say, *guapo*, it is OK. It is done. It is over now." José-Luis smiled and kissed Tom's hand gently.

"Donatello worried he would get sick in the countryside or bitten or something and he would not get back to the town in time for treatment. He told me that if anything happen, I must learn to keep living, and when I will be ready, he said, find a new husband."

José-Luis looked away. He still held Tom's hand, but he was looking out of the window on the other side of the coach now, way off into the distance across the lights of all those tidy little suburban homes with all those normal families living normal lives. Comfortable. Safe. Leaving men like José-Luis and Donatello out in the rain. Because they would be a danger to their children, to their husbands. José-Luis sighed.

"I wished I would have been stronger. I wished we would have moved somewhere else. Brazil maybe? Perhaps it is better there for people like us?"

They sat in silence now, both looking out of their respective window in opposite directions but still holding hands. As if they were watching out for danger from all sides. Men of their sort had to stick together and had to look out for one another. No one else would. Especially now. Tom caught sight of a large monolith on a billboard. He'd not seen it before, but he knew what it meant. The coach had moved on before he had time to read the writing at the bottom.

"Someday I will find my lover," José-Luis said suddenly. Tom stiffened. Slowly, José-Luis turned back to look at Tom. Tom's eyes were down fixed on some spot on the table. He looked up at José-Luis and seemed to be rather hurt.

"Don't be sad, *guapo*." José-Luis put a finger under Tom's chin to raise his head. He looked fondly into Tom's eyes. "We are not lovers. We have good sex, great sex. I like that. I like it a lot." He grasped Tom's hand to his chest and blew him a kiss. "I want us to have lots more too. But for lovers it is different. When you have sex with your lover, you do it for both of you or maybe just for him. When friends have sex, they do it for themselves. We are friends. And that's enough. I like it that way."

José-Luis could see the tears in Tom's eyes. He knew too that they were not for him. He slipped his arm round Tom's shoulder this time and hugged him close, kissing him on his forehead.

"You have your lover out there too, Tom Bright, someone special who is just for you. You will find him when you are brave enough to see. I know you will."

He wiped away a tear from Tom's cheek and then kissed him again. "Maybe he will be there waiting for you in Weymouth?" José-Luis suggested. Tom sat up abruptly. But he had no time to ask José-Luis what he meant.

"Are we nearly there yet?" Jason, the soundman, had come forward in the bus. He and the rest of the crew were clearly bored and perhaps tired after their long flight and then waiting for the tour bus in the cold.

"You're just like restless kids, you guys!" Tom replied. "It's about three or four hours to Weymouth from here. More if you get stuck around Winchester," he added, trying to see where they were through the rain. He wiped the condensation off with the back of his hand and pressed his face against the glass because it was dark outside, cupping his hands to shield his eyes from the lights in the bus.

"Is he waiting for you in Weymouth?" whispered José-Luis close by Tom's ear, as he settled back in his seat and nestled his head against Tom's shoulder. He wasn't being deliberately unkind. He just felt that there was some unfinished business here somewhere. He hoped that he would be able to help Tom with whatever it was. "Maybe he's been waiting all this time?" he mused.

"What makes you say that?" Tom was sitting up straight, clearly uncomfortable about something.

"Nothing, *guapo,*" José-Luis replied, though he now suspected there was more to it. "I just wondered why we are going to Weymouth. Where is it, anyway?"

"Well," Tom began, "it's where I grew up. Julia thought it would be a good idea to hold a charity event there. It would make a good story... for the press, apparently."

"So, the newspapers are interested in where you grew up?" José-Luis asked.

"Yes… well," Tom looked at his hands on the table in front of him. He slipped out from José-Luis's arm. "Oh, I don't know. It just seemed like a good idea. I don't know anymore." He put his head in his hands and ran his fingers through his hair.

"Hey, *guapo*," José-Luis put a hand on his shoulder, "it is alright. It does not matter. Do not get upset. I am sorry."

Tom looked at José-Luis and took his hand. "No, really, it's OK. I don't know why it makes me feel so uncomfortable. I just have a feeling in my gut about it all."

José-Luis waited for him to say more.

"But it was Julia, you know," Tom went on.

"Julia? What?" José-Luis asked.

"Who suggested the trip." Tom replied. He wasn't sure who he was trying to convince.

"It does not matter to me, *guapo*," José-Luis said gently. He gave Tom a peck on the cheek and settled into his shoulder again. "Wake me up when we get closer. We do not want any of your fans seeing you cuddled up with another man, *guapo*!"

"Please don't joke about that sort of thing."

"Hey, *guapo*, I am sorry. Is it that serious? Do you really have a man in Weymouth, then?"

"No… yes…"

José-Luis laughed. "OK. So, which is it?" He sat up and looked at Tom, waiting for some kind of explanation.

"It was a long time ago. We were at school."

"And?"

"And nothing really. Last time I saw him, I gave him a quick kiss. That's all. I think we were a bit tipsy. We'd been for a drink. Only because it was the end of term, and we were now old enough to go into a pub. He didn't react the way I'd hoped. We were only 18, just kids really."

"Just kids?"

"Anyway, I don't think he was that way."

"Well, if he is not *that way*, why worry?"

"I don't know. Maybe he'll try to blackmail me."

José-Luis laughed again. "Look, *guapo*, if this man is not our kind, he is probably married by now with a wife and children and a house just like those out there." José-Luis gestured through the window at a blanket of suburban security stretching away from the road in all directions. "He won't want to out himself to embarrass you."

"What if he asks for money?"

"You say no and you tell Julia to do her job. You pay her enough to handle the press for you."

They both fell silent for a while.

"Was he fit?" José-Luis asked suddenly, sniggering. Tom snorted.

"What is that supposed to mean?" he asked turning to look José-Luis in the face.

"You know. Was he handsome?" José-Luis was laughing properly now, his white teeth sparkling in the semi darkness of the coach. Tom flushed slightly. "He was, wasn't he?"

"Well, yes. He's a bit taller than me. At the time, he had broad shoulders and strong thighs."

"And you were 'just kids'?" José-Luis slapped the table and laughed out loud. "I am sorry," he added, looking at Tom's face. He was clearly uncomfortable with the memory. José-Luis shook a finger at Tom. "Do not worry, *guapo*. You are fit and handsome too. He will love you."

Tom looked troubled now. He was lost in thought again, staring at his hands on the table in front of them. José-Luis looked through the coach window. They'd just passed a massive billboard which had caught his eye. Staring back at them was Margaret Thatcher's fifteen-foot face above the headline *'Family Values'*. Tom had seen a piece in the newspaper about something called Section 28. It didn't sound promising.

"This does not look a friendly country for our kind." José-Luis had read the billboard too. "He is not going to say anything."

"I wish I could be sure..."

"Anyway. He probably moved away years ago... You did!"

When the A-Level results came out, Paul waited all day till he thought everyone else had been to school to look at the sheet sellotaped to the glass doors of the teachers' entrance. He was worried about going to get his results, not that anyone else should see them, but he just didn't want to see any of his classmates just then. His head had been confused since the day of the masked ball, and he yearned for a bit of peace and quiet for a while. He'd hoped that maybe some of the people he'd known from school might still be around in Weymouth. Perhaps he would see them, and they could still be friends or something. He walked along the seawall, sometimes just sitting, waiting.

Many times, he replayed the last time he and Tom had been together. He was taken unawares when Tom had kissed him. If he could go back, he would be better prepared. And he wanted another chance. He wanted that kiss. If only he'd not had a drink first. He'd no experience with alcohol. Apart from anything else, the little he knew about drinking made him nervous that he would lose control and people would see the real Paul. The Paul who loved Tom and wanted to be with him. If he had another chance, he would kiss Tom in public. He wouldn't care what people thought. That's what he told himself. Over time, he locked those thoughts away. They were too painful. He doubted he would ever get that chance again. As a successful singer, after all, he could have the pick of anyone. And what he didn't want to think about was that maybe Tom had grown out of Paul. Even that he'd grown out of men.

By the end of September, he was ready to set off for Bournemouth. He wasn't looking forward to it particularly, though he thought the change might do him good. He'd wanted to study English at first and then teach. He loved reading still. It was his comfort now. And he wanted to help kids understand that all literature was for them. Whoever they are. Even Shakespeare had wonderful things to tell them. But he'd been scared. He'd admitted to himself he was afraid in case he came across another Charlie Donaldson or Peter Tipler. And the students would know about Paul's deep-down thoughts and desires. He was ashamed of how he'd felt with the jockstrap that night when he was younger. And he didn't know how he would manage if he had to try and teach fit and handsome young men. Working backstage, though, he could hide. He wouldn't need to talk to anyone else because he'd have to keep quiet for the actors. They were the ones who would tell the story for the audience. He liked that idea. So, Bournemouth it was, and the Dorset Institute of Higher Education.

"Don't you go getting married before you get your qualifications now!" his mother had said half-jokingly, though secretly she was hoping he'd find a nice girl to settle down with when he'd finished. He set off for the station, weighed down with all his stuff. He told his mother not to come and see him off; after all, she had to look after his Dad. The train was pretty empty. He'd tried to schedule it so he could arrive in good time to settle in before he'd have to go and find something to eat at the halls of residence. When he got to the halls, there was a bit of a queue. He waited patiently till he got up to a desk with a girl who couldn't have been much older than him, holding a ruler and trying to match names with room numbers on a vast piece of paper she had on the desk in front of her. She smiled at him when she looked up, appreciating his physique as much as his honest face. Tracing the name from one side of the sheet to the column of room numbers, she told him where his room was and instead of handing him onto the boy sitting next to her with a big board of keys hanging from hooks, she found the key herself and handed it to him, smiling as sweetly as she could. Still holding on to the key fob, she told him to come back and see her if he had any questions, any at all, once he'd dumped his stuff. It was girls on one floor, she said, adding that she was on the floor directly below his, and then boys on the next alternating all the way up to the top of the building, apparently. Paul was relieved. He was used to hiding in plain sight amongst boys. He waited patiently for her to release the key, smiled at her as nicely as he could, picked up his case and made for the stairs. He hadn't gone back down to the hall when he'd found his room. He decided he'd unpack and settle in a bit.

It was a few weeks before he actually bumped into any of the other girls. Like Charlotte, a drama student. She was pretty, down from somewhere up north. She had a strange accent, anyway. She'd tried to make conversation, but Paul didn't know what to say. Answering in monosyllables and not knowing what question to ask in return. He smiled a few times, put his hands in his back pockets trying to look relaxed. Eventually she'd said she had to get going otherwise she'd be late for a lecture. He'd smiled and held up an outstretched hand as a sort of goodbye wave. He didn't see Charlotte again. It left him feeling awkward. Walking down to breakfast one morning, he'd overheard some girls talking about coaxing someone out of their shell. That made him even more nervous around girls. He started to time eating to be early in the morning and as late as possible in the evening. That would reduce the chances of him being cornered.

Although he would never admit it, Paul knew that he was physically attractive to girls of his own age. He was tall with broad shoulders and narrow hips. This made him feel awkward. Without his old friend's help, he had no idea about fashion anyway. Apart from the occasional splash of *Masculin II*, more for his own comfort than to attract others. He wore unflattering sweaters and baggy jeans to draw attention away from his torso and his strong thighs. His hair was always clean but never well-cut or styled. He just wanted to blend into the background and get on with his life, alone if needs be. The only women he felt comfortable around were middle-aged and older women who posed no threat to him. Who would not want to chase him, he thought. He even convinced himself that all he needed was to make it to forty and he'd be safe. He'd have to keep himself to himself so that no one would try and 'bring him out of his shell'.

He missed the freshers' drinks party. It wasn't deliberate it turned out, he'd had to go home that weekend because his father had had a bad turn. His mother had told him he didn't need to come home, she'd understand if he was trying to settle in and all that. His father had been bedridden for almost as long as Paul could remember, but still relatively healthy. Everyone was sure he'd last for years yet. He thought he shouldn't leave his mother to try and manage on her own, though, that would be unfair while he was gadding around in Bournemouth. That sort of set a precedent or just became an excuse. And he went home almost every weekend from then on. Things changed a bit in his second year. He was in digs not far from the station but had managed to get some general backstage odd-jobbing work at the Hippodrome. He'd only go back to Weymouth perhaps once a month, just to see that everything was alright. And to avoid his fellow students, especially the girls.

To begin with, Paul's room was just for sleeping and reading. He had a growing collection of books, of course, in addition to what he needed for his course. But the walls stayed blank until he received a postcard from Lucy. She'd been on a college trip to Paris and, she wrote on the card itself, the picture reminded her of Paul and his friend, Tom. Paul turned the card over to see three men planing down some varnished wooden floorboards in an exotic-looking room. They were stripped to the waist and concentrating hard on what they were doing. He knew about the Impressionists but had never heard of Caillebotte or the picture *Les Raboteurs de parquet*. He was fascinated. How physical the work appeared and how intriguing an assumed conversation between the two figures towards the front. The exterior scene beyond the window and wrought ironwork. With some digging, he found an A3 version at the gallery where the painting was normally housed. So, he'd written to them in the best French he could muster from various bits he found in phrase books and dictionaries in the library. It went onto the mantlepiece of the chimney breast opposite his bed. This encouraged him to look more at art. That and the student discount at the local *Athena*. Originally, he'd thought it was a trendy fashion shop, so no use to him. But he'd read in the student magazine that they had new stock in. He didn't buy much, though he ended with a poster of one of Monet's *Haystacks*. It made him think back to that summer in Bramdean, even though his auntie's farm was fruit not corn or wheat. He'd wanted the version with the haystacks under snow, but they only had them in the summer evening sun at the shop. He added to it postcard-sized views from different times of the day and of the year. Later, he also stumbled across a reprint of Edmund Leighton's *Tristan and Isolde*, which he pinned above the single bookcase in the room. All the pictures were stored away in a large tube when he moved back in with his mother, of course, and Paul thought little more about them.

His room, both in the halls of residence and in his digs, was largely silent. He didn't even have a radio. Other student rooms around him would be blaring out the latest chart toppers or heavy metal. Even classical musical. His remained mute. He'd no great collection at home, either. What music he did play was largely from musicals. Mainly, because his closest friend had been such a great singer. He'd bought his first ever cassette tape *The Rocky Horror Show*, which he told people he associated with getting him into lighting and special effects. In time, that had encouraged him to look at what LPs his parents had. But somehow, since leaving school, he had no longer wanted to think about music. Peggy had found the tape of *The Rocky Horror Show* almost completely unravelled in his waste basket that summer before he went to Bournemouth. Paul had said that it had caught on the mechanism in the cassette player. Before he could rescue it, almost all the tape had got caught up on the small spools. He didn't look at his mother when he told her. And she didn't ask.

His father finally died in the summer vacation before his final year. He'd helped his mother with all the arrangements and had offered to stay on after the start of the term. But she insisted he go back.

"It's your final year, Paul. Dad wouldn't have wanted you to mess it up now."

As it happened, he didn't mess it up. Even though he made sure to go and check up on his mother as many weekends as possible, he still passed all his exams comfortably. When the results were posted on the notice board in the main building, some of his fellow students were asking who was this guy with the great degree?

He was offered a pretty good job too, staying on at the Hippodrome to help with lighting and special effects. He'd almost had an unexpected big break as an actor whilst in Bournemouth, too. His prodigious knowledge of Shakespeare had been discovered quite by accident one summer. As acting stage manager, his duties included understudying all the parts – in theory at least. There was never really any danger of having to go on, and even then, the assumption was that the understudy would have to read from the script. One matinée, however, Brutus or rather the actor playing him, was indisposed. An unpleasant bout of crabs, it turned out, making it impossible to stand still and look stately. So, on he went. He surprised everyone when he didn't need a script nor a single prompt and captivated both audience and cast alike. The girl playing Portia was particularly intrigued by this young, virile understudy, and engineered a wardrobe malfunction in the hope of being taken advantage of. It back-fired, sadly. Paul sized up the situation quickly and asked the dresser to sort it out instead.

When it was suggested he might actually appear more regularly, even read for the part of Shylock in the *Merchant of Venice*, he backed out completely and resigned. His resignation was not accepted, of course, he was already a very capable and therefore valuable lighting engineer. Instead, they changed his contract to reduce the risk of actual stage appearances to emergency understudy. Even then, restricted to four performances a quarter at most.

Somehow it never came to it again in spite of the rather turbulent and colourful lives of some of the actors.

After a year or two, and still a little uncertain about the risk of being forced on stage, he'd got the chance to move back to Weymouth. Besides, it was his vocation, he decided, to be in the background all the time. To stay in the wings, to make it work but not be showy, to stand back and let others take all the applause. It was also a sensible option that meant he could move in and look after his mother. She enjoyed the company and the feelings of security. She fussed over him though:

"Now, don't you ever worry about bringing a nice young lady back here anytime," she said rather too regularly. "This is your home too, you know, and I just want you settled before I can pop off and join your Dad."

Paul tried not to let it annoy him. After all, that's how it went for normal people: university, a job, courting, getting married, having children, even a mortgage. It all made such perfect sense. Paul explained quite plausibly that working in the theatre meant he was inevitably busy when everyone else was out enjoying themselves. And his mother had an old-fashioned view of actresses. Peggy was worried, though. To her knowledge, Paul had never had a proper girlfriend. In fact, she could only remember one date and that had been arranged as a foursome with his schoolfriend, Tom. What if he was one of them after all, she thought. To keep such thoughts at bay, she nagged him to find a date even more often. At least, she told herself, that Tom had moved away.

When he'd first come back, there were other women interested in him. He'd bumped into someone from school only the other day in Sainsbury's.

"Vickie! You know, I was Vickie Freeman back then."

"Oh yes," Paul said; he'd tried to suppress that memory long ago.

"Well, I've a kiddie now," she continued, brightly. "Dad's buggered off, though. One of them sailors on the cross-Channel ferries. Gets me pregnant, the bastard, then sods off back to France. Doubtless a *Mam'selle* in every port."

"Sorry..." said Paul. That was all he could think of.

"Oh well, no point in crying over spilt baby milk, I always say."

This was meant to be humour. Vickie laughed, though Paul didn't until it was obvious he was only laughing out of politeness. He was beginning to wish he'd gone down a different aisle.

"So," Vickie carried on unperturbed, "do you get out much?"

"No, not really..."

"Well, there's always the pictures!" she smiled at him lewdly, "I don't get sick on sweets anymore," she added, presumably another attempt as humour.

"Oh, right..."

"How about tomorrow night? I'll have to check my diary, of course..." she chuckled.

"No, sorry... I work see. I'm at the theatre. I do all the lighting and stuff."

"Oh, right..."

And that was the way it went. Someone would corner him by the meat pies or cleaning products and suggest they make up for lost time after all these years. He'd need reminding who they were, and he'd have an excuse. In the end, people stopped asking. They just forgot he was there. Which was the way he preferred it. His mother couldn't understand it, of course. Even given an understandable bias, she knew he was handsome underneath it all, especially if he shaved more regularly and kept his hair trim, like he used to. And he was a strapping, young man – broad shoulders, narrow hips, strong arms and legs. He was definitely a catch. She was convinced he was just a little shy.

Daytimes, when he wasn't working, he'd usually take himself off somewhere. Once he'd learned to drive, he would venture out of Weymouth, down the coast perhaps, or into the countryside. He enjoyed his own company, or at least his own company was undemanding. It was too painful to go and sit on the seawall these days, even though he still loved the sea. Sometimes staring out from a headland somewhere, as if waiting for someone to return. Kahedin under white sails returning to sooth his aching heart. So long as the sails had been changed. That's all that mattered.

Sometimes, he might even see if he could get a decent view of the ferry port without being seen himself. He'd watch the sailors, once they tied up and all the passengers were gone, chatting amongst themselves perhaps. Or having a quiet stroll, smoking a cigarette, watching the pretty girls go by. Or popping into the gents, maybe. He also tried joining an afternoon book club. He was disappointed, though. First, the choice of books was terrible. Having made the mistake of buying his own copy of the first title, he'd re-joined the library. It was uncomfortable taking out books with racy pictures of handsome, fit men on the front with go-to-bed eyes. And even after the first one, he realised that these were not the type of book he wanted to read. That being said, it didn't seem to matter whether he read the book or not. Most of the others didn't. This was not a book club, he soon decided. This was about older women exchanging cakes and chatting about trivia over a cup of tea. He finally left when he realised that he was becoming the centre of attraction. He hadn't noticed at first. Each time he turned up, the women would already be seated and it didn't take long to realise that there was a space for him between two different women.

If truth be told, he was lonely. But he didn't know what to do about it especially when the book club was such a let-down. He didn't know how to find let alone keep friends. Not since schooldays had he been close enough to anyone to be able to talk freely and enjoy an easy friendship. Never very talkative, he was even losing the ability for small talk. His work colleagues were all married it seemed, and when not working, would be out with the family, or drinking, or rowing with their partners. Some even had affairs. Not terribly discreet, if it involved a secret assignation backstage. Was that normal life? He was very organised and dependable, and clearly extremely good at his job. Everyone was used to his reclusive ways. They just assumed he would be there when needed, but they rarely saw him arrive in the morning and knew he'd be the last to leave. Clearing and tidying as he went.

When they built the new pensioner bungalows near the cemetery, it didn't take long for Mrs Armstrong to apply for one. It would make it easier to visit her dead husband, she said, and the house was too big for her anyway. Paul accepted this without fuss. He didn't feel that she was throwing him out but was pleased that she was trying to move on. In his turn, he found himself a modest flat about a ten-minute walk from the theatre. As you came in from the stairs, there was a small vestibule where he could hang coats and things. This led to a decent sized lounge big enough for his books, and a bedroom to the right where there was a double bed, the first he'd ever slept in. The other side of the lounge was a small kitchen and leading off that, a bathroom. There was fire escape off the kitchen, the door next to the bathroom. He could keep milk out there when it wasn't too hot to keep it fresh. His mother thought the fire escape made it vulnerable to burglars. But Paul had explained that it was three floors up and that the fire escape was visible from public roads on three sides, so she felt more reassured. He didn't tell her that it connected with those of the neighbouring buildings.

When he'd moved into the flat, he'd unpacked the posters and cards he had from university. He was careful about how and where he hung his pictures, dismissive of a single picture lost in the middle of a vast expanse of wall. He found a larger print of the *Raboteurs*, which he put above the bed in his room. He took himself back to *Athena* to see what else might appeal and to *Habitat* to get some of the fold-away, stackable bookshelves which everyone was talking about. He couldn't decide between Hammershøi's *Interior, Strandgade 30, 1901* and Vermeer's *Woman in Blue Reading a Letter.* In the end, he bought a reprint of both. The Hammershøi he hung on the wall opposite the bed next to the door. He imagined looking through the door, like in the painting, and seeing an isolated figure somewhere beyond. He tried not to think about who the figure might be. About who he wanted the figure to be. He had a wedding photo from his parents on his bedside table. He looked at it for a long time, not at Peggy and Eddie smiling back into the camera, but at a couple committing to one another with everyone presumably happy for them.

The Monet *Haystacks* reprints went above the fireplace in his living room. It was perfectly acceptable to put the main poster centrally on the chimney breast and then arrange the postcard-sized prints beneath it. The Vermeer went closer to the big bay window, which seemed to make sense given what it depicted. It always caught his eye if he'd been looking through the window, daydreaming. He imagined getting a letter from overseas someday. Of reading it, looking out of the window towards the sea where a sailboat with white sails would be approaching the harbour. He found a print of Van Dyck's *Self-portrait with a Sunflower,* which intrigued him. He imagined the sunflower as a light revealing some truth, the artist with his back to the viewer, looking over his shoulder having tried to hide something which was now out in the open for whoever chose to look. That went near the door out into the small hallway. He'd come across a very small reprint of Caravaggio's *The Incredulity of Saint Thomas* which he admired for the realism of the figures. Though doubting Thomas's finger in Christ's wound made him queasy. He put it in the small hallway near where he hung his coats, because he thought the lighting seemed to reflect the shadows in the picture itself.

The Leighton *Tristan and Isolde* he put near an arrangement of the bookcases. These were two stacked vertically and then two more side-by-side. So, the reprint went into the crook of a sort of L shape of bookcases. He felt the painting complemented the literature on the shelves themselves. Then he found a reprint of Holman Hunt's *The Light of the World.* He moved the Leighton over to the wall opposite the fireplace near the door to his bedroom replacing it with the Holman Hunt by the bookshelves. There was no television. And to begin with, no way to play music or listen to the radio. Except when he went round to see his mother, or was answering a direct question from a colleague, he might go days without speaking at all.

The flat suited Paul, especially with his books and pictures out on display. Approaching thirty now – it was 1986 after all and getting on for ten years since they'd left school – he moved into his own space, alone, part of normal life for him now. Not a bachelor pad as such. There'd not been even a hint of a date let alone a girlfriend or someone to share the double bed with throughout those ten years. Paul was content though. Tuesday to Saturday in the theatre till late. Sunday he would generally visit his mother, and Monday was when he could do those domestic things like shop, or go for walks, or just watch for that someone from across the sea. He was becoming increasingly reclusive and withdrawn.

Like his Bournemouth rooms, the flat remained silent. One Monday, Peggy dropped round panting a little from the three flights of stairs. She had a small parcel with Paul's name but her address. Paul made her some tea, while she sat expectantly wondering what was in the parcel. She thought she recognised the writing. But it wasn't quite Jessie's. The parcel itself was also small, square and hard. And it rattled if she shook it. It turned out to be a CD. Almost without looking at it, Paul handed it to his mother saying it was from Lucy and Auntie Jessie.

"Is this one of them new records then?" she asked, turning the CD over quizzically. "How can this tiny thing have as much on it as a vinyl LP? The hole in the middle looks a bit big, though, for a normal record player." She read the letter enclosed with the CD without asking Paul if he minded and then picked up the CD again to look at the front cover. "It's that Tom you used to be so friendly with," she said, "*Latin Romance*," she read. She didn't notice Paul hesitate as he came in with her tea. He put the cup on the coffee table and went back into the kitchen to pour a cup from himself. And to compose himself once more before sitting down with his mother. "Oh, that's nice," said Peggy, taking a sip of her tea, "nice of them to send it to you. I expect you've already bought it, though, haven't you? Him being a friend and all."

"Err, no actually," Paul answered, trying to sound relaxed. Peggy put her cup down in its saucer and looked round the room.

"Have you got a record player, then? Something you can play it on for me now?" she asked, handing the CD back to him.

"No," he said, taking the disc and putting it face down

on the coffee table. "It's a CD player now, Mum. I don't have one, though."

"Pity," she said.

Paul liked Olwena. He didn't find her threatening at her age, and she didn't ask any awkward questions about his private life. She was friendly and not like the women at the book club at all. Olwena had been a widow for some years now, having nursed her husband in the final stages of dementia. With nothing else to do, she'd become depressed. She couldn't help mulling over what might have been if she'd been braver. But then she loved her children, and that wouldn't have happened. She'd finally volunteered to help out with bits of sewing and things at the theatre. She liked being around the theatre. As a girl, she'd loved musical theatre, especially pantomime. It wasn't the fairy-tale princesses that attracted her like other little girls. She was fascinated by the notion that the principal boy was in fact played by a girl. Even with all the traditional thigh slapping, she'd wait all year till the next pantomime came to see who they'd be. They were less domineering and uncouth, she thought, than real men. There was a gentleness to them despite their outward appearance that she found appealing. She wanted to be Cinderella and have the principal boy fuss over her shoes or something. As she grew older, though, her parents had frowned on the apparent fixation with pantomimes, and she'd been obliged to stop going.

Arthur Prichard was the elder son of a neighbour across the road. He'd left school with no qualifications and had found work at the port. Olwena Jacobs had barely noticed him but was introduced by her mother: "You could take that nice young man from across the road to the school dance," she'd suggested, and even gone and asked his mother when they met at the laundrette. He was no Prince Charming. Though shouldn't that have been a girl anyway? And so, her new life began, and what could have been was over. Arthur did take her once or twice to the pictures when they were courting. Once they married, he refused to go anywhere near the theatre which he thought of as a den of iniquity full of actors with loose morals. Saturday evenings he would have a bath and then they would have sex. Olwena accepted this as a routine duty never thinking it could be enjoyed let alone a sign of intimacy between two people who loved one another. They had two sons and then the sex stopped altogether. She accepted that husbands, Arthur at least, would find other interests like fishing and magazines. When they were six and eight years old, she'd taken the children to see *Jack and the Beanstalk* at Christmas. But Arthur forbade them to go again. He did not want, he said, his sons to be corrupted by the ne'er-do-wells and effeminates on stage. She didn't complain, though she missed it. Their sons had moved away a long time ago and rarely came back to visit, when their father became unwell. Olwena therefore nursed Arthur alone. So, when she'd washed and changed him and put him to bed in the evening, she would knit for grandchildren she would rarely see. She might even watch television. Her favourites were the lady detectives or scientists, women who know what they're about, wearing smart trouser suits, efficient and self-assured, gentle but their own boss. She'd have liked to have met someone like that. Things might have been very different, she thought.

Olwena loved her family, nonetheless. Duncan, the elder of the two sons, married an ambitious lady, Rhonda, and they'd moved back to Wales when she was elected Cardiff city councillor. Their children now spoke with a distinctly Welsh accent that she found alienating. Richard had married a Spanish girl, whose family were originally from Chile but had fled Pinochet. The children had her dark complexion and almond eyes. If they came for the sea in the summer, they tanned very quickly. Gabriela worked at an embassy, Olwena thought, somewhere near Chelsea and not too far from the Natural History Museum. She was a sweet girl and treated her mother-in-law with kindness and respect on those few occasions when they met.

Doing odd jobs now in wardrobe, Olwena was almost enjoying some of the life she'd always wanted. Most of the cast adored her and would bring chocolates or even flowers for their favourite 'auntie'. It was only Paul, though, who would spend real time with her, and sit and chat with her. At least he would let her talk at him and occasionally respond with a "Yes" or "Oh, really?" She'd bring in a flask of tea, which was always stewed and unpleasant, and some homemade cupcakes, which were just as bad. He wondered if they were close enough for him to tell her. They'd talk about the shows that were booked and who might be coming. Sometimes,

Paul might explain to Olwena if there were any tricky bits of lighting or special effects he needed to create. He was also kind to her.

There was a large, south-facing window in wardrobe to let in as much light as possible. An anti-fade blind was hung before it, casting a golden glow across her workbench and the room as a whole. Paul was there one day when she was struggling with repairing one of the dancer's skirts. It was difficult to see the old stitches on a seam which had come apart. Olwena pinned the needle to her blouse and stood in front of the window, the seam and skirt held taut between her hands as she bent over to try and make out where the old stitching had been. It struck Paul immediately: this was so similar to the pose on his Vermeer picture. He made a mental note to find a card with the same picture on it.

A few weeks later was Olwena's birthday. Paul took a box of chocolates and his card to her that afternoon. She put down what she was working on, wiped her hands on her apron and sat down, clearly pleased that he'd remembered. She carefully slit the envelope open with the blade of a pair of scissors and took the card out. She read the message inside first and, grinning, turned to thank Paul. He dismissed it and said Happy Birthday again. She closed the card and looked at the picture on the front. The woman in the blue dress, in front of a big window not unlike the one there in wardrobe, with something in her hand.

"The other week," Paul began, "when you were mending the skirt and had to stand up to get the light, it just reminded me of this picture."

Olwena was squinting to see what was in the woman's hands.

"It's a letter," said Paul. "I think it's supposed to be from the person she loves."

Olwena gasped, dropped the card on the workbench and stared through the window. Tears seemed to be forming in her eyes. Paul was confused.

"Olwena," he said standing up and wondering if he should put his hand on her shoulder, "are you alright? I'm so sorry. What is it?"

Olwena touched his hand while she composed herself.

"I'm fine," she said, smiling up at him, "really. It's nothing." She paused and sighed. "You weren't to know. Just I used to write to someone very special."

She patted his hand now and stood up. She fussed over the tea and opened the chocolates to share with him. She tried hard not to show any emotion. She liked Paul a lot and knew he would not deliberately want to hurt her. She found his company easy and though she never asked, she hoped that someday he would find that special one. To lighten her mood, she leaned forwards and turned on the CD player that was balanced on the window ledge. She'd sometimes like to sit and listen to a CD recording of the show that was coming to the theatre. She turned to sit down again and saw Paul mouthing the words to himself.

"You always know the words!" she laughed. He flushed slightly.

"It's the only type of music I listen to really," he answered, and by way of explanation, "Mum and Dad had them all on vinyl at home."

"My favourite was *West Side Story,*" Olwena told him, "the awful tragedy of two lovers who weren't supposed to love each other!" She took the needle she'd stuck through her blouse and threaded it with black cotton to begin mending the seam of the skirt.

"I bought myself a CD player," Paul said, "thanks to you!" He smiled at her and she winked at him. "Well, it was about time. Someone sent me a CD and I didn't have anywhere to play it," he added. "Since then, I've got quite a collection of musicals. And bits of classical music that I've heard and liked."

"I like the ballet," said Olwena without looking up from the costume. "My favourite bit is the *pas de deux* from Tchaikovsky's *Swan Lake.*"

"That's a love story too," said Paul, "where the lovers are doomed."

"That reminds me," said Olwena, standing up and taking the newspaper from her bag. She rattled it under Paul's nose in excitement.

"Look at this!" she shouted, "that Tom whatsit is coming."

Paul was only half listening but took the paper she offered and glanced at the pictures on the front page. He blanched.

"You alright, Paul? You look as though you've seen a ghost."

"No, no, I'm fine. Just been a bit under the weather recently. I'll feel a lot better once I've had a nice cuppa."

There was Tom Frampton or rather Bright as he was known nowadays staring back out at him. He was coming for his first ever UK tour starting in Weymouth for some kind of lavish, 'home-coming' charity event. He hadn't changed. The clothes were smarter, of course, and fashionable, with wide lapels against padded shoulders. His hair was still as thick and wavey, and he'd clearly had work done on his teeth which were perfectly straight and presumably white and blemish free. His lips were as they'd always been. He desperately wanted to touch them again. In one of the photos inside, he was standing with a mic on a stage and behind him were a group of Latin American musicians: a bandoneon, a marimba, timbale, and a guy with various tambourines and maracas standing up. Paul hadn't followed Tom's career particularly, except for the CD that Lucy and auntie Jessie had sent, of course. But was vaguely aware that he wasn't a popstar like Bolan when he was alive or Bowie. He'd left the UK as soon as he'd graduated from Guildford and settled, according to Olwena who seemed to know these things, in LA "...or somewhere over that way. Near Mexico anyway."

"Well, well!" said Olwena flicking through the newspaper. "Our big celebrity here at our theatre. Fancy that!"

Paul had played the CD Jessie and Lucy had sent only once. It was too painful for him to hear the voice he remembered so well. Slowly, he'd pulled the CD cover from the plastic case and, standing in the bay window facing out to sea, he'd scrutinised the lyrics. He wondered if the lyrics might refer to him. To Paul. To the young man Tom had kissed. He struggled with the Spanish trying to equate the words to the French he knew. There was something about the song *¿Dónde estás ahora?* that moved him, but he didn't know why. Searching intently, wondering what the songs meant, he began to feel tearful. He packed the CD away and busied himself tidying the flat. Sometimes he caught himself wondering what the lyrics meant. He tried his best not to.

What Olwena had spotted in the paper turned out to be true. At the stage meeting a few weeks later, Rob, the stage manager, went through the list of upcoming shows and then made a lot of fuss about a three-night set with the great Tom Bright. The star was even paying for several weeks' worth of rehearsals here in Weymouth before opening what was to be such a big show, Rob had told them. Weymouth was not typically the venue for Latin music. They'd had some Russian Cossacks a few years ago and a group of singers with *Songs of the Auvergne* the year after that, but the theatre had remained half empty. Ballet was unheard of. The pantomimes were still a mainstay over Christmas. And other than that, they tended to host touring musicals or repertory productions. But generally, they lost out to Bournemouth for the big music shows and certainly anything out of the ordinary. So, there was quite a lot of excitement.

"It says here," Frances, the manager of front-of-house, was reading from a different paper, "that this Tom Bright went to Jordan Hill Comp. I wonder when that was? He doesn't look that old, does he?"

"You never know with photos, though, do you? All air wiped and touched down."

"Air brushed and touched up, Danny."

"Isn't that where you went, Paul?" Frances was looking at him standing towards the back of the stage coiling some wires. Everyone turned to look at him.

"Er... no... I don't really remember... well, not with that name, anyway. I was doing technical subjects, anyway."

"He looks like one of them gay boys to me," said Danny.

"What are you talking about, Danny?" Frances flicked her newspaper and glowered at him.

"You know. A shirt lifter, a nine-bob note, a bum boy..." Danny was trying to think of all the names he could think of. Terrence was looking at him, wishing he'd stop. Paul sat in silence. He was used to letting things like this wash over him. The funny jokes, the lisping, the mincing. If he didn't react, then it would soon stop, and he wouldn't have drawn attention to himself. It was the story of his life, in a way, so he thought he no longer cared.

"Shirt lifter," Danny was explaining to Frances, "is a bloke who comes at you from behind and has to lift up the back of your shirt to..."

"Yes, thanks, Danny, I think I get the idea," Frances said. "All very childish, if you ask me."

Some of Danny's more graphic names and explanations now started to make Paul feel uneasy inside. He was already unnerved at the thought of Tom being here in Weymouth and at the theatre. He didn't really know how he would react when he saw him. Or how Tom would react to him, either. 'Just don't show any emotion,' he told himself. 'Pretend you don't know him... you don't care.' This made Paul sad all of a sudden. He leant forward, his elbows on his thighs, and his eyes fixed on some random spot on the floor. Danny was all set to carry on.

"All very exciting, boys and girls," said Rob at which most of the staff rolled their eyes. They didn't like being patronised by the stage manager.

"So, when were you there, Paul?" Frances was still determined to find out as much as they could. But when she looked over to where Paul had been sitting, there was no one there. He'd disappeared as usual into the wings somewhere, probably winding loose ropes or checking for rubbish or something.

"Funny that," said Frances.

"Did you know him?" asked Olwena the next day.

"We were in English together," Paul answered.

And they didn't speak of it again.

The tour bus was enormous and blocked most of the car park. Paul stopped and shifted the backpack on his shoulder before going into the theatre. There were lots of people milling around which put him a little on edge. He was circling round in the wings, trying to get to the stairs backstage and the safety either of wardrobe or preferably his workspace above the stage in the loft. He didn't get that far yet though. He slowed down when he caught sight of a shortish but well-built guy. He looked like a lean rugby player from behind. Not one of those big guys who runs and shoves the players from the opposing team. He was smaller, but you could imagine he would be quick on his feet. Paul couldn't see his face yet. He was wearing a short-sleeved shirt, his muscled, hairy arms and strong neck exposed, showing a Latin complexion.

His backside, Paul couldn't help but notice trying not to dwell too long there, looked strong and firm.

Paul shifted uneasily as he realised the man had turned his head and was looking straight at him. The man smiled broadly, his even white teeth almost lighting the gloomy stage.

"Hello," he said, his accent was Spanish maybe, "you must be Paul, our lighting wizard?"

"Err, yes. Well, I do the lights, anyway. I'm not sure about *wizard*. Pleased to meet you."

"José-Luis, Tom's choreographer." He held out his hand which Paul just looked at, as if not knowing what to do. José-Luis felt no slight. He was getting used to Anglo-Saxons. Americans would shake hands, the British rarely did, and not even straight men in either culture would kiss one another when greeting. As Paul stepped forward, José-Luis was vaguely aware of a masculine fragrance in the air. Not unpleasant though he didn't recognise the scent.

"When you have time," José-Luis continued, "I want to talk to you about the lighting and about the effects for different points during Tom's performance."

"Yes, sure," Paul tried to look relaxed. He'd caught José-Luis's eye briefly and shifted a little uneasily. He felt drawn to the hirsute choreographer, who seemed genuine and caring, and he was already beginning to feel less on edge. He smiled back and, surprising everyone there, he stepped forward and shook José-Luis's hand, a strong, manly handshake, the type José-Luis was unaccustomed to outside Colombia. Taken aback by this, José-Luis went to hug him. But Paul was too quick and already stepped back to a safe distance.

"Everyone knows where to find me," he said, vaguely waving towards his colleagues. He turned and was gone.

Work was pretty busy over the next day or two; there was a lot to plan and manage. Usually with Rob, Paul met José-Luis and Tom's manager just to get a general overview of what was needed. He could fill in the details as the rehearsals proper got underway. He always carried a cheap A6 notebook that he could slip into his back pocket and where he would keep all his detailed notes. José-Luis found it rather cute and endearing how protective Paul was of it. He once snatched it out of Paul's pocket just as a silly joke. Feeling the close contact, Paul span round and snatched the notebook back in one fluid movement before José-Luis realised what was happening. There was an uneasy pause for a moment. And then both José-Luis and Paul had laughed. It was a delicious moment, particularly for Paul. José-Luis was sensitive enough that he didn't put a hand on Paul's shoulder as he enjoyed a shared unfamiliar moment with the inscrutable lighting engineer. When he thought about it, José-Luis realised that he liked Paul a lot. It was not just that he was handsome and physically attractive in such an understated way. There seemed to be something strong and dependable underneath the shy and reserved exterior. Something that was worth getting to know.

Initial rehearsals went surprisingly well, with everyone really appreciative of the lighting. Very quickly, they stopped noticing and just took it for granted that it would work, and it would look exactly as they'd wanted even when they hadn't realised that those were the effects they were looking for. Olwena noticed that Paul had started to dress better for some reason, the sweaters no longer hanging off him, the trousers sitting more snuggly around his waist and thighs. She thought nothing of it. But it was true.

Paul had plucked up courage to go into some of the more fashionable shops around Weymouth. He'd even gone so far as trying on a pair of jeans to check the fit. The salesman drawing back the curtain and looking at him appraisingly made him uncomfortable. At least it confirmed, though, that this was his size. He was very aware of the salesman looking at him still, so he spent little time looking at t-shirts and sweaters. Instead, he guessed the size of his chest and bought a couple of plane white t-shirts and hoped for the best. On the way back to his flat, he stopped at a barber's. He looked at all the different photos around the mirror once he was in the barber's chair with a cover over him wondering what the least obtrusive style might be. In the end, he'd asked the barber to give him a general cut and tidy up the back. The barber had obliged, but with little enthusiasm. At least it was a lot neater, Paul thought, without looking at the mirror being held behind his head for him to inspect how the back had turned out. He just wanted to get out of there and back to the flat. The next morning, he got up earlier than usual. He brushed his hair carefully but was too worried that it would look a mess if he washed it. He knew the jeans would fit perfectly well and was pleased when the white t-shirt he picked up did as well. If anything, it was a little too snug. He made a note to get a bigger size if he bought any in future. He was so anxious with his new look that he arrived a good 45 minutes before anyone else at the theatre.

Tom and José-Luis were working on something centre stage that afternoon when Paul had appeared looking for Rob, the stage manager. He crossed discreetly upstage, skirting the back wall, his eyes fixed on where he was walking. Tom noticed him straight away, abruptly interrupting the discussion with José-Luis. The choreographer followed his gaze, appreciating the masculine tautness of Paul's upper body and his strong legs. He smiled to himself and turned back ready to carry on talking with Tom. But Tom was transfixed. José-Luis coughed.

"*¡La boca!*" he sniggered. Tom looked round and saw José-Luis laughing at him. He snapped his mouth shut and averted his eyes for a few seconds while he tried to compose himself.

"So," he began lightly, "where were we?"

"Well, I was talking about the opening number," José-Luis was still laughing, "but I think you got distracted."

Tom smiled at him. "Let's get back to work," he said and patted José-Luis's chest.

A loud wolf-whistle stopped everyone in their tracks. Even Paul looked around.

"Well, Paul Armstrong," Frances shouted across the stage, "look at you! Who's the lucky lady then!?" Paul blushed and turned away. "Don't you scrub up well?" Frances continued. This was the best bit of gossip she'd got hold of for ages. She'd convinced herself that he was gay or something. He'd never mentioned a girlfriend, and no one had seen him out about Weymouth with anyone. Seeing him make an effort like this she thought meant a young lady was in his life at last and that she'd bought his clothes. But it would have to wait for another time. Paul was already gone.

"Is it true?" Tom asked José-Luis abruptly.

"Is what true?" José-Luis was still trying to work through a particularly tricky piece of choreography and hadn't been paying much attention. He was tracing his feet across the floor and turning first this way and that, imagining the music in his head.

"Is Paul going out with someone? ... With a girl?" Tom grabbed José-Luis's hand, stopping him in his tracks, to stress the urgency of this request for information.

"I don't know. Ask him." José-Luis was surprised at how insistent Tom was.

In general, Paul had continued to be even more elusive when Tom was around. In his turn, Tom was frustrated at the feeling that Paul was ignoring him. When he'd realised that Paul was not only in Weymouth but actually working in this very theatre, he'd decided how much money he would offer him to keep quiet about their kiss. There'd been nothing to it at the time, of course. Though over the years, Tom had realised that if truth be told, he'd hoped that stolen kiss would lead to so much more. Coming back to Weymouth and seeing Paul again rekindled all those happier memories. With the realisation that Paul was actually avoiding him, his fears about being outed abated a little. Paul had forgotten all about that kiss, he convinced himself. He'd moved on, he thought. Maybe even married or settled with a nice girlfriend somewhere. After all, he was even more handsome and fitter than Tom remembered. He told himself he was relieved, but there was enormous sadness too. It was all too confusing. Tom didn't know what to think or even how he felt. José-Luis had noticed the negative mood and told Tom he needed to snap out of it, whatever it was, though he was beginning to understand a lot more than he admitted.

"*¡Mira!*" said José-Luis, a little frustrated with Tom now. "Paul is not going to be seeing any woman."

"How do you know that?" Tom almost shouted back.

"Calm down," José-Luis told him. "Just look at the way he acts. I'm pretty sure..."

"Really?" Tom insisted. "You know that, do you, for certain?"

José-Luis looked at him and shook his head, his hands on his hips. "What's it to you anyway?" he asked. Getting no answer, he turned and walked off to find the other dancers and rehearse with them.

Around this time, José-Luis sought Paul out in his workroom, realising that he was probably the first or certainly one of very few who'd been allowed in there.

"Morning, *pollito*," José-Luis began as if this was perfectly normal and he'd been there many times before, "I hope you don't mind me coming to find you here." Paul was British enough to dismiss the intrusion as unimportant, going so far as to clear a space for José-Luis to sit down.

"It's just Tom and I have been working on a new number for the finale."

Paul got his notebook out, as José-Luis watched his hands closely. They were strong, like his arms, but also sensitive José-Luis felt. His fingernails were spotlessly clean and, although clearly not manicured, were trimmed and even. The choreographer began to explain – with the benefit of hand gestures and facial expressions to add emphasis where needed – what they planned. A sensual dance with Tom alone at first but then joined by a partner, a single spotlight on him and the partner joining him in the light, dry ice swirling around the stage to obscure everything else and to keep the focus on Tom and his partner. 'Here we go,' Paul thought, 'I'd best train someone up to work with me on this lot.' José-Luis stood and mimed the sorts of movements that the partner would make once they had come onto the stage and approached Tom.

Paul watched him carefully, his eyes fixed on José-Luis's feet as they caressed the floor. He followed the choreographer's movements closely, looking up occasionally at hand gestures even glancing occasionally at José-Luis's torso and midriff. He sat down as Paul busily took notes. Even though he shuffled the chair round closer to Paul, José-Luis had to turn his whole head sideways to read what Paul was writing. At one point, he couldn't quite see what Paul had written. He reached across the desk and took Paul's hand simply to move it out of the way so he could read what was there. It was a perfectly natural move, and Paul did not immediately pull his hand away. José-Luis was aware when he did, that he didn't do so hastily. He just moved the hand to start correcting his notes and writing new ones.

Paul was very aware of what had just happened. It was what colleagues or friends might do. For him, though, there was more. He habitually avoided physical contact especially with other men. Somewhere in his memory, though, he remembered that same feeling during those awkward moments when he and his old school friend had touched, intentionally or by accident. It was not just the localised touch of another boy, but it was the way it spread through his senses, lasting for quite some time after it had originally occurred. Leaving a dull yearning. Once José-Luis had left, and they'd agreed on the types of effects Paul should create, Paul was briefly taken back to one special summer. He and Tom had been helping Paul's auntie out after his uncle died. Every night, he recalled, when the chatter had died down and they lay in the darkness, he'd wanted to reach out, just a few inches surely, for that same kind of contact. He had to be careful when he met José-Luis from then on, since maybe the choreographer would not like too much physical contact from him, he thought. And yet, something made him want that contact more. He wished he understood these things. If the urge became too strong, though, he would remember the look on Danny's face as he reeled off one pejorative term after another.

"Where's Tom?" Julia asked as she crossed the stage.

"Don't know," answered Rob and carried on with what he was doing.

"It's important!" insisted Julia, "I've got him an interview with *Melody Maker.*" This announcement was met with almost complete silence. Everyone just carried on what they were doing. "Look! Do you know how difficult it is to get *Melody Maker?*"

Frances walked onto the stage, stopped and folded her arms.

"Do we know you, love?" she asked.

Julia looked Frances up and down, clearly trying to control her outrage. How could an international star like Tom Bright put up with these provincials? Doing some research before her interview, she'd assumed that Tom was from leafy Surrey if not Guildford itself, since that's where he'd studied. She thought his Latin American music, bucking the trend of mainstream popstars, made him quirky and interesting. She would be horrified to discover that he'd finally chosen that direction as the result of a crush on a Mexican waiter in a restaurant in Godalming. And since she didn't see that listening to his songs was part of her brief as PR agent, she'd never thought about his lyrics. Nor how artfully ambiguous they were.

She paused. Then she walked purposefully over to Frances, holding her hand out.

"Hi, I'm Julia Dulwich," she said, "pleased to meet you... And you are?"

"I'm Frances," Frances answered but didn't shake hands, "I'm the front-of-house manager."

"Oh... And do *you* know where I could find Tom?"

"Not a clue, love," said Frances and turned to go about her duties. "Maybe he's having a nostalgic look round where he was born."

Tom had found his way down to the seawall. He sat and looked out to sea not knowing what he might be looking for. He'd been a bit surprised and hurt when José-Luis had told him they were just friends and not lovers. Tom had thought they were in a relationship. So, effectively, they were going steady. And who knows? Maybe someday they'd settle down together? That was what he'd been thinking. Now he had to face the prospect that he had no one. He felt a little ashamed that he'd callously assumed José-Luis would be happy to be his partner with Donatello unfortunately no longer around. He realised just how selfish he'd been.

However, this wasn't the real issue. He'd been trying to avoid admitting to himself what was really upsetting him. It was a foolish idea to come back to Weymouth, he now realised. He'd told himself that Paul had nothing to do with it. It was about coming home and acknowledging where it all began with *The Girl from Ipanema*. Many of his fans hadn't realised he was from Weymouth; like Julia, they thought he was from Guildford or even London. So, this was an opportunity to set the records straight. With that, though, he was still not being entirely honest.

All those years ago, he'd turned over and over in his head the painful memory of that last afternoon backstage before the end of school. He'd told his mother he thought he was having a migraine to get out of going to the ball itself that evening. Even though he had no history of migraines. Kissing Paul like that haunted him still. Why had he done it? Did he think Paul wanted him to? And then there was his reaction. Had it been so disgusting that he'd thrown up? Then, some while later, he began to wonder if there might be a different explanation for Paul's illness. After all, they'd had a few drinks beforehand, and they were giddy at the thought of leaving school. Perhaps Paul had just been surprised. After all, he'd been so close, holding him, making sure he didn't fall. That was the first time Paul had come up so near, so intimate. Tom ached to be with him again. Even just to know, once and for all, whether there'd been anything between them and could be again. He didn't want to think he might be wrong. That Paul had in fact moved on and found someone else. If only Paul would give him some kind of sign. The tiniest indication that he wanted to be with him, that's all. They could build on that. They would be happy, he just knew it.

Tom sat watching the small sail boats not far from the shore. Over to his left, a ferry was manoeuvring into the port. The sailors would tie up and then look around for anyone who might be looking for some fast fun – man or woman. Tom had no appetite though. He hung his head and, covering his face with his hands, he sobbed. Shaking uncontrollably, tortured by not knowing, yet wanting Paul. In his songs, there was an unmistakable yearning. Perhaps Paul had listened to his music? And so, perhaps he knew how Tom felt about him. How much he still longed for him. For the first time in years, Tom admitted that it was not just for anyone, for any man. He longed to be with Paul. And that's why he'd come back to Weymouth. If he could pick up the trail again, he just prayed it would lead to Paul.

Both Paul and Olwena had been surprised by how long the rehearsals were scheduled for. Because it was the beginning of the tour, apparently, Tom's manager had booked the theatre in Weymouth for those extra weeks leading up to the first performance. This made it difficult to start with since they had to clear up from whatever Tom Bright's crew had been doing during the day so that the evening performances could go ahead coming to the end of the run for the previous show. But then, rehearsals were also interrupted with Julia dragging Tom off to the local radio or television station. He was a sort of local celebrity after all, and it had been a long time since he'd been in these parts. Even his parents had moved further down the coast into Devon. So, there'd been no reason to come back till now. Every time Julia came on stage, the backing singers and musicians just accepted the interruptions and carried on as best they could.

José-Luis was always very patient. Though, as a perfectionist, he was always nervous when it came to new choreography. The theatre staff were intrigued. They weren't used to hosting Latin American music and the dancing looked alien, not the macho, bull-fighting stereotype they'd imagined. Equally, they were surprised by what appeared to be a budding and unlikely relationship between José-Luis and Paul. They were used to the lighting engineer just moving around quietly, there when needed, though no one had called him, and hidden away in the loft above the stage when they were doing other things. So, José-Luis shouting up from the stage to say he was 'coming up to find you', jokingly adding 'make sure you are decent, and you are not doing anything you shouldn't', was a source of some amusement. The lighting engineer was too dour and cold and detached for there to be any gossip as such.

Despite himself, Paul found this rather refreshing and not irritating or embarrassing at all. Even though sometimes, it seemed that José-Luis was up there on some pretext rather than for any serious reason. Paul even found himself hoping that he'd come up. Despite their obvious differences, they just seemed to be comfortable in each other's company, and that's what Paul loved. He didn't understand the South American guy's ways or mannerisms, but it had been such a long time since he'd felt so at ease in the company of another man. Olwena noticed a change in his mood. She would never want to be intrusive, but she hoped he trusted her enough to talk with her if needed, and most of all, she wanted him to be happy.

Paul was surprised one day to see José-Luis unannounced, as it were. He'd got so used to José-Luis's cheery voice and engaging smile when he turned up at his door, that seeing him sad and upset that day wrong-footed him. He didn't really know how to react or what to say.

"Are you alright, José-Luis?" he said eventually.

"I'm OK, thank you. It's just..."

Paul looked at him. What was he supposed to say? "Just?"

"Today is a sort of unhappy memory," he said.

"Like an anniversary?" Paul saw just a single teardrop land on his worktable. "Did someone die? Was it one of your parents?"

Without thinking, he stood and walked round the table. Crouching down again, and putting his hand on José-Luis's knee, he said:

"Do you need to talk about it?" surprising himself as much as anyone else.

"This was the day my husband was lynched in Colombia."

Paul had exhausted all the supportive gestures he could think of. He felt slightly awkward leaving his hand on José-Luis's leg this long. So, he stood up and perched on the table next to him resting his hands in his lap, trying to think of the right words.

"Oh my God, that's appalling. It sounds absolutely terrible. I am so, so very sorry. It must be horrible for you... each year, just thinking about it. Is there any way I might help?"

Surprised at the sincerity in the voice, José-Luis looked up at Paul and smiled. It was exactly the type of thing he'd wanted to hear from someone, though had not expected it to be Paul. He risked rubbing one of Paul's hands.

"Thank you. That is very kind. Today is a difficult day for me. That is all."

"Do you want to get out of here for a bit? Maybe a walk by the sea? Along the seawall is... was my favourite place."

"No, it's OK," and then he added, "it's not really good for me to be out in the daytime. It would be too risky. If they send me back to Colombia, I will not be safe."

Paul was confused, though he'd heard something about José-Luis coming with the tour bus on the ferry rather than on the plane with the others. He hadn't thought anything of it. Putting two and two together, he said: "Surely you could ask for asylum?"

José-Luis huffed. "With your government?" he said quite reasonably, "I heard the new Home Secretary even attends some arrests of illegal immigrants in person..."

"I suppose so." Paul leant forward and put a hand on José-Luis's shoulder. He didn't really know what else to do. "Don't worry. You're safe here. Promise."

"You're very kind, Paul, you know that, don't you?" José-Luis looked up into his eyes, his expression and tone very serious.

"I... Well, I just try to be helpful," Paul replied. "I want you to feel safe here, so that you can get on with your work."

"It's more than that," José-Luis stood up, and Paul took a step back to give him room. "I understand now why he... I mean, there is something about you that makes people feel safe." Paul didn't answer.

It was only later that Paul remembered and wondered about José-Luis talking about his 'husband'. He'd never really thought about it but couldn't quite get his head around two men marrying in a conventional sense. His mind kept wondering back to his parents' wedding photo. Which man would wear white? Perhaps it was just a figure of speech? He was pretty sure he'd not heard of two men marrying in Britain. He liked José-Luis and felt comfortable with him. Knowing now that he liked men not women as normal people do didn't change his attitude towards him at all. Paul wasn't like that.

"Thank you. I feel better now. Yes, Paul, I feel very safe with you. I'm so grateful that we came here." José-Luis stood up, wiped his hand across his face, and turned to leave. "I need to go and check how things are going with Tom's costume. For the final number."

"Anytime," Paul called after him.

"What do you think of Tom Bright's trousers?" Olwena asked a few days later as they sat drinking her special tea and, today, rock cakes. Paul was a little ill at ease. Olwena picked this up. "I mean, you know, these Latin trousers with the reflective strip down the side." Paul relaxed. José-Luis had warned him about these trousers, and Olwena was altering Tom's, adding a reflective strip along the outer seam of each leg. Even she thought it looked a bit tacky.

"Well," explained Paul, "the effect will be quite dramatic. The challenge is having a single, static spot. So that you can't see their faces. That will probably mean they can't see each other either, not until the last minute." Olwena bit through the thread when she'd finished the first leg rather than use scissors. She held the trousers up and shook them to encourage the creases to drop out.

"Here, stand up," she said, her teeth clenched holding a dozen pins she'd removed one by one from holding the reflective strip to the trouser leg as she'd sewn. "Turn round."

Paul did as he was told. She held the trousers against his waist. He knew this was important for her to get an idea of how the trousers would hang, so he tried to avoid the reflex to move away and avoid her touch. It was just a habit.

"Hmmm," she said, the pins still in her mouth, "good job they're not meant for you." Paul wondered what she was getting at. "About an inch or so on the waist and maybe two on the length." Without thinking, Paul looked behind and down at his feet to see what she meant.

"Well, they're not for me," he said, perfectly reasonably.

"I could do with checking the length with the shoes as well. It's so difficult without him being here. But with the flare in the leg, you really need to know how the hem will sit. On the shoe at the front and then against the heel at the back." She fussed around a bit and managed to find some Cuban-heel shoes. "What size are you?"

"Ten," Paul said, without thinking of what was coming next. Olwena went back to the basket. Finally, she stood up again, her back stiff with bending at an awkward angle.

"Here. Put these on please, it'll give me a better idea." Dutifully, though checking the door to make sure no one was coming, he put on the red, Cuban-heel dance shoes and stood up. "Round you go," Olwena said with a stirring motion of her right hand. Paul turned round and she held the trousers against his waist again before dropping them a little lower. She bent down to check the length against the heeled shoes and put a guide pin in. He wasn't comfortable with her hands on his buttocks, but he stayed as still as he could. To distract himself,

"I know these are not for me," he said, "but I'm taller than Tom." This was the first unprompted mention of the name. Olwena looked up at him carefully.

"Yes, I know. Do you think I'm stupid or something?" she smiled. She wasn't angry, of course. "About inch and a half, maybe two," she said.

"Yeah, that's about right," said Paul.

"Don't ever fancy being on stage yourself, then?" Olwena asked, as she was folding the trousers again, putting them back on her workbench to shorten a little.

"Not really," said Paul, then he added, "it'd have to be something really special to get me on stage. I'm perfectly happy backstage, out of view, just doing my bit." Olwena was quiet for a minute of two. She took a sip of her tea and grimaced slightly. Looking out of the window at nothing in particular,

"You never know," she said.

As the week of interrupted rehearsals went by and the previous booking finished, most people began working late and were still round in the theatre well into the evening before walking back to the hotel where they were all staying. Paul got into the habit of making sure he was the last to leave, tidying up as he walked softly from the stairs across the stage itself and out of the stage door. For now, and with this production, he was always relieved to be going back to his own flat. In fact, few people knew where the flat was; they just knew he must be local. And that made him feel safe.

He picked up props and bits of clothing, plastic cups even. No one quite realised that he did this, but the cleaners were always grateful that they didn't have to tidy up after all those arty people. They knew these people were not normal and you never knew what you might find dropped on the floor or half-hidden in a waste-paper bin. Generally, he would put discarded items of clothing on any bit of scenery or chair or whatever was to hand. It was too dark to identify who they belonged to or if they were costumes or someone's own clothes. That evening, though, a short-sleeved shirt and a pair of trousers seemed familiar. A pair of cotton boxer shorts – unusual in the UK at that time – caught his attention. They smelt like something he remembered. Without thinking, he'd pressed them gently to his nose and took a deep breath, trying to identify where he knew the scent from.

An unexpected noise interrupted his reverie. It didn't bother him, as such, he was just a bit surprised. He was usually pretty careful to make sure everyone had left before he did his rounds. As it happened, he was clearly not the only one who'd tried to make sure there was no one else about. He walked towards the noise, without thinking about the pants still pressed to his face. There was no need of course to tread particularly carefully – he'd been moving around undetected for years. Somehow, though, this evening put him a little more on edge. As he walked forward, he could hear low pitched repeated noises. He thought he recognised the noise from his times alone at night in the dark in his own bed. But even from where he was, he could tell there were two people. Peering cautiously around one of the flats at this side of the stage, he quickly pulled his head back into the shadows. He didn't want to interrupt or to be seen. Slowly, slowly, he bent his head forward again though.

There were two people, two men, completely naked. One, shorter, well-built and hairy, was lying almost on the back of the one lying on his stomach underneath on a prop basket with a dark dust sheet over it, his hairy chest against the other man's back. They were both drenched in sweat and very vocal, clearly enjoying the close proximity. Although he'd only ever seen José-Luis clothed, he recognised him immediately. The strong back, narrow waist and hips, and as he could see now, hairy buttocks. And, of course, he'd found his clothes just a few minutes ago, he now realised. He was fascinated, attracted maybe – he didn't really know – how the hairs seemed to grow denser between the cheeks. He had an urge to reach out and touch him. Feel his back and down to his bottom. To caress him gently. Show him affection. It took him a little longer to recognise the guy underneath. It had been many years since he'd seen him naked, he realised, and he was now a fully grown man. It was Tom.

So this, he realised, was how men have sex. He automatically tilted his head at a slight angle as if to get a better view of something, but then straightened up again, feeling he could see a little too much that way. José-Luis was thrusting deep into Tom still. Paul was curious, that's all, and wondered if it hurt. But Tom wasn't complaining. As he looked more closely, he could see that their hands were clasped, José-Luis's covering and folded over Tom's, their fingers locked together. José-Luis seemed to be getting more insistent with the movements of his lower body and finally, almost like a jolt or a spasm, José-Luis let out a long, loud grunt, practically stood up and exhaled. Slowly, he stopped thrusting and kissed the back of Tom's neck, running his fingers from the nape of Tom's neck up through his hair. It was exciting, and unselfishly, Paul took pleasure in their pleasure and for them. He couldn't explain it. José-Luis moved back and off Tom and stood aside while Tom recovered a little and stood up too. Paul stepped back to avoid being seen and catching a glimpse of rather too much of the two lovers. When he looked again, José-Luis was now on his back, his legs around Tom, who was the one thrusting back and forth in his turn. Tom bent forward and they embraced and kissed, but Tom didn't stop moving or making low, unintelligible groans. Both men were totally focused on each other. In that moment, at least.

Paul was conscious that he should not be watching. Despite his own lack of knowledge and experience in such things, he felt he was intruding – albeit unintentionally – into a very personal and private act. For whatever reason, he wanted to watch. He wanted to see them relaxed and enjoying each other. Not for any salacious reason – that sort of thing just didn't occur to him. He'd never bought any porn either here or in Bournemouth when he was a student. He just felt that there was something reassuringly natural about seeing them acting this way together. It was like some big question or some significant worry had been answered. He felt relieved and happy. It looked perfectly normal for them to be so close and to be doing what they were doing. He smiled to himself.

Paul slowly withdrew into the darkness. He still had the boxers pressed against his nose and face. He carefully placed them on the floor where anyone passing that way – hopefully Tom, of course – could reclaim them. He felt a heavy weight on his shoulders; he didn't know why. He was genuinely happy for them. That they had each other. He was happy too that José-Luis had found someone else after what happened last year. But there was also a deep sadness in him which he didn't recognise although he'd felt it before. As he made his way towards the fire escape, he heard Tom climax, and he imagined them in each other's arms, catching their breath, kissing, caressing each other's heated bodies. It was cold outside, which froze a tear on his face. As he wiped it away, he realised he didn't know he could feel like this.

Back in the theatre, José-Luis and Tom were lying exhausted side by side on their backs on the prop basket lid. José-Luis turned on his front and pulled himself up on his elbows.

"See, *hermoso*, we have fantastic sex," he was smiling, looking down fondly on Tom's face. "I hope you enjoyed it too!"

Tom snorted and kissed José-Luis's hand. José-Luis did not withdraw his hand, but shifting his weight onto the other arm, he stroked Tom's face gently, metaphorically trying to smooth the furrows on his brow.

"Find your lover, Tom Bright, find him. He's out there. I know he is. Waiting." Tom tried to look relaxed and smile. "He may be closer than you think," José-Luis added as much to himself as to Tom. In his turn, Tom slid gingerly off the basket, checked the black cloth for tell-tale stains, and walked onto the stage to find their clothes. Picking up his boxers, he went back to José-Luis and, laughing, "Look, you animal!" José-Luis was folding the black cloth ready to put somewhere appropriate in the backstage area. He looked over to where Tom was waving his boxers in the air. "You must've just tossed these aside carelessly onto the floor when you tore them off!"

Tom was laughing now as he shook his own boxers out, bending slightly, getting ready to put them on again. He stopped, though, almost overbalancing, falling heavily on the foot he'd been about to put into one leg of the boxers. José-Luis looked up at him.

"Can you smell something?" Tom half-turned his head, as if listening for something in the darkness.

"You mean other than this, *guapo*?" José-Luis stood bandy-legged, like a child who's got wet pants sitting on the grass.

"Not that, you dirty bugger!" Tom laughed, but he still looked concerned and puzzled. "I can't place that scent. But it's familiar somehow."

3

Tom didn't know if he believed in coincidences or not. Time after time, he'd had to admit how grateful he was when he was told to sit next to Paul on that first day of secondary school all those years ago. Otherwise, he thought, Paul would never have spoken to him. He just wasn't like that. Tom shuddered. He didn't want to think about it. If he took that to its logical conclusion, of course, he'd have to admit that being born in Weymouth was such a gift. How else would he have known Paul? But then coming back and seeing Paul again had been too painful till now. Paul wouldn't even talk to him. He desperately hoped that that would change.

Then, there'd been the time he was trying to play a cajón outside the theatre in San Diego. José-Luis, recently arrived from Colombia via various stops in Central America, had been passing at just the right time. He'd come over to him and suggested they change places. And when they'd fallen into conversation, José-Luis had admitted that his sense of rhythm came from his dancing. He'd demonstrated a tango later that day at a Latin American bar near the historic old town, explaining to Tom that the dance had come from Argentina. Originally danced between two men. Was that a coincidence, he wondered? All too soon, though, he was brought back to reality and the hotel restaurant sitting opposite Julia, his PR manager.

"Yes, really. Look!" Julia was reading the broadsheets over breakfast. "The Conservative Party Conference this year is in Bournemouth, a mere 35 miles or so along the coast. How amazing is that?" Really? Thought Tom. There'd be the usual sabre rattling about being tough on crime and a safe pair of hands for the economy. He'd also heard that Thatcher was brewing something up about family values even before he'd seen the billboard just outside Heathrow.

"The nuclear family," Julia continued as if on cue, *"consists of a father, a mother, and 2.2 children."*

'What's .2 of a child, anyway?' Tom thought.

"Britons should embrace what for generations had been seen as normal family life. In so doing, Britain will be great again."

Tom snorted, and Julia flicked the newspaper pointedly. Tom wondered briefly where he might fit in with all this family values stuff. Would he ever have any children? Did he want children? He hadn't really thought about it that much. There was time for all of that, he decided. He was only in his twenties after all. But then – he wasn't listening to Julia anymore – José-Luis had been very happy with Donatello, and they didn't have any children. For a moment, Tom wondered if men *could* marry men in Colombia. He thought not. It was probably just José-Luis normalising things. Donatello was a respectable doctor, after all. Well, until the bigots got him. Tom shuddered again just thinking about it. How could anyone do that to another human being?

He suspected José-Luis was so devoted to Donatello that he used the term 'husband' to show it. José-Luis had made it perfectly clear that he didn't normally sleep with other men. He was completely faithful to Donatello when he was alive. Now that he'd gone, José-Luis said, he thought that Donatello'd want him to enjoy life as best he could. Thinking about it now, Tom understood what José-Luis had said about sex and love. He wanted to be loved, he thought, really loved. For someone to want him so badly. And for him to be as devoted to another man as José-Luis had been to Donatello. Men like them seemed to be forced to live outside society, he thought, while having to survive somehow inside it. Yet all they were doing was following their hearts. Surely José-Luis's love for Donatello was just as natural and just as pure as any other couple's up and down the country, with or without 2.2 children?

He looked at Julia. Her hair was scraped back into a French knot, her blouse buttoned right up to her chin, and her jacket was crisp with gold anchor buttons. Her lips were moving, but he'd closed his ears. He didn't need to listen to that stuff. Tom didn't think she was the type to have children either. So, in that respect anyway, he thought, they weren't that different.

"Isn't it time you went to the theatre?" Julia was looking over the top of the newspaper. "Tom! Are you listening to me?"

"Yes, of course. How interesting... So, I best be off. I was going to wait for José-Luis."

Julia frowned very slightly. Tom misinterpreted the look on her face.

"OK, OK, I'm going. I'll just clean my teeth and grab my jacket. He can join me when he's ready."

Coincidentally, earlier that morning across town in his flat, Paul had torn the *Family Values* article from the newspaper and burned it on the stove in the kitchen.

There'd been a softer side to Julia Dulwich when she'd started working for him, Tom reflected as he made his way to the theatre. She'd been naturally deferential. She would ask Tom his thoughts and seek his approval if she had plans for a press release or launch event. Her dress sense was very Laura Ashley with long flowing skirts, frilly blouses and looser fitting jackets. All it needed was a basket over her arm and a bicycle. And the smell of freshly baked cakes, wafting round her head like a pearl necklace. Tom simply thought she would become more autonomous as she got used to the job and to his ways. He didn't pay much attention to how she dressed, though, beyond thinking it rather Home Counties housewife. He liked to think he treated everyone the same, nothing too formal, based on mutual respect and consensus. And with Julia, it was just the same, though he'd hoped she'd drop the doe-eyed look when she was hanging on his every word.

They were on a short tour in Canada, when things seemed to have changed, he reflected. Vancouver, Edmonton, Winnipeg, Toronto and then Montreal. Julia had gone the extra mile and taken care of all the accommodation as well as the publicity. This was her first tour since she'd joined Tom and the crew. Tom was very impressed and took her to dinner as a thank you. She looked very glamorous while Tom had come straight from the theatre. She blushed when she noticed him looking at her cleavage; he was thinking she would catch a bad cold with so much flesh exposed. He had felt responsible somehow. Not that this display might have been for him, but whether he should have leant across the table and covered her up with his napkin. She'd brushed her hair back with her hand, wearing it loose and down. He'd also been worried at the thought of having to protect her honour against any whalers who might drop by and get drunk, before he'd remembered that Winnipeg is land-locked and unlikely to see much passing trade from lust-ridden seafarers. She blushed again when she caught him chuckle to himself, misinterpreting what that meant. At one stage during the meal, Tom got the impression she was flirting with him. He put it down to the wine and thought no more of it. He'd never really considered himself attractive to women. The screaming teenaged girls were part and parcel of what he did. But there was nothing serious. On the other hand, he didn't even know when another man was interested in him. These were dangerous times for casual encounters anyway, he reflected. And he was too afraid that the press might get hold of it and blow his cover. 'That would be something for Julia to get her teeth into,' he thought. Then shuddered again.

"So, does everyone socialise together?" Julia asked Greg, the musical director, a few weeks after starting. Greg looked at her for a moment or two.

"Not really, no. When we're touring, we spend a lot of time together on planes or tour buses. So, after that, we quite like to do our own thing."

"And how about Tom?" Julia said casually.

"What do you mean?" Greg asked.

"Does he socialise with anyone?"

"You better ask him." And Greg walked away to discuss something with Jason, the sound engineer. Tom found her behaviour over the coming weeks rather strange. But as she grew in confidence, he had to admit she was very good at finding opportunities to promote his work. She was also very protective and would not be intimidated by promoters or music industry types. He made sure she knew how much he appreciated all of this, though he wasn't ready to take her to dinner again. At least not on his own.

Late one evening when they were wrapping up rehearsals for a new show, most people having left for the night, Tom and José-Luis were alone in a side office, discussing some last-minute changes to routines. They were standing close. José-Luis leaning in towards him, whilst Tom was showing him something he'd spread out on the office desk. Wrapping things up, Tom turned, put his arms round José-Luis's waist, and they kissed.

"I was just wondering..." Julia walked into the office with some early versions of the local papers, head down browsing the headlines. She looked up and stopped. Tom and José-Luis looked round, unconcerned, Tom's arms still round José-Luis.

"Hi Julia. I didn't know you were still here," Tom replied nonchalantly. "OK, so shall we discuss it now, or do you want to do that tomorrow?" Only then did he take his arms from José-Luis and turn to face her.

"Oh, no, sorry... Tomorrow is fine." Clearly a little taken aback, Julia averted her eyes. She turned slowly and left.

"What was all that about?" asked José-Luis.

"Search me," Tom answered. "I'm sure it'll keep though. So, what shall we do this evening?" And they made arrangements to meet later. Discreetly, of course. Tom didn't like the press sniffing round his private life.

The next morning, Julia managed to get Jason on his own this time.

"So, well, it was a bit odd last night," she started. Jason looked at her trying not to show that he didn't really care. She carried on regardless.

"I went to ask Tom something, and that foreign guy was there."

"Look, love," sighed Jason, "we're abroad. We're all foreign here. *Which* foreign guy?"

"That Mexican dancer chap. The short one." She tried to sound casual.

"He's Colombian. What about him?"

"Well, he and Tom were a bit close. And then they kissed." She was trying to gauge Jason's reaction.

"It's showbiz, love," said Jason, turning to get on with something else, "Better get used to it."

"What's up with him?" Frances, the front-of-house manager, asked Terrence, one of the quieter stage crew, looking over the top of the day's paper at a very pale Danny slumped on the table. Terrence rolled his eyes back at her.

"Burning the candle at both ends recently," he replied. Danny snuffled, raised his head and looked from Terrence to Frances.

"Oh, for goodness' sake, Danny," Frances huffed, "either pull yourself together or take the day off sick."

Danny roused himself again.

"What's wrong, anyway?" Frances added.

"He was out with the *lads* last night," explained Terrence, emphasising the word 'lads' deliberately. "They were partying till quite late. Lots of Tequila apparently."

"What's that when it's at home?" Frances wasn't sure if it was a drink or something you ate or even sniffed.

"It's a type of alcohol," Terrence said, "clear and a bit like petrol. It's from Mexico apparently."

"My God!" Frances laughed, "first our international celebrity, Tom Bright, and then an exotic foreign drink. It's all happening in Weymouth! Whatever next, I wonder?"

Danny groaned, his head on the table between his arms.

"Serves you right, then," Frances looked pointedly at him, completely unsympathetic. As far as she was concerned, the job came first. You could only ever drink too much when there wasn't a show or rehearsals the next day.

Loud noises came from off stage, and the musicians and dancers walked across chatting in Spanish and laughing and joking.

"Hey, Daniél!" called Carlos cheerily, "you no singing and dancing today?"

Danny finally sat up and waved over to the musicians: "Morning, guys. Must be something I ate, that's all."

Everyone tried not to laugh. Rob, who'd come onto the stage to join them now that the others had arrived, had put a large glass of water on the table in front of him.

"Been out with the musicians and dancers every night this week," Terrence offered by way of explanation to Frances and Rob, sitting down at the table with them. Frances couldn't believe her ears.

"Danny?" she asked, "with all of our exotic friends there?"

Terrence nodded. "Taking a walk on the wild side," he added, barely able to stop a broad smirk spreading across his face.

"The things is…" Danny said at last, holding up his hand.

"Don't strain yourself there, tiger!" Frances laughed.

"No, the thing is," Danny repeated, "I've been thinking…"

"Steady on there, Danny," Rob said, "first Tequila, now thinking…"

"He's been exploring his feminine side, haven't you, Danny?" Frances was enjoying this.

"No, look, seriously," Danny was adamant he was going to say his piece. "I know I was a bit hasty the other day…"

"What?" Terrence interrupted, "you mean talking about *shirt lifters* and *queers*, and all that kind of thing?"

"Yeah, well," Danny winced and looked down at his hands a bit sheepishly. "OK. I was wrong."

There were a few moments' silence, whilst everyone tried to take in what Danny actually seemed to want to say.

"They're not that bad when you get to know them," he explained.

"When they buy you drinks, you mean!" Terrence and Frances were not letting him off the hook that easily.

"No, really, they're a good crowd and decent fellas," Danny said, sitting up straight now, his hands together in front of him on the table. "No funny business… You know… They're just normal blokes. Out for a good time, see."

"Good for you, Danny!" Rob said, slapping him on the back. That wasn't such a good move, and Danny looked as though he might be physically sick. He took a long swig from the glass of water. "That's all it takes," Rob continued. "A bit of understanding and letting people be who they are."

"Exactly!" said Danny, trying to forget his hangover, taking another mouthful of water. "Alright, *amigos*!" he shouted back towards the musicians who were still chatting easily with one another. He stood up, swallowed hard and went over to join in with his new friends, putting an arm round Gabriel's shoulder, one of the other musicians.

"He doesn't realise, of course," Terrence said, looking at Frances, "they're not all gay. In fact, I think it's only those two over there," he nodded his head in the direction of two rather strong, masculine looking backing singers. Frances followed his gaze.

"Oh wow!" she answered, "you just can't tell, can you?"

"Yeah, well," said Rob, "what does it matter anyway? So long as they do their job. That's all I care about."

Greg and Jason had just arrived and went over to join the musicians and talk something through. Or perhaps just to share a joke or two. Soon, there was a lot of loud laughter and back-slapping. Frances rolled her eyes and smiled broadly at Rob:

"Wonders will never cease," she said as she tidied the magazine away, "Danny's seen the light!" Rob laughed too, and she made for the front of house. She had some posters and adverts to sort out. Julia had had the cover of *The Face* made into a poster with Tom looking over his shoulder, the light coming from somewhere in front of him. Frances wanted to find an excuse not to use it. But in the end, she found she couldn't.

When Tom arrived at the theatre, most of the crew were gathered on stage waiting for him and José-Luis to arrive so they could get started. Frances seemed to be keeping everyone entertained. So, Tom went and joined them.

"Right, everyone, listen carefully. We've only got three more clues to go," Frances shouted to anyone who'd listen. There was usually a copy of *Equity Magazine* somewhere in the theatre, and the crossword was one of those clever ones that had both cryptic and simple clues that fit into the same grid. Frances was working on the simple ones. It helped pass the time. The dancers and musicians didn't really pay much attention. After all, English was not their first language. They'd show willing sometimes, though.

"So *'Unrequited love at epiphany'*, 5 letters, first letter *'V'*..." she read.

"*Virgin,*" said Danny.

"Really? What's that got to do with *unrequited love?*" Greg asked.

"Well, they're not getting it. That's why they're a *virgin*."

There was a collective groan and rolling of eyes. "You're the last of the great romantics, Danny," Frances said. "And anyway, it's got six letters." Still, no one had any other suggestions. They couldn't understand the clue, let alone work out the answer.

"Are you sure these are the easy clues?" Jason asked.

"Of course. We've done the rest!" said Frances.

"*'Unrequited love at epiphany'* beginning with *'V'*..."

"When's epiphany?"

"January sometime. Not long after Christmas and New Year."

"*Viola*" came a muffled voice from above them.

"Thanks, Paul," Frances shouted back. Tom smiled to himself. He remembered how proud he used to be when, after much argument in English lessons, Paul would come in with some intuitive but profound interpretation. Those were happy memories, and he couldn't help smiling to himself briefly. He wished he could speak to Paul. Like he used to. It had been so easy back then. Tom imagined he could even cope with just being friends from now on, though he knew he wanted so much more than that. There was no doubt now that Paul was avoiding him, but he wished he wouldn't. Tom tried to resist the temptation to look up and see where Paul was.

"Shit!" he said, before he could stop himself, the front legs of his chair banging noisily onto the stage as he sat back forward. "Of course! We did *Twelfth Night* at school." Tom wished he hadn't as soon as he'd said it. Frances gave him a knowing look. Danny didn't understand what *epiphany* had to do with *twelfth night*, but he thought it best not to ask.

"Viola! Of course. She disguises herself as her dead brother and falls in love with the Duke. He can't fall for her because he thinks she's a man. Meanwhile, Olivia, who the Duke loves, falls in love with Viola dressed as a man..." Tom almost gabbled.

"What?" Danny looked completely confused.

"It's OK, Danny," said Frances, "that's Shakespeare for you."

Danny nodded wisely to Frances but wished people wouldn't dress up and make life complicated.

"Last but one," said Frances in a loud voice to everyone, "you listening, Mr Armstrong?" There was no reply, of course, but she knew Paul well enough to know that he would be.

"So, another one about love. *'Forbidden love on ancient shores'*, seven letters, and if *Viola's* right, that means the fourth letter is *'A'*." She sucked the top of her pen, trying to look as though she might have any idea what the answer could be.

"*Romeo,*" said Vince, one of the backing vocalists.

"That's five letters," said Frances.

"*Juliet*, then." Carlos, the bandoneon player offered.

"Six letters. And neither of them has an *'A'* in it." Rob added, walking onto the stage at last. He'd been listening from the wings.

"Wait a minute," Rob liked to think he could actually tackle the cryptic clues and not just the simple ones, "*ancient shores... ancient shores...* that could be here. This is the Jurassic Coast after all." Frances looked at him disapprovingly. Tom flushed slightly.

"*Phaedra... P H A E D R A*", Paul shouted, spelling it out before anyone could ask how that fit. "Married to Theseus, but falls in love with his son, Hippolytus."

"How did he know that?" Frances asked no one in particular but looking pointedly at Tom. She checked the answers, upside down on the back page. "Bloody Hell, he's right!"

"Thanks, Paul," she shouted back, as she folded the paper,

smoothing it down on the table with a satisfied smile. She tapped the pen on the tabletop in no particular rhythm. She scribbled large swirls over a piece in the daily tabloid about family values and Thatcher's call for normal family life.

"Isn't there another clue to go?" Terrence asked, the other stagehand working with Danny was clearly getting into it.

Tom looked pensive, as Frances began to open the paper again at the crossword puzzle. She smoothed out the page and was checking where the missing letters were when Tom stood up and said:

"I think I better ring the hotel." He wandered off into the wings.

He was worried about José-Luis. Apparently, the new Home Secretary down the road in Bournemouth was trying to prove her credentials as a tough-thinking, tough-acting minister. Julia had announced it at dinner last night. This included immigration control. Julia had said it was high time someone took control and stopped all of these foreigners taking our jobs. No one really cared what Julia thought. José-Luis was not exactly illegal. But then he wasn't totally legal either. He was travelling on a temporary tourist visa. He'd probably outstayed his welcome already and should definitely not be working. Tom and Jason had thought that airport immigration tended to be more switched on. Everyone agreed, therefore, he should travel with the bus, as a foot passenger if necessary, and come through the more relaxed border controls at ferry ports. Tom and José-Luis, however, were both worried that it might only be a matter of time till he would be picked up and questioned. Tom rang the hotel and became even more worried when the receptionist said he'd left about fifteen minutes earlier, accompanied by a short, dark-haired lady. 'Wasn't that exactly the description of the Home Secretary?' he thought. He was beginning to panic. But Frances said she would check the schedule of speakers at the Tory Conference and see if the Home Secretary could in fact have come over to Weymouth.

A few minutes after Tom had put the 'phone down to the hotel and come back slowly onto the stage, a worried look on his face, there were loud foreign voices from the direction of the stage door. José-Luis sauntered in talking animatedly in Spanish, a dark-haired lady on his arm with similar olive complexion and beautiful eyes. They were both gesticulating wildly with their free arm. José-Luis looked round at the startled faces staring at them. Switching to English, he smiled:

"Look who I have just bumped into! What a coincidence, here in this town in England at this time and eight thousand kilometres away from home.

"This is Dana-Beatriz de la Anunciación," José-Luis stepped aside and, gently removing the hand she'd slipped through it, waved his right arm theatrically through the air making a showy gesture to introduce her and bowing like the prince in a pantomime. Tom looked at the lady next to José-Luis, his brow slightly furrowed. He felt he was missing something. Like: who was she, how did José-Luis know her, and what on earth was she doing in Weymouth of all places?

"Pleased to meet you," Tom said, nevertheless, holding out a hand to Dana-Beatriz. He wanted to ask for a bit of an explanation but thought that might be rather tactless. She curtsied briefly towards him as she held out her hand in return. He obliged and kissed it lightly.

"Dana-Beatriz and me, we trained as dancers together," José-Luis added, helpfully. Carlos seemed to need no introduction. Instead, he launched into a piece slightly more upbeat than the tangoes he'd been playing in rehearsals, shouting something in Spanish which Tom couldn't quite understand. She beamed at him and, holding her arms up against her chest her hands clenched in loose fists, she shuffled a little in a sort of dance in time to the music.

"We used to dance competitions as little children," José-Luis said. "Shall we show them something?" He looked at Dana-Beatriz who nodded back enthusiastically in response. "What would you like to see us dance?" He took Dana-Beatriz's hand again and led her to a space centre stage.

"No, no, no, you've got to do it properly," Gabriel shouted over.

"True," said José-Luis, "especially with such a fine lady." He bowed to Dana-Beatriz, who bowed her head back at him. "Paul," José-Luis shouted, looking up to the loft above the stage. Paul's face appeared. "Would you be so kind and light us? Please?" Paul hadn't actually said so, but José-Luis knew he would. He was warming to the reclusive lighting engineer, respected his skill in creating the atmosphere that he, Greg and Jason wanted even if they were not always able to describe it perfectly, and he liked his kindness towards the lonely Olwena. That showed the type of respect for family that he dreamed of. He saw a sadness in him too which he couldn't quite fathom, but which he felt he recognised from Tom. And he was still unsure whether Paul was in fact the mystery man in Tom's past. He was certainly handsome and strong. The strong silent type, he speculated.

Rob helped Danny and Terrence move most of the bits of furniture off the stage whilst everyone went down into the auditorium to sit a few rows back for the best view. The Latin musicians sat towards the back and whispered arrangements to one another whilst all the furniture moving was going on. Olwena had come down to see what all the commotion was about and was sitting on the end of a row, still holding the stitching she'd been working on. Paul's face peered down through the gloom looking onto the stage from above, though no one seemed to notice.

"What shall we dance?" José-Luis looked over to the musicians.

"*¡Porro! ¡Porro colombiano!*"

"Really? We're not really dressed for it."

"Please! Remind us of home," said Angelo.

Dana-Beatriz picked up one of the black dust cloths and made to tie it in a rough knot around her waist.

"No, wait!" Olwena put down her sewing and rushed back onto the stage. She pinned the dust cloth like a peasant skirt from Dana-Beatriz's skirt band with swathes of cloth hanging from the waist across the hips to make it look theatrically authentic. Dana-Beatriz turned this way and that to see the makeshift skirt swish sensually back and forth. Delighted with the effect, she flashed her beautiful teeth at Olwena, who looked down and fussed with the skirt once more. She hurried back down the steps to join the others before the musicians started up.

"Hey, Olwena!" José-Luis called after her. "Look, you've dropped this." He bent down to pick up a small, lady's handkerchief. "What's this? J.B.?" he asked, as he looked at the hankie. The initials were in white silk thread in one corner, edged with drawn thread work.

"Oh, yes, that's right," replied Olwena, slightly flushed, "it's mine." She stuffed it back into her sleeve and took her seat at the end of the row, not looking at anyone else. Paul wondered about the hankie and the initials J B. He couldn't quite work out why they seemed familiar.

The stage was in complete darkness for a minute or two. Paul had been watching the musicians during rehearsals, so he knew that they didn't play from a musical score. Each was lit by a single spot from above, and a general soft-filter light from offstage left. There was a single spot in the middle of the stage, with the two dancers slowly circling it, their faces lit up whilst their bodies were still half in the shadows. Gradually, rising from their feet, they were each lit individually, but their faces were left in shadow. The *porro* itself was more a folksy dance, the others decided, and so they clapped politely but without any great enthusiasm. The musicians were delighted, though, and jumped to their feet clapping and whistling loudly.

After what seemed like hours, they sat down and picked up their instruments again. Carlos played a sort of interlude, while Dana-Beatriz started to take off the temporary skirt. Olwena hurried back on stage to help. As the other musicians joined in, the music came to a clear point where Dana-Beatriz and José-Luis took hold. This was a milonga, much faster than the crew were used to during rehearsals when first José-Luis and then Tom danced with one of the female dancers. The two dancers were bathed in a single light which followed them around with fixed footlights sending a pattern across the stage a little like a chess board. José-Luis seemed to lead Dana-Beatriz from one light area on the stage to another, missing out the darker spots in between. Some of the steps were similar to the familiar tango they'd watched, but it was all a lot faster. With the rhythm of the music and apparent movement from a trick with the lighting, the crew loved it. Danny and Terrence even got up and danced down one of the aisles, badly, but with great gusto. Tom was relieved, though, that he wouldn't have to try and go that quickly.

Finally, they came to what everyone recognised as the tango José-Luis had been working on with Tom, or at least the same rhythm and melody. The pair danced a routine they'd never seen before, though. It was absolutely breathtaking. Dana-Beatriz and José-Luis stayed cheek-to-cheek no matter how much they moved and turned, their legs seeming to twist and flick, drawing imaginary half-circles on the ground. It came across as ritualistic, Paul thought, but it had such an intense meaning that he felt something in the pit of his stomach. They danced as one. Paul's lighting caressed their bodies as they moved together, somehow their respective brows casting shade over their eyes, adding to the emotion and mystery. While at the back and around the wings, uplighters threw light around the whole stage, giving the impression of an enclosure, a prison almost. They had each other, holding each other close, the audience like voyeurs watching something they shouldn't, something private and personal. The whole effect was stunning. The lighting added to a sensuality about the whole spectacle, with the uplighters being drawn downwards to point horizontally across the stage as Paul felt the music coming to an end.

The couple stood panting slightly, an arm around one another's waist. José-Luis whispered something in Dana-Beatriz's ear and looked back towards the musicians. After a few words in Spanish, they all looked over to Tom. He realised that José-Luis and Dana-Beatriz had been discussing whether he should dance with her. This was awful, and he swallowed hard, his mouth suddenly dry. Singing he could manage but dancing with a professional made him feel vaguely ill. José-Luis was an exceptional teacher, but what he'd just danced was at another level. Reluctantly, though with no other choice he felt, Tom slowly returned to the stage and walked towards Dana-Beatriz who looked at him with that captivating smile and held out an encouraging hand towards him. She didn't speak. But José-Luis told Tom just to dance the routine they'd been working on. Paul leant forward, resting his chin on the guard rail that most of the guide ropes were tied to. Tom took up his position, head slightly down, and waited for the solo bandoneon to start. The uplighters round the stage were now pointing upwards on alternate diagonals like an open-weave basket. There was a single wide spot centre stage, focused on Tom's upper half to begin with. Dana-Beatriz fixed her gaze on him, and zig-zagged, *ochos* José-Luis called them, towards him. It reminded Paul of Salome dancing for Herod, and he wondered who would lose their head over this particular dance. The crew in the auditorium held their breath.

Standing directly opposite him now, still looking at his downturned face, she stopped, bringing her two feet together. The single spot widened, embracing both dancers, but still leaving their eyes hidden. Bending into the standing leg, Tom made a slow rondée with his right leg. Once both feet were back together, he stepped forward, ball flat, standing no more than a few inches away from his partner. Her head was now looking down, her eyes towards her right hand. Waiting. Paul looked on, watching Tom's every move. In his turn, Tom looked down at his partner's right hand, taking her hand in his left, he slowly insinuated his right forearm under her right arm, and pulled her gently towards him. She kept her head towards her right; he looked left, as his cheek slowly touched hers. And they danced. Dana-Beatriz moved in response to Tom almost as sensually as she had with José-Luis as the music covered the stage. But Tom was coming towards the end of what he could remember, a feeling his partner could sense. In one fluid movement, José-Luis took over from Dana-Beatriz. She stood back, beaming, and continued to watch the two men dance, her hands clasped excitedly across her chest. This clearly didn't seem odd to her. After all, she'd often seen the dance done by two men. Nor to the others, either, who had almost mistaken the partner switch as part of the routine. They didn't seem to notice either that José-Luis was now leading, and Tom was being led.

But Paul knew. Perhaps it was easier to see the difference from his vantage point. Without having to concentrate on moving the spot, he shifted how he was standing and rested his chin on his hands. The feeling in the pit of his stomach grew. It felt heavy and alien. He couldn't take his eyes off the two men, haunted by the mesmerising sound of the bandoneon. He didn't know why, but suddenly he could feel tears pricking at the back of his eyes. He tried to hold them back, to bury them, to focus on something else. He could see only Tom and José-Luis. It completely entranced him. He could see only the dance. Two men dancing. And he could hear only the bandoneon. As they moved, he realised just how beautiful it was. It wasn't disgusting or unnatural. It was as beautiful as any dance he'd seen before. Coupled with the lone bandoneon wrapping everything in an emotional mist, leading the dancers across the floor, each holding the other firmly but with the gentleness of lovers. Paul felt his stomach lurch.

He remembered the story in the *Illustrated Children's Bible* at school. Saul falling from his horse, having to be led into Damascus because he couldn't see. Then, just as Jesus had said, he knew what to do and the *scales*, Paul remembered, *fell from his eyes*. He thought of the Van Dyck portrait in his flat, the artist looking over his shoulder hiding something, yet revealing it as the sunflower lit everything up. He was shaking now. He couldn't bear to watch the men dancing anymore. He felt before he heard it stop. A tear fell on the casing of the spotlight he'd trained on the men. It sizzled noisily.

He turned abruptly and sank to the floor. Somewhere down there on the stage, there were hoots and shouts and clapping. He clasped his hand to his face and sobbed, great deep uncontrollable sobs. He was worried someone would hear, so he clapped the other hand over the first. He was now blind with the tears that spilled out and down his face. He couldn't stop himself. His whole body seemed to lurch as years and years of emotion just burst out. There was nothing he could do. So long as he hadn't felt anything, he'd been safe. It didn't matter that he was unhappy. He was safe and no one would hate him or sneer or be disgusted by him. He wanted to be normal. No, not that. He'd wanted his life to be accepted as normal. He'd wanted it to be real and so to be beautiful. For others to see that it was naturally beautiful and perfectly normal.

As the noise and the clapping began to subside, he turned himself over onto all fours, pushed himself up onto his knees, and grabbing the guard rail for support, he stood up with considerable effort. He walked towards the wall high above the front of the stage and disappeared into the gloom. A door here led to the lighting balcony above the auditorium. He could see his colleagues in the front rows of seats. But he couldn't look at Tom and José-Luis. He was too overwhelmed. Occasionally, he sobbed. He waited in the gloom. He couldn't face the world out there quite yet. Gradually, everything went quiet, his sobs subsided, and he went back to his solitary workspace. Safe again, or so he thought.

On stage, Dana-Beatriz was hugging and kissing the two men in turn. "Beautiful! Beautiful!" she said in English, the first and only thing she'd said. As the clapping and adulation subsided, José-Luis took her arm and began to lead her back towards the stage door. They were both chatting easily in Spanish, their heads together as they walked. Reaching the flats stage left, Dana-Beatriz turned and blew a kiss back towards the assembled crew. "Thank you! Thank you!" she shouted. "Good luck with the show! Break your legs!" She searched Olwena out specially and curtsied prettily as she mouthed '*¡Gracias!*' and blew a kiss. And she was gone.

When José-Luis came back, it was some time before he had answered everyone's questions about Dana-Beatriz, how long they'd danced together back in Colombia, how they'd bumped into each other again in Weymouth of all places, where she was going next, all that kind of thing.

"Yes," José-Luis agreed, "it was such a lucky chance. We haven't seen each other since I left Colombia. I didn't know she will be in England when Tom decided to come back to Weymouth for this charity event." Tom wondered if he had actually decided, or whether it was fate that had brought him back. Was this a coincidence too, he thought?

"And then to find her here, in Weymouth, it is too incredible." José-Luis beamed at the musicians. Gabriel joined in at this point.

"My cousin say he thought she was coming to Britain for a concert. But dancing is not so popular here right now."

"It say in *La Cronica* that she goes to France, Italy and then Spain after she leave here," said Carlos.

"Everyone goes to Spain!" said Gabriel.

"That's right," Carlos replied, "they are our brothers and sisters."

"Only since Franco has died." Gabriel shuddered a little.

"He not like our kind," one of the burly backing singers added.

Putting their instruments down, the musicians, dancers and singers carried on talking together in animated Spanish about Spain, about Dana-Beatriz, and dancing as they left the stage and went outside to smoke.

Finally, José-Luis and Tom were left alone together:

"She was a good friend to Donatello, also," José-Luis explained to Tom, not without some pain. "She said she had learned from some other people that I'd had to leave Colombia quickly, saying friends tell her that there had been some hangings in the villages where she knew Donatello and the other doctors worked. She have put two and two together, she said, and realised I'd had to leave because Donatello must have been one of the doctors killed." Tom hugged José-Luis, who buried his face in his shoulder. He didn't cry; he sighed, sad but tired of all the pain.

"Anyway," José-Luis said, stepping back from Tom a moment later. "Come on everyone! Now you've seen how it's done," and he winked at Tom, "time to get back to work."

Just then, Julia came striding across the stage. "Is this going to take long?" she asked, scarcely hiding her impatience.

"Well, we have a few hours' rehearsal to do," Tom

replied. Julia eyed José-Luis unpleasantly. Jason was busy with the mics but stopped and turned towards Julia.

"Always thought she was a closet Tory," he said to no one in particular. But of course, Julia had heard.

She huffed. "Someone's got to keep this country's borders tight," and turning back to Tom, "I'm going back to the hotel. Come and find me the minute you're finished here. We're booked for an interview with Wogan this evening. We'll need to leave about four at the latest. This is prime time! This is important."

Members of the crew all made rather childish gestures as Julia strode loudly from the stage.

"We best get a move on, then," said Tom. He walked upstage to where Jason had positioned the mics and it wasn't long before the musicians were playing, the backing vocalists swaying as they produced a bed of sound, giving Tom's vocals a depth and richness that was important in larger venues. The running order was beginning to take shape, though Greg was still wanting to change things around to build up towards the final number.

"This is the new release, and we need to contextualise it appropriately," Greg scolded Tom a little for sounding a bit tired of all these changes. Jason glanced across to Frances as he rolled his eyes. She nodded agreement.

Once Greg seemed to be happy, and Jason had said the sound was good, Tom left to find Julia back at the hotel. She had changed and was now in a red bolero jacket over a white tailored blouse with a double string of pearls, low-heeled patent leather shoes and French navy slacks. She was pacing the reception area impatiently, holding a jacket for Tom. He could afford to look casual as a celebrity and slip the jacket over his t-shirt and jeans, she thought, but she had to look professional.

"What was all that about?" Tom asked when they were in the car and heading off to London.

"What do mean?" Julia retorted, clearly cross about something.

"Back in the theatre. Keeping borders safe and all that nonsense?"

"It isn't nonsense at all. We need to be careful." She was wiping imaginary dust from her trousers, picking invisible fibres from her jacket sleeves. "Besides, you don't want your reputation tarnished by scandal..."

"What scandal?" Tom looked at her and waited for an explanation.

"Well, for a start, illegal immigrants..." she began.

"What are you talking about?" he interrupted.

"That Spaniard..."

"He's Colombian."

"Whatever. I've not seen any papers. These theatre types and degenerates..."

"Alright!" Tom was angry now. "That's enough. You're not my keeper, you know. You just deal with publicity."

"What do you mean 'just'?"

"I won't ask you to explain what you mean by 'degenerates'. But remember: you work for me, you don't manage me, you don't tell me what to think or who to hang around with. That's none of your business." Tom surprised himself with how direct he'd said all this.

She opened her mouth to say something, but he carried on:

"You've done an excellent job for me... till now, anyway. But theatre people are a bit loud and a bit showy, I thought you'd have known that. It goes with the territory. So, get used to it... Or move on."

With that he turned away and looked pointedly through the window on his side of the car. The conversation was over. Julia looked at the back of his head. She'd wanted to say more. To explain how dangerous it was to allow all and sundry into the country. But she thought better of it. She turned away and stared through the window her side, tapping her fingers impatiently on the arm rest.

She liked to think of herself as part of the new Thatcher generation, and so above petty squabbles with celebrities. Part of being a new woman in the 80s, though, meant that someone had to be vigilant and make sure that society was protected. Liberals may well think we should embrace all sorts and throw the borders open to any Tom, Dick or Ricardo, but not her. British values and British culture were under threat – that was one of the things they were talking about, she'd heard, at Bournemouth at that very moment. Affirmative action was needed, she believed, to keep undesirables out of the country and protect against bad influences from within. In her view, José-Luis ticked all these boxes. She'd started too to become suspicious about Tom Bright himself. But she needed the job, she accepted, for now at least.

They stopped off at a service station to get some sandwiches and a drink. Tom went to the toilets and left Julia to queue in the café. Neither spoke as they ate. When they arrived at Television Centre, Julia strode on ahead. Tom caught the eye of the chauffeur and looked up to Heaven. The driver laughed but said nothing. Tom strolled into the building, not really caring where she'd gone. However, as soon as he was through the big glass doors, a rather effeminate P.A. came towards him, clip board in hand, and ticked something off, presumably Tom's name.

"Tom Bright, lovely. I'm Craig. I work on *Wogan*. So, if you'd like to follow me, please, Tom."

Tom did as he was asked. 'Bet Julia loved you!' he thought with a wry smile.

Coming out of the lift, there was Julia talking to a small group of people waiting to be shown into the green room. She pointedly ignored Tom, who had to get his own drink, and keep himself company till he was called in.

The interview went well, Wogan as affable as ever. Tom warmed to him immediately, even though he'd previously thought of him as middle class and slightly stupid when he'd heard him on the radio. But he was smart, Tom could tell. Although Julia hadn't briefed him, Tom managed not to say anything that she felt she'd have to recover from the next day with an appropriate press release and so forth. Tom too had relaxed a little and even picked up a mic when Wogan asked him to give them a song. Unrehearsed and unexpected, Tom exchanged a few words with the band and then walked back centre stage.

"Well, this is a surprise!" He exchanged a smile and a thumbs up with Wogan, who nodded appreciatively. In his turn, he'd warmed to Tom Bright, which is why he'd tried his luck and asked him to sing unprepared.

"I wasn't sure what I should sing really. But then, you know, being back in Weymouth for our first gig on this tour, I thought I'd sing something different from my usual set. I got my first break, I suppose, in a school musical production," he explained, "and for the audition, I started with Lulu's classic *You Know You Make Me Wanna Shout!"* The audience started to applaud. Tom held his hand up until the clapping had died down. "But I'm not going to sing that now," he smiled, "Instead, here's something I once sang for a very, very special friend back in school. My big crush, if you like. No, that's not fair," he added almost to himself, "It was much more than that. It's the love of my life." He looked down at his feet. "Still is." He didn't know whether he'd said too much. He'd said it now. All he'd always wanted to say, and now he admitted it to himself. The millions who tuned into Wogan didn't seem to matter now.

The band started, and he came to from his thoughts. He smiled out to the audience and putting the mic into the stand, danced a few basic *bossa nova* steps, before he gave an intimate rendition of *The Girl from Ipanema,* as if no one else were there. Everyone felt something, though. It was almost as if he was singing just to them. Wogan and his audience loved it. Julia looked on from the wings, her lips pursed. She'd almost hoped Tom would make a fool of himself. But he hadn't. He was a complete, and very talented, professional.

Back in Weymouth, Paul's mother sat in her living room watching the television. Like many others in the retirement bungalows, she'd made herself a pot of tea which she brought in on a tray with some digestives ready to watch *Wogan*. She secretly fancied him herself. She'd been surprised to see the young man on the settee opposite Wogan. She recognised him from somewhere. But it took her about five minutes or so to realise who it was. And so she'd sat up, fascinated as the young man she'd not seen for many years answered all the presenter's questions with confidence and good humour. The only time she'd heard him sing was in the school performance. Paul hadn't even played her the CD Lucy had sent. So, when Wogan asked him to sing – which even she could see was a surprise – she paid a little more attention, interested to hear how he sounded now. 'His big crush? What an odd thing to say on prime-time television,' she thought. Then, 'I wonder why Paul never mentioned Tom having a girlfriend? They were so very close all those years. Right up to the last day, it seemed.' Putting her cup down in its saucer, she said out loud "I wonder..."

With Tom off to London and his interview with *Wogan*, everyone had returned to what they'd been doing before. José-Luis had nothing else to do. He didn't want to go back to the hotel alone, though. And he didn't really want to kill time with Frances and the stagehands.

"Knock! Knock!" said the choreographer, wrapping a knuckle against the doorframe to Paul's workroom. Paul turned away and tried to look busy.

"By the way, thank you," José-Luis said with a short bow.

"What do you mean?" Paul asked.

"For the impromptu lighting," José-Luis explained.

"Oh..." still Paul didn't look up. "Oh, well, that's sort of what I do."

"True. And everyone knows how good you are. But you had not seen and you had not heard most of that before."

"Well... you know... I just tried to pick up on the music."

"Mother blocks daughter's wedding, which would have given her the pip!... Eight letters: *H*, something, something, *I*, something, something, something, something..." The voice was slightly muffled from down on stage.

"Paul?" Frances said a little louder, hoping he'd heard.

"Havisham... H-A-V-I-S-H-A-M," said Paul, almost distractedly.

José-Luis looked at him. He knew from past experience, even over the short time he'd been here, that Paul would be right. He had no idea why. "Shall I tell them?" he asked.

"No," Paul answered, "I'll let them know sometime."

José-Luis nodded. Instead of sitting down, though, he went back out of Paul's workroom, leant against the guard rail and shouted the answer down to Frances.

"Tell Paul 'Thanks'," Frances shouted back up to him. Paul knew they wouldn't understand how the answer fitted, but at that moment, he really didn't care.

José-Luis came back and sat opposite Paul. Neither of them spoke for two or three minutes.

"So," José-Luis broke the silence, "who is this *Havisham*?" He exaggerated the *H* as Spanish and French speakers sometimes do because that's what they're taught.

Paul sighed more to himself rather than anyone else, and looked up into José-Luis's face, avoiding his eyes.

"She was a frustrated old spinster... jilted on her wedding day... Spends years in her white dress surrounded by the trappings of a wedding morning that had never happened. Presumably she was waiting for her fiancé to come back. She tries to frustrate a possible loving relationship between her adopted daughter, Estella, and this guy, Pip, who loves her."

"Pip?"

"Short for Philip."

José-Luis nodded slowly.

"'*To give someone the pip*' means to annoy them," Paul added.

José-Luis raised an eyebrow, then: "From a book?"

"*Great Expectations*," Paul answered, staring at the table in front of him. "Dickens."

José-Luis looked at him, his eyes narrowing. "Like 'waiting'?" he asked. Paul nodded. "...and just waiting for something to happen, but not doing anything about it?" Paul thought for a minute or two and nodded again.

"Ah," José-Luis tilted his head back slightly and raised both eyebrows, though Paul didn't notice. He wasn't looking. They sat for a few more minutes, neither of them saying anything.

"And what did you think about the dancing?" José-Luis asked.

Paul had gone back to rewinding some electric cables that he'd wound and unwound repeatedly for the last five or ten minutes. He thought carefully about what he should say. Eventually, he thought he knew. He looked up past José-Luis's face towards the wall, still winding the cable:

"She's very beautiful. Did she know you back in Colombia?"

"She is beautiful, true; she dances beautifully too. And, yes, we know her back in Colombia. She and I, we have danced for many years as partners back then."

Paul nodded. It was all he could think of doing.

"I didn't mean her," said José-Luis.

Paul paused for a moment. "Oh, Julia?" he said, finally, "I'm sure she's OK. Her bark is worse than her bite. She just seems to want to get the best publicity for Tom."

"Bullshit!" José-Luis looked cross, leaning menacingly across the table towards Paul, his knuckles turning white as he weighed down on them. Paul looked away, shocked, trying to avoid confrontation. He knew what José-Luis had meant, but he didn't want to admit it. He liked José-Luis. He felt relaxed when he was around. He didn't want to make him angry. Avoiding all possible conflict his whole life meant he didn't know how to deal with it now.

"I... I don't know what to say..." Paul stuttered.

"I was not talking about Julia. You know that. I was not talking about dancing with Dana-Beatriz. I was..."

"Please. Don't..." Paul hung his head, "Please..." his hands suddenly limp on the table in front of him.

"What are you afraid of, *pollito*? Why do you run away? Why do you hide from the truth?"

"Please, José-Luis. I'm confused. I don't understand." Paul was searching for an explanation, it seemed, on the desk in front of him.

José-Luis sighed. He folded his arms across his chest and looked back through the doorway. He thought it was probably best to leave Paul for now and started to walk towards the door.

"It was very beautiful," Paul began, slowly, weighing each word carefully.

José-Luis turned to look at him. He was sitting, staring into space, his eyes beginning to fill up again. "What else did you think it would be?" José-Luis asked.

"I don't know..." Paul began, "I just didn't expect it to look like that. Two men dancing together. Up close. It looked normal. As though it was meant to be."

"Why would it not be *normal*?" José-Luis seemed genuinely surprised, but Paul wasn't really listening.

"I never knew that it could be so beautiful, so natural. I wasn't expecting that. It was very beautiful," he repeated.

"How did you *feel*, though?" José-Luis asked, looking carefully at Paul's expression. Automatically, Paul put a hand flat on his stomach. Although he'd been crying, he seemed to be more alive than at any time since they'd arrived.

"It was exquisite. To think that two... I'm so confused. I've got such a headache." Paul rubbed his forehead and tried to massage his temples. He kept staring into the middle distance, the tears now rolling down his cheeks. He didn't even try to hide them now. "All my life, other people have said what's right and wrong. They told me what to like, how to act, what was beautiful and what was ugly, abhorrent, unnatural. Against Nature. Not God's will. Everyone else seemed to know what to do, what was right. They all live normal lives. The men go home to their wives. The women have 2.2 children and kiss the men when they get home. That's how it should be. It's natural that way. That's the way nature intended it." José-Luis went over to him and put a hand on his shoulder. He could feel Paul automatically stiffen.

"Relax, *pollito*. Don't be afraid. What is normal? Surely, if it is beautiful, it is natural? Nature gave us beautiful things to enjoy."

Without thinking, Paul put his hand on José-Luis's. "I don't know anymore. I'm so tired."

Paul felt he was going mad. He liked listening to Tom's music. He would even sometimes imagine Tom was singing to him, just for him and no one else. The songs on the CD, although in Spanish, seemed to speak to him, he felt, though he didn't know what Tom was singing. And had only managed to translate a few lines. But men don't do that sort of thing. That's how he was brought up. He'd been confused when he'd caught José-Luis and Tom together in the wings. It didn't look unnatural, though. Not to him. They were enjoying it. They were happy together. But that was them. And he knew that other people wouldn't think it was natural.

The dancing was different, though. Maybe it was the mournful music. Maybe it was his own lighting arrangement, feeling something as José-Luis took hold and led Tom through the dance. Whatever it was, it was all so special, so emotional. He'd never believed two men could look like that together. And the crew and musicians and theatre staff had all thought it was wonderful too. Two men together. No one seemed to think it was disgusting. No one turned away. Or spat on the floor. Or folded their arms with contempt. Everyone saw that it was beautiful. Paul felt exhausted.

"Tell me what it was like at school with Tom," José-Luis interrupted his thoughts.

Paul suddenly looked up at him. "It was... How did you know?"

"It has been obvious since we first got here. And some things which Tom said on the way."

Again, Paul looked down and stared into the middle distance. What had Tom said? Had he spoken of the summer they'd had together? Paul rolled his head back slowly, as if trying to relieve some sort of stiffness, but actually remembering Tom's hands smoothing cream across his back and shoulders. Had Tom talked about anything at school? Even the kiss? That one and only and final kiss? Before he'd run away? Before Paul had lost him? Paul felt José-Luis's hand on his shoulder and came back into the room.

"Has Tom said anything?" Paul began with some urgency. "He mustn't know about this."

"About what?" asked José-Luis.

"About me... About how the dancing made me feel. About me remembering..."

"Remembering? What do you remember, Paul?" José-Luis rubbed his shoulder gently. He could feel the tension release as somewhere deep down Paul was letting go of something.

"We were very close," Paul began. He let his hand drop into his lap. José-Luis turned and perched on the desk beside him, waiting for him to continue.

"Go on," he said.

"We met on the first day at school. I suppose it was just a coincidence that we were put together. I don't know what it was, but we just seemed to hit it off. We did everything together. For Tom, it was easy."

"What do you mean?"

"He was always out-going. You've seen him, too. People like him. And when they find out he can sing... and act too... they like him even more."

"Is that why you liked him?"

"Not really. That was just Tom. I thought he was very talented, of course. That he would go far. At the end of the day though, to me, he is just Tom. And I..." Paul paused for a moment, trying to compose himself. "Whether he's an international star or not, it wouldn't matter to me. But I felt happy with him back then. We were good friends."

"Were you ever more than just friends?"

Paul looked up at José-Luis, a question playing across his face. "What do you mean?"

"Can I be truthful with you, Paul?" Paul nodded his head hesitantly and turned his gaze downwards again towards the floor. "Let me guess. You were the best friends. You were always together. Yet you were afraid, Paul. You were afraid to be true to yourself or to Tom."

"No, it's not like that." Paul was blushing. But he was also close to tears again. "Please..." he begged, and tailed off, he couldn't say anymore. He turned his back towards José-Luis and rested his face against his hands on the back of the chair, trying not to sob noisily again. He wanted to be alone. So he could go back to how things were. When he was just lonely, and he didn't feel anything, and he was safe.

"You were afraid, and you decide to be a friend. Only a friend. But you wanted more. You had to hide – even from yourself. You had to pretend. But be careful, Paul," José-Luis turned Paul round and putting a finger under his chin made him look into his eyes. "You have to do something before it is too late."

"Too late for what?" Paul asked, still looking into José-Luis's eyes as if searching for an answer. Or at least just for some kindness to leave him be and not ask him anything else.

"Until it is too late for the real Paul to live. You will kill him, Paul. You will stifle him. You will suffocate all that pure love. Let him breathe. Let him be free."

Paul bowed his head, his face in his hands.

"I don't know what went on when you and Tom were at school together," José-Luis thought a little about how he should continue, "but whatever happened, you must be true to yourself. Tom knows you avoid him." Paul made to protest, but José-Luis held his finger up to stop him saying anything. "Yet, you say you think our dance was beautiful. In fact, it touched you so deep that you cried. You sobbed here all on your own."

"How did you...?" Paul asked hurriedly.

"You have to let go of your fear, Paul." José-Luis stood up from the table and crouched before Paul, trying to meet his gaze and encourage him to look up at him. "If what you had at school meant anything to you, then you can have it again."

"I don't know," Paul turned away, trying to escape, "I'm so confused. Your dance was so beautiful. I never thought..."

"Sorry, I'm not interrupting, am I?" Olwena stood in the doorway. Seeing José-Luis, she looked at him and continued, "She's so beautiful that lady."

"Dana-Beatriz, yes."

"That's the one. And I loved that folk dance... the puro."

"*Porro.*" José-Luis had stood up and was looking at Olwena a little irritated. Composing himself, he went on, "It was so clever of you to attach the skirt that way, though," and he smiled at Olwena. She blushed slightly. He stood now to block her view of Paul. He stepped forward and took her hand sliding it through his arm and turning her to leave.

"So, Paul," he was looking back over his shoulder, "I'll see you on stage at five. Once everyone's gone."

"Right. OK. Five." Paul didn't know what he was saying.

"That's half an hour, Mister Armstrong."

And José-Luis led Olwena away, telling her about folk dances in Colombia, and the costumes people wear in the villages. Olwena was delighted and leaned into him, wanting him to tell her more. As they walked slowly along the corridor towards wardrobe, José-Luis could hear Paul mumbling to himself:

"Please, I just want to be left alone... I was fine before... I just want it to be alright... Please..."

By five o'clock, Paul had all but forgotten José-Luis had told him to be down on stage. His head was still spinning though, and he'd had to concentrate very hard that afternoon to do what was needed for the production and rehearsals. He'd tried to make sense of their conversation and of the feelings he'd had when he'd seen Tom and José-Luis dance together. It seemed to mean so much to him, he thought, because he'd never thought that two men dancing together could look that way. Could look so normal and so beautiful. The sex was somehow different. He'd known about that sort of thing. But sex was private. An intimate moment between two people. So, you didn't see it. And it had to be hidden away, that was the only way it could be legal, he'd read. The dancing was different. There was music to accompany it, making it just like any other dance. Though that music was special. It made everything seem so emotional. And then, everyone had clapped and shouted and said how much they loved it. Two men dancing. It was out in the open, and people thought it was wonderful too. Paul caught himself tearing up again. He fished for a handkerchief in his pocket and blew his nose.

"Come on, Señor Paul, it's gone five o'clock!"

Paul looked over the guard rail and saw José-Luis beaming up at him as usual, one hand on his hip the other shining a torch right into Paul's face. He was calling him onto the stage. Automatically, he stood up straight withdrawing his head from over the guard rail. Paul wished he could stay up there where he was. He felt hidden. Nothing else mattered. He was safe there. On his own. After a minute or two, and José-Luis waving the torch light around, he picked up his things, turned off the lights, and went down. His heart was beating just that bit faster.

"So, Señor Paul," José-Luis said with an exaggerated swagger. He was walking back and forth in front of Paul, almost like a matador eyeing up a bull. He stepped forward and was about to take Paul's hand, but Paul started and automatically took a step back. José-Luis smiled.

"OK, let us try something else. You heard of a *bossa nova*?"

"I think so," Paul said. He seemed to remember something from when he was at school.

"The rhythm is pretty easy: *slow, a quick-quick, slow, a quick-quick.* It is not that common, but it will get you moving." José-Luis demonstrated and told Paul to do the same. He nodded his head slightly in time with José-Luis clapping and moved in the way he thought José-Luis had.

"No, no!" José-Luis had one hand on his hip and was wagging the index finger of the other. He stepped forward closer to Paul.

"Now," he put a hand on each of Paul's hips, who immediately took a step back. "Oh my God! I'm not gonna do anything to you. Relax!" They both took half a step forward, and Paul looked away as José-Luis put his hands on his hips again. "Now... that way," and he nodded with his head towards his right, "*slow, a quick-quick*...And back the other way," he nodded to his left, "*slow, a quick-quick...*" As Paul stepped as he had before, still nodding his head slightly to mark the beat, José-Luis twisted his hips first one way and then the other, forcing Paul to swivel as he took the sidestep. After a few moves back and forth, José-Luis let his hands drop and clapped the beat.

"Good! Good!" he clasped his hands together and looked Paul straight in the eye. "Now, for the Latin dances, this part of the foot," and he raised his left foot, holding onto Paul's hand, and tapped the ball, "he never leave the floor. You scrape it like this." And he demonstrated once more, counting the basic rhythm again. Paul watched his feet carefully. He was clearly concentrating very hard. When it was his turn, he did his best to keep the balls of his feet on the floor, 'caressing it' José-Luis had said, which wasn't easy in his trainers. José-Luis then told him to vary direction. Instead of side to side all the time, he said he should step forward, then to the right, step back, and then to the left. "Like a box," he said. Each time Paul did what José-Luis demonstrated. When he'd finished two such box movements, José-Luis stepped forward again. This time, he went to take Paul's hand in his. As if he'd been stung, Paul pulled his hand back and stared at José-Luis. José-Luis sighed. He shook his head slightly, looking down at the floor.

"¡*Mira*! Let me tell you something," José-Luis caught Paul's eye and held his gaze for as long as Paul would allow. "When I was a boy, my father and my brothers, they beat me. Every day. They say me that the beating, it is going to make me a man. I did not believe them. My father never beat my brothers. But I learned then to pretend to be a man. To walk like a man. To play football and not to go dancing in the school hall." Paul looked up briefly. "I stopped being José-Luis. I stopped being me.

"But then, I stopped to have friends, too. I was frightened that I would not be a man with them. I was afraid that they would not like me, that they would tease me, or worse. Then I move away to college in the town. The first day, I meet Donatello. He makes me relax, he makes me laugh. And I like to make him laugh, because I was falling in love with him." José-Luis was staring at the stage. He smiled to himself, but it was a sad smile. "But

I couldn't say nothing," he continued, looking straight at Paul. "I have to hide. I have to pretend to be a man in case Donatello doesn't like me no more.

"I love Donatello, but I was scared to tell him. I thought it was easy just to be friends. I wanted to be with him, to touch him. I wanted him to touch me. I was scared because I didn't want him to hate me for who I am. For loving him. But also, I know that it was not acceptable for a man to love another man. I know my family would reject me, or even worse. I didn't know what to do. I thought I was going mad. How could I live my life with so much fear? How could I lie to myself for the rest of my life? *Vivir con miedo... A life lived in fear* and all that.

"I miss him so much, Paul. I have lost him for ever now, but at least we had some precious times together. Please," José-Luis held out his hand to Paul, "Let me show you how to dance too.

"Then one day, there was music in the street. Donatello was still in his science class, and I was waiting for him. I love that music," and he started to click his fingers and step in time to a remembered tune. "And I dance. And people stop and they look. They start to clap too in a big circle around me. I am happy because I love to dance." José-Luis demonstrated a *bossa nova,* with his arms up close to his sides and his hips moving, Paul thought, independently of his feet. It looked fabulous, even though it was so simple. Paul found himself clapping along. *Slow, a quick-quick...* José-Luis smiled and winked at him.

"So, then I hear his voice. My friend, Donatello. The friend I love but I have to pretend we are just friends. And I stop. I am afraid. I am scared what he will think.

And Donatello, he steps forward, and he takes my hands and he moves me like I was moving before until I carry on. He step back – he is not good at dancing – and I see the joy in his eyes as he watches me, his friend. Though dancing is not for real men.

"When we were walking back to the dormitory, he looked at me and he say,

"'I love you when you dance.' I smile, I am a bit embarrassed. And he lift my face up to his and he say,

"'I love you, José-Luis. I want us to get married.' And he kissed me. Right there in the street. Just like a man does with his girlfriend."

José-Luis stopped for a moment and dabbed at his eyes. "At first, I do not understand what that kiss meant..." Paul put his hand on his arm,

"It's OK, José-Luis. We can stop now if you want."

But José-Luis shook his head.

"No, Paul. We go on. He saw me dance and he realise we are just the same. Him and me. We are not like other men. We are not just friends, even though I'd tried so hard to hide it for so long. I wanted him so badly." José-Luis stopped again. He blew his nose and stuffed his hankie back in his pocket.

"We have to move away then. To Bogatá. To be together and live together. He told me I should go and be a dancer. He carried on to be a doctor." He stared into the distance. His eyes searching for something. "The day we graduate, Donatello, he take me to the church near our dormitory and inside he give me a ring. We had to be quiet so no one would see us. But we managed to kiss behind the statue of San Sebastian."

He fell silent, still looking off into the middle distance. Paul came over and put his arms around José-Luis.

"It's OK. It's OK. You're safe now."

José-Luis smiled the same sad smile and, tapping Paul's arms, he said they should get on. Paul had a lot to learn. A hand on his hip, Paul's eyes were directed at the floor between them. He blinked several times before he looked up. He stepped forward and took José-Luis's hand.

"Thank you, Paul. Now... here's how to come alive again."

Before they finished and went their separate ways, Paul had learned the basics for a number of Latin dances, even allowing José-Luis to take hold and lead him round the stage a little. They finished off with some basic steps from the Argentine Tango. Paul recognised it immediately. It felt strange doing this dance of all the others. This was the dance he'd seen the two men, José-Luis and Tom, dance together. Just like partners or lovers. This was the dance that had stirred him. That opened his eyes and made him come alive. He concentrated very hard now. He wanted to learn.

That night, lying in his double bed alone, Paul imagined dancing like that with Tom. He wished he could. He jumped out of bed and searched for the CD he'd hidden. He turned it over a few times, thinking. Then, he found the CD player and, turning the volume down very low, so as not to annoy his neighbours, he put the CD in and pressed *Play.* Tom's voice began quietly and filled the room. Paul straightened up and stood back to listen. Soon, he couldn't resist it, but he moved as José-Luis had been teaching him, changing the step and pace for the different tracks on the

CD. Paul wished Tom could be there with him. But he knew that soon he would be off for the rest of the tour. And Paul would go on as he had before. Safe in his loft above the stage. Being just a friend again. A former friend.

A few days later, Tom and José-Luis were having breakfast together at the hotel. There was no sign of Julia, which neither of them particularly minded.

"Oh my God! That's revolting," José-Luis pushed the pork sausage to one side, "I cannot eat such a thing!"

"Not what you said last night," Tom was pretending to read the paper.

"Do not be disgusting," José-Luis feigned shock. Tom put his paper down and blew José-Luis a kiss. "Stop it!" he said, looking around anxiously, "You'll have Julia after us."

"OK, I'm sorry. Where is the old witch anyway?" Tom said, half distracted.

"I do not know. But she frightens me. I am sure she is plotting something." José-Luis was serious.

"No, don't worry," said Tom, picking up his paper again. "Her bark's worse than her bite."

"*¡Caray!*" said José-Luis wide-eyed, "That is so strange."

"What is?" asked Tom.

"Paul said exactly the same thing."

Tom put his paper down again and looked over to José-Luis.

"When have you spoken to Paul? How is he? Why won't he talk to me? He's avoiding me, isn't he? Is he alright? Does he need anything?"

José-Luis held his hands up in surrender. "*¡Oye!* One question at a time." José-Luis carried on eating what was left of his breakfast. He was thinking.

"Has he always been a... what is the word? ... a recluse?" José-Luis waited for Tom to answer.

"No." Tom thought for a moment. "He's always been quite shy. But it was never like this. Him skulking around backstage, not really talking to anyone. Hiding away up in that gloomy loft space above the stage. Shouting crossword answers down to the rest of the crew." They both laughed.

"Does he talk to anyone now? Does he have a family?" José-Luis asked.

"Only his mother," said Tom. "His father died ages ago according to my mother. He'd been ill for a long time anyway. There's that woman in wardrobe."

"Olwena? Well, he is kind to her, and he listens to her. But I do not think he tells her anything personal. Or how he is feeling. Hopes, fears. Nothing like that." José-Luis went quiet.

"Why do you ask?" Tom wanted to know more.

"Do you still love him?" José-Luis asked without answering Tom's question. It seemed so natural, and yet so blatant. Tom looked at him. He swallowed and opened his mouth to speak but couldn't think of anything to say.

"It does not really matter for now. If you care for him, though, then you need to be very careful," José-Luis added.

"Why? What's wrong?" Tom said at last.

"When people are afraid to live and to love," José-Luis began, "they decide to hide away. To keep their feelings hidden. To be alone and pretend everything is OK. They may even start acting a part. To be normal. You know, the devoted husband, in their normal houses."

Tom looked at him, "And?" he said.

"This almost happened to me."

"But Donatello...?" Tom asked.

"When we first met, I loved him, of course. But I wasn't sure if he was or wasn't... you know what I mean. I was so much in love with him, though, that I decided I would always be his friend, so I could be with him and close to him forever."

"Is that so bad?" asked Tom.

"¡*Mira*!" José-Luis went on. "Life has been easy for you..." Tom made to protest, but José-Luis just carried on. "Yes, so you pretend to be a womaniser. You have your image. But basically, it does not matter. You can live your life however you want."

"Not if Julia had her way," Tom snorted.

"I'm serious. Life is OK for you, Tom Bright. You have a lot of love around you. For people like Paul, it is not like that. He is afraid to admit his feelings. He wanted to be friends, just like I did with Donatello, and then you ran away."

"That's not fair..." interrupted Tom. But again José-Luis carried on.

"It does not matter now. I believe that is how Paul sees it. It gets worse though," he said, looking reflective.

"How so?" Tom asked.

"Because now he does not know anything different. He does not know what his feelings are. He does not know what is right and what is wrong." José-Luis looked at Tom. "He may even think he is alright. Being alone, hiding in the wings. He knows you will leave when the show is done. So, it is better for him to stay as he is. He won't get hurt, but he won't be happy. I do not think he knows how to be happy anymore."

"What can I do? He must be so alone and so miserable." Tom said, genuinely worried about Paul.

"I do not know," José-Luis looked thoughtful. "I think you will have to be very patient. Do not try to force him. Encourage him."

"I'll try. But it won't be easy. He keeps ignoring me." Tom was nervous.

"Let him know you love him," José-Luis added. Tom made to object, but José-Luis would not have it.

"I do," is all Tom said. Despite himself, Tom took José-Luis's hand across the table and squeezed it gently. "I think I understand," he continued. "I was always the outgoing one. Paul was always quiet. God," he looked at José-Luis, "if only I'd known. I thought... when he..." Tom felt for his handkerchief. He didn't want to cry in public.

José-Luis put his finger to his lips. "Sssh. We do not know anything for certain. All *I* know is that Paul has made a life of being alone and apart from others. You can help him. You need to let him see it is perfectly acceptable to be Paul. You may have to lose him, though. For his sake."

Tom looked at his hands on the table. He was trying not to cry still. He felt so desolate. All he'd wanted when they were younger was to be with Paul. He thought he could manage. But the thought of rejection was too much.

All the confusion. The lying to himself and to everyone else. Lying about this tour, even. Now he didn't know what to think. He knew he still loved Paul the moment he'd seen his broad shoulders, the short hair above his strong neck. The neck he wanted to touch and stroke. Had he been so wrong? he wondered. Had he made Paul miserable? That thought was too much to bear. Even worse, would he have to let Paul go? For Paul's sake, even if it broke his own heart?

"I'll try," he said. "But..."

"That is all we can do," said José-Luis. "Give it time. And be patient."

José-Luis poured the last of the coffee and they both drank in silence. José-Luis went back upstairs to get a sweater for the theatre. When he got back down, Tom stood up ready to leave the table still holding his coffee cup. Without thinking, he leaned over and grabbed the half-eaten sausage.

"That is disgusting," José-Luis said again and screwed his face up. Tom looked at the sausage, pulled a face and put it back down on the plate.

"Anyway," José-Luis was gathering his things together, "he is a pretty good dancer, you know. A natural, I would say."

Tom nearly dropped his cup. "Paul Armstrong? A dancer!?" Tom shouted towards José-Luis's back as he made to leave the restaurant.

"Moves his hips like a pro!" José-Luis minced towards the door. An elderly couple looked at him and frowned.

"It's alright. He's not well," Tom mouthed at them, moving his index finger round in exaggerated circles near his temple. Waving briefly, he rushed out after José-Luis.

"Oh, sorry, I was looking for Rob." Paul was standing in the office doorway with his exercise book of notes in his hands. Recognising the voice, Tom shot round and looked up into Paul's face. He was weary and his expression must have betrayed something which he'd not intended.

"Err, no. He's not here at the moment." Tom cleared a space on the table and pointed to the chair the other side from his. "Listen, why don't you take a seat and wait. I'm sure he won't be long."

Paul was backing out from the doorway. "No. It's alright. I'll catch him later." His face looking down towards the floor, he tapped the doorframe with his hand before moving away.

"No, Paul, please... wait..." Tom stood up and went to the door. Paul was near the end of the corridor already. "Please, Paul, wait... Can't we just talk? Can't we just be friends?" Tom thought he saw Paul turn his head just a fraction before he turned the corner and was gone.

"Oh, shit!" Tom said to himself and punched the doorframe. As he walked slowly back to his seat, he nursed his knuckles which were smarting now. "Oh, fuck, that was the wrong thing to say, too!" He slumped back into his seat. "Why is love so fucking difficult?" he groaned.

"Sorry. Mr Tom?" Olwena was at the door holding a pair of trousers.

"What!?" he said a little too abruptly than he'd intended. Looking round to see who it was, he went on. "Oh, sorry. Olwena, isn't it?" Olwena nodded, still a little unsure.

"Is this a bad time?" she asked.

"No, no, sorry. Please, come in."

"I can come back at another time," she said, almost bowing her head slightly.

"No, really... I... I was just feeling a bit sorry for myself." Tom stood and showed her to the chair opposite him. She sat down cautiously.

"So, Olwena, how can I help?" Tom smiled, leaning forward, legs apart and his elbows resting on his thighs. He tried to look calm and interested. Almost as if he had to make a conscious effort, he smiled at her and looked her in the eye. A genuine, but a sad smile, nonetheless, she felt.

She put her sewing on the table and smoothed out the fabric. "I'm sorry, really..." she began, but Tom waved his hand and smiled more broadly.

"I just wanted to check the length of these," she said, holding up the Latin trousers for the final number. "I thought I should before I stitch the light reflecting strip down the side."

"Oh, God," said Tom, looking at the trousers, "I'd forgotten about the light show! I'll look like some kind of glow-in-the-dark stick."

Olwena laughed. "I'm sure it'll look wonderful," she said. "And Paul will make it all work for you." Tom stood up rather abruptly, she noticed. Without thinking, he took his trousers down. Then he stopped suddenly and held the trousers in front of himself, hiding his boxer shorts.

"I'm so sorry, I wasn't thinking," he said apologetically. "Forgive me!"

"There's no need," said Olwena kindly, "I've seen it all!" She handed him the trousers which he slipped on.

He did up the waist and the fly and stood with his arms out to the side for her to inspect.

"Sorry," she said again, "could I ask you to climb onto the chair, please?"

Without saying a word, Tom stepped up onto the chair.

"Won't be a minute," said Olwena, leaning over and pinning a new hemline. As it was, the trousers were actually a little long. She took the tape measure she had draped round her neck and measured the turn up. "I knew it!" she said triumphantly. Tom was rather startled and looked down from her to his feet alternately.

"Knew what?" he asked.

"Paul's exactly an inch and a quarter taller than you. Mind you," and she smoothed down the cloth down his front and then across his buttocks, "you're about the same size for the rest of the trousers. He's a little broader. Not much though."

Tom wondered how many other people were close to Paul. Knowing his inside leg measurements and other personal details. He stepped down from the chair and changed out of the Latin trousers again. As he handed them to her, she looked up into his face:

"Do you mind if I say something, Sir?" she asked.

'Here we go. I wonder who else is going to tell me how to run my life,' he thought. Out loud, he answered, "Please, go ahead," he answered, "but please, just call me Tom."

She smiled, more to herself than to him.

"For men like you," she began. Tom looked up at her a little surprised. "Love is much more difficult than for other people."

'Oh God,' he thought. 'How many people know about my disastrous love life around here?'

"I hope you don't mind me saying this, Sir... I mean, Tom."

"No, no... please." Tom tried not to look cross. 'This is priceless,' he thought, regaining his composure and trying to adopt an affable air.

"You have all the standard stuff – Does he love me? Is he right for me? Shall I say something first, or will that frighten him off?" She was trying to drape the trousers so that they would keep the crease marks, and so she wasn't looking into his face. "We all do that," she said, quietly. "But then for men... like you," she repeated, "There's more. You've got the worry of all the people around you. What will *they* think? Not just about your partner – that's the same for everyone, of course, you want the people you love to approve of your choice – but that your partner's another man. Then on top of that, you worry whether it's natural to love like that. And if you haven't said anything to the one you love, whether he will be appalled and hate you." She was standing straight now, the trousers hung over her arm, "And the last thing," she said looking into his face at last, touching his arm, "You don't believe you're worth love because of all that."

Tom didn't know what to say. He just looked at her, his mouth open.

"Must get on. Sorry, Tom, I've taken up far too much of your time already. Can't sit around chatting all day!" She was about to leave, when she turned, not looking directly at him. "What was it that German chappy says?" She drummed her fingers against her bottom lip as she tried to remember. "I know. *Love is possible only if two persons communicate with each other from the centre of their existence,*" she said. "And remember, that doesn't mean a lot of talking, either." And she was gone.

Tom sat there, staring at the wall. He kept switching the desk lamp on and off while he was trying to make sense of everything that José-Luis had said about Paul over the past day or so and Olwena had said just now. Had they ever communicated then? he wondered. He tried to think back to their school days, to the summer on the farm, to sitting on the seawall. So many times, he'd wanted to reach out. He wanted to hold him, a simple show of affection. And after all, Paul had asked whether Tom would miss him and hadn't wanted to go straight home from the farm. Surely, he felt, surely, they'd communicated. Paul must have known he loved him, Tom was convinced. Yet he'd reacted badly when Tom had tried to show his love and kiss him.

The thought began to dawn on him, slowly at first, that he may have misinterpreted what had happened. Was he so self-centred that he hadn't noticed that Paul was unhappy and afraid about showing his true feelings? Tom felt unsettled and fearful. He didn't want to lose Paul again if there was any chance at all that Paul might love him. Back at school as they were growing up, maybe they just hadn't believed in themselves enough. Now, and thinking about what José-Luis had said, did he love him enough to let him go? Perhaps Olwena was right. He was starting to wonder how much he really loved Paul. Whatever happens, he said to himself, I must try. So he knows he is loved and worthy of love.

"I just don't want to face life without him anymore,"

he said out loud before he realised it. He looked around to make sure no one had heard.

Paul refused to do any dancing when other people were around, of course. So it tended to be later on towards the evening. José-Luis was patient and would wait. He was a good pupil, though, and quick to learn. José-Luis had taken it gently, focusing on routines Paul would know from the show they'd been rehearsing. He was impressed, too, and was enjoying the time with Paul. He was beginning to understand his feelings for the dour lighting engineer with his narrow hips, broad shoulders and the most enticing eyes he'd seen for a long time. Feelings of friendship and affection, wanting him to be himself. That was all, really. He realised, too, that he just felt safe with Paul, in his strong arms and against his broad chest. He'd not felt so safe for a very long time. He liked that feeling. In his heart of hearts, he knew that loving Paul meant wanting him to be happy. He hoped that would be with Tom.

He said nothing of this to Paul. But he was glad that Paul was a lot more relaxed about being in hold and the two men touching. José-Luis had a cassette player that he would bring to their lessons with music he'd recorded from their own musicians. So Paul was becoming very familiar with some of the numbers and could even dance some of them as a leader. José-Luis enjoyed that. He enjoyed, too, being in Paul's strong embrace and giving in to his dance leads. Even though he knew, of course, what they were meant to be dancing.

That day Tom was at some publicity event, though Julia was mysteriously absent for most of the proceedings. And while he waited for Tom to get back, José-Luis was practising an Argentine tango with Paul to a distorted cassette on his player. Paul no longer had to count the steps but was becoming a lot more confident and led with ease. Today, they were going to dance under a single spot which Paul had strategically positioned to provide a circle of light mid stage. He'd also switched on the uplighters. They shone diagonally at different angles from almost horizontal near the wings to almost vertical centre stage. It produced a mesmerising effect to the extent that an onlooker may be confused about what they were seeing until they got their bearings.

"Now, *guapo*," José-Luis took his hand and led him into the spotlight. "Tell me. Who do you dance for?"

Paul thought. "I dance for me, I think," he looked past José-Luis and down to the stage. "And perhaps for…" he trailed off. José-Luis waited to see if he would say anything more. After a few minutes, he inclined his head to one side and looked into Paul's face.

"Let us say," he began, "that you are dancing for the one you love." Paul looked at him and flushed slightly. "No," José-Luis continued, "I want you to dance as if you were dancing with your lover." He dropped Paul's hand. Taking hold of Paul's arms, he shuffled them both around a half circle, so they were each facing the opposite direction.

"Now," he let Paul's arms go, "you are going to start over there in the wings, and you are going to come towards me as the music plays, like you have seen me do before." Paul squeezed his bottom lip between forefinger and thumb, concentrating on what he was going to need to do. "And then when you take hold, you are going to lead me as if I am the one you love." Paul went to say something, but José-Luis stopped him. "It does not matter that I am not the one you love, *guapo*," he went on, "part of dancing is to make everyone believe I am the one. You saw how I danced with Dana-Beatriz."

Paul looked around nervously just to check that no one was, in fact, watching them.

"Paul," José-Luis said. Paul looked over his shoulder to where José-Luis was standing. "Pretend you are dancing with the one you really love. Really and truly love. Not me."

Paul turned abruptly and walked back to the wings, as José-Luis had instructed, while José-Luis himself went to the cassette player and switched on the music. He walked quickly back to his position in the spotlight centre stage and counted them in. Paul stepped forward on the ball of his foot, swivelled and moved forward again. When he was opposite José-Luis, he traced the rondée, moved forward to join José-Luis and took hold. But three steps into the dance, José-Luis broke hold and stepped back.

"No, no, no... fuck it, Paul! You have to help me."

José-Luis strode to the cassette player, shaking his head, his hands on his hips. He was looking at the floor as he came back to face Paul. It was a few minutes before he raised his head and looked Paul in the eye.

"I like you, Paul, I like you a lot," José-Luis stroked Paul's cheek. Paul didn't move away this time. "So, you need to remember that. Not because it's me. But because someone likes you, Paul Armstrong, they like you a lot." He walked in a tight circle, his eyes on the stage again. When he'd come full circle, he looked at Paul again. "And, you are not going to like this, but there is someone who loves you a lot, too." Paul looked away. "So, let us leave that for now.

"We have been learning a lot together. You are a good dancer. From those first steps when you counted the beat, and you would not look up and you would not move your hips. You have come a long way, Paul. You should be proud of that. Not many men manage that." Paul didn't say anything. His brow furrowed, he kept his eyes averted.

"But *you* have got to play your part now," José-Luis continued. "Yes, it would be nice for those of us who love you to see you happy. Comfortable in your own skin." José-Luis was almost talking to himself now. "More, though, for your own sake. You owe it to yourself to let go. Allow yourself to be happy, Paul. It is about time." Finally, José-Luis looked up and tried to make Paul turn towards him.

Paul was uncomfortable. He couldn't look José-Luis in the eye. Head down, arms folded across his chest, there were a lot of things going on in his head. But he didn't walk away. He didn't leave the dancefloor.

"¡*Vale*!" José-Luis walked to the back of the stage again, rewound the cassette and lined it up at the beginning. He was afraid he might have pushed Paul a bit too far. If he lost him now, he could see Paul shutting down again. Alone, lonely and afraid, regretting missed chances. Longing for the love he was afraid to give himself, but which he deserved.

Paul didn't know what he felt. Automatically, he felt he had to work hard to show José-Luis that he was grateful for his efforts and the attention he'd invested in him. No one else had. Well, not since Tom had left the first time. Without knowing how, though, there was something else which was almost overwhelming. He wanted to dance. When he'd seen José-Luis and Tom dancing, he couldn't understand why he'd been so moved. It was beautiful and that was unsettling. For the first time in his life, he'd found a way to be himself truly and honestly and without worrying what other people thought. He'd tried all his life to downplay what he felt and what came naturally to him. He'd told himself that that's how real men behave, how they move, how they act. Sometimes, though, he admitted that he didn't want to stand out, or for anyone to suspect him of being anything but 'normal'. When he was dancing, he felt free. He could move in a way that seemed to be perfectly normal, even expected. He could relax and give himself over to emotions he didn't know he was able to feel. And, he realised, he'd never danced with a woman, only a man.

"Please, José-Luis…" Paul said quietly. José-Luis kept his back to Paul. His stomach was turning over and over. He held his breath. If Paul was willing to jump, he wanted to be there to catch him. "Please. May we try again?" Paul asked simply. "Please would you give me a second chance?" José-Luis wanted to go over to him and hold him and tell him that everything would be fine from now on. But he couldn't turn round just yet. He didn't want Paul to see his tears.

Paul continued: "If there's time. If it's not too late."

"It is never too late, Paul," José-Luis said, finally

controlling his emotion. 'Well, almost. Do not miss this chance, Paul,' he thought. Though kept it to himself.

"Now, *pollito*, dance," José-Luis added, trying to sound positive. "But dance like you mean it. Don't dance for me. Dance for the man... for the one you love." He started the music, and as he walked back centre stage to take up his position, he indicated Paul's starting position in the wings. Paul returned upstage left and listened for his cue. José-Luis watched him come slowly towards him, hips slightly forward, the balls of his feet on the floor. Before him now, he watched as Paul bent slightly into his supporting leg, traced a wide rondée, perfectly balanced, then drew his feet together, the ball of his foot never leaving the floor. Gently, but firmly, he led José-Luis towards him, a tighter hold, his right arm lower down José-Luis's back, almost on his waist, his left arm bent so that their hands were raised slightly above their heads, and gently drew José-Luis's cheek into his chest. He hoped his heart wasn't beating too loudly. And without warning, Paul thought he could see Tom in his arms, about to dance cheek to cheek. He tried to concentrate and come back to the moment. Listening intently to the music, he took a silent breath and, lifting his body almost imperceptibly but enough to signal to his partner that they were starting, he moved slowly backwards, pulling his partner gently but firmly with him.

José-Luis didn't count the beats of the music this time. He didn't mentally follow the steps, either. He gave himself up to the dance, Paul leading him, coaxing him, sometimes moving away to give him room to dance a more intricate sequence, blocking a step, inviting

José-Luis to stroke his foot against Paul's calf, lean in and flick a *gancho* between his partner's legs. He was no longer in a small provincial theatre on the south coast of England. There was no theatre. He was in Donatello's arms. He sighed and leant into Paul's chest, safe, quiet, transfixed. Breathing in the vague masculine scent of his partner, suffused with the honest sweat of much effort. Even when the music had stopped, Paul held him close for an extra minute or two. José-Luis was breathing heavily, his heart thumping in his chest. Paul was too.

The silence was broken with whistling and clapping. Paul let go of José-Luis and stepped back as though he'd been caught doing something he shouldn't. Staring over his right shoulder, he looked round to see Tom coming towards them in the centre of the stage. The light from the stage behind Paul and shining towards Tom, Paul's expression was hidden.

"Bravo! Bravo! That was awesome... Paul, I never knew..." Tom stepped forward a little quicker now. "No, Paul, please..." Tom held his hand out to the man he knew he still loved. But Paul was gone. Evaporated, as usual, into the shadows offstage. José-Luis put his hand on Tom's shoulder, kissed his cheek, and was about to say something when they were interrupted by a kerfuffle from the auditorium. They turned to see Rob failing to stop five or six border officials striding quickly down two of the aisles in the stalls. Tom automatically stepped in front of José-Luis to hide him.

"You can't just barge in here, you know," Rob was saying, still trying to stop the nearest officer from getting to the stage.

"Yes, we can, Sir, we have a warrant for an illegal immigrant. Now, hand him over, and we'll be on our way."

Tom was desperately trying to think what he could do to save José-Luis. Or at least, to buy him some time. He knew that it would be hard to argue for José-Luis once he was in custody. He was trying to think who would deal with an asylum hearing and whether that would work. The officers were coming closer. There were six of them. Big burly blokes. He and Rob wouldn't be able to stall them for very long. He panicked. He turned to yell at José-Luis to run and hide. The lights seemed to have moved and he was blinded for a minute or two. When his eyes adjusted, the stage was empty. Just the vaguest wisp of dust swirling where José-Luis, Tom could've sworn, had been standing just seconds before. He scrunched up his eyes, trying to peer round the spotlight that was still flooding the space that moments before the two most important men in his life had danced so breathtakingly. Nothing. Nothing, that is, except a vague scent which Tom thought he recognised. As he leant forward to try and see to the back of the stage, it grew stronger but then disappeared almost as he stood up again.

"Now, gentlemen, if you tell us who you're looking for, maybe we could help," Tom said, straightening up and turning to face the officers again, trying to control his breathing. He could see Rob looking startled too.

The first officer stopped and took out his warrant. "A Mr Esperanza," he read, "Mexican, illegal entry to the UK, and we have reason to believe he has been working professionally without a work permit."

'Colombian,' Tom said in his head. "Well, how extraordinary." He said instead, a little theatrically. "Did you know this, Rob?" He looked at the stage manager, who shook his head.

"Mexican?" Rob said, "I don't think there's anyone fitting that description here, officer."

The other five officers were now on the stage. They fumbled around with the flats and pushed against the backdrop. They shone lights up into the loft above the stage. A couple of them ran around backstage, checking all the dressing rooms, Paul's workspace and wardrobe where Olwena worked. They made a lot of noise as they ran up and down stairs on either side of the stage. It was almost farcical.

"Nothing, Sir," they said, returning to the stage. The first officer looked from Rob to Tom. He wasn't sure what to make of it.

"Mexican, officer, working illegally, you say?" Tom said quickly, trying to look thoughtful. As if this was all new and unexpected. "We'll certainly keep an eye out. Rob, could you get the officer's contact details, please, in case we get any news of an illegal Mexican anywhere?"

Rob showed them out, smiling now and polite, breathing a little more easily. Almost automatically, he tore up the piece of paper with telephone number and so forth that one of the officers had given him and threw the pieces into one of the bins in the auditorium. Tom was still confused, stepping forward slowly, looking thoughtfully towards centre stage, before he sat on the edge, his legs hanging over into the front row of the stalls.

"Jesus!" was all Tom could say. "How did that happen? Or did I just imagine it all?" Rob seemed to be as confused as he was.

"Bloody Hell!" Rob said at last, relieved and starting to tidy things on stage, ready to leave for the evening. "That was a close one. Thank God for Paul, that's all I can say."

Tom left Rob to lock up the theatre and made his way back to the hotel. It was unsettling anyway to have immigration officers barge in. Even worse, though, not knowing what had happened. And how José-Luis had disappeared right before their eyes. He didn't sleep that night, worried about José-Luis, but more so wondering what Paul had had to do with it. After such an amazing dance, too? Tom couldn't remember the dancing itself, he realised. What they'd danced or how they'd moved. However, the emotion behind the way the two men had danced with one another woke something up deep down inside. Something he'd not been aware of before.

4

Lying next to one another, Paul was tense.

"What shall we talk about?" asked José-Luis. Paul looked over to him and tried to think of something to say. It struck him as an odd question when there they were two semi-naked men next to one another in the same bed.

"I know," said José-Luis, and before Paul knew what was happening, José-Luis was under the duvet. Paul felt him move down in the bed and put a hand on his pyjama bottoms. He didn't know what to do. This is not happening, he said to himself. But then realised, felt more than anything, that it was very real. Closing his eyes, he lay back and took slow even breaths till he felt he could hold back no longer. He tried to shift in the bed underneath José-Luis but couldn't. It was too late. The most extraordinary feeling of release and warmth spread throughout his entire body. It was some minutes before he felt uncomfortable and guilty. He didn't know why. It just seemed natural to feel that way.

José-Luis appeared again next to him, wiping the back of his hand across his mouth. "That wasn't so bad, was it?"

Paul snorted and, despite himself, smiled at José-Luis. He let out a long breath as he lay back and closed his eyes for a few moments. He didn't know what to say, whether he should thank him. He opened his eyes after a minute or two and went to lift the duvet up and go down the bed himself. But José-Luis dropped his arm on the duvet, stopping him. He leant on his other arm and looked at Paul.

"There is no need for that. We have plenty of time. Just relax." Paul smiled back at him and began to open his mouth, but José-Luis put his finger on Paul's lips. "Sssh!" he said gently, "do not be afraid, Paul. I want to show you how to be yourself."

"I don't understand," said Paul, "What do mean 'be myself'?" he asked.

José-Luis thought for a moment. "I am sorry, Paul, that was wrong of me," he said.

"No, really," Paul looked serious, "I just don't understand."

"Perhaps I am wrong, Paul," José-Luis was stroking Paul's chest gently. As a friend. "I do not think you have ever had sex before. I mean... with someone else, with another man."

Paul didn't react straight away. "You're right, José-Luis. I never thought sex was right for people like me."

"Why?" José-Luis put his head on one side, genuinely surprised. But then he thought he understood. "You mean, you do not think it is right for two men to have sex?"

Paul flushed.

"So, what did you think about Tom and me when you watched us in the theatre?" José-Luis asked. He'd suspected that the someone who'd been watching them have sex some days ago was Paul. He'd recognised a hint of aftershave when he'd cleaned himself up and followed Tom onto the stage. The same fragrance that lingered all around the flat. Paul's reaction the night before just confirmed it. Paul shifted uneasily in the bed.

"Be honest," José-Luis added. Paul thought for a few minutes.

"I liked it," he said simply.

"Is that all?" José-Luis laughed out loud. "Come on, Paul, even *you* can do better than that!"

Paul was shocked and looked at his hands, embarrassed.

"Do not worry, Paul," José-Luis said, shaking his head gently, "I will not tell Tom if he has not already guessed." They both remained silent for a few minutes.

"I mean," he began. He glanced surreptitiously over to where his parents' picture had been turned to the wall. "Fuck! It was amazing... I wish..."

"No, no," José-Luis replied, "No 'I wish' or 'if only'. Life is what it is. There is no point in regretting what has been done already. Or complaining about what *might* happen if you do not do something to *make* it happen or to *stop* it happening."

"I know. You're right," said Paul.

"But just be careful not to let life slip away in future." José-Luis folded his arms and raised an eyebrow at Paul, who shifted uncomfortably.

"It just felt so good," Paul added at last. "I mean, you just looked so happy. And you were obviously really enjoying it."

"And for men like us," José-Luis continued, nodding, "it feels a lot more than that. When it is not just sex, it is even better."

"How do you mean?" Paul asked.

"When you love someone, sex is part of giving yourself to them. And they give themselves to you too. That feels very special." José-Luis lay back on the bed and smiled, remembering what it had been like back in Colombia.

"Are you going to teach me about love?" Paul asked after a few moments.

José-Luis laughed. "No, I cannot do that. I will teach you about sex," he said and tickled Paul under the duvet. Without thinking, Paul turned away. When they'd settled back again, José-Luis went on: "Anyway, you know about love already."

"What?" Paul was surprised.

"You just do not realise it." José-Luis winked at him and leaned over to turn off the bedside lamp. He smiled and lay down, getting comfortable. Paul did the same, though his head was spinning. Five minutes, ten minutes passed. He began to wonder if what had happened before really had or whether he'd imagined it all. He was trying to make sense of what José-Luis had said too.

"And tomorrow morning," José-Luis said suddenly through the darkness, "there are some things you need to buy at the pharmacy. I give you a list. Men like us need to be careful and take precautions!" He leaned across and kissed Paul's forehead. "Night, *pollito*! Sweet dreams."

Paul woke once in the night. The moon was streaming in through the window and shone on José-Luis's shoulders. Paul wanted to reach out and touch his back, caress it, trace the hairs with his finger. Without thinking, he leant over and kissed his shoulder. José-Luis shifted slightly. He didn't wake up, but the duvet slipped and showed his boxers now tight across his perfectly shaped buttocks under his broad back. Paul followed the hairs with his eyes down to the small of his back, converging over his buttocks. Carefully, so as not to wake him, Paul pulled the duvet gently over him. He kissed the duvet covering José-Luis's shoulders this time.

"Night, *pollito*!" Paul said.

After the relief that José-Luis had avoided arrest, Tom began to wonder about things. Paul remained uncommunicative. Did he actually have a part to play in José-Luis's disappearing act when the immigration officers had arrived? Asking anyone else about José-Luis's whereabouts seemed too risky. Yet with Paul hiding away all the time, there was no way he could ask him. Besides, someone must have told the authorities that José-Luis was there. And that could only be someone associated with the theatre and the production. This made Tom nervous, though he had an idea who it might be. If he made a fuss, would that damage his own reputation, though? He didn't really care about being accused of sheltering an illegal immigrant. He did care, though, that someone outside his team might start to ask questions about his relationship with José-Luis.

There was more, though. He was still a little upset that José-Luis had made it perfectly clear that they were friends not lovers. He was beginning to wonder whether he just didn't understand relationships after all. As a closeted man was there more than just sex? Around the time Tom was admitting feelings for Paul, José-Luis had also started mentioning that true love – whatever that is – might actually end up being prepared to let someone go. Was there something more to this? Tom wondered. An ulterior motive? Did José-Luis have designs on Paul? Was he trying to exclude Tom or prepare to cheat on him? Tom felt very alone. There was no one he could ask about any of these things. Except Paul, when they were younger. He felt he'd already damaged any potential closeness there. Why had he even mentioned being 'just friends'? That wasn't what he wanted at all. If he spoke to anyone else, like Olwena in wardrobe, he'd effectively out himself. And he'd spent so long trying to keep that whole area of his life secret. He was now desperate, though.

He started to remember how easy it had been at school. He could tell Paul almost anything. Yes, he lusted after him too he realised now. But that wasn't the only thing. Until that kiss right at the end, his friendship with Paul was not really about sex or kisses or anything like that. It was about being so comfortable with someone that you felt they would be there for you whatever happened. As he realised now, thinking of Paul disappearing down the corridor and what José-Luis had said about him shutting down and not being the person he could be or deserved to be, it was also about being so much in love with someone that all you want is for them to be happy. Whether or not, Tom realised, that happiness includes you and what you do.

"Oh hi," Tom said uncomfortably as he walked into wardrobe hoping to find Olwena. He shuffled from one foot to the other. Olwena stood and moved costumes from a chair to make space for him.

"Sir... Tom, there you go. Have a seat," Olwena sat back down holding the clothes to her chest that she'd just picked up. They sat in silence for an uncomfortable two or three minutes. Then,

"So, err..." Tom began, wiping the palms of his hands on his jeans, "So, are you from round here?" he asked, wishing he could have come up with something better.

"Oh yes," Olwena said, "Girls High School as it was at the time, and all that."

"Did you not think of moving away?" Tom went on, searching for something neutral.

"Not really," she said becoming more pensive. "I'd hoped for something... someone."

Tom looked at her.

"But they... Well, you don't want to hear about me!" she laughed and smiled, though there was a real sadness about her expression. "Is there a problem? Do you need me to alter something?"

"No, no, everything's fine. I just wanted to ask you something." Tom was looking everywhere but Olwena's face. "I wonder if you could give me a little advice."

"Well, if I can. Ask away," said Olwena, and she tapped Tom's knee. She put the costumes down on the workbench and clasped her hands in her lap, focusing on Tom.

"You know what you mentioned the other day?" he began. Olwena's face remained neutral, but she nodded briefly to encourage him to go on. "So, just suppose I loved someone here in this theatre," he began. Olwena's expression still didn't change. "And, of course, after the show in Weymouth, I'll be off touring round the UK. And I might not see them for a while. And, you know, as you say, I need to keep communicating..." Tom shifted nervously and fell silent. Olwena waited patiently.

"So, you want to know how to keep in touch?" she prompted after another pause. She turned back to her sewing. She was marking out alterations to one of the dancer's costumes with tailor's chalk and was now trying not to look up at Tom so that it would be easier for him.

"Well, yes... sorry, that sounds a bit silly."

"Not at all," Olwena touched his knee again, "nothing's ever silly with things like this. So, what do you need to know?" She could tell that Tom was nervous, so she hoped that by seeming to carry on with her stitching that would encourage him to relax and get to the point.

"How do I keep in touch with them?" Tom said, hoping Olwena wouldn't ask for any more detail. "I don't really want to send letters here to the theatre..."

"Oh, that's easy," Olwena said, and Tom smiled and relaxed. But when Olwena didn't carry on straight away, he sat forward in his seat encouraging her to carry on. "If you ask Rob," she said, "he's got everyone's address. He'll tell you."

"Of course," Tom slapped his forehead. He was trying to keep it light. "I never thought of that."

Olwena looked at him indulgently. She knew he was trying to avoid confirming that he was talking about Paul. "Be careful, though," she said, "letters may not get you what you want."

Tom squinted slightly trying to see her expression against the light. "How do you mean?" he asked.

"Oh, nothing," Olwena said wistfully. "I tried to stay in touch with someone very dear to me through letters. It was someone I had fallen deeply in love with at school. And I honestly believe that they loved me just as much. I know this sounds silly now, but we exchanged handkerchiefs. We'd read it somewhere. That it was like exchanging a lock of hair or something very personal. But then, you know, it wasn't so easy back then. They got married and moved away. I wrote, trying to keep my letters safe in case the partner found them. I wanted to say so much more. Finally, the letters just stopped coming."

"I'm sorry," said Tom, looking down at his hands in his lap, "What happened, if you don't mind me asking?"

"When the last but one letter didn't get a reply, I sent another. A last hope. I just wanted to know that they were alright. Safe and happy. I almost begged them just to tell me that."

"Were you more than just friends?" Tom surprised himself with such a direct question. Olwena stopped smoothing the garment on the workbench before her. She turned towards the window. Wardrobe was always bathed in a yellow glow, with the anti-fade blind hanging down to bench height. She took the card down she'd sellotaped to the wall and looked at the woman in the picture with a letter in her hands. She smiled to herself, lost in memories and thoughts. Putting the card down on the bench, she looked out of the window again, her skin tone altered by the yellow light. A natural sunbeam found its way round the edge, and as she turned back towards Tom her head was framed in light.

"Just be careful," she said, "Don't leave here without making sure he... they know exactly how you feel. That way, they'll know your letters are genuine. That you love them." She turned back to the costume in front of her. Taking a threaded needle she'd pinned through her cardigan, she began to sew along the chalk lines. Tom was unsure he'd heard her correctly. "Anything else I can help with?" she added.

Tom stood up abruptly and wiped his hands again down his thighs as if brushing off imaginary crumbs. "No, that's really helpful. I wouldn't have thought about asking Rob." She turned to face him, looking a little confused. "About the address," Tom said quickly.

"Of course, there is another way," Olwena said suddenly as Tom was already in the doorway. He turned.

"What's that?" Tom asked.

"You could just ask him directly himself," and Olwena returned to her work and left him to his own thoughts. Tom smiled, holding on to the doorframe as if not quite ready to leave. He was interrupted by the tannoy.

"Oh there!" Olwena said as if they'd not spoken about anything important, "Mr Jason is calling you down onto the stage." She smiled at him kindly.

"There you are, Tom!" Jason looked slightly annoyed. "I've been looking for you all over the place." Julia looked up from the paper and raised an eyebrow. "Thing is," he said, "I need to do a sound check with one of the new mics Rob's just bought. Some nonsense about the ones I brought being 'incompatible' with Health & Safety. Do you mind?"

"Do you need one of the numbers from the show?" Tom picked up one of the scores he'd left on the table centre stage.

"Doesn't really matter," Jason replied. "Just a few bars. Anything will do. *A cappella*. I've already checked the musicians. Just sing something."

Tom followed Jason towards the front of the stage to the mic stand. Jason stepped aside to let Tom adjust the height and angle to suit himself, and then dropped down into the auditorium to go over to the desk and adjust levels as needed or check on the sound quality. Tom waited patiently for Jason to signal to him he was ready for the sound check. Olwena appeared in the wings holding the skirt she'd been working on when they'd been speaking just before. Everything seemed to go quiet as though people knew that Tom was about to sing. He tapped a few times on his thigh, nodding his head to the same rhythm, as if he was listening to the musicians counting him in, lifted his head towards the mic and closed his eyes ready to sing.

Just two or three phrases in and everyone stopped what they were doing and looked. Olwena stood, mouth open, watching the young singer closely. Rob came to the wings to see who it was with a voice like that. Jason looked up from the desk in the auditorium pulling one earphone from his ear, and Frances appeared in the central door to the stalls, folding her arms and leaning against the door frame. Even Julia put her paper down. From the opening bars of *¿Dónde estás ahora?* there was not a sound anywhere else in the theatre. With no accompaniment, no backing vocals, nothing. It was something they'd not heard before, an unfamiliar style even. It was mournful and somehow deeply personal. Although the stage crew couldn't understand the lyric, along with the musicians and dancers everyone began to think of someone they'd known. Someone they really loved.

"He could stop traffic with a performance like that," Frances said to herself.

"It's bloody amazing," Terrence replied from behind her, making her stand straight and glancing sideways at someone she'd never heard express any appreciation for a performer. "I bet he wrote it for someone. You know, a girl or something."

Or something, Frances thought. "Yeah, he definitely had someone in mind," she answered out loud.

When he'd finished, Tom was completely oblivious to the effect he had on his colleagues, as if he'd been singing for himself. Olwena sniffed and hastily retrieved a handkerchief from her sleeve, while Frances, Terrence, Rob and the musicians all erupted into applause. And even Julia nodded appreciatively to no one in particular. Jason took off the headphones, coughed slightly, and shouted from the back of the stalls:

"Well, I don't think we've any complaints there, Tom!" His voice was a little unsteady. He tried hard to sound relaxed. "You've certainly kept that little gem a secret."

"Oh," Tom looked around, suddenly self-conscious, "it's nothing really. Just an old song from one of the first albums. It just came to me then. Not sure why." He looked down at the stage in thought.

Leaning on the guard rail high above the stage, Paul was watching from the shadows. He recognised the track and now, he felt, he understood what it meant. And why it was so important to him. He withdrew from the patch of light coming up from the stage below and turned, deep in thought, to go back into his workspace. He sat down, switched off the light in his little workroom, and tried to understand what he was feeling. Life was slipping by. He wondered if he had the courage to change things or whether he would just have to go with it. "I love you, Tom," was all he said in the dark. "Please don't go without me this time."

Admitting this to himself for the first time shocked him, and he sat back abruptly, switching his desk light back on and momentarily blinded by its light. He blinked for several minutes, trying to adjust to it. Did he really think – or even hope – that Tom would declare some kind of love for him and want to do the live-happily-ever-after bit? What about José-Luis after all? Would Tom be so heartless as to cast him aside? And what would José-Luis make of all of it? Paul shook his head. This was madness, he thought. He didn't want to think about being left behind again. He would cope. After all, he'd coped for all these years and would manage again. Blinking back the tears now, which he told himself were due to the bright light, he took the *Tom Bright Charity Show* notebook from his back pocket and tried to read through it. He wanted to make sure that he hadn't missed anything. Whether it was for Tom Bright or anyone else for that matter, Paul was meticulous, and he wanted the lighting and special effects to be flawless. It was professionally important. That's what he was all about. Until now.

He slammed the book shut on his desk, surprising himself by the noise it made and automatically looked around to check if anyone might have heard. 'Maybe,' he said to himself, tapping the edge of the book against his lower lip, 'making sure that the production is perfect is my escape? The way to protect myself?' He didn't want to pursue these thoughts too far. Instead, he decided he should do a detailed check that everything was in place. Here, backstage and front of house. By the time he was high up in the auditorium looking down on the stage where he could see Frances reading through her paper and Danny trying to strike up a conversation with one of the female dancers, he felt better. He smiled to himself. 'I'll survive,' he thought, 'I always have before.'

Although Paul was hanging around a little longer than he would normally before going to the theatre, José-Luis faced a long day alone. He'd given Paul a food shopping list when he'd seen what Paul had on offer. That way there was at least something he could cook and eat. Paul had struggled to find the types of cheese and cured meats, let alone the bread. There wasn't much call for it in Weymouth. But he tried his best. And after a few days, Paul would liaise with Tom to get José-Luis some fresh clothes. Tom and Paul were both very careful, though, to avoid attracting attention. Tom was beginning to suspect that Julia might have been behind the arrival of immigration officers. He had no concrete proof for now. It was her attitude and her tone and the way she took every opportunity to insult José-Luis and to point out that he was an illegal immigrant. This was not entirely fair, though Tom knew that if it came to it, they would find it difficult to counter the claim in court.

On the second day, Paul helped José-Luis push back the furniture in the living room to maximise the space in the middle. That way, José-Luis could go over more than just in his own mind the routines he'd choreographed. He was careful not to draw any attention from neighbours during the day. He used his Walkman to listen to the music and tried to tread as softly as possible. Apart from all of that though, José-Luis liked spending time alone in Paul's flat. He wanted to get to know him, what he liked and how he spent his spare time. He was grateful to Paul for what he'd done. He knew enough about him to realise that that was the type of person Paul was. He began to love him for it. Not as a lover, certainly not as a replacement Donatello, but just as a really good, reliable friend. Even more than that, as someone that he wanted to be just as happy as he'd been himself with Donatello. He wanted Paul to be happy in himself, too. To be whoever he wanted. If that meant being with Tom, he would be very happy for both of them. He knew, though, that he had to be very careful. He'd got used to trying to coax Tom out of his shell since they'd arrived in Weymouth, particularly since he now realised that it was Paul who he'd loved and still longed for. With Paul it was different. He seemed more fragile, in a way. Dependable, intelligent, likeable even. But not his real self.

After a day or two, he started noticing the pictures around the walls and tried to understand what they said about Paul. Monet's *Haystacks* dominated the room to some extent, though José-Luis didn't think there was much to them. Except the haystacks staying in the same place and just the weather and lighting changing around them. Of course, it made him think about Paul's artistic sense the way he'd arranged the smaller prints in relation to the large poster. He couldn't quite fathom why the predictability of the harvest would appeal. *Les Raboteurs de parquet* above the bed made him chuckle. Right above where they'd slept were three semi-naked men, muscly, glistening with sweat. 'How appropriate, but I bet Paul doesn't see it that way at all,' he thought. He was hiding something, José-Luis felt, just as the Van Dyck self-portrait in the living room showed. Everything about the pictures told his story. Some aspect of Paul's life. The question was, José-Luis wondered, how much of all this was Paul aware of himself?

They'd come in via the fire escape and the door in the kitchen. So, he'd only found *The Incredulity of Saint Thomas* when Paul had gone into work, and he finally decided he wanted to know what was behind that particular door. The light was poor in the dimly lit vestibule, but he thought he recognised the picture from his college days. It was about faith, he seemed to remember, or rather the lack of it. Brother Gabriel, with his strong jaw and the hairy ankles under his Franciscan habit, had been teaching from the Gospels and was talking about the Apostles. Thomas, he'd explained, doubted that the figure they'd met on the road was really the resurrected Christ. He'd wanted to see and feel for himself the very wounds Christ had suffered during the crucifixion. Brother Gabriel told all the boys in his charge that they should never doubt the all-embracing love of God.

"God loves all of us," he'd said, in his gentle Castilian accent. "No matter who we are," he'd added, looking directly at the young José-Luis. "We need to trust Him, to jump into the unknown if necessary. *Un salto de fe.*"

José-Luis winced at Thomas's finger poking into the wound and the concentration on the men's faces. Christ holding Thomas's arm to avoid too much pain, presumably. Why on earth had Paul bought it? José-Luis wondered. Going back into the living room and spotting the CD player, he looked round for the CDs to see what music his new friend listened to on his own. He found one of Tom's early CDs almost hidden away under a pile of classical music. He flicked over the tracks. *¿Me quieres?* was underlined. He took the CD out so that he could read the lyrics on the insert. How odd! He thought to himself. Paul doesn't read Spanish, I'm sure. Yet there are some very personal love songs here. *"Do you love me?"* Of course, doubting Thomas. Poking at the emotional wounds. I wonder. On the bottom of the lyric sheet, *"Where are you now?"* was written in English in Paul's careful script. Glancing up the list of tracks, José-Luis found that track too.

Carefully, he replaced the CD where he'd found it. Right there on the same shelf was a small Spanish-English, English-Spanish dictionary. He looked around and found a pen. *"Si, está aquí. Y te quiere"* he wrote on the first page.

Turning back towards the bedroom door, he saw the *Tristan and Isolde.* He looked at the picture of the courtly lovers, taken aback by the detail, and drawn by the simple expression of early love he thought he could see in their eyes. The harp was almost a barrier for Tristan preventing him from getting any closer to Isolde. A barrier that Tristan presumably had to get over. The scene must be early on in the relationship, he thought, and he wondered whether it would last. He'd not noticed the figure of King Mark off to the right at first. And he just thought that it was some busybody interfering. He squinted to make out the commentary printed in very small type at the bottom of the picture. Then he went over to the bookcase and searched through the books till he found a reference book about early English literature. Flicking through, he found the story he was looking for. Reading the commentary, he was touched by the thought of Tristan desperately waiting for the boat to return. The boat he hoped would carry Isolde (also known as Iseult, apparently, he read) back to him. The loyalty of Kahedin, but the deliberate deceit of Iseult aux blanches mains. Tristan dying from a mortal wound that Isolde could have cured. And then she'd died of a broken heart.

The story made him think. He wondered if his mother had lied to him like Iseult aux blanches mains. If so, why would she do that? Suddenly, another thought struck him. Suppose his mother hadn't lied, well not really, but hearing that a doctor – any doctor, not necessarily Donatello – somewhere had been lynched, she'd wanted to protect José-Luis. That was the only way she could think of to persuade him to leave. The love of a mother would lead her to do anything she could to save a child, he concluded. After all, she knew that his father and brothers were increasingly hostile to him. He felt nauseous, though. Maybe it wasn't Donatello, and José-Luis had abandoned him? That was too much for him to bear. José-Luis hoped desperately that Donatello understood. From his own perspective, his love was still stronger than ever.

For now, though, he didn't know what to do. He had to think. Just as he was putting the book back on the shelf, he stood back up straight. "*¡Por supuesto!* Of course!" he said out loud, "Dana-Beatriz!". She wouldn't lie. If Donatello wasn't dead, she'd have contacted him to find out why José-Luis had left, surely? She'd have found out where he was. He didn't know whether to be relieved or even more sad. He tried to distract himself by concentrating on the choreography. He took the *Tristan and Isolde* picture down and, propping it on the floor under where it had been, he turned it to face the wall so that he wouldn't have to look at it.

Unable to concentrate though, José-Luis sat down heavily on the sofa. Was Paul Tristan waiting for Tom to return from beyond the seas? Is that why he was so obsessed with the story? He had to help Paul. That much he knew. Was there still time to save him? He looked at the Van Dyck and saw the artist staring back at him. He walked back into the bedroom to get a sweater and as he turned to come back to the lighter and warmer lounge, he noticed the Hammershøi *Interior, Strandgade 30, 1901.* That was the saddest picture of all. A figure from behind in the next room, in the shade, alone. Like Paul, José-Luis thought, in his workspace above the stage. Alone, lonely even, and cut off from anyone else.

As José-Luis sat and looked out of the window, the sea just visible across the tops of several buildings, he wondered why Paul and Tom kept playing this game. It was a bright day and there were many small sailing boats crowding the sea just offshore, buffeted by the wind. It was obvious to anyone, he felt, that they had very strong feelings for one another. And it seemed particularly cruel to José-Luis – having lost Donatello and, rejected by his family, having had to flee his home – that they would not want to take advantage of a much more liberal society in Europe. It was very simple: they love each other, so why are they not enjoying it?

José-Luis loved each of them. Although he didn't like to admit it, he'd used Tom to begin with. He was so distraught at losing Donatello and leaving Colombia that meeting Tom had come just in time. He realised, though, that sooner or later he would have to be honest with him. Being on his own in France and on the ferry, he knew he had to let him down gently. He suspected that Tom loved him. Let's face it, though, he told himself, Tom only thought he loved José-Luis. They were both on the rebound. And now José-Luis understood the reason Tom was acting the way he did. All those years apart and yet he was still hopelessly in love with Paul. Now that he'd met Paul for himself, José-Luis could see why.

José-Luis turned back to the room. He picked up the Tom Bright CD and idly read down the list of tracks. Last but one was something he didn't recognise: *La primera vez que vi tu rostro*. He slipped it into the CD player and sat down to listen. It was slow and almost melancholic. It reminded him that early on the first morning he'd been here with Paul he'd woken to see the first rays of the sun creeping through the window. The light had played across Paul's face, still sleeping. Yes, he was very handsome in an understated way. Because of that, José-Luis thought, he was even more attractive. As Tom's voice smoothly sang the melody, José-Luis cast his eyes round the room for no particular reason. But as he looked through the door to the bedroom, he caught sight of something under the bed. Going to investigate, he found the copy of *The Face* with Tom, looking over his shoulder, staring back at him. He thought for a moment. Paul must have shoved it hastily out of sight when they'd first arrived. He was too upset and flustered to notice. His attention returned to the track on the CD as it was coming to an end '*...y duraría hasta el fin de los tiempos*'.

He had to think of a way to get Paul to relax and come out from the shadows. But he knew that wasn't going to be easy. He'd already seen, and Tom had told him how it was at school, that Paul had escaped into literature. José-Luis glanced round the room at the pictures and over to the bookshelves. Literature and art, though, are not real life. 'We react to what we read or what we see, that is all,' he thought. José-Luis had to show Paul that he could be part of life, an active player in real life. He wouldn't need to be content with watching artificial stories or paintings which capture an idealised version for his entertainment. He could make a decision to be part of what was going on and shape his own destiny. To start with, he could stop avoiding Tom and tell him he still loved him as much as when they were at school.

Although Paul had taken shyness to the next level and didn't know how to escape from the safe little world he'd built up round himself, José-Luis could tell that he was genuine and loyal underneath it all. It was easy to lust after him. But it wasn't just a physical thing. José-Luis had felt that there was so much more to Paul, and he could sort things out even when no one else could. And more caring than almost anyone he knew. As he showed when they danced, too, he was just as emotional as Tom. Maybe in time José-Luis could fall in love with him? The problem, though, was that Paul still loved Tom, of course. And what about José-Luis himself? Paul reminded him of Donatello, of how safe he'd felt in his arms. Just like when they were dancing the last time in the theatre, and Tom had caught them. He wiped away a tear as he admitted quietly to himself that he was still in love with Donatello. However hopeless it was, he wanted him so badly. He would never find anyone like him. Across the rooftops he caught sight of several sailboats tacking across the bay, their white sails waving to him. At least, that's what it looked like. He restarted the CD on the same track and wept silently to himself.

"So..." Julia drawled, as she put her bag down next to Frances's paper. Frances chucked her pen down on the table and sat back in her seat. She didn't particularly want to talk to Julia, but clearly, she was after something.

"That little number the other day was pretty impressive," she said.

"Which number?" Frances asked, not even trying to hide that she wasn't actually that interested. She knew exactly which number. Everyone had spoken about it all that afternoon.

"You know," Julia cajoled, "That little Spanish thing."

"Tom's famous for Latin American music. There's a fair few *little Spanish things*." Frances was trying to think of an excuse to get up and leave without appearing too rude.

"What was it now..." Julia looked up for inspiration, "*¿Dónde estás...?* Something."

"*¿Dónde estás ahora?*" Frances corrected. "Love song, apparently." She picked up her newspaper pointedly, hoping Julia would take the hint. *Where are you now?* was the title, apparently, one of the musicians had explained to her. But she wasn't going to give Julia the satisfaction of knowing what the English version of the title was.

"Any idea who it was for?" Julia persisted. Frances put down the newspaper again rather loudly.

"Look. What is this all about?" she said looking up at Julia, ignoring the tone in her own voice.

"Just wondered..." Julia said, noncommittally, walking slowly around the table. "And this Paul character? The moody one with the tight t-shirts?"

Her eyes narrowing, Frances looked up at Julia trying to read her expression.

"What about him?" she asked eventually.

"Well, he and Tom...?" Julia said, trying not to sound too interested.

"He and Tom what?" Frances was losing her patience.

"You know... There's clearly something going on between them." Julia was fishing, Frances could see that now.

"Look. All we know is that they were at school together, years ago." Frances thought carefully before she went on, "They were in English together, apparently, that's why Paul always knows the crossword clues." This didn't entirely make sense, but it was all she could think of to try and divert the conversation away from her colleagues.

"Is that all...?" Julia was asking when Danny shuffled noisily onto the stage. Julia tutted loudly and rolled her eyes at Frances. In return, Frances raised a quizzical eyebrow back and tilted her head to one side. She found she was becoming increasingly defensive where the people she worked with were concerned.

"Look. Maybe we could grab some lunch sometime?" Julia suggested. "To give us a little privacy."

"I don't think so," said Frances, appalled.

"Why not? You can't be *that* busy in a two-bit provincial theatre like this." Julia could barely hide her contempt.

"It's not that," Frances said, turning back to her paper, trying to show that the conversation was now over. "I just don't like you."

Danny hurried off stage again, but even so could not hide the sound of his loud laughter.

Paul sat nervously in the bedroom. When Tom had left all those years ago, Paul had given up. If he couldn't have Tom, he didn't want anyone else. And that meant just keeping himself to himself. Then he could feel safe, or so he kept telling himself. So, he'd missed all the growing up that everyone else had been doing. Last night was his first sexual experience and if honest with himself, he wanted more. He wanted to feel what he'd seen Tom and José-Luis enjoy back in the theatre. He didn't want to think over what José-Luis had said about love. He wondered if he had been in love all along, but just without realising it. He was confused too about how he felt towards José-Luis. He'd told him to check where the fire escape went, just in case. He'd made sure that he remembered to warn him that in an emergency, he shouldn't just head straight down to the carpark, but follow the bits that joined up with the next property and led across the rooftops. He cared about José-Luis and was worried that they'd try to find him again after the fiasco at the theatre. Did that mean he loved José-Luis? Yet he felt so sad for him losing Donatello. He'd have done anything, he realised, if he could get the two men back together. All of these emotions were so new to him, though, especially the sex. He didn't know what the rules were, what he could and couldn't do. What was allowed. At the same time, though, he still felt deep down that this was not what they should be doing.

José-Luis gently told him to take his pyjamas off as they prepared to go to bed that night. Doing as he'd been told, Paul also took the precaution of turning the photo of his parents towards the wall again. He sat on the end of the bed with the *Boots* bag at his feet, waiting for José-Luis to come back from the bathroom. He shivered a little. He didn't know whether it was nerves or the cold. When he finally came into the bedroom, José-Luis had stripped to his boxers. He smiled at Paul as he placed his clothes neatly on a chair by the door. Paul tried to smile back. He was desperate not to look at José-Luis's chest and his muscly legs. Picking up the *Boots* bag, José-Luis stood close to Paul and checked what he'd bought. Paul could smell José-Luis. It was making him feel heady. His heart beat a little faster as he remembered catching José-Luis and Tom making love in the theatre.

"¡*Bien, guapo*! Good!" José-Luis said as he took some of the things from the bag and put them ready on the bedside cupboard. He walked back in front of Paul and bent to kiss him. In his turn, Paul stretched up automatically parting his lips slightly, ready to receive José-Luis's tongue. After a while, José-Luis stepped back, kissed Paul gently on the forehead, and began to take down his boxers. Paul was transfixed. José-Luis dropped the boxers at the foot of the bed and took a step forward.

"It's OK. You can touch it. It doesn't bite."

Paul looked up into José-Luis's face.

"Go on. I want you to."

"But..." Paul hesitated, despite himself, not daring to take his eyes from José-Luis's.

"But what?"

"But... Tom."

José-Luis laughed, but not unkindly. He'd not thought that Paul would believe he was Tom's lover. It hadn't taken long for him to notice that whenever Tom appeared, though, Paul would dissolve into the background somehow. He recognised the look on Tom's face when Paul was there, however briefly. Nor had it taken him long to realise that this was the man back in Weymouth that Tom denied. Seeing the newspaper clippings on the cup-stained coffee table when he'd walked into Paul's flat the first time just seemed to confirm it. And finding *The Face* hidden under the bed. He wondered if he should tell Paul that this is what he'd meant about love. Though he was worried that the two of them, Tom and Paul, were in danger of losing one another again, maybe forever. He wanted to bang their heads together.

"What about Tom?" José-Luis knew, of course. "¡*Mira*! Tom and me, we have sex sometimes, and we both enjoy it. But I do not love Tom and if he would be truthful, he does not love me either. Our hearts lie somewhere else. I know you have lived a quiet life, Paul..."

"Does it show?" Paul blushed, still concentrating hard to look into José-Luis's face and not let his eyes drop, even though that was exactly what he wanted at that moment.

"I knew that when we shared the bed last night and I..." José-Luis continued. Paul shifted uncomfortably. "It's OK. We all have to learn sometime. Just like the dancing, *pollito*, it takes practice."

José-Luis bent down and caressed his face with his soft touch. Taking Paul's hand, he placed it gently on his own stomach. Paul was confused and uncomfortable, but he didn't take it back. Without thinking, he began to let it run down José-Luis's pelvis, feeling the hair and the muscles underneath. He moved his hand aside to José-Luis's thigh automatically but then finally took hold of his scrotum.

"*¡Oye!*" José-Luis took a step back, laughing, "not so rough!"

"Sorry," Paul whispered hoarsely. It was all he could manage.

"I want to teach you, Paul. I want to show you what you can do and how special life can be."

Without thinking and without taking his eyes from José-Luis's, slowly Paul moved forward and, opening his mouth, tried to mimic what he'd learned last night. José-Luis sighed and gave himself up to the moment, his hand gently on the back of Paul's head.

"You've done this before," José-Luis laughed. Paul made to move back and deny it and try to explain but José-Luis's hand gently kept him where he was. "Let's both enjoy it together," José-Luis said, "that feels very good."

When José-Luis began to moan and shift more noticeably, he let Paul's head go and started to breath more rapidly. "Careful, Paul, careful. I'm so close..." But Paul didn't stop. Eventually, laughing, José-Luis withdrew. He crouched before Paul and kissed him again. Paul stood up, erect and excited about what he thought was coming. José-Luis smiled, stood up straight again and went to the bedside cabinet. He came back and sat at the end of the bed, taking a condom out of its foil pack and unrolling it on Paul's penis after kissing it gently. He moved back onto the bed and, putting a pillow under his pelvis, he lay down on his front. Paul watched, waiting till he could touch José-Luis's shoulders and back.

"Now," José-Luis had propped himself up on his elbows briefly and looked over his shoulder. "Just like you saw Tom and me do."

Paul had no time to think about what José-Luis had just said. He lowered himself onto the bed and began to caress and kiss José-Luis's back, from the shoulders down his back and onto his buttocks. He slowly moved on top of José-Luis and pushed gently inside. José-Luis smiled to himself as he let out a small sigh, his head resting on his hands. Pushing himself up again, he turned, and they kissed as Paul began to move back and forth. Once or twice, José-Luis stiffened slightly and kissed Paul's hands that he held in his own. Paul stopped and apologised.

"It's OK, *guapo*," José-Luis whispered, "it's OK, please, I love it."

As Paul climaxed rather more quickly than he'd expected, José-Luis let out a gentle laugh and thanked Paul. They both dozed with Paul still on top of José-Luis. After a few minutes more, though, José-Luis moved him off, kissed his chest, and covered him with the duvet. They both drifted into a very peaceful sleep.

Some hours later, Paul woke to find José-Luis standing by the bedside cabinet. The moon was flooding in through the bedroom window, and highlighted his beautiful, strong body. He was erect and had just put on a condom before walking to the end of the bed. "Now it's your turn," he whispered. Paul rolled onto his back as he watched him bend over the bed towards him and kiss him on the lips. In a single movement, it seemed, José-Luis pulled Paul down the bed, his legs either side of José-Luis's strong body. As he felt José-Luis push in gently, he grasped the bottom sheet either side of his thighs.

"It's OK!" José-Luis kissed him again. "Relax. Enjoy it."

Paul lay back and put his hands onto José-Luis's chest, stroking the hair. As José-Luis quickened, he lent forward and Paul caressed his back, loving the feel of his sweat. To Paul's surprise, they both climaxed together. José-Luis chuckled and lay gently on top of Paul for a few minutes. Then he rolled over to his side of the bed and lay on his back, cleaning himself off.

"I love you," whispered Paul.

"Sssh!" José-Luis held a finger over his lips, raising himself up on his elbow. "No. We both love someone else," he said simply and lay back down. "You know," he went on a few minutes later, "you're only the third man I've ever slept with. We all have to be careful. Men like you and me and Tom. I read it in a magazine back in the US before we came here. We should not have swallowed, of course, but at least now we are being safe. Thank you, though. I love the sex with you and Tom. It helps." They lay next to one another, the moonlight shining across their bodies. Eventually, they both fell asleep once more.

Some while later, Paul woke up. Still drowsy, he could smell someone next to him. Not an unpleasant smell; musky, vaguely sweaty, but wholesome. He breathed in and stretched his legs down the bed. Somehow the smell made him think back to the summer he and Tom had worked on the farm in Bramdean with his cousins when they were still at school. Half asleep now, he reached slowly across the bed till he found José-Luis's hand. He gently slipped it into his own. Slowly and softly, he stroked the fingers with his thumb. To his surprise, he felt the thumb on the other hand rubbing his fingers in turn. As he drifted off to sleep again, he felt more alive than he had for as long as he could remember.

Over the few days that José-Luis was with him, Paul started to see things differently. At first, he would oversleep, José-Luis waking him up with coffee. Real coffee after he'd seen to José-Luis's shopping list, though it hadn't been easy to track down a coffee pot and filter. But then he began to set the alarm. Something he'd not done for years. Not since his school days. When it went off, he'd wake up immediately and turn it off. He liked to be alone with José-Luis breathing peacefully beside him as the day outside began to get busy. Intuitively, he knew that this is what he'd always wanted. To wake up next to another guy. To be comfortable. No matter how much they snored or sweated or whatever – not that José-Luis was irritating in that way – just to be close and secure with someone.

As José-Luis slept on, Paul might slip an arm around him and pull him close. He might kiss him gently so as not to disturb his sleep or rub his shoulder or stroke his hairy chest. It was just about being close to someone, someone that you felt a connection to and who you knew you could trust. If José-Luis had turned towards him in the night, he might instead turn over too and snuggle his back against José-Luis's chest. As if responding to the warmth of Paul's body, José-Luis might move his arm across Paul's shoulder or upper arm and draw himself closer. He wouldn't wake up. It just seemed natural. In this position, Paul would feel the effects of the morning down against the small of his back or his buttocks. Whereas before, this would have made him freeze momentarily whilst he considered how best to move away and get some space between. Not that he'd ever been this close to another man. Well, not since that summer when he and Tom were teenagers. Now, though, it made him feel alive. It was what men like him do, after all.

That thought made Paul sad, though. He wasn't coping well, he felt, with Tom being so close every day in the theatre. Part of him wanted to sit down and talk. Ask if they could turn back the clock a bit. Try and explain what had happened all those years ago in the school hall. It was even more depressing to think about that now. All those years where he'd been on his own. This solitary life seemed just as normal to him until now. Having Tom there, though, had thrown all of that into disarray. He wanted something more from life. From Tom. And yet he was afraid. Afraid that Tom had moved on. That Tom no longer cared for him. Paul, just a lighting engineer in a provincial theatre on the south coast of the UK. In a dreary theatre, kept alive by pantomimes and summer specials.

Almost without thinking, Paul shifted slightly so that his back was touching the hairs on José-Luis's chest. To stop it tickling, he moved closer still which made José-Luis move in his sleep and come closer, putting an arm not just round Paul's shoulder, but around his stomach. Paul's body responded automatically, making him hold his breath hoping that José-Luis would not feel him against his forearm as he slept. As he relaxed and began to breathe more easily again, Paul felt almost overwhelmed by an anxious feeling. A feeling that he might lose out again. He liked José-Luis. He liked him a lot. It wasn't just the physical side of things. He almost knew that José-Luis had been kind enough to take his hand, metaphorically, and introduce him to the life he'd never had but had always wanted. Now he was scared that that life was slipping away. And he didn't know how to stop that happening. Gently, he moved José-Luis's arm and slid quietly out of bed and into the kitchen.

José-Luis half-opened his eyes. Watching Paul's naked back and bottom disappear through the doorway, he sighed to himself. He knew he couldn't make things happen between Tom and Paul. They would have to work that out with and for each other. He hoped, though, that he might be able to help Paul get over all those years of self-denial and self-imposed celibacy. He liked Paul. He could show him how two men make love, how they might make one another feel special. He might even be able to let him glimpse how special Donatello had been for him. He was afraid, though, that Paul may be too entrenched in this small-town loneliness to be able to change. To be himself and allow himself to be and to find happiness, even when it was there, ready for the taking.

Paul walked through the kitchen and into the bathroom. He stared into the mirror and wondered who it was looking back at him. He'd made an effort, he admitted to himself now, to look better, more attractive, his hair tidier and his clothes better fitting. He frowned. Had Tom even noticed? He washed his face, the water still cold this early in the day. He dried himself off and flattened his hair with his hand, trying to make it look neat again. He turned one way and then the other to see if he had a better side. He stood up straight and looked at his broad chest. His wide shoulders narrowed through his torso down to his hips. He looked the part, at least, reasonably fit, a real man. Was it enough? Paul looked straight into the eyes looking back at him from the mirror. "Will it work?" he said to no one in particular. "Surely I'm better as I am." Tom will move on, presumably without him. It'd have been better if he'd not come to Weymouth, perhaps. It was all a bit much for Paul. He didn't want that. He didn't want to be left alone again, the man he loved going off and living the life he'd wanted to share with him.

"Are you alright, Paul?" José-Luis shouted from the bedroom. Paul wiped his face again with the towel.

"Yes, I'm fine, thanks. Just couldn't sleep." He called over his shoulder.

"Come back to bed," José-Luis said, "I'll warm you up."

"No!" Paul said a little sharply. "Sorry. No, it's fine, honestly. You go back to sleep. I'll make some coffee for us both in about half an hour or so."

Paul wrapped a bath towel round his waist and went back into the living room. He closed the door to the bedroom softly, turned to sit on the settee and stared out towards the sea for a while.

"Erm, Tom," Paul shifted nervously at the office door holding a letter. Tom turned round immediately and stood looking up into Paul's face.

"Paul, how... Please, come in... Sit down," Tom cleared a space at the table and moved some papers from the chair opposite. He pulled his own chair out for Paul to sit on whilst he sat on the other one. Slowly, Paul sat down and felt the warmth from the seat through his pants.

"I've got this for you," he held up an envelope. "It's from José-Luis," he added, leaning forward in a whisper. "There was one for Luisa too. And for Carlos."

"Jesus! Why don't we just tell everyone...?" Tom began, but Paul interrupted.

"He trusts them," he explained, "they're all from Central America somewhere."

"I suppose so," Tom nodded.

"I left their letters at the stage door... You know, so they didn't necessarily know they'd been delivered by me." Paul turned and looked down the corridor in each direction. "Anyway. Here. I thought I should deliver this one in person," he smiled awkwardly as he handed Tom the letter.

Without breaking his gaze, Tom took the letter, brushing against Paul's hand. Paul didn't try to move his hand away to avoid Tom's touch, like he'd done so many times at school. Tom opened the letter and scanned it quickly. He looked up at Paul, clearly relieved.

"Oh, thank God, I was so worried about him," he said.

"I'm sorry," said Paul, sitting down now.

"What for?"

"I should've told you." He dropped his gaze to his hands. "I suppose I was worried that the news would get out. I'm so sorry. I wouldn't have wanted you to worry. You of all people."

Tom looked across the table. He dared to reach out and touch Paul's hand properly now, stroking it with his index finger.

"So long as he's safe. That's all that matters." They didn't say anything for a few moments. "You don't think *I* told the police, do you?" Tom whispered to Paul, leaning forward slightly.

"Oh God, no!" Paul replied, a little too loudly. They both looked round and checked the door. "Sorry. No. Of course not. I guess I was just being overprotective. He's been through such a lot."

"Did he tell you about Donatello?" Tom asked.

"Yes," Paul looked briefly into Tom's eyes. "God, that's awful. It's barbaric even."

"I know." Tom turned away for a moment. "I hope he finds someone."

Paul gently stroked Tom's shoulder. "Anyway, what does he say?" he asked. Tom picked up the letter again.

"He's making changes to the routine, telling me I need to do this and then to try that. He never stops!" Tom laughed. Paul smiled too.

"Has he taught you these new steps?" Tom asked.

"No," Paul replied a little shocked, "I'm no dancer,"

"Rubbish! I saw you..." Tom looked into the envelope again and pulled out a room key. "And this is his hotel room. He wants me to get him some clean clothes. I expect he's been working up quite a sweat over at your place..."

"Perhaps we need to get him onto the tour bus when you set off," Paul tried to change the subject.

"I don't know," admitted Tom, "I get the feeling they'll be watching us like hawks."

Paul felt awkward about referring to Tom's departure. Tom sensed as much.

"There's plenty of time before then," he said, and "We don't need to think about that now!" This was perhaps a little too earnestly, and they both fell silent for a few minutes.

"Look, I'll empty my backpack and you can take it at lunchtime to get the clothes... If you've nothing else going on." Paul began. "Then I can take them back this evening. It won't look odd me carrying my own backpack."

"Sounds like a plan to me!" Tom stood up and made to put his hand on Paul's shoulder. But Paul had moved away automatically, perhaps being more business-like now that there were things to be done.

"This is all my fault," Paul added.

"Why?" Tom was puzzled.

"I don't know. I'm sorry. I should've said something."

"Will you stop saying 'Sorry'!" Tom laughed. "It's like Olwena calling me 'Sir' all the time. I feel like some kind of tyrant."

"No, you're not that. Nobody thinks that," said Paul, "You never were like that," he added looking down at the floor remembering things and not realising how tender this sounded. They fell into an awkward silence again.

"That song," Paul said. "What...?"

"Now it's my turn: Sorry, Paul, which song?" Tom smiled.

"Stupid me!" said Paul and ran his fingers through his hair, but not looking at Tom now. He sat down again, his hands on the desk. "The one you sang unaccompanied the other day for Jason's sound check."

" *¿Dónde estás ahora?* What about it? Do you know it?" asked Tom.

"No... I mean, Yes... I..." Paul flushed slightly.

"It's OK. You can be honest," Tom's mood was lifting. "We go back a long way, after all." Tom wasn't sure it was a good idea saying that. But he had to try.

"I... It..." Paul stuttered. He couldn't find the words.

"You know, when I wrote it, I dedicated it to someone very special." Tom had put his hand onto Paul's. He wondered whether he could say any more. Whether he should just try. "Most of the tracks on that album..."

They were interrupted as Rob came into the office. Paul immediately withdrew his hand and stood up, turning.

"There you are," said Rob, "couldn't find you anywhere. Hello Paul. Not like you to be late these past few days."

"Sorry, I've not been sleeping very well," he mumbled.

"Guilty conscience?" Rob joked, winking at Tom. "Frances was right then!" Paul glanced at Tom.

"Funnily enough," said Tom, coming to Paul's rescue, "I've found it a bit stuffy at night too this past couple of days."

Paul left Rob and Tom to talk about whatever it was Rob needed to discuss. As he crossed the stage to get to his workspace in the loft above, Frances was sitting at the table centre stage with Danny and Terrence. She was making little progress with the crossword and was having to look surreptitiously for the answers on the back page to fill them in.

"Paul! Paul!" she said delighted when she spotted him. "OK. Here goes: *Haughty lady but not the Queen.* Six letters, fourth one is *N*."

"Bennet," said Paul. "Elizabeth Bennet. *Pride and Prejudice*," he added, as if that explained it all to Frances.

"How does he get the answers so quickly?" she muttered to herself. Danny seemed to be counting letters on his fingers. Frances hit him across the head with the paper.

Terrence followed Paul upstairs. He wanted to learn something about stage lighting, and when they weren't too busy first thing, Paul would show him some of what he does. He called Terrence his apprentice, which made him feel special. To be like Paul with lighting and stuff would be amazing. Meanwhile, hearing heavy footsteps approaching, the rest of them all turned to look into the auditorium. Julia strode down the nearest aisle and up onto the stage, dropping her bag on the paper Frances had just put down. Frances sighed and pulled the paper free, putting it onto an empty chair instead.

"Julia!" Rob appeared from the wings, stopped and

folded his arms, "I've told you before. Staff and performers should use the stage door, not the doors to the box office."

"What's the difference?" Julia protested, "surely it's all the same when there's no performance on?"

"You sign in and out at the stage door. So, if we have a fire or something, we know who to account for. It's for your own safety."

"Or we could always just leave you to burn," Frances said to no one in particular, though Danny sniggered. Julia glared at them, picked up her bag and strode off to sign in at the stage door. Frances rolled her eyes at Rob. A few minutes later, Julia came back on stage and dropped her bag onto the paper on the other chair.

"Any news from the Brazilian?" she asked.

"Who's that?" Danny asked.

"That queer little dancer," Julia explained.

"I didn't know he was from Brazil?" said Danny, looking round at Frances and Rob for explanation.

"Nor did anyone else," added Frances. "You know, Julia, some people would find your words offensive."

"Where is he?" Julia ignored her. "Someone must know."

Danny shrugged his shoulders. "If you mean José-Luis, he just disappeared. He's not from Brazil, though. Ask the musicians." Julia tutted and rolled her eyes.

"More Brazilians, I expect." She muttered under her breath. Danny was going to correct her, but Frances shook her head, glaring at him.

"Anyway, I need to talk to Tom," Julia sighed, pulling the cuffs of her blouse down so they could be seen under her jacket sleeves. It was important to look professional. Danny checked his shirt sleeves too.

"He's in the office," Rob answered, "I've just left him." As Julia collected her bag again and made to walk off stage once more, he turned to Frances.

"Paul's in, by the way," Rob said.

"Late again!" Frances observed. "Yes, I know. He's just provided the missing answer for the crossword," she added, wiping the dirt from Julia's handbag from the paper a second time. "Think he's found a girlfriend at last?"

Rob shrugged his shoulders and left the stage to go back to his desk in the wings to collect his fire safety notes.

"He's certainly changed over this past week. New jeans that actually fit, new t-shirt, new haircut. Got to be for the benefit of someone he fancies," Frances said as he disappeared into the wings.

Just then, Tom appeared upstage. "Anyone seen Rob? I was with him a minute ago and forgot to ask him something... Ah, Julia, you'll do," he said as he came centre stage not looking at her directly. Julia stopped and turned. She looked at him impatiently, unimpressed to think that she was a substitute for that oaf of a stage manager.

"I need to talk to you about some interviews," she said loudly, cutting him off.

"OK, that's fine. Could I ask a favour, please?" Tom asked.

"Go on," she said without much enthusiasm. Tom pretended he hadn't noticed.

"Well, when you see Rob next, could you ask him for Paul's address, please?" he was hoping she wouldn't ask why. He hadn't worked out a reason that he was happy with yet.

"Paul?" she asked. "That oddball who does the lighting?"

Tom clenched his fists. He tried not to react. Frances tutted.

"Paul Armstrong. Got it?" he answered.

"I'll make a note," she said, turning to go off stage to the office, thinking Tom would follow. "It's not urgent, is it? You just missed Rob, incidentally. I'm sure he'll be back soon."

"OK, that's fine... whenever," Tom pretended to be looking at a score on the table in the middle of the stage as if it didn't matter, "just, you know, when you next see Rob. Paul's address. Yeah...?" Frances craned her neck to look at Tom's face. Why, she wondered, would he want Paul's address after all this time?

Julia looked at Tom suspiciously as she made a note on her *To-do* list in her *Filofax*. She didn't really know anything about the reclusive lighting guy. At least he wasn't like that faggot of a Spaniard, she thought. She looked up from her *Filofax*, tapping her finger on her lips trying to remember what Frances had told her. That was it! Tom and Paul had been to school together. Tom must want to keep in touch. Weird, she thought. And why doesn't he just ask Paul directly?

"Can we go to the office now?" she sighed. Tom followed her back to where he'd just been, smirking knowingly at Frances as he went. She'd rolled the newspaper into a cone and had it on her head like a witch's hat.

"OK, everyone, all performers on stage please," Rob was clapping his hands to attract attention. "Staff, please stay too. We all need a last-minute refresher on safety."

Frances huffed but stood back a little to let the dancers

through in front of her. Using the tannoy in the wings, Rob called any other colleagues down from other parts of the theatre.

"As you know everybody, the show is approaching very quickly now." There was a general murmuring and some excited exchanges. "It's going to be an amazing performance. I just know it is! I've watched you all, and Weymouth doesn't know what's about to hit it." Frances wasn't sure that was what he meant but didn't say anything. "Now there are just one or two things you have to remember. Terrence, can you go to the fire bell, please?"

Terrence had just come back onto the stage after a session with Paul. He turned and went backstage again. On Rob's signal he sounded the bell. There were different variations depending on whether they were really on fire or just practising. It all depended on how many rings and how long each ring lasted. The musicians muttered something to each other; they weren't sure they understood which version related to which problem and plan of action. But they decided to keep quiet about it. Rob also explained how staff would be told about any bomb scare or similar threat. The police were telling all pubs, clubs, and entertainment venues to be extra vigilant with the Conservatives just up the road in Bournemouth. Apparently, if there was a suspicious call, they were all supposed to check obvious places for a possible bomb.

"Sod that!" said Frances. "If some nutter plants a bomb, I'm not looking around till it explodes in my face."

"The Conservatives don't expect us to be policemen now, do they?" Danny asked.

"No," said Terrence, "they're just asking us to do our bit till they can get her!"

Julia turned and glowered at Terrence, crossing her arms across her chest.

"But if we're all looking for bombs, who's going to 'phone them?" Danny added quite reasonably he thought.

"Look! It's just a precaution," Rob said, exasperated.

Eventually, he came round to the stage itself. Tom appeared at this point and tried to keep out of the way, downstage, near the stage left wings. Rob showed everyone the marks which Danny had carefully put on the stage with marker tape. Then, he walked over slightly left of centre stage, taking his time to emphasise the effect of what he was about to say.

"Paul," he shouted up and waited till he could see Paul's face over the safety rail. "Can you come down, please? We need to show them the quick way off the stage." He grinned, while Frances tutted. She'd seen it all before. "So, as you can see, there are no real markings here," and Rob brushed the stage with his foot to emphasise the point. He then decided to jump up and down on the spot. Frances laughed to herself at the thought of what would happen if Paul pulled the lever at that precise moment.

"As you can see," Rob carried on, still jumping occasionally, "the stage is perfectly safe. However," and he took a couple of steps to the side and made sure no one was near where he'd been jumping, "if you could, please, Paul." Next minute, on exactly the spot he'd been standing, the stage opened up. Two hinged flaps dropped into the void. There were some appreciative gasps while people tried to get a glimpse into the hole that had just appeared. "OK, thanks Paul." Just as soon as it appeared, it was gone again. More cautiously this time, Rob walked across the space and made a single, gentle jump.

"So, ladies and gentlemen, yes, the stage is perfectly safe normally. But just don't get on the wrong side of Paul or you might end up down the hatch!" One or two of the musicians laughed. Frances and Terrence stood impassive and waited for it all to be over. Tom, however, was transfixed, suddenly deep in thought. He looked at where the hole had been. Just as Rob said, no sign of it now. Then he turned to look into the auditorium. He was trying to decide if he could hide the chute from where he was standing so anyone coming down the aisle couldn't see.

"You alright there, Tom?" Rob asked as everyone got on with whatever they'd been doing before the safety drill.

"Yeah, fine, just thinking really," Tom replied. "I didn't know you had a trapdoor here. I guess it must be for pantomimes."

"That's it," Rob replied, "I can't remember it being used other than that. Paul'd know though."

Once Terrence had gone back down to the stage, Paul walked round for a word with Olwena.

"Hello, stranger, how nice to see you!" she said, standing up to pour tea and opening a Tupperware container with some scones. Paul swallowed and went and sat down.

"I'm sorry I've not popped in before," said Paul, staring at the scone she'd just put before him.

"Oh, don't worry, I know you've had other things on your mind," she sipped from her cup, smiling over at him.

"The thing is," he began. But she held her hand up to stop him. She stood up and walked out into the corridor, taking ten paces or so in either direction as if she was checking for something.

"We can't be too careful," she said as she sat down and picked up her cup again. "Ew, this is cold." She put her cup down and picked up Paul's. Walking over to the sink, she poured both away. She left the tap running and as she came back, she started the sewing machine. The racket was incredible. "Walls have ears," she winked at Paul as she tapped her index finger against the side of her nose. "Now," she said, coming close so he could hear, and speaking rather loudly over the din, "How's our friend?" Paul gave a broad smile. He wasn't used to such kindness, he thought.

"He sends his love," he said, not entirely untruthfully. José-Luis had mentioned her once or twice, and he spoke of her fondly. "It's all a bit strange, all of this."

Olwena looked serious now. "There are some occasions," she said, looking at her fingers, "when the law needs to be 'interpreted' with real people in mind."

"How do you mean?"

"I'm just saying," she continued, "that there are times when you have to do what's right. There's a lot in this town who wouldn't like men like José-Luis. He's foreign, for a start, and a dancer... a beautiful dancer!" Olwena trailed off, smiling to herself as if she was remembering something special. Paul was concentrating hard to hear her above the commotion of the tap and the sewing machine.

"And, of course," she pursed her lips as if she'd tasted something unpleasant, "there's plenty of folk who don't think men should go with men at all." Paul stiffened slightly, but she pretended she hadn't notice. "Or women with women." She was deep in her own thoughts again now. "Live and let live is all I say," she said, "Love is love. So long as it's genuine, that's all that matters." She moved forward in her chair and put her hand on Paul's arm. "Life brings enough challenges every day, so everyone deserves to love and be loved. No matter what. That's all I meant to say. I don't care what that Julia woman thinks or that lot over in Bournemouth. You deserve to love the one that's right for you," she patted his arm again and smoothed down the cloth on her worktable. As if to emphasise the point: "And that means you too, you know!"

Paul's eyes opened wider as if slightly shocked by something. He wasn't used to looking into people's eyes and understanding what they meant. But Olwena had turned back to her work.

"You know," she said, almost to herself, "I don't think I believe that old saying."

"Which one?" Paul prompted after a few minutes.

"You know the one... about love and loss. How does it go?" she rested her hands on the cloth in front of her and looked out of the window trying to remember the words.

"*Better to have loved and lost...*" Paul began.

"That's it... *than never to have loved at all.*" Olwena looked up straight into his eyes. "I regret losing the one I loved," she explained, "and sometimes I wonder if it'd been better if I'd never met them."

Paul stood up abruptly. As if something she'd said made him feel uncomfortable. "Sorry," he said, "I have to go. Get back to work."

"You off?" she smiled up at him, "Thanks for coming round, love. I'll have a proper brew tomorrow and some rock cakes. Give him my love." And she winked at him. He tried to smile as he turned and left. Walking along the corridor heading back to his workroom and away from the noise of the sewing machine, he could hear music from the stage. He recognised the lead in from the bandoneon.

"Tom! Tom!" Luisa, his female partner for the finale, was trying to wake him out of his daydream. Carlos was waiting for the signal to carry on with the melody.

"Oh, sorry. I was miles away... I don't know what's wrong with me lately," he said coming to.

"You are worried about José-Luis, that is all. We all are. Do you know where he is?" she asked.

"What? José-Luis? No, why? Should I?" Tom was not making sense. Luisa sighed and waited for him to take his position. She nodded to Carlos.

Tom took the hold, and they began to dance. But moments later, Luisa broke away and stepped back.

"Look, do you want to do this later? I do not mind, really." Luisa tried to be patient, but something had got into Tom, she felt, and the dancing wasn't working. She was used to him being a little wooden, but this was too much. It felt like he was just going through the motions.

"No, sorry. Really. It's OK. When you're ready please, Carlos, from the beginning, please."

Tom tried to concentrate as best he could. He'd danced the routine so many times, it should have been easy. He knew now though that it wasn't just the steps that mattered. He knew Luisa could feel it and all the dancers could see it. He tried to slow the thoughts in his head and to focus on how he was moving, how Luisa was moving, and responding to her, the way José-Luis had taught him. The way José-Luis had danced with him. He had to stop thinking like that. It wasn't fair on Luisa, or anyone else for that matter, he thought. He managed to snap out of it for a while, and he felt Luisa relax more. As they both became less tense, she started to dance more naturally and with more sensuality. She touched his shoulder more delicately, she brushed his cheek with her own, as if coaxing a lover. At last, the dance seemed to be working.

When he'd heard the music, Paul had started to look down to see Tom and his partner on stage. He wasn't surprised when she stepped back and spoke to Tom, a little impatiently, Paul felt. They started to dance again. After a shaky start, they seemed to be getting into the mood more. It began to flow. But something was still not quite right. Paul could sense it. When he'd watched Tom and José-Luis, it was deeply moving, and he'd felt something inside that he'd never felt before. Or at least, that he'd never allowed himself to feel before. It had hurt in the pit of his stomach. He'd tried to look away. To escape and be safe again. But he couldn't. He had to watch, mesmerised at something intangible. He'd seen many conventional couples dancing, a woman with a man. He'd admired the skill and wondered how they felt in each other's arms. But Tom and José-Luis together was all very different.

There'd been a deep connection between the two dancers, between the two men. An unexpected emotion shot through with passion and joy and a feeling that, at last, life would be alright. He was alive, and he was free. Paul had felt that too when he and José-Luis had been practising. It felt natural for them to be together. The dance had taken over, and it became a way of showing maybe not that José-Luis and Paul loved each other, but that two men could. Tom was dancing well now with Luisa. But that impression wasn't there. It was technically accomplished, Paul admired it, but it was barren. Paul wanted to be the one to show Tom how the dance was meant to be once more.

Tom and Luisa finished to the expected applause and whistles from the stage crew and from fellow performers. Luisa seemed satisfied for now and joined the other dancers. She took something out of her bag and left the stage to find Rob.

"Mr Rob," she said when she found him at his prompter's desk in the wings, "Could you make sure Mr Paul gets this letter, please?"

"What is it?" Rob asked taking the envelope she'd handed to him.

"Mr Paul will know," she smiled and went back to the dancers and musicians on stage. They needed to make plans for how they might rehearse their other numbers. The ones that didn't involve Tom.

Meanwhile Tom stood for a moment, hands on hips, his eyes down on the stage. He knew it had not felt right for him. He knew there was something missing. It was true, he thought, he was missing José-Luis, and he was very worried about him and what would happen to him next. That wasn't it, though. He understood now what José-Luis had said on the tour bus. They have sex. They enjoy the sex. But they are not lovers. It had seemed harsh at the time. It was true, though. He could see that now.

Pulling himself together, and without thinking, Tom glanced up to the stage loft. He saw someone move back from the guard rail. He knew it was Paul. Paul had been watching them dance. He knew too that Paul had seen that they weren't really dancing together, how he'd struggled with Luisa. He thought back to a few days before when he'd watched José-Luis and Paul dance. How beautiful it had looked, once he'd got over the fact that here was Paul, the shy kid from school, dancing like a man. And with another man at that.

He felt wretched. Like that teenager all those years ago, he was lost. He'd had to give in to the realisation that he was 'one of them', as Peter Tipler used to shout across the schoolyard. He loved men not women. That was unfair, though. He didn't love all men. He loved Paul. He loved him now more than he had back then. Paul had grown up to be everything Tom had expected. It wasn't just that he was even fitter and more handsome than he had been back then. But he was so very kind and resourceful. You knew you could rely on Paul for anything, and he'd be there. In those few exchanges they'd managed, it had felt real. It had felt like they were made for each other. Like they had never been apart. He wanted to hold him now and tell him how much his love had grown. Even over these past few weeks. It was almost unbearable. He was suffocating. The dance hadn't worked with Luisa. But it would work with Paul. That's what he wanted. That would make it right at last.

Deep in thought, Tom walked slowly off the stage to the office. He'd worried about coming back to Weymouth. It made sense, he thought, since he'd been to school here and this was where he'd performed first. He couldn't remember though who had decided they should start in Weymouth. To spend more time rehearsing here in preparation for the rest of the tour. Was it Julia? Or had he manipulated the situation? His family had moved away a long time ago. Gwen said she would come over to Weymouth for the show. But Bob wouldn't. Tom had given up on that idea. Had he known that Paul was here, he wondered? Or perhaps just hoped. José-Luis had asked on the tour bus when they were driving down from Heathrow. Not in so many words, but José-Luis knew him well. It was all too much, and Tom put his head in his hands and wept silently. How could he show Paul that he loved him? That his life up to this point was all about coming back to find him?

"Morning!" Paul said sheepishly, scarcely daring to go beyond the doorway. Tom looked up and tried to smile. Paul didn't notice how troubled he was yet. "There's another letter here from José-Luis. Probably more changes to the choreography." Paul handed Tom the letter and was just turning to go off to his workroom when Tom stopped him.

"Paul, please..." Tom was searching for the right words. Paul turned back, concerned by the tone of Tom's voice and, now that he looked properly, by the way Tom looked.

"Are you alright, Tom? You look as though you're about to throw up."

"Oh fuck, Paul, I've done something really stupid," Tom was too anxious to say any more.

"What's wrong?" Paul asked, taking a step into the office, hesitating to put a reassuring hand on his old friend's shoulder. Tom slumped forward, his head in his hands.

"Look," he began, "You know when you and José-Luis did your Houdini act the other day when the immigration officers arrived?"

"Yes... What about it?" Paul was not particularly concerned about José-Luis right now, but he was more worried for Tom.

"Well, the way I see it, it had to be someone close to the show who tipped them off." Tom looked up into Paul's face to gauge his reaction.

"Go on," Paul said frowning at the thought.

"Well... I've been racking my brains. Who'd stoop so low...?"

"That evil Tory bitch!" Paul interrupted, his arms folded across his chest now and looking like thunder.

"It gets worse," Tom whispered hoarsely. Paul strained forward and waited for him to carry on. When he didn't say anything else, Paul said:

"Hey, buddy... Don't worry. It'll work out, I promise."

Tom couldn't help himself now. His head resting on his arms folded in front of him on the desk, he sobbed noisily. Paul went up close and put his hand on Tom's shoulder as he leant forward to comfort him. It was such a natural gesture that Tom did not react to his touch as he would have done any other time. All he wanted was Paul to take him in his arms and tell him it would be alright. That he would keep him safe. That José-Luis would be alright. Saying it would all work out had touched him so much.

"Come on, Tom, it can't be so bad. Tell me what's happened, and we'll work out what to do about it." Paul stood back to give Tom some room as he raised his head once more.

"You won't hate me?" Tom said without thinking.

"I could never do that," Paul replied immediately, and flushed slightly.

"You won't be angry with me?" Tom was almost pleading as he turned to where Paul was standing.

"Of course not. Whatever it is. I promise." Paul spoke softly and kindly. Tom turned his gaze to the floor.

"Well, without thinking, I asked Julia to get your address from Rob," he slouched into the chair, relieved almost to have told Paul the worst.

"Ah," Paul responded. He wondered why Tom would want his address but decided he didn't need to think about that just now. "OK, look. I took the precaution when José-Luis first moved in to show him all the escape routes. We keep a bag packed with some of the clothes you got for him near the door that he can pick up quickly if needed." Tom relaxed, listening to the assured way Paul seemed to be describing the situation and the detailed precautions he'd already taken to keep José-Luis safe. "I'll pop back at lunchtime and just check things are OK for now and tell him to be extra careful. I sort of knew he couldn't stay with me forever... You know, till you move on from Weymouth, that is. And I've been talking to Lucy and Steve too."

"Who are Lucy and Steve... Oh, yes, I remember, the nympho... But what's it got to do with them? What can they do?"

Paul looked round nervously, he walked over to the door and checked both ways along the corridor. "Let's just say," he half-whispered, "we've got a backup plan."

Tom was so relieved. He knew Paul would sort things out. This was one of the reasons he loved him so much. Really loved him. If the plan meant Paul and José-Luis running off together, that was fine. Tom would be devastated, he knew, but so long as Paul was happy. After all these years. He wondered if he dare stand up and throw himself into Paul's arms. But Paul was gone.

"Such a pretty thing," Olwena said.

"Who?" Paul asked. He'd just taken a swig from his cup, grimaced and put it back into the saucer on the worktable.

"Luisa," Olwena said, smiling to herself. "She was telling me about José-Luis."

Paul remembered what Tom had said when he'd delivered the first letter. It seemed that everyone knew more than Paul would have hoped.

"You know," Olwena continued as if she'd read his thoughts, "they all hate that Julia woman. Carlos has even written a song about her!"

"Really?" Paul looked at her, and she winked at him. "They all think she's got it in for José-Luis because she's jealous."

"Jealous?" Paul looked puzzled.

"Don't ask me," Olwena said sighing, "what do I know about such things?"

Paul looked at her trying to read what she meant. He suspected she actually knew more than she was saying. He was even more worried about José-Luis after what Tom had said. Now Olwena had just told him that the dancers and musicians were all suspicious of Julia. He needed time to think and work out what to do if the worst should happen. He loved José-Luis. He was starting to see that he loved him in a different way to how he felt towards Tom. He was such a good friend and he'd taught him so much. He smiled when he thought about José-Luis or when he got back to the flat and was there with him. With Tom, though, he had butterflies in his stomach just thinking about him. He wished he knew what Tom thought. How Tom felt about him.

"She's such a lovely dancer," Olwena repeated suddenly, interrupting Paul's thoughts. "And she's had such an interesting life! Just listen to me going on."

"She is a lovely dancer, you're right," Paul reassured her.

"She's not happy, though," Olwena said looking straight into his face this time. "She's not happy with your Tom." Immediately Paul felt defensive, though he had to admit, what he'd witnessed earlier was not good. They'd danced better than that before. "It's very important to her, you know, as a dancer, that the dance is right. She's been writing to José-Luis, you know."

"Yes, I know. I sometimes wonder if I'm turning into a postman!" Paul laughed as he said it. If the threat to

José-Luis weren't so serious, all this secret toing and froing would be a farce.

"I think she'll want a word with you about that," Olwena stood now and took her sewing to the ironing board. "Off you go now. I think she'll be up to see you after they've finished this number!"

Paul stood up and made his way to the door.

"And Paul, dear," Olwena said as he was about to leave. He stopped and turned towards her. "Give our friend a kiss from me!" she said, brightly. Paul coloured slightly and, looking towards the floor in thought, he turned once more to leave.

"Oh, and another thing," Olwena had put the iron down. Already in the doorway, Paul turned again to face her, "Now don't you let him get away from you a second time!"

Paul sighed despite himself and this time walked out into the corridor. He suddenly wondered who the 'him' was that Olwena had just mentioned. As he made his way to his side of the stage loft, sure enough, he saw Luisa coming from the stairs. He watched as she leant cautiously over the guard rail before pulling her head back quickly. She wasn't used to heights. Seeing Paul, she smiled at him.

"Hello Mr Paul. I am coming to see you, please," she said. "I am talking to José-Luis," she added.

"You best come through to my workspace," Paul said, showing her through the door before him and bowing his head slightly.

Gradually, performers and stage crew left for the evening. There was not much more they could do tonight. Tom had gone back to the hotel and got something to eat. But he was restless. He walked down to the seawall and looked out over the sea. One or two men came past, and Tom was aware of them eyeing him up. He didn't turn and look, though. Tom knew he didn't want any casual encounters. Sex with José-Luis was wonderful, but it was a diversion. It was true. They were friends not lovers. Tom had to admit that he'd used José-Luis. However much he liked him and cared for him. Tom knew that he had sex with José-Luis for his own pleasure. It wasn't really for José-Luis at all. As the evening wore on, it grew cold. There was rain coming, Tom remembered from when he was a child and the air had suddenly turned chilly. He turned to go back to the hotel. As he passed the theatre, he decided he'd go in and sit there for a while. See if he could clear his head.

There was no one else there. He turned the light on in the office and sat for ten minutes or so. He was restless, though. Leaving the office and walking across the stage, he suddenly found himself climbing the stairs up to where Paul had his workspace. He stood in the doorway for a moment and wondered if he dared go in. Walking as quietly as he could, he took a few steps into the small room. There was a vague smell of aftershave, which he breathed in and closed his eyes. *Masculin II* – he remembered at last. Tears rolled down his cheeks as he realised that Paul had carried on buying it. And it was Tom who'd picked it out for him. He stood in silence for a moment, opened his eyes again and scanned the room. The neat boxes of tools and lighting bits and pieces. A small pile of cheap exercise books. Tom took one down and opened it. Paul's neat writing. Everything in complete sentences. Tidy, fastidious almost.

When he replaced the exercise book, something caught his eye. There was a white t-shirt hanging from a peg in the corner. Paul was now completely in black, of course, as the performance approached, he thought. And before he knew it, he'd taken the t-shirt from the peg. He hesitated, checking behind that there was no one there, straining to hear any movement in the theatre. Reassured, he turned back into the room. His heart was beating faster now. He took the t-shirt in both hands and raised it to his face. He closed his eyes and smelt Paul. Quietly, he lay his cheek against the t-shirt. He wished Paul were here now. He wished he could tell him how much he loved him. How he'd come back to Weymouth hoping to find him again and explain.

By the time Tom had made it downstairs again, it was very late. He didn't want to go back to his lonely room in the hotel. He sat in the office wondering if there was anything productive he could do. Check musical arrangements, perhaps? Go through the show in his mind and critique for himself each bit. There didn't seem to be anything. He was lost in his thoughts when he heard footsteps coming towards him.

"Oh, it's you," Rob said, brushing some rain from his jacket, "I saw there was a light on and thought I'd come in and check."

"Yes, of course, sorry," Tom stood up, "I've just been finishing off." He looked at his watch. "God, is it that time? I should be getting back."

"You seem preoccupied," Rob said, "is there something you need to talk about?"

"No, it's fine. Thanks." Tom tried to smile. "I always get nervous in the run up to a show."

"There's more to it than that, if you don't mind me saying?" Rob was leaning against the doorframe, his arms folded across his chest.

"I'm just tired," Tom offered, "Really." Then, sighing and looking down at the table, he went on, "It wasn't a good idea to spend this long here... in Weymouth."

"I get the impression you had to come, though." Rob said. Tom looked up at him, taken aback with what seemed like a personal remark.

"How do you mean?" Tom asked.

"It's just there's been a look about you. Maybe more so since José-Luis has had to go into hiding. You seem exhausted. Not just physically tired – you know, everyone's been working really hard. But strangely, emotionally tired too." Rob was still resting against the door, wondering if he should not have said anything.

"Oh, God. I don't know." Tom looked up at the ceiling and folded his arms behind his head. "I was in love here once. As a kid. I don't know whether I expected to find the person here or not."

Rob didn't say anything for a while. He was trying to think of the right words. "I think you have found them again," he began.

"Rob! Rob, where are you?" It was a woman's voice this

time coming down the corridor to the office, a mixture of excitement and panic.

"In here, love," shouted Rob. His wife, Gemma, appeared, a little out of breath. "You alright?" he asked, rubbing her shoulders.

"There's something big happening," she said, "over by the flats at the seafront. There's police cars and then what looks like a big posh limo. It seems to be some kind of raid or something. With top brass over from Bournemouth. There's cameras and all sorts."

"Shit!" said Tom looking scared. "José-Luis!" he added as he ran to the stage door. Outside it had started to rain heavily now. He picked up a towel near the stage doorman's window which he tried to cover his head with and ran out into the wet.

"Can we just lie quietly tonight?" Paul said, putting his arm round José-Luis.

"What's wrong? Don't you like having sex with me?" José-Luis asked.

"No... Yes... I mean, I love it. I've loved everything about it. I love all the different things we've done. It's just I'm a bit on edge right now. I don't really know why." He turned to José-Luis and kissed him, pulling him closer. "I'm so glad you're here, though. I'd go mad on my own."

"You know," José-Luis began, "since you love him so much..."

"Please." Paul put a finger on José-Luis's lips. "Please. Let's not talk about that now. Please."

José-Luis took Paul's hand and kissed it gently. He was worried that he'd not been able to watch Paul and Tom together in the theatre. Force them to be with one another and talk clearly about how each felt for the other. Time was running out. He knew. He wished he could do something before Paul slipped back into his life as a recluse.

"Don't be afraid," he whispered. "You deserve to be happy. You deserve to love and you are certainly loved." He sat up and moved Paul's arm from where it lay. Instead, as he lay back down, he put his own arm behind Paul's neck and around his shoulder, pulling him tight towards him. He stroked his hair gently, kissing his forehead every now and then. They could hear the rain outside getting louder and more persistent.

"It's OK, *pollito*," whispered José-Luis, "You're safe with me."

They must have dozed off. The next thing Paul knew, they were shocked awake by loud banging on the door.

"Open up. Police."

The banging continued. José-Luis jumped out of bed and made for the kitchen and the fire escape, pausing only to scoop up his clothes from their usual neat pile and the bag they'd packed for emergencies. Paul was out of bed too, stumbling as he tried to wrestle with some of his own clothes. He managed a t-shirt and a pair of briefs. It would have to do, he thought.

"I'm coming. I'm coming." He shouted back to the door as he heard the first thud as if someone was trying to break in. Finally, checking that the fire escape door was closed, and pulling the kitchen door to behind him, Paul switched on the light and went to open the door. Pushing him aside, four or five uniformed officers – immigration officers, not police, he noticed – spilled into the flat. They seemed to be everywhere as Paul followed them back into his lounge.

"What do you want? What are you looking for?" he stammered. A woman's voice behind him made him jump. As he turned round and tried to cover his briefs with a cushion from the armchair, he saw a short, stern looking woman, her hair swept back ferociously into an uncompromising bun on the back of her head. He thought he recognised her but wasn't quite sure.

"Can I help you?" Paul asked.

"We're looking for your foreign friend," the Home Secretary announced. A camera man was following her, though was not filming at that point.

"Sorry, I don't..." Paul began.

"Look," the Home Secretary stared straight at him, clearly angry at something, her square jaw twitching slightly as she clenched her teeth. "Don't try to be clever. We know he's in here."

"Ma'am," one of the officers, who'd been searching the bedroom, came back into the lounge holding a pair of boxers. The Home Secretary clicked her fingers and pointed at the boxers. The officer duly handed them to her. She carefully put a finger under the waistband, trying hard to have as little contact with the boxers as possible. She turned them to examine them a little and pulled her head back with distaste at some of the stains she saw. She held them up and looked at Paul triumphantly. The cameraman started to film at this point.

"Well?" she asked, "What's this? Whose are these?"

Paul went to say something, but instead his mouth just opened and closed.

"They're not yours," she continued, sensing she was on to something given how nervous Paul looked, "given your underwear." She nodded towards the cushion, making Paul feel even more uncomfortable.

"I... They're..." Paul swallowed. His mouth was dry. The woman looked at him, expecting an answer.

Just then, the kitchen door was pushed open and the officer who'd gone to check the bathroom pushed someone into the room. Paul didn't dare look in case it was José-Luis.

"Found this one coming in from the fire escape, Ma'am," the officer said.

The Home Secretary turned and looked at the man, her head to one side, waiting for an explanation. He was bare chested and had a rather cheap-looking towel round his shoulders. He placed a milk bottle on the table, raindrops running down the sides and onto the plastic tablecloth, and took the towel to carry on drying his hair. He stopped again, though, and looked at what the woman was dangling at arm's length in front of her.

"They're mine, thanks," Tom said, snatching the boxers from the Home Secretary's finger. Paul was trying hard to remember to breath.

"What?" the Home Secretary was beginning to sound even angrier.

"He was just coming in from the fire escape as I came out of the bathroom," the officer said.

"Yeah," Tom smiled, "we keep the milk out there to keep it fresh."

Paul was trying to take all of this in. He watched Tom, admiring how calm he was.

"Sorry," said Tom, "I'm Tom Bright. I'm here for a show in a couple of days." He held out his free hand to the woman, but she refused to shake it.

"Do you often leave your boxers in other people's flats, then?" she managed.

"No," Tom laughed briefly, "No. Paul's an old school friend." He went to slap Paul on the shoulder, but automatically, Paul had moved out of the way. No one seemed to notice. "Isn't that right, Paul?"

"Err, yes," Paul answered at last, "Jordan Hill Comp... Just down the road."

The Home Secretary was looking from one to the other. She was trying to decide whether this was plausible or not. She looked suspiciously into the bedroom where there was clearly only one double bed, ruffled with duvet and pillows all over the place. She returned to look with obvious distaste on her face at the two men.

"Paul lets me stay here..." Tom explained, "when it gets a bit loud outside the hotel. You know," he laughed again, "all those screaming fans."

The Home Secretary turned smartly on her heels, knocking into the cameraman, who quickly recovered and turned off the camera. Silently, the officers gave up their search and began to leave the flat, dropping unceremoniously anything they might have picked up as they'd effectively ransacked the place. The one who'd pushed Tom in from the kitchen strode past once more, banging his helmet against the glass lampshade which shattered and fell to the floor. The naked bulb shone directly onto Tom's head, lighting up his face, and as he moved to shake bits of glass from his shoulders and out of his hair, caught the water droplets on his torso.

"Fuck me!" said Paul, relieved that the flat was empty, and José-Luis seemed to have escaped once more. Tom looked at him and they both burst out laughing. Mainly with relief.

5

"I told you, Julia. What on earth did you think you were doing?" Tom was furious and pronouncing words very carefully, trying not to lose his temper. "In case I didn't make it crystal clear last time, your job is to look after my public image. Not to police who's around, what they are…" Julia was looking extremely uncomfortable, but she remained tight-lipped. "… or, in fact, who they sleep with!"

There was a slight hint of distaste on Julia's face now. Frances had heard all of this and tried to busy herself unobtrusively with the legs at the side of the stage and whatever else was close at hand. Danny was sweeping the stage slowly as he always did.

"As I suggested on the way to London, if you don't like these people, you really need to move on, Julia," Tom was starting to realise that there was more going on here. "I can't trust you anymore." There, Tom felt, I've said it now. Being honest made him feel good about himself.

"I'm trying to look after your best interests!" she retorted.

"Meaning?" Tom was glowering at her now. She felt uncomfortable with a side of Tom she'd not seen before.

"The press would have a field day if they learned you'd been harbouring some dodgy foreigner," she shouted. She didn't want to think that maybe that wasn't the real reason.

"It was you, wasn't it?" Tom looked threatening. Being honest seemed to have made things clearer for him now. Julia took a step back.

"You told immigration. And then..." It was as if things were becoming clearer for Tom. Julia walked around the table. It made her feel safer to put distance and an obstacle between herself and Tom.

"And then... You get that witch over from Bournemouth for some publicity at Paul's."

"I beg your pardon? That was the Home Secretary." Julia sounded affronted.

"And that makes it right? That makes sneaking around and snitching acceptable?" Tom was shaking his head in disbelief. Suddenly, he looked up at her: "So, you did do it! You disgust me."

"Someone had to do something positive. To be responsible." Julia huffed.

"You're unbelievable," Tom had gone from anger to disbelief. He felt he needed to make a stand. For other men like him. "How could you stoop so low? Be that despicable?"

"Despicable? Me?" Julia looked genuinely affronted. "What about your disgusting little fairy friend?" She'd taken a newspaper from her bag and now slammed it on the table between them, trying to look authoritative and triumphant. "Look! Look here!" She pointed at the headline. *"The Gay Curse,"* she read, picking the newspaper up again. "You call me despicable? And all the time, that filthy little queer's been spreading his germs all over the place!" She tossed the newspaper back on the table.

"Don't tell me," Tom smirked, "You think these guys brought it on themselves." Tom looked her in the eye. "You do, don't you?"

"Well, it's not..." Julia had folded her arms and was trying to avoid eye contact.

"You really are something," Tom began. "People are dying. Wasting away in their beds, and no one knows how to help them. Not many people *want* to help them even. And *you* think they deserve it." Julia looked up at him defiantly. This was not the Tom she'd grown accustomed to: conciliatory, leaning towards more softly spoken, malleable. Something or someone had clearly annoyed him. A raw nerve had been touched, and he was taking it out on her. It never occurred to her that she might have brought his anger upon herself.

"I don't believe this," Tom went on. "And I thought you were supposed to be educated?" Tom was struggling to find the right words now. "Do you actually read the newspapers or just stop at the headlines and the gawdy photos? Do you actually *know* what's going on during this crisis?" Tom had picked the paper up and was leafing through it. He was looking to find one of those depressing interviews with Larry Speakes, feigning ignorance while making it perfectly clear that the Reagan administration had no intention of doing anything to tackle the pandemic. Tucked away towards the sports pages was a short article titled: *Speakes Plays Dumb Again: Reagan Aid Ignoring AIDS.* Tom flicked the newspaper to invert it along the centre crease and pointed out the short piece to Julia. "Look!" he said, "it would be funny if it weren't so outrageous." Julia glanced at the headline but refused to comment. "Do you know what I think? I think you're all heartless hypocrites. I hope you and all of your right-wing cronies rot in Hell," said Tom, barely hiding his contempt.

Julia leant forward as if she wanted to say something, but Tom held up his hand.

"I don't want to hear it, Julia. You're done as far as the music business is concerned. I'll make sure of it. And if you know what's good for you, you won't show your face around here again. You'll be hearing from Mannie, and Leonard will send you your P45 and make good your money." Tom folded the paper again and tossed it casually across the table towards her, picking up the pen that someone had left and scribbled angrily across the *Gay Curse* headline. "And if I hear one squeak about me and homos, queers, degenerates, anything, I'll sue you for every right-wing padded shoulder, every chrome-plated button, and every Tory penny you and your whole family have got."

She looked shocked.

"Oh, and just so you know, Mannie and Leonard are Jews. I hope that's alright with you people. I'll be asking Mannie to look at breach of confidentiality too..."

She turned on her heels and strode across the stage towards the wings and the stage door, muttering "Fucking fairy!" under her breath,

"...and defamation," Tom shouted at her back.

Quietly pulling Danny with her, Frances backed off stage. Above them, Paul's face looked down. He was leaning back slightly. In black now for the shows, he was even more difficult to spot in the shadows. He felt safer that way. But he was pensive. It was some minutes before he turned round and went back into his workroom. Tom was pacing round the table. He wanted to go and pull Julia back so he could dress her down some more. He just couldn't get over how a person would snitch on someone they knew like that. He picked the newspaper up again and skimmed the article. 'As if people like us haven't got enough to deal with,' he thought. 'Where will all of this end?' He flung the newspaper back on the table and turned. He looked up towards Paul's workspace in the stage loft. 'Please,' he said to himself if no one else, 'I need you more than ever. We need to be strong together.' He sat at the table, staring at the paper. 'Oh God. I've not felt this alone since the last day at school. I need you, Paul.'

It was late when Tom had got back to his hotel room after running over to Paul's place in the driving rain. He'd half hoped that he could've stayed. He even thought that Paul would have let him stay. Would have wanted him to stay, even. But he was shocked at what he'd just witnessed. Maybe José-Luis was right after all. It was easier for people like him. A celebrity who was and wasn't like everyone else. Allowed to do and be who he was. Somewhere above him he could hear Bowie on a radio... *If you say run, I'll run with you...* He was afraid now for José-Luis, who must be cold and frightened somewhere all on his own. It must seem like Colombia all over again. And this was supposed to be a liberal, Western democracy. And yet he was having to hide. He didn't know what would happen now. Somehow, though, he knew that he wasn't alone with this problem anymore. If nothing else, perhaps he and Paul could be there for José-Luis.

"Thank God you had everything set up!" he'd said to Paul when things out in the stairwell and hall had quietened down, and they were sure the Home Secretary and her entourage had left without José-Luis.

"He'll be alright for now," Paul had reassured him. "We'll have to think about what to do next." And suddenly Tom felt tired.

"I'd best go back," he'd said, but regretted it as soon as he had.

"You'll catch your death like that," Paul had replied. He'd disappeared into the bedroom and come back with a thick sweater and a t-shirt. He'd dried Tom's hair, made him some tea, and watched him dress. Tom tried not to spend too much time fondling the clothes Paul had offered him. He was glad, though, that he wouldn't have to go back cold and wet. He began to warm up a bit and even acknowledged the strange notion that Paul's clothes wrapped around him and keeping him warm and dry was a good omen. Paul was there for him, he concluded. And comforted by that thought, Tom had left.

Back in his room, Tom couldn't sleep. The rain had stopped outside, and there was a full moon breaking through the clouds now and then. On such occasions, a cold, silvery light would soak the room in an eerie brightness. Tom lay on the bed, Paul's sweater round him still. The scent of *Masculin II* coming off the t-shirt. He found it soothing and pulled the sweater closer around him. He wasn't sure what he felt at that precise moment. He just knew that he'd never felt so desperate in his whole life before. José-Luis's safety was paramount, that much was clear. But he was afraid that he was missing something with Paul, with how to show him how much he loved him. He didn't want to leave Weymouth without him or lose him this time. Yet he couldn't think of the right words to say.

Tom still was in denial about why he'd come back to Weymouth. True, this is where it all began. This is where he was born and where he'd gone to school. And this is where he'd first sung in public. *The Rocky Horror Show* of all things. But surely there were lots of people who'd first sung at school but who didn't need to rush back as if it were something significant in their careers. This is where he'd met Paul. He knew that, but it still felt too raw to admit it. It didn't matter now why he'd felt it was a good idea to come back. He was here. If he was honest with himself, he was lonely and afraid. AIDS was ravaging Los Angeles, and it had spread everywhere. Already, so many of the people he knew were dying. He'd been so scared of outing himself that he'd been very careful about who he met and who he slept with, fortunately. Until José-Luis had come along, that is. He'd managed to get one of the early HIV tests before he and José-Luis had started a physical relationship. And he knew they'd both been completely faithful since then. Well, until now perhaps. Tom thought about how he felt if José-Luis and Paul had been sleeping together. He decided he really hoped they had. Just so that Paul would know what it was like to be intimate with a man. He hoped that Paul had felt whole because of it.

With Tom and José-Luis, it wasn't just a physical attraction, though. For Tom, he'd thought there was more to it at first. He was aware that José-Luis had fled Colombia, although they didn't talk much about it. He felt relaxed in his company. So much so that sometimes they didn't even feel the need to talk. He liked having him around and missed him when they couldn't share a bed. He loved the sex and the physical side to their relationship, true. Monogamy was never talked about as such, but for Tom, that was all he'd ever wanted. But right from the start, there was something missing he now realised. He almost felt he could do without the sex. It was the closeness he valued. It was being with him, knowing he cared about him, laughing at his jokes. He genuinely thought he loved him. That this is what love was about. Sex is wonderful, but it's only a part of it. Even before all of this had happened, he knew this even though he'd not wanted to admit it.

When José-Luis had dropped the bombshell and told him that they were not lovers, Tom had been hurt. Now, though, he realised what José-Luis meant. He'd convinced himself that he'd have happily spent the rest of his life with José-Luis, and he'd have been faithful and caring. All of those things that loving couples do. But now it was becoming clearer to Tom that he really wanted to be a loving couple with Paul. That's all he'd ever wanted. After all, that's why he'd come back to Weymouth. Just on the off chance that Paul would still be there. And if not, that Mrs Armstrong would be here, and he could ask after him. He felt ashamed of himself that he'd used José-Luis in a way, like an insurance policy if his quest to find his first love had ended in failure.

When they were kids, he'd wanted Paul so badly. To feel his body, to make love and give each other pleasure like only they could. He didn't know this for certain, but he felt intuitively that they would be able to. It was only since he'd come back to Weymouth, though, that he'd realised there was so much more to their friendship. Even without sex, he'd have walked across hot coals just to be with Paul. Though they never touched, Tom felt safe with him. It was almost as if there didn't need to be anything physical between them. This was love, surely? This was real love.

He rolled over towards the window, pulling Paul's sweater tight around him. In the light of the moon, he could see a pair of José-Luis's boxers under a chair in the corner. He smiled to himself – 'His underpants get everywhere!' he laughed. He picked them up and put them in with his laundry in the bag in the bathroom. He hoped it wouldn't be long before he could give them back to his dear Colombian friend in person. He stopped. He suddenly realised that he loved José-Luis too, but in a different way. José-Luis was one of his best friends, he now understood. He wanted him to be happy. He wanted him to escape to somewhere nice and warm – he'd hated British weather, he said – and find another Donatello. A few days ago, he'd just wanted him there, though admittedly it was maybe for sex. It was different now. He wanted for him what he'd want for himself. Whatever that might be.

"Hey, look at this!" Rob hurried onto the stage rattling a newspaper. He shook it out so he could read the article buried on the third page. "*Miss Dulwich*... that's the lovely Julia, isn't it...? Anyway. *Miss Dulwich has announced her intention to move into politics. Tom Bright, the popular musician currently on tour in the UK, said he fully supported this move and wished her good luck for the future."*

"That's not how it happened," said Frances.

"What do you mean?" Rob and Danny said at the same time.

"You were there, Danny. Tom had a real go at her!"

"Oh yeah, I remember now," Danny realised as the penny dropped.

"So, what happened, Frances?" Rob asked. He was slightly deflated that no one was impressed with what he'd found in the paper. Frances liked to be in on all the gossip. She rubbed her hands down her trousers in preparation to tell everyone what had gone on.

"Well, after all that business here where they tried to arrest José-Luis and then what happened at poor old Paul's flat."

"What was all that about?" Rob asked, confused. "What's that got to do with it?"

"What? Paul's flat?" Frances couldn't believe that Rob hadn't heard.

"Either! Both! Whichever. Come on, Frances, what's all this about? And what's it got to do with the lovely Julia?" Rob had folded the paper and dropped it on the table. There was a picture of the 2001 Space Odyssey monolith on the front with the *"Don't Die of Ignorance"* line underneath.

"So, Julia came in as normal a couple of days after the Home Secretary and her merry men had turned up at Paul's flat looking for José-Luis..."

Suddenly, something dawned on Rob.

"Oh my God!" Rob said, his mouth open in disbelief, "So, that was what was going on?" Now it was Frances's turn to want to know more.

"I'd come in here to see why the light was still on in the office and bumped into Tom," Rob went on. "When Gemma rushed in and told us about the police cars and things, Tom went white. He just ran off. He must've been going to Paul's."

"Apparently, Julia had put them onto him," Frances added. "Got that new Home Secretary over from Bournemouth, with TV crew and all. You know: to make a big show of it."

"A lighting engineer? What would he have to do with anything?" A look of horror spread across Rob's face, and he blanched this time. "Oh fuck, I've just remembered something else, too," he said, sitting heavily on one of the seats round the table.

Frances looked at him, surprised there might be something more she didn't know. "What?"

"Well, Tom told Julia to ask me for Paul's address. I don't know why he wanted it..."

Frances widened her eyes. She was starting to get the bigger picture, she felt.

"Anyway. So, Julia comes in and before she's had a chance to smooth her pearls and buff up her shoulder pads in that day's power suit," she began, "She was looking a bit smug if you ask me. Self-satisfied."

She stopped when she spotted Paul out of the corner of her eye, moving cables around. In his backstage black outfit, she wouldn't have noticed him if his face hadn't turned towards them at that very moment. She waited till he had disappeared into the wings on the far side of the stage. Frances leaned forward conspiratorially and lowered her voice.

"Tom just let her have it. She went on about AIDS and filthy gays and all that crap. You know all the sort of rubbish that Thatcher and her dimwits peddle."

"The bitch!" offered Danny. Frances and Rob exchanged a knowing glance. They liked the new Danny.

"So, anyway," Frances continued, "Tom sacked her!"

"No!?" said Rob, then: "Serves her right. The stuck-up, sanctimonious bitch! You're right there, Danny," Rob was getting angry now too.

"I know," Frances said with a smile, "she really is a piece of work. She virtually admitted she'd snitched on José-Luis and sent the pigs to Paul's flat."

"What a shit!" Danny banged the table with his fist. Both Frances and Rob looked at him, taken aback by his outburst.

"OK, OK! Calm down, tiger," Frances began.

"No," Danny said, "it really pisses me off. I wasn't into fairies..." Frances rolled her eyes to Rob.

"You've said that..." Frances started.

"No, I mean, I'm still not... You know what I mean." Danny seemed to want to make a point. "Anyway, before all these musicians and dancers turned up. But some of them are really decent blokes. We've had a few pints together. Never any funny business, just a good laugh!"

"Well," Rob grinned, "there speaks the voice of the people! Good for you, Danny!"

"Good riddance, anyway," said Frances, "she was something else, that woman."

"Who? Thatcher or the lovely Julia?" Rob had picked up the paper and was holding it up. "Look at this. Thatcher's picture right next to the AIDS advert! Maybe *'Don't Die of Ignorance'* refers to her?"

A few days later, when the dust had settled a bit, Rob came looking for Tom on stage. Frances, Danny and Terrence were sitting at the table centre stage as usual. Tom was sitting there too, distractedly going over the music to various numbers though with no real enthusiasm.

"'Tis better to have loved and lost...," Francis read, raising her voice as she always did when she was doing the crossword. *"But not very sporting*. Eight letters. Fourth letter *'N'*, fifth letter *'Y'*."

Tom was sitting on the other side of the table, so Rob decided he'd wait for a few minutes.

"Anyone," said Danny, "That's got an *'N'* followed by a *'Y'*."

Frances looked at him admiringly. "Close. But it's only got six letters."

"...than never to have loved at all," Tom said absent-mindedly almost to himself.

Frances and Rob looked over to him and then at each other. Rob was worried that Tom was emotionally on the edge.

"Tennyson," Paul's voice appeared from somewhere, "Alfred Lord. Two *'N'*s."

"Thanks, Mr Armstrong," Frances shouted back as she wrote in the letters. "He's bound to be right," she added to no one in particular; she'd stopped checking on the back page even. "Amazing what an honest, working-class education can do for you," she muttered to herself. Sucking the end of the pen, she looked up: "Oh, I get it... '*sporting*' as in '*tennis*'. And it's a Tennyson quotation."

"He's wrong though," they heard Paul add. Frances looked up from the paper in surprise, and Rob glanced towards the stage loft and Paul's workspace.

"Now, there's a turn up," said Frances to Rob, "our elusive lighting wizard adding commentary now. 1986 really is a year of change!"

She glanced sideways at Rob. He was staring across the table. Following his gaze, they both watched Tom with his hand over his mouth and, apparently, trying to hold back tears.

"Come on," said Frances, slapping Danny on the back with the magazine, "we've got work to do out front." She and Rob stood up and marshalled the others off the stage. They'd both thought it wise to leave Tom to his thoughts for five minutes or so.

"Erm, Tom," Rob said when he came back on stage a little later, "Can I have a word? In the office maybe?" Tom followed him in silence, glad for some kind of distraction.

"This letter arrived at the box office for you," he said, handing Tom an A5-sized envelope with an airmail sticker on the front. It felt quite bulky, as if there were a card or something like that enclosed with the letter. Tom didn't recognise the writing. It looked foreign, though, not how they'd been taught at school. And judging by the stamp and some writing on the back, he could see it had come from Spain. After a lot of squinting, he decided it was from Dana-Beatriz, the dancer José-Luis had met by chance in the hotel. He opened it and sure enough, there was a short covering note in what he assumed to be Dana-Beatriz's rounded, florid lettering.

"Mr Tom Bright, it was so nice to meet you all. I know that your show will be a fantastic success. You are a lovely dancer too! Please, Mr Tom, can you give this letter to José-Luis. It is very important for him to read it. He must see it as soon as possible. Thank you. God bless you all. *Todos Mis Abrazos.* Dana-Beatriz de la Anunciación." He shook the A5-envelope over the desk and a letter dropped out with *"Señor José-Luis Esperanza"* on it in different writing this time.

Tom sighed and ran his fingers over the envelope.

"Everything alright, Tom?" Rob was still standing half-way to the door.

"Yes... yes..." Tom said, only now realising he was still there. "Well, I hope so, anyway. I think I need to go and talk to Paul."

"He's been a bit quiet lately," Rob said, "I mean, even more so than normal. What's going on?"

"Oh, it's all that silly nonsense with the police and everything, and that old witch flying round on her broomstick," Tom said, not really thinking.

"The lovely Miss Dulwich, you mean?" Rob laughed. "Yeah. Good riddance. Even Danny thinks she's a shit. Do you know, I reckon she'd sell her own grandmother if it got her five minutes with Margaret Thatcher."

Tom laughed in spite of himself. "I could well believe it," he said, "some people, though, are absolutely incredible. No compassion. Nothing." He picked up the letter from Dana-Beatriz and the one for José-Luis and followed Rob out of the office. He could do without all of this, he thought, with a show to put on.

Back at his prompt desk in the wings, Rob began to think. Finally getting rid of Julia, and José-Luis having to go into hiding somewhere seemed to have taken their toll on Tom's mood. As stage manager, Rob felt responsible to make sure the show went on. There was more to it than that, though. He'd grown genuinely fond of Tom and the dancers and the musicians. It was true that they'd been here longer than troupes were normally. But they were just nice people. José-Luis himself was a breath of fresh air and a lot of fun. And as far as Rob was concerned, he could sleep with whoever he liked. *Live and Let Live*, that was Rob's motto. They were all blokes at the end of the day. And there'd never been any 'funny business', as Danny had pointed out.

Everyone was talented, of course. They wouldn't be putting on a professional show otherwise. But again, this was different. They'd never seen anything like these dances or heard this type of music in Weymouth before. The most exotic thing they'd ever had was a Christmas Show from *The Black and White Minstrels*. It made Rob cringe just to think about it. There was something about Tom, though, and the way he sang. Even Gemma thought so when she'd popped in one lunchtime to bring Rob something to eat. "Mournful," she'd said, "but really beautiful. Makes a change from the stuff in the charts right now."

What about Paul? He'd come with glowing references from Bournemouth which Rob had initially found a bit suspicious. When he'd 'phoned his opposite number over there, though, most of the call had been spent with the

Bournemouth lot wondering how they could possibly find anyone as good as Paul. Rob soon came to realise that whatever was needed, Paul would deliver. Before being asked sometimes. He was so good that it was easy just to forget he was there. Well, until even the performers would come and tell Rob how unique that strange lighting guy was. Everyone sang his praises. So, the fact that he was a little shy and kept himself to himself was neither here nor there. Frances had found out that Tom and Paul had gone to school together. And Rob had assumed that the frosty atmosphere was probably due to some teenage fight over a girl. Now, though, he just didn't know.

If they were benders, 'Good luck to 'em!' he thought. It wasn't the easiest time to be gay. Even Gemma had said: "Aah, isn't that sweet!" when he'd talked to her about it. He wasn't sure whether he could or even should mention it to Frances. It was none of his business, after all. He was beginning to get anxious though. If they did like each other that much, they better get their act together pretty soon. All this moping around wasn't helping. And if they weren't careful, Tom would have buggered off again. Rob couldn't help smiling to himself that he'd thought "bugger". Then it dawned on him just how hard it must be if virtually everything could be a joke against who you are. Rob just hoped both Paul and Tom could be happy.

"I'm sorry," Tom said rather formally. Paul looked up from some wiring he was doing, slightly startled. The room was almost completely dark except for the anglepoise which had lit Paul's face, hands and the cables he was working on. They'd reverted to their usual stand-off since the incident at Paul's flat, though Tom had hoped that would be a new beginning.

"Look, I'm sorry, I really didn't want to disturb you in your work," Tom spoke slowly and as if talking to a stranger who commanded his respect, not someone whose salary he was effectively paying. Paul stood up, wiped his hands on his shirt, and swivelled the angle-poise lamp head up and round to provide some more general light.

"What can I do for you?" he asked and reaching for his exercise book, "Is there something about the lighting that needs changing?"

"No. Listen, Paul, this is nothing to do with lighting. It's a letter. From Spain. It's for José-Luis."

Tom handed the letter to Paul, who took it automatically and looked at the name on the front.

"From Dana-Beatriz, I expect."

"No. No, it's not," said Tom.

Paul looked up at Tom, expecting some kind of explanation.

"She sent a covering note, and her writing is different," he said.

Tom felt uneasy up here. He couldn't quite tell why. Though last time he'd been on his own, he couldn't help looking around at the tidy room, mainly to avoid Paul's gaze. Everything seemingly in its place. He could smell the scent that had been haunting him since they'd first arrived even stronger than ever. Taken aback slightly, he smiled to himself. His heart was beating a little faster too.

He felt it was probably a mistake to be so close in such a confined space, but at the same time, that's what he'd wanted for so long. And for them to be alone.

He started looking at the shelves distractedly, not really seeing any of the neatly stored items. Next to the collection of Paul's signature cheap exercise books, he came across a pile of programmes and took a few off, just to fill the awkward silence really, and an excuse not to leave quite yet.

"These shows from here?" Tom asked casually.

"Mostly," Paul said.

"Did you light all of them?" Tom was trying to keep a conversation going.

"Yes," Paul said.

Suddenly, Tom dropped the programmes to the floor. He'd not been expecting it. Both he and Paul bent down to pick them up. More by luck than judgement, they managed to avoid cracking their heads together. Paul couldn't avoid the familiar smell of Tom. Different, older, but close enough to what he remembered from that heady summer in Bramdean.

"Oh God, I'm sorry. I'm so clumsy. I think it's nerves..." Tom said, trying to shuffle the programmes into some kind of order.

The last programme Tom handed back to Paul to put back on the shelf in its neat little pile was from *The Rocky Horror Show*, their school production. Tom held his breath, desperately concentrating on the simple movement and hoping that his hand wasn't trembling too noticeably. It may have been the light, but Tom was sure Paul had blushed slightly when he'd taken this last programme from his hand. He tried to work out what was going through Paul's mind, though Paul was looking away, down at the programmes he was sorting together before returning to the shelf. Paul looked up and saw Tom looking intently at him. He smiled briefly then averted his gaze once more.

"Here," said Paul, standing up again and stepping aside. "Have a seat." He pulled his own chair from the desk and offered it to Tom. It was still warm. Tom tried not to betray any of his feelings as he sat on the same spot where only a few moments previously the man he'd lost and hoped to find again had been sitting. Meanwhile, Paul perched on the edge of the desk. He was lit by the light of the anglepoise, his strong jaw and cheekbones in relief. He picked up the envelope again and weighed it in his hand.

"I thought you might know where to find him," Tom added, as a belated explanation for why he'd come to Paul's workroom. He really was hurt that Paul kept avoiding him, that was true. And having conspired almost to help José-Luis escape a second time, he'd just hoped that Paul and he could get a little closer, maybe. Or at least that Paul might give him updates on how José-Luis was doing and that sort of thing. Whatever had gone on in the flat between Paul and José-Luis didn't matter to Tom. Paul wasn't married with kids and a mortgage, after all. But somehow, it also made Paul more remote, unreachable perhaps. There was a connection between Paul and José-Luis which Tom didn't understand. Perhaps he was jealous? Paul was tapping the corner of the envelope on his chin, thinking.

"Why don't we take it together?" Paul said.

Tom looked up at him. He wasn't sure he'd heard correctly.

"When are you free?" Paul went on.

Tom swallowed, hoping Paul hadn't noticed. "Well, as soon as, I suppose," he answered. Trying to be calm and nonchalant.

"We best wait for it to get dark. Can you get out of the hotel without anyone noticing?" Paul asked.

"Yes, yes, of course."

"No, I mean it. No one must see you or follow you." Paul looked serious.

Tom was puzzled for a moment. This all seemed unreal. Like some kind of murder mystery.

"Are you sure that Dulwich bitch has left Weymouth, for instance?" Paul continued. Tom looked up at Paul, surprised to hear him mention Julia at all, the more so because he referred to her in that way. Paul clearly had feelings in there which Tom had never realised.

"Yes, she's gone to Bournemouth to be with her chums."

"OK. 9 o'clock then. If I tell you which way to walk, that should throw them off."

"Is all of this really necessary?" Tom felt vaguely ridiculous.

"Look. They've had two attempts to arrest him. The last one at my place left the Home Secretary herself with egg on her face."

"Could've been worse!" Tom mimicked holding something unpleasant between thumb and index finger, scrunching up his nose in mock distaste. They both laughed. That felt good. Soon, though, Tom had to snap out of it and listen carefully to the instructions Paul was giving him, no matter how much he felt this all to be over the top and excessively cautious.

Tom did exactly as Paul had instructed that evening and met him at quarter past nine after a very circuitous route through town on the path down to the seawall heading towards the ferry port. After another five minutes, though and much to Tom's confusion, they doubled back and made for the headland. There was a row of beach huts, some brightly painted, others a little worse for wear. Paul kept looking behind as they walked past the huts, even checking the space between them. Tom didn't feel this was a joke anymore. Instead, he began to feel uneasy too. Eventually, about two-thirds of the way along, Paul stopped and quietly knocked. José-Luis was delighted to see them when he opened the beach hut door. Even more so when he saw them together.

"Enter! Enter!" he said and stood back to let them go in. Paul looked over his shoulder again, just to check they had not been followed. Tom stepped inside, beaming, and wanting just to talk and catch up on things. He looked round for somewhere to sit. The beach nut was rather sparsely set out. There was a camp bed, where presumably José-Luis was sleeping, a rather small table, and two director-style folding deckchairs. Paul made towards the camp bed, but José-Luis held him back. He hugged and kissed each of them in turn. He was happy to have company, of course. But he hadn't expected to be with the two men he'd most wanted to be with recently. He kept hold of a hand of each of them. Like children in a playground.

"This is so lovely," José-Luis was saying, "especially you two together at last."

Almost without thinking, Paul walked away to the bed. Tom tried not to notice. Besides, José-Luis's excitement was too infectious. He'd missed him more than he'd realised, and so it was good to see him again.

"My friends!" José-Luis went on, "unfortunately, I can offer you nothing to eat or drink."

"That's not true!" said Paul, taking the rucksack off his back and resting it on the bed. He unpacked a bottle of wine, some water, bread, cheese and ham, and some fruit. José-Luis took the food and sniffed at the ham.

"I love you, Paul, but your meat is *awful*!" he said, holding the ham out at arm's length. Rather like the Home Secretary with his boxers a few nights before. Tom and Paul looked at one another and laughed. José-Luis didn't see what the joke was. He'd said many times before that boiled ham was a particular abomination. It felt good, though, to see them relaxed and sharing a laugh together, even if he felt a little excluded. José-Luis poured some wine into each of a strange assortment of glasses and cups. "To friends!" he said and swigged back the wine. He pulled a face slightly when he'd swallowed it.

José-Luis turned to Tom.

"So," he said, "Paul told me all about your *¿Dónde estás ahora?* Unaccompanied performance. I wish I would have been there!"

Both men froze. Paul, because he didn't want Tom to know either that he'd been so impressed with the number or that he spoke to José-Luis about such things. And Tom, because he was afraid José-Luis might say who the song was dedicated to.

"Yes, well…" Tom began, trying to think how to steer the conversation somewhere else. "Jason wanted to check something, and I couldn't think of anything else. You know, anything that people weren't sick of hearing."

Paul turned away and tried to look busy, rooting in his rucksack for something.

"I have only heard you sing it once myself," José-Luis went on. "I suppose anyone who listens to it will imagine that it is being sung specially for them."

There was an awkward silence. After a few minutes, Paul had regained his composure and turned round to remind José-Luis what he needed to be doing.

"Now," Paul's tone became rather serious as he gave José-Luis his instructions for the coming days. "My cousin, Lucy, will be here from the end of this week with her camper van. Clive and the kids won't join her for another week. So, you can alternate who sleeps where. You in the campervan a couple of nights, and Lucy here. Then Steve and Janet will be down, staying in their fixed caravan the other side of Black Head. Then you can swap with them too, every third night." José-Luis was looking at Paul's lips, concentrating hard, nodding occasionally to confirm that he'd taken it all in.

"Keep them guessing, eh?" Paul patted his arm. "We'll keep you out of harm's way."

"It's like a bloody military operation!" Tom said, but Paul shot him a warning look and he didn't say anything else. They all chatted a bit about how rehearsals were going, and about the new publicity person, while Tom shared out some of the peanuts he found at the bottom of the rucksack. Both Tom and Paul had decided not to tell José-Luis about what Julia had been up to. José-Luis asked how the finale was going, and suddenly Tom stood dramatically and slapped his forehead.

"We've got a letter for you," Tom said, "I almost forgot! That was the whole point of coming. I'd forget my own head..." Taking the letter from Paul's rucksack, he handed it to José-Luis, who looked puzzled as he took it. He turned it over without thinking to see the front. As if someone had flicked a switch, the colour drained from his face, and he sat down heavily all strength gone from his legs.

"José-Luis, what's wrong?" Paul asked, going over to him, putting a hand on his arm. Tom didn't really know what to think but went over too and sat next to him.

"Is everything OK?" they both asked at once.

José-Luis looked up at each of them in turn. His mouth was open, but he didn't seem to be able to say anything. His eyes looked shocked or perhaps scared. He looked at the envelope again still not opening it but tracing a finger across the writing on the front.

"It's Donatello," José-Luis whispered at last. Tom and Paul looked at each other. "This is his writing." Still José-Luis didn't open the letter. Tom took his hand.

"It came today with a note from Dana-Beatriz. From Spain. She said we had to bring it to you as soon as possible because you would want to read it."

Still staring wide-eyed into space, José-Luis looked down at the envelope and turned it over slowly. Then suddenly, he tore it open frantically and flicked over what it said. They both stood up and waited for him to say something. He looked up from one to the other, almost as if he expected them to be able to explain what he'd just read.

"I must go to Spain," he said simply. Then: "Please help me," was all he could manage after that. He was sobbing and rocking, now, holding the letter close to his chest. "Please..."

"Of course, we will," said Paul, sitting down on the other side of José-Luis again, his arm around his shoulder pulling the Colombian towards him. Tom raised his eyebrows at Paul as if waiting for some kind of explanation. But Paul wasn't looking. He glanced round the small beach hut, as if he were looking for something. Then he stood up abruptly and paced up and down as if he was trying to work out what to do next. "We must do it properly this time, though. We'll need to get you a visa and things. But we'll manage it as quickly as we can. I promise."

José-Luis looked up at Paul, his eyes puffy and red, and then at Tom, who nodded enthusiastically without really knowing what was going on.

"Now, where's your passport," Paul carried on. "We'll need that, I suppose."

Tom wondered what Paul meant and wished he'd explain. But he felt comforted that he seemed to have made a plan already. And he somehow knew that it would be something sensible and helpful. José-Luis went over to a small leather bag. The rest of his luggage was back in the hotel, unless the Home Office had seized it. This was what Tom had managed to bring, thinking that it must be important since José-Luis had always kept it close to his chest when they were travelling. José-Luis fished out a large wallet with his passport and some other papers.

"Here," he said, handing them to Paul, and shaking too much to be able to sort out what was needed, "take it all. Please, just help me."

"Of course, we will." It was Tom who said it this time. He gave José-Luis a hug in his turn and stroked his head. He still wasn't sure what was going on, though he trusted Paul implicitly. "Don't worry, we'll sort it all out." Paul was sitting at the table and going through the various papers just to check what José-Luis had given him. Tom tried to comfort José-Luis leaving Paul to work out whatever he'd decided. Eventually, regaining something of his normal gentle optimism, José-Luis hugged them both. Then he went back to the camp bed and lay down, drawing his legs up towards his chest and muttering something to himself in Spanish still clutching the letter. Almost in unison, Tom and Paul stood and went towards the door.

"No. Wait." José-Luis said, his voice hoarse. "*¡Por favor!* Take this letter. Show them how this is important. I must get to Spain." He looked from one to the other and then went back and lay on the narrow camp bed once more. He kept muttering "Please help me. I must get to Spain." They left, closing the door quietly behind them, Paul still looking around to check no one had seen them. Looking at each other for a moment, they then turned and set off back towards town in silence.

"Lucy and Steve? Your cousins from Bramdean?" asked Tom after a few minutes.

"That's them," Paul tried to sound relaxed. "It was the best I could do, just to keep José-Luis hidden. Moving about between different places seemed like a good idea."

"Yeah, great," said Tom, "but how are you... are *we* going to manage all of those arrangements? The visa and things?" They walked back along the seawall without saying anything for a while.

"I've a feeling Olwena's daughter-in-law works at the Spanish embassy," Paul began at last, taking Tom rather by surprise. "I could really do with talking to her about it. I'm just nervous though. I'm not sure I can trust her. I don't want anyone to know José-Luis is still around."

"Sounds like the only option we have right now," Tom said still staring at the pathway in front of them. Then, turning to Paul and gently putting a hand on his arm to get him to turn and look him in the face, "You know, Paul, you have to learn to trust people again. At least, those of us... You know, the people who care about you. I know that's not easy given your experiences in the past..." Paul looked away, and Tom hoped he hadn't spoken out of turn. "Anyway, what's your gut feeling?"

Paul didn't really know. He thought for a moment and then said: "Yes, you're right," he smiled briefly at Tom, making him feel they were indeed in this together. "She's very caring and certainly won't want anything bad to happen to José-Luis."

"We've had some pretty unexpected chats recently," Tom said, almost to himself. "I trust her." They walked on a little way in silence.

"What do you think of this letter business, though?" Tom asked. This was one of the big questions on Tom's mind at that moment. "Donatello's dead and buried years ago back in Colombia. Perhaps they had friends and he'd given them a letter in case anything ever did happen to him." Paul looked doubtful. Tom was trying to think of a plausible argument. He went on: "...and they'd brought the letter with them to Spain, hoping to find José-Luis?"

Paul stopped for a moment. "I'm not so sure," he said. "You read Spanish, though, don't you? Should we read the letter, do you think?"

"I don't really like to," Tom shook his head. "From a dead man, and all that. Save it for the embassy, perhaps?"

Paul nodded and they walked a little way in silence again. Paul turned to look out over the sea. His mind began to wander, starting with Donatello and how devoted he and José-Luis had been to one another, then thinking of his own quiet empty life. He'd longed for Tom to return. He couldn't understand why he'd left so suddenly. And not a word all these years since. Perhaps that's what he'd meant just now about his 'experiences in the past', Paul wondered. At least he'd known Tom was still alive. So, there was always a chance. He'd finally given up hope, though, and resigned himself to being on his own from then on. He'd blamed himself for a while for not making his feelings clear. But then, he wasn't really sure that Tom had loved him the same way. It had been such a shock seeing him come back. He didn't really know what to do now either. It was difficult for him to snap out of the reserved, unemotional way he'd lived all his life. He was just confused. He wished he knew what to say and what to do. Just to let Tom know how he felt. Here looking out over the sea with Tom. He looked down at his hand and then at Tom's. Perhaps he could slip his into Tom's. Not say anything, just hold hands and turn and look out to sea together. Nothing else. Pulling himself up, he told himself to stop thinking about himself and concentrate on what needed to be done for José-Luis.

"You remember we used to spend ages down here?" Tom stopped now, turned and looked out to sea. Paul stopped too. He still desperately wanted to take Tom's hand, to feel reassured, maybe to let Tom know something of his feelings. But he couldn't do it. Sensing something, Tom turned back and for a few moments stared at Paul's profile against the lights back in Weymouth. He wanted to stay here forever with Paul. He loved that profile, loved everything about him. He was kind, thoughtful, resourceful. He was Paul and whatever else, Tom loved him. He didn't want to go back to Weymouth. To normality and, most importantly now, to living a lie. He stepped closer to Paul. He wanted to feel his touch. The warmth of his body against his. His heart was in his mouth. He was going to give him a proper kiss this time. Just to know, once and for all, where he stood.

But it was too late. Paul had just turned and was strolling slowly back towards the garish lights in town, his head down, thinking, José-Luis's wallet clutched to his side. Tom wanted to shout and scream, even run up to Paul and force him to turn around and look him in the eye, to hold his head in his hands and kiss him. Surely, that would be communicating like Olwena said? Surely,

Paul would know how he felt? As Paul walked on, head still down, Tom could see his free hand down by his side, his fingers flexing.

Two days later, Olwena and Paul were on the train to London. Paul had bought them both a cup of tea – a British Rail plastic mug with a tepid cup of something that tasted a little metallic. 'No change there then,' thought Paul. Olwena finished her digestive and wiped her hands on her hankie. Paul noticed the J.B. embroidered at the corner. When she saw him looking at the monogram, Olwena smiled to herself and tucked her handkerchief back into her sleeve.

"So, Paul," she said, looking him straight in the face across the table between them, "are you going to tell me what this is all about, dear?"

"I'm sorry, Olwena, I should've said," Paul looked down into his lap, then out of the window. He'd not said much to her back at the theatre, just that he needed to go to the Spanish embassy and maybe she'd like to come along and see her daughter-in-law. Now that they were on the train, though, he felt he owed her more of an explanation.

"Look," he began, "I really am sorry I didn't say anything before... It's just..." He trailed off again. But she waited patiently. She didn't want to push him and risk the strong, silent treatment she'd become accustomed to with Paul.

"I need to tell you some things, and I really need you to keep all of this to yourself. Promise?" Paul looked directly at her across the table between them.

"Of course, I will. You know you can trust me, Paul," she replied. She felt a little exposed now without some stitching to do. Could he, though? He was so out of practice, he thought, he didn't know how to tell who he could trust anymore.

"Remember Dana-Beatriz?" he went on after a deep breath.

"Oh, yes, that pretty young thing with the gorgeous eyes who danced with our José-Luis."

"Well, she forwarded a letter, see, for José-Luis," Paul was still trying to weigh up how much to tell her. "He was very upset by the letter."

"What did it say?"

"I don't really know." Paul had it in his rucksack along with José-Luis's papers, but he wanted to keep that secret. "All I know is he needs to go to Spain as quickly as possible."

"And so, is that why we are going to London?" Olwena asked.

"Yes, I need to go to the Spanish embassy. It's for José-Luis, though, not for me."

"You should've said, silly, I could've 'phoned Gabriela," Olwena said, satisfied that things were starting to make some kind of sense. Paul looked down again, colouring very slightly. He was picking at the formica on the table.

"I already did," he said, barely looking at her. "I'm so sorry, Olwena. I've been so worried."

"Oh," she said, and adjusted her coat and bag. Paul couldn't tell if she was angry or not. "Well, if it's to help José-Luis, then I'm sure it's all above board." She didn't sound convinced, but she smiled across to Paul. "And it'll be nice to see the kiddies! Will we have time?"

Paul hadn't thought of that. He didn't even know where they lived in London. It suddenly dawned on him that he'd only been thinking about José-Luis. He felt very selfish. He didn't really want to get back to Weymouth that late, but he thought he owed it to Olwena at least if that's what she wanted to do.

At the embassy, they were met by a handsome, if abrupt young man in uniform, his peaked cap down over his eyes, who asked their names and what business they had.

"We're here to see Señora Prichard," Paul said, "I booked an appointment via the telephone."

" *¿Con quién?*" The young man was searching up and down a list of names he had with office and telephone numbers.

"Señora San Martin," Olwena corrected. The man looked up at her and nodded.

He offered them a seat and disappeared through a large, oak panelled door. Five minutes later he returned, took his seat again behind a large desk without a word and carried on reading whatever it was he had in front of him. He didn't say anything else to Olwena or Paul, like how long they should wait and when Gabriela would come. Opposite them was a large, dated exhibition about cork oak, with black and white photos from left to right telling the story of cork production in north-eastern Spain, its resistance to fire, and planting it in other regions to protect other trees.

Another five minutes and Gabriela came through a different door, a pad and pen in her hand. She smiled at her mother-in-law and walked over to kiss her lightly on both cheeks. Stepping aside, she asked them to come through to her office, which was behind the door she'd just emerged from apparently. Paul followed the two women who were silent now as they walked back through the door.

"So, Mr Armstrong," Gabriela sounded neutral and business-like. Olwena said nothing but sat a little way back so as not to interfere.

"The thing is," Paul started. "I don't really know where to start."

Gabriela put her pen down, linking her hands together on the desk in front of her, and waited patiently her head tilted slightly to one side.

"The thing is, I'd like to get a visa for Spain."

"You don't need a visa to travel to Spain, Mr Armstrong."

"No, sorry. It's not for me. It's for a friend. He's from Colombia."

Gabriela looked at him for a minute or two. "You must tell your friend that he will have to come to the embassy himself. The office is open..."

"No, you don't understand," he interrupted. Gabriela raised an eyebrow.

"You see, the thing is, it's not safe for him to travel in public."

"Mr Armstrong, you are not making any sense. There are procedures which have to be followed." She glanced at her mother-in-law, who was looking at the clasp of her handbag, trying not to listen. "We cannot let just anyone go to Spain."

Paul leant on the desk and put his head in his hands, before sitting back upright, shocked at himself for this momentary lapse of professionalism.

"I'm sorry, Gab... I'm sorry. Our friend's husband was murdered in Colombia. Betrayed by his own family and lynched." Olwena gasped and put a hand over her mouth, staring in disbelief at the back of Paul's head.

"Is she..." Gabriela's tone changed very slightly.

"He." Paul said.

"Is *he* in any danger?" Gabriela asked, simply and without any hint of surprise. "Why does he want to go to Spain?"

"I don't know. Oh, I've messed this all up. The Home Office are looking for him..."

"Mr Armstrong," Gabriela stiffened slightly, "you are not asking me to break the law, are you?"

"No, no," Paul said quickly, holding both hands up to emphasise his denial, not looking at Olwena as he remembered her words from a few days ago. She looked down at her shoes. They all sat in silence for a few minutes.

"I'm sorry, Mr Armstrong," Gabriela was gathering her pen and pad together as she stood up.

"No, wait," said Paul. He picked up his rucksack and took the letter out. He handed it to her. "Please," he stood up too, "Please. Read this."

"What is it?" she asked.

"I'm sorry," Paul said, slumping back into his chair, "I can't really read Spanish... without a dictionary."

Gabriela took the envelope and sat down again. Turning it over, she took the letter out and read it through quickly. With a sharp intake of breath, she looked across the desk at Paul.

"We must get your friend to Spain as quickly as possible," she said, setting down her pad and starting to write. "I need his passport... I assume you have that at least? And any other papers."

Paul rummaged in his rucksack. He brought out the large wallet and took out José-Luis's Colombian passport. A set of passport photos fell out at the same time – apparently taken in Paris because José-Luis had thought he might need a visa to travel on to the UK. There were other bits of official-looking paper, a driver's licence and an identity card. He slid them all across the desk to Gabriela. She picked them up and examined them one by one.

"*¡Bien!*" she said, "these should do. Come back the day after tomorrow, and I'll see what I can do in the meantime." She looked across at Paul as he went to say something more and then over to Olwena. "Maybe there's a different way of doing it. *¿Mamí?*" she said. Olwena sat up and looked back at her daughter-in-law, "why don't you come and stay with us for a night or two? The children would love it. Really. And Richard's always saying he wishes he could see you more often." Olwena beamed at her, but then looked at Paul as if to see if he approved.

"If that's alright with everyone?" Paul said, relieved.

"That's settled, then. I suppose you have no luggage, *Mamí*?" Gabriela smiled. "Don't worry. We can go via High Street Kensington on the way home and pick you up a nice nightie. Something special."

"Oh, well..." Olwena looked a little worried.

"It can be an early Christmas present," Gabriela was collecting all of the papers together. Paul took out his wallet.

"How much do I owe you?" he said.

"You're not trying to bribe me, are you, Mr Armstrong?"

Paul couldn't tell whether Gabriela had become suddenly cold again or perhaps just joking.

"No, no, I just meant for the visa and things."

"Good point!" said Gabriela, "one moment, please." She left the office for a few minutes and came back with an official looking ledger. Looking at José-Luis's passport, she made out a receipt, tore it out, and handed it to Paul. He was still holding his wallet.

"No need," said Gabriela, and stood up again, holding her hand out to Paul. He stood and took it, thanking her for her patience and understanding. He kissed Olwena lightly on the cheek and made to leave.

"Mr Armstrong," Gabriela said. He turned, his hand already on the doorknob and the door half-open. "Your friend's husband is not dead." She'd shown him out before he realised what she'd just said. She closed the door behind him, and the handsome man in uniform looked up from his paper, touched his cap, and wished him a good afternoon.

Paul was glad to be on the train home by himself. He liked Olwena a lot, and he knew now he owed her an enormous debt for being there when he'd spoken to Gabriela. He was aware too that being able to trust someone was actually a big relief. At that moment, though, he needed to think. He couldn't understand Gabriela's final comment. How could Donatello still be alive? It didn't make sense. Yet, if there had been some kind of misunderstanding, he should be happy for José-Luis. All they had to do was to get him to Spain. Simple really. The easiest would have been the tour bus. After all, that's how he got into the UK in the first place, surely? But then presumably the Home Office would be watching out for it now that they were onto José-Luis.

The external compartment door opened, and Paul was brought back out of these musings. A young couple negotiated the steps from the platform almost at the same time that a young man, slightly drunk, appeared at the internal door to the corridor. Everyone glanced briefly at everyone else. Paul was near the window, facing the direction of travel. The young couple, a black man and his white fiancée, sat opposite about halfway along the bench seat. The other man sat on the same side as Paul, at the partition to the corridor at that side. The couple spoke almost in a whisper to one another. The man had a newspaper across his knee with the *"Don't Die of Ignorance"* advert on the front. Paul and the other man said nothing, each staring out of their respective sides of the train. Another five minutes or so, and with a lot of door slamming and a single whistle blow, it pulled out.

They'd just left Clapham Junction when the young man shifted in his seat noisily. He leant forward, and speaking directly to the young woman, said rather loudly:

"You can do a lot better than him, love," nodding in her fiancé's direction but not looking at him. Paul sat up in his seat. "You don't want to be having little coffee-coloured nippers now do you?" The couple tried to ignore him. "Eh! I'm talking to you." The young man was sitting further forward, almost touching the knees of the man opposite. He shifted in his seat and said quietly to his girlfriend, "Just ignore him. He's had a bit to drink."

"Eh!" the young man said again. This time talking at the man. "I'm talking to the organ grinder, not the organ grinder's monkey."

"That's enough." The young man and the couple both looked round, surprised at Paul's intervention. "It's getting late," Paul went on, "why don't you just settle down and leave the rest of us in peace."

"What's it got to do with you?" the man was becoming aggressive.

"Look, just calm down. These people have done nothing to you. Just leave it."

"It's OK, really," said the young black man, smiling at Paul.

"Shut the fuck up, you!" the man pointed menacingly at Paul. And turning to the man opposite: "Oh, so the ape can talk, can he?"

The black man looked at him. "Look, we don't want any trouble. We're just on our way home. So, let's all just leave it."

"Who do you think you're talking to, boy? I didn't say you could speak to me."

The black man turned away and rolled his eyes to Paul. At this, the young man stood up and shoved the black man's shoulder. Paul stood up and stepped between them.

"That's enough, mate. Either you sit down and leave the rest of us in peace, or maybe you need to find yourself another seat in another compartment." Paul slid the door open. The draught from the corridor blew in, and the young man sniffed the air. Leaning closer to Paul, he sniffed again.

"Perfume!" he said. Paul didn't answer. "So, a nancy boy, eh?" Although a good five or six inches shorter than Paul, he squared up to him as he said: "You take it up the arse, mate? That what you like?" he spat on the carriage floor. "That why you're defending the darkie? They all got big ones, ain't they?" He leered suggestively as he looked from one to the other. Paul pushed him out into the corridor and slid the door shut again. He stood against the door till the young man had staggered further down the carriage, shouting the occasional obscenity. Eventually the noise subsided, and Paul took his seat again near the window.

"Are you two OK?" he asked.

"Yes, thank you," the black man said. His fiancée was looking down, a tear fell on her lap. "Hey, honey, it's alright, he's gone now."

"I'm really sorry about what just happened," Paul said. "It makes me very angry when people judge other people. We're all minding our own business in this world, just trying to get by. And when you find someone special, no matter who or what they are, you just want to be with that person. Not with idiots like that telling you what to do." Paul surprised himself and sat back in his chair, slightly embarrassed.

"That's true that, mate," said the black man. "Thanks." He hugged his fiancée who looked over at Paul shyly and smiled. "Thank you," she said quietly. The newspaper fell to the carriage floor, and the man leant forward to pick it up. Both he and his fiancée looked at the front page. Surreptitiously they each glanced over at Paul and seemed to sniff involuntarily.

After a few minutes, Paul noticed a change in their attitude. The girlfriend moved to sit on the other side of her fiancé, and he crossed his legs away from Paul. They both gave Paul furtive and, he felt, judgemental glances before whispering to one another. Paul wondered what this was all about. He'd not particularly wanted their gratitude, and he didn't see himself as a hero. He'd just reacted to a situation which he found unacceptable. He thought over what had happened and sat back with that same familiar feeling of being condemned, being on the outside. He wondered if the couple had taken seriously what the drunk guy had said. Did they really think he had designs on the man? It was preposterous, yet Paul had heard it so many times before. Not specifically applied to him, but to other men. It seemed, to Paul at least, that it wasn't enough to be judged for their sexuality. There seemed to be a view that they were all predatory. Just then, he caught sight of the newspaper still on the man's lap. He sighed and, folding his arms across his chest, pretended to fall asleep so that they wouldn't feel embarrassed.

The couple got off at Basingstoke. Paul settled into his seat in the corner again. He was still a bit angry. He had no time for prejudice and definitely saw no reason why someone shouldn't love whoever they wanted. Love happens. It's not something that you can legislate or control. And love doesn't need to mean sex, either. That was fun, he knew that now. He even understood how it could be delicate and generous and special when it was between people who really loved one another. Surely that couple knew that? Or maybe 'normal people' with 'family values' didn't think that way?

He put his head in his hands. He was tired. He wished he was at home, in bed. It would have been nice to be in bed with José-Luis, but only to have someone else there with him. He liked him so much, he'd enjoyed his initiation into sex, but he didn't love him that way. He wanted the best for him, that was true, especially now that there seemed to be a real chance José-Luis could be reunited at last and so unexpectedly with Donatello. He was so happy for José-Luis. He almost wished he could be there when he met up with his husband again. Really, that's all he'd ever wanted for his friend.

So, maybe that was a different kind of love? He certainly cared enough to bend the law slightly as Olwena said. He envied José-Luis, going back to Donatello, though. Being happy together and safe now. All he knew was that he, Paul Armstrong, didn't want to be alone anymore. He looked out of the window at the sky darkening over the fields. He wanted to go home to a partner who would hug him when he told the story of the drunk in the carriage and the young couple wanting nothing to do with him. He wanted his partner to tell him everything was alright. Not to worry about what other people thought. After all, they had each other, and that was all that mattered. He felt slightly ashamed of himself. More than anything right then, he wanted some kind of sign that Tom would look out for him and be there for him. Not so much physically – Paul could look after himself in that department – but emotionally. He wanted Tom to protect him from the disapproving eyes of others, the whispered condemnation, the contempt on the faces of the couple he'd just been sharing the carriage with. He wanted to know that Tom felt just as strongly about this as he did.

As they drew into the next station, he looked up to see where he was and recognised the platform before he saw the sign: Winchester. He slumped back in his seat and, looking out at the faces of commuters walking down the platform, he wondered who they were going home to. Wives, husbands, children in their neat little houses to eat dinner together. To watch television, have a glass of wine and then go upstairs to sleep. Ready to do it all again the next day. Did they love the family they were going home to? Did they know what love meant? Had they felt the breath of a lover next to them? Or the thrill of seeing them again? Paul was afraid now.

Winchester. The last time he'd been here was with Tom years before. That perfect summer on his auntie's farm. Paul sighed. He loved Tom. He always had. He wanted Tom now, in this draughty railway carriage. He wanted to hold him, feel *his* breath on his neck. It wasn't José-Luis he wanted beside him in bed, it was Tom. Did Tom love him as he'd done at school? Was Paul enough for him? How would he know? Could he trust the feeling he had in his gut? He'd seen a different side to Tom when he'd sacked Julia. Here was the man who cared about people. Who defended José-Luis. Would he defend him, Paul, against Julia? Against a world that didn't think two men could love each other? Who couldn't have family values together? Paul sobbed quietly in the dark. He wanted to know that Tom loved him as much as he loved Tom. Was it ever that clear? Or did you just have to take the risk. Close your eyes, jump and hope for the best. Take a leap of faith.

When the train finally pulled into Weymouth, it was already evening, and the sun was beginning to set. Paul didn't really mind it getting dark. He was usually content to be alone with his thoughts. Lately, though, he was unsettled. He took a detour via the seawall and leant against the railings to stare out towards the horizon. He was surprised to see a small sailing boat moving quite quickly towards the harbour. He wasn't far from the beach hut, and he wondered if José-Luis might be there or at the caravan. He craved the touch of another man, though he felt some compunction. José-Luis was convinced he was on his way back to be reunited with Donatello. So he felt it would be unfair. He wondered how Tom felt about having sex. Paul wanted to do all the things José-Luis had taught him with Tom. To try more. To see what they'd both been missing. He now realised that that was not enough. He loved Tom and wanted a real relationship. He wanted them to be together, to enjoy sex of course, but also to want to spend time with one another, with or without sex. To be happy to sit without having to speak, just being content with each other. If it was only the physical, he thought, then he really wasn't interested. He knew how to be alone. So, when the troupe moved on, he would manage.

A man in his thirties or maybe early forties was walking steadily but slowly along the seawall. He was fairly handsome and seemed to be looking appraisingly at Paul too. He slowed down opposite Paul and looked back once or twice, hoping to catch Paul's eye. Paul didn't look, though. He didn't want sex right now. He knew where to get it, though, if it came to it. But that made him sad.

There was still enough light to see the boat and its sails, but he thought it could be dangerous now for it to be out on the sea. It was blustery, and the boat was having to tack to make any progress in the breeze. Paul watched as it zig-zagged towards the shore. It must have been an effect of the light, because each time the boat changed direction, the sails changed from black, or dark grey, to white. He wondered if the black sails were intended for him or for José-Luis. He didn't want to think about that now. He really hoped that José-Luis would find happiness in Spain.

Paul kept thinking about going to see José-Luis after all. He wasn't looking for sex, which would just be a diversion anyway. He needed to talk to someone who might understand. He'd been alone most of his life. He knew how to do that. He didn't want to be reduced to cruising for casual encounters. He hoped that it would never come to that. But he wanted to love someone and be loved. Even José-Luis had said that lovers were more than just bed friends. He'd also been content with his life before Tom had come back. He didn't know what to do now. So, he and Tom finally understood perhaps why they had been so close when they were young. Paul realised now that he'd failed to trust Tom before, and he was at fault. He'd been scared and decided to hide, live on his own, avoid temptation. Now he was less sure. He was afraid that Tom would leave and that would be it. At the same time, he still wasn't sure that Tom felt the same way about him as he did about Tom. He hadn't been very friendly, he knew. Yet Tom now knew where he lived and how to keep in touch. That was something. Perhaps Tom was put off though and wasn't interested anymore. Paul didn't want to think about that. He wiped away a tear which he told himself was from the breeze coming off the sea. It was time to get home. He just wished there was some kind of sign to tell him what to do. He wished he didn't have to keep going over these thoughts again and again.

As night finally drew in, and Paul had ignored another couple of men, he stared a little longer out to sea watching the moon slowly start to dapple the choppy waves. Finally, he turned and headed back to town and his flat. It was really quite dark now. He was so tired that he wouldn't notice the empty space in his double bed. His route took him past the theatre which wasn't too far from his flat anyway. Usually at this time, the theatre would be in darkness, a few security lights inside for the caretaker to do his rounds. And during the days there were bobbies on the beat, so that the local policeman could peer in through the glass doors at the front and check that everything was in order. But tonight, there was a glow from the front as Paul approached along a sideroad. Rounding the corner, suddenly Paul's face was lit up with neon across the front of the awning: *Tom Bright,* it said. Having been used to the dark, he had to squint holding up his hand to shield his eyes from the dazzling lights, the gusty breeze pressing his shirt flat against his broad chest made his trousers cling to his muscly legs. *Tom Bright* had come back to Weymouth. To his theatre. What a coincidence.

Paul and Tom had visited José-Luis, this time in the campervan, and Paul had explained everything that had happened. All bar what Gabriela had said right at the end. He still didn't understand what she could possibly mean. He wondered whether to confide in Tom. But rehearsals were now at that critical stage where everything, Tom thought, just seemed to be going wrong. So, Paul kept himself to himself in his workroom, looking down from the guard rail occasionally just to see how the finale was going. He felt more comfortable looking at Tom now. It was almost like old times, except that they were both older, more experienced, and perhaps a little world-weary. Keeping everything inside is exhausting, Paul knew. But he was also afraid. It all seemed silly, though. Paul knew that Tom and José-Luis had slept together, presumably on many occasions and not just on a prop basket in some provincial theatre. And Tom knew that Paul and José-Luis had at least been very close in Paul's flat before the Home Office raid. Perhaps, Paul wondered sadly, perhaps Tom didn't love him. Perhaps that kiss had just been a mistake.

"Do you have a minute?" Paul had waited for the dancers and musicians to break for lunch. Tom looked stressed and was just about to make a curt response, when he realised it was Paul.

"Yes... yes, of course. What is it? Something wrong? Something with the lighting?"

"No," said Paul, "nothing to do with the lighting. You look tired, Tom, are you OK?"

Tom was about to shake this off. He was fine, just a bit nervous, with the opening night looming and performing back in Weymouth professionally for the first time. But then he realised. Paul had actually called him by his name. He smiled up at his old friend.

"I'm absolutely fucking knackered," he said, standing up and dropping the pen he'd been writing with on the table, "I'm always like this before opening night. But there's just something about this gig. About being back here. I'll be so relieved for José-Luis when he gets to Spain. But I'm jealous of his friends there. I wish I had someone..." He tailed off and ran a hand through his hair. He desperately wanted to reach out to Paul, to hold his hand, just to connect with him. They needn't look at each other. That would be acceptable, surely? He still loved him, he knew that now, more than ever. But he was scared it might be too late. Paul was ready to make some excuse and back away, as usual. However, he stopped. He was worried about José-Luis anyway, but he was worried too about Tom.

"Do you have time for a bit of fresh air? Maybe a quick stroll down to the seawall?" Paul asked. Tom's stomach lurched. Like we used to, he thought, but was afraid to say.

"Great idea!" he managed. Then, "so long as we're not walking bloody miles round the Wrekin and back!" They both laughed. Tom even managed a slap on Paul's back as they made for the stage door. Paul didn't flinch or stiffen, he noticed. Five or ten minutes later, they'd passed the port and were at the seawall with that sweeping view towards the headland.

"Do you remember..." Paul began, but then stopped. Tom tried not to react. "I've been coming down here, you know, while you were away... overseas... and..." The claxon on the ferry sounded and the seagulls screeched loudly as they took off in fright. 'And...?' thought Tom. But the moment was lost.

"Anyway," said Paul, suddenly more serious. "I didn't tell you everything that happened at the embassy." Tom looked at him. "I couldn't really. Not while José-Luis was around."

"That reminds me," said Tom, trying to keep it all casual, "isn't Olwena supposed to be back today."

"Tomorrow," said Paul.

"So, what else?"

"I was just getting ready to leave. For a while, it was touch-and-go, and I was pretty down about it all. When I handed Gabriela the letter, though, it all changed."

"Yes, so you said." Tom was close to losing his temper. He was tired, it was good to be out in the fresh air. And it was special being with Paul. Especially now. But he'd heard all of this already. He just wanted to be quiet with Paul, that's all.

"Sorry, I'm repeating myself," Paul said, as if he'd read Tom's thoughts, "I was literally about to walk out of the door, and Gabriela called me back and..." Paul paused for a moment and turned Tom to look him in the eye. "And she told me that José-Luis's husband, Donatello, wasn't dead."

"My God!" It took a minute or two for Tom to realise what had been said. He grabbed Paul's arm. "What? How is that possible?"

"You remember, though, José-Luis was just in shock.

He couldn't speak or look at us, he just kept saying he needed us to get him to Spain. As quickly as possible before the end of the month."

Tom released his grip and turned and hugged Paul close. Paul was his oldest friend and they'd just got some tremendous news. Paul didn't pull away this time. He held Tom close, he wanted to make him feel safe and relaxed. It was Tom who finally released his hold and said:

"We best be getting back. My God, that's amazing. I'm going straight to the ferry port now and getting him a ticket." Tom started to run back towards the terminal, like an excited kid in the playground.

"But won't you need passport and things?" Paul shouted after him.

Tom turned and carried on skipping quickly backwards looking more like a kid, whilst shouting to Paul.

"I know one of the guys at the ferry," he shouted. Even from a distance, Paul could see Tom tweaking his eyebrows suggestively.

"Mind your step! Turn round. Go on!" Paul was laughing now and more worried that Tom would trip and hurt himself if he wasn't facing the way he was going. 'And you've got dancing to do,' he thought.

As soon as she got back to Weymouth, Olwena went straight from the station to the theatre. Paul was on stage going through his notes for the show in his exercise book. Standing close to him was Tom, a hand nearly touching the small of his back. She smiled to herself. 'Like normal people comfortable with one another,' she thought. 'That's better.' She hurried over to them.

"Do we need to go somewhere more discreet?" she asked quietly.

"Perhaps you and Paul could meet upstairs somewhere?" Tom suggested. "I'm a bit tied up down here."

Paul nodded, and Olwena took herself off up to Paul's workspace via wardrobe, so she could drop off her new overnight bag and coat. She waited patiently for Paul to come up.

"Look," she picked up the large brown envelope she'd put on the table when Paul came five or ten minutes later. "Gabriela's given us a Spanish passport." Paul was impressed. This was much more than he'd hoped for. "He's also got an ID card, and naturalisation papers."

Paul gave Olwena a brief hug. "That's amazing, Olwena, thank you so much!"

"Nothing to do with me," she said, though did wonder if her connection to Gabriela might have had something to do with it after all. "I reckon it was that letter."

"Did Gabriela read it to you?" Paul wondered.

"No," said Olwena, "but it's in the envelope with everything else. She did say something about relatives of hers. The family came from Chile, you see, and I think many of them suffered a lot under Pinochet and his henchmen. I think something struck a chord. She told me about an uncle of hers who was supposed to leave with them and come to Europe. But the uncle's lover had been *disappeared*, I think she called it. So, he refused to leave. He said he would not leave until he'd found Angelo and brought him to safety. Oh, Paul. It was awful. Some weeks later they saw a picture of the uncle lying in his own blood outside their apartment."

She shook the envelope over the table to see if she'd forgotten anything, trying to distract herself. Paul too didn't know what to say. He felt a sudden rush of anger, exactly as he'd felt on the train. Olwena noticed Paul's expression. She leant across the table and took his hand before he could pull away.

"It's OK, Paul. At least we know that Donatello didn't die horribly. And we all want to help our little friend get to him!"

As she shook the envelope, as if on cue, Donatello's letter fell out first. But then came a smaller envelope. It was unsealed and there was no name or any writing on the front. Olwena picked it up and took out what looked like a small business card. Printed on one side was the Spanish proverb: *Vivir con miedo es como vivir a medias.* She showed it to Paul. Neither knew what it meant. On the back, handwritten in English, it said: *Don't be afraid anymore,* and then the letters: *G S M*.

"What do you think that means?" asked Olwena. Paul had heard it before, he was almost sure. But he didn't want to talk to Olwena about it right now. There was too much going on in his head.

"I'm not sure. What do you think *G S M* stands for?" he asked instead.

They both fell silent for a minute or two.

"I know!" said Olwena suddenly, "or I think I do anyway. It's *Gabriela San Martin,* of course, that was her maiden name."

"And the name she's known by at the embassy," Paul added.

He sat down in his chair and looked up at Olwena. "Well, perhaps it has something to do with the letter? Anyway, it doesn't matter. I'm just so relieved," he said, "now all we need to do is get José-Luis safely on the boat and out of here."

Olwena bent over slightly, "For you to do all this, you must be very fond of him." There was a glint in her eye, which Paul was not completely happy with. "Men like you need to stick together." She stood up and was about to leave when she turned: "And how's your friend, Tom, taking it all?" she asked. Paul was too surprised to wonder what had made her think of Tom.

"Oh, he's fine," he replied, "thanks."

"Come on, José-Luis, you don't want to miss the bloody ferry after all this!" Tom was anxious for José-Luis and whatever was waiting for him in Spain. But he was also aware that he and Paul needed to get back to the theatre as quickly as possible. Rob at least would be on tenterhooks. José-Luis was unhurriedly getting out of the back seat of Steve's car. He was a different man from only a few days before, happy, relaxed, smiling broadly. He looked like some kind of exotic god emerging from a carriage not Steve's little car. His hair had been swept away from his face, his olive complexion glowing, emphasised occasionally by his beautiful broad smile. Walking round the back of the car, Steve opened the boot, and José-Luis picked out a new leather holdall with *José-Luis E* near the clasp. He stumbled through the entrance doors to the ferry terminal, giddy with excitement. Paul and Tom looked at one another concerned. Paul leant forward just to check that there was no one like the police coming. Even Tom was worried.

"Now, concentrate," Tom said almost like a teacher to an unruly child. José-Luis stood to attention, and Paul smirked. "This envelope has your Spanish passport, your Spanish ID card and naturalisation papers." He took the passport out and told José-Luis to put the rest away safely into his holdall. "Don't lose them!"

"Oh, and José-Luis," Paul interrupted. José-Luis swung his whole head round towards Paul now, who was trying to contain he's own vicarious excitement. "Donatello's letter is in there too." José-Luis lowered his eyes for a moment.

"Thank you," he said. "Donatello is not dead, it was all a horrible, terrible but wonderful misunderstanding. It was a colleague we knew working in a village nearby. That is also horrible. But at least..." They all knew what he was going to say. Again José-Luis looked down, clasping the passport in his hand. He felt guilty somehow that his joy had had to come at the expense of someone else's pain. He didn't even think about all that time he'd suffered, thinking Donatello had actually died.

"But after that," he went on, "Donatello, he had to get out of Colombia as quickly as possible – he was next on the list, his family had made certain of it. He write me that he will wait in Cuenca till the end of the month. So, till next Friday. If I don't get there, then he will understand.

He will accept that I have found someone else. And he will be happy for me."

They all stood in silence for a moment. Separately, both Paul and Tom were taken aback by this level of love for someone. Donatello and José-Luis were truly in love with each other. Even to the point of letting go, so long as the other one was happy. For Paul, it was disturbing to think he might just be close to being with the man he loved only to lose him again. He wasn't sure he would be so generous just to hope for his happiness. Meanwhile, Tom remembered José-Luis telling him he had to be prepared to let Paul go, if that's what it took for Paul to find himself. He was ashamed that at the time he suspected José-Luis's motives. Now, though, he realised just how special José-Luis was. He'd never really complained about the hand they'd all thought fate had dealt him. Instead, he wanted to be there first for Tom, then for Paul. To help each of them in the best way he could. Tom cleared his throat. Paul looked away, trying to hold back a tear too.

"OK. Well, that explains the ticket to Cuenca, then." Tom said, pointing to the envelope José-Luis had still not stored away safely in his holdall. He took it back again from José-Luis's hand. "Here are your tickets: for the ferry, the train to Paris, Paris Madrid, and then from Madrid to Cuenca and Don..." He stopped for a moment, unable to continue. "And, in this envelope," a catch in his voice still, "You've got francs and pesetas for the journey." He took a smaller envelope from his inside pocket and handed it to José-Luis.

"Write to us," Paul said. "Tell us when you are happy. With Donatello."

"Tell Donatello," Tom added, but he stopped. Had Paul really just said 'us'? He tried not to read too much into it, even if he had. He continued: "...and tell him that we'd love to meet him someday. Perhaps, now that you're *Spanish*," he said, tapping José-Luis's passport, "you can both come back and visit us here in Weymouth." José-Luis suddenly stopped fussing with the different envelopes and looked straight at Tom, who was trying to pretend he hadn't meant anything in particular by the 'we' and 'us' in those statements. Paul turned so neither Tom nor José-Luis could see the expression on his face.

The ferry's imminent departure was announced, and the last passengers were boarding. José-Luis hugged them both and kissed each on the lips, "I love you guys!" he whispered. With a hand still at the back of each of their necks, he looked from one to the other. "Now, you stop fucking about! You hear me? Don't let love slip away again! Don't be afraid this time." Paul remembered the little card from Gabriela. He didn't want to live half a life anymore.

The seamen were starting to prepare to cast off, throwing the mooring ropes onto the ferry. Without the ropes, it would soon start to drift away from its moorings. They held it against the mooring for now. José-Luis ran down to the control point, showed his ticket and passport, and was waved on board without a hitch. It had worked. He turned around to wave, almost dropping his papers and his luggage in the process. Both Tom and Paul lurched forward automatically as if trying to stop things falling even from this distance. The gangplank was drawn in, the side gate closed shut, and the ferry drew away. José-Luis was gathering up the papers he'd so nearly dropped into the harbour and stuffing them unceremoniously back into his bag. He paused when he noticed a picture he thought he hadn't seen before. He tried to make out what it was and beamed over to Paul and Tom, waving. Paul had put a postcard-sized reprint of *Les Raboteurs de parquet* in with all his stuff. José-Luis was blowing kissing to them both. Next minute, with a low rumble and churning up a substantial wake behind it, the ferry accelerated away, and he was gone.

They watched until it had cleared the harbour and was out into the Channel. As they'd stepped forward as if to catch José-Luis's stuff, they'd shifted positions and were now still standing very close almost facing one another. Neither of them moved till the ferry was out of sight. Tom could feel Paul's breath on his face and the hint of a smell of *Masculin II* in his nose making him giddy. He wanted Paul. He knew it wasn't just seeing José-Luis off that made him feel lonely. Almost without thinking, he raised his hand and was about to lay it gently on Paul's chest, but Paul turned, averting his gaze, and walked back to the car where Steve was waiting to drive them back to the theatre. Tom wiped away a tear. Probably at seeing José-Luis happy and on his way to his lover, husband and best friend in Spain.

Steve flicked away his cigarette, pushed himself upright from perching on the bonnet of his car and climbed back into the driver's seat. "Well, that's that, then," he said, in a matter-of-fact sort of way. Paul looked at him in disbelief across the car roof. Then he opened the door his side and got into the passenger seat again. Tom took a seat in the back. On his own, this time.

"That was a bloody good adventure!" Steve was looking over his shoulder as he reversed out of the parking space, so he didn't notice the look of horror on Paul's face this time. He wished his cousin would keep his stupid remarks to himself and just drive. Turning round again to face the way he was going to drive, they headed back towards town. No one spoke. Tom watched the seagulls and the heavy sky idly as they drove along the harbour front. Turning to look out of the opposite window, he caught Paul looking at him in the rear-view mirror before quickly turning away. It was strange. Again and again, Tom caught a brief glimpse of his school friend's blue eyes staring back at him for just the briefest of moments.

The relief at seeing the ferry pull out of the harbour with José-Luis safely on board was slowly replaced by a different feeling for Paul as they drove back. Although only a few days, he'd enjoyed having José-Luis around. Even without the sex, he was good company and good fun. When he'd had to move into the beach hut, Paul had to focus on keeping him safe and his whereabouts secret. Then on trying to arrange for him to get to Spain. Now all of that was suddenly gone. Paul felt empty once more but unsettled too. He wondered if it had all been too quick and whether he'd learned enough from José-Luis. He wished he was sitting in the back with Tom, holding his hand, just so they could be together and be happy for José-Luis at least. Or preferably, as they began their own life as a couple. He didn't know what he was thinking and was so distraught at José-Luis's story too that he'd told himself Tom would be leaving soon. Without him. And it would be best to get used to being alone again.

He couldn't think what else to do. He knew what living alone and being lonely meant. He'd had years of experience with it. Waiting, watching and hoping. But now he was afraid that Tom would leave him a second time. Rejection would be unbearable. Was José-Luis right when he kept hinting that Tom loved him? Paul didn't know whether he was brave enough now to take that leap of faith. He imagined he could feel José-Luis's strong hand on the back of his neck still and he wished his friend could tell him what to do now.

"So," Steve broke the silence when they were about halfway back to the theatre, "was Twinkle Toes a fairy then?"

"What!?" Tom blurted out, a little too abruptly. Apart from the emotion of seeing José-Luis safely clear of the harbour and on his way to find his husband again, he was becoming increasingly frustrated at the surreptitious glances from Paul. Couldn't they just look into each other's eyes? Would that be too much?

Paul meanwhile was taken aback and glared at his cousin next to him. He'd been used to ignoring remarks like this. If he didn't react, then they weren't about him, he felt. Just now, though, Tom so close he could almost taste him and José-Luis so recently off on his way to be reunited with Donatello, he felt a sort of defensive solidarity he'd not known before. He glanced quickly back towards Tom.

"Hey, look... We need to get back to the theatre as soon as, really..." he said, trying hard to sound neutral. Steve frowned a little and nodded his head. He assumed Paul was being a bit sensitive towards Tom Bright in the back. Steve wasn't worried about Paul that way. After all, he was an engineer and that was a really macho job. Tom, though, was in showbiz, and everyone knew that that type was a bit dodgy. He leant forward and turned on the car radio to cover the awkward silence. Jimmy Young was interviewing some Tory minister about the controversial proposals for the Local Government Act, something they kept calling Section 28. Steve swore and retuned to Radio 1.

When Steve parked up by the theatre, Paul thanked him for all his help. Tom noticed that Paul stiffened when Steve went to hug him. What now, he thought, they were cousins after all. Paul agreed to go over one evening for a meal in the caravan with his cousin's family, and even take a bottle of wine. When Steve suggested he could bring 'his young lady' too, Paul gave a quick laugh and briefly glanced over at Tom before looking away. Tom waited beside the car. It would be perfectly natural for them to walk back in together. Paul hesitated. In the car, and thinking about what José-Luis had said, he'd made up his mind that he'd take Tom's hand as they walked back to the theatre. That was all he could think of, but desperately hoped it would be enough. Or at least, a start. Turning towards Tom, something caught his eye across the carpark over Tom's shoulder, and he turned away again. He smiled briefly, frustrated once more, and wondering if they'd ever be able even just to talk things through. He stuffed his hands in his pockets and walked off alone into the theatre. He felt drained now, frightened that Tom would leave again, and very alone without José-Luis to confide in.

Tom stood on his own now watching Paul's back as Steve pulled out of the carpark and set off west towards the holiday villas. He wanted to cry out, he wanted Paul to take him in his arms and say "We did it! We helped our friend. He's going to Spain to be re-united with his husband at last. Now it's our turn." Instead, Paul was striding steadily back across the carpark to the stage door. Tom felt so unhappy. He wondered if José-Luis had been right after all. Surely if Paul really loved him as José-Luis said then he'd have shown some kind of affection. As it was, he'd just walked back into the theatre as if they were strangers. It was almost too much to bear. 'Give me a break!' he wanted to shout. He could feel the tears pricking his eyes. He felt like screaming and howling. Maybe it was all too much, and he was just too tired.

Something caught his eye though. Turning to his left, way across the carpark the other side of the boundary wall, he saw a group of girls waving at him enthusiastically. He wished he could have just slipped inside the stage door himself. He realised he owed it to them to go over, though. Slowly, he walked across the car park to give himself time to compose his thoughts again. Preparing to sign photographs or magazines, he fixed a professionally friendly smile. That might at least delay his heart breaking. A gracious and generous performer, he offered each of them a complimentary ticket. At least that way, they soon left him alone, chattering loudly as they walked away together into the centre of town.

"Why, Julia Dulwich!" Tom said looking up from the score he'd been writing on at the table centre stage, "What an unpleasant surprise. Oh, and I see you've brought your minders... just in case."

Wearing an emerald-green brocade jacket and navy trousers pleated at the waist, she had a police constable at each shoulder. She came striding onto the stage towards him, the two constables struggling to keep up.

"Where is he?" was all she said.

"Sorry?" said Tom, tilting his head slightly, as if he didn't know what she was talking about. Upstairs, Paul had been explaining to Terrence how to control the dry ice maker, and where he'd need to be above the auditorium to manage the spotlights, especially for the finale. He made sure that Terrence was well prepared, just in case, to manage it all on his own. They had come out to the guard rail when they'd heard the heavy footsteps cross the stage. Frances edged forward in the wings, Rob close behind her, both wanting a ringside seat for what they thought was about to happen.

"I thought he told her never to show her face round her again?" whispered Rob.

"He did," Frances hissed back, "that's why she's brought the pigs!" Rob was a little shocked but decided not to challenge Frances. The policemen were only doing their job after all. And judging by the look on their faces, they weren't enjoying it much right at that moment. For a minute, Rob wondered why they kept looking towards each other. But there were more important things to think about right now. He didn't want to miss a minute of what was about to happen on stage.

"I have an arrest warrant here for your little *friend*," she announced, making a gesture to signal quotation marks around the word 'friend'.

"Julia, if you have something to say, vile and odious

as it may be, then say it. Don't talk in riddles and keep us all guessing." Tom was calm, which made everything seem even more tense. The inevitable explosion seem even more threatening.

"I know you're being deliberately obtuse," she almost spat back at him. "But it won't help. This authorises me to take José-Luis Esperanza into custody." She waved the warrant triumphantly above her head before smacking it down onto the table. Danny flinched, just offstage on the opposite side to Frances and Rob, drawing a finger across his throat and miming strangling someone. Julia was clearly not welcome among the crew.

"Not you, surely," Tom queried, "but your little *friends* here?" He mimicked her hand gesture. Most of the musicians and dancers on stage backed into the wings. They wanted to know what was going to happen. But this was clearly a very difficult situation which might get out of hand at any moment. And as foreign nationals, they felt it safer to keep well away.

Julia leant on the table in front of Tom and was about to speak.

"Not sure that colour suits you, you know," Tom pointed his pencil idly at the brocade jacket. Without thinking, Julia jabbed her chin onto her chest crushing the jabot of her blouse to look. Frances bunched up her shoulders as if she was expecting a door to slam or something, waiting for Julia to start screeching.

"Look, I have reason to believe that Señor Esperanza," she spat, her distaste visible in every fibre of her body, "is working in this country illegally, that he entered illegally, and so we have to enforce the law."

"Well, *if* that were all *true*, I couldn't agree more," Tom looked innocently at her, relishing each moment. "Anyone know where José-Luis is?" he addressed no one in particular but anyone that might be listening.

"No," came Danny's muffled voice from off stage.

Tom smirked and shrugged his shoulders, "Sorry, love, can't help you there." He looked back at the score in front of him. This conversation, he was telling her, was over.

"I will take this place apart," she threatened, jabbing an angry index finger at him and barely controlling the pitch of her voice, "if you don't tell me where that little Mexican..." Colombian, thought Tom, looking up again with feigned surprise on his face; Spaniard now, thought Paul "...*deviant* is." Suzie walked onto the stage and folded her arms, looking quizzically at Julia.

"Ah, Suzie," Tom gestured towards Julia, "meet Julia Dulwich, she used to work for me... apparently. Julia," he smiled insincerely at her, "this is Suzie Bickerstaffe, she handles publicity for me. She's very good, you know. And so much nicer than her predecessor." Suzie stepped forward offering her hand, but Julia just looked her up and down and turned back to face Tom. "None of the problems we had with the one before," he added spitefully returning once more to his score.

"Pleased to meet you, I'm sure," Suzie wiped her hand on her skirt, "You get that jacket from Dorothy Perkins?"

"It's Jaeger, actually." Julia said without taking her eyes off Tom's face. Suzie pretended to be surprised. She only had a vague idea about who this woman was, but Julia's manner right now spoke volumes.

"I'll ask you one more time," Julia was now leaning

threateningly on the table in front of Tom, speaking very slowly and deliberately, "where is the little freak?"

Tom still didn't rise to the bait. "Freak?" he turned to the stage around him, "Any freaks here?" he asked. There were a few minutes silence. Then,

"Me!" Olwena stepped out of the wings, biting the thread from stitching a pair of Latin trousers.

"And me," said Frances, coming back on stage and folding her arms, staring at Julia. Others did the same. Danny took the opportunity to come over to stand with Frances and Rob. Even Terrence shouted: "And me!" which surprised Paul who turned round to see him leaning over the guard rail angrily shaking a fist. Tom kept his composure. He folded his hands across his chest, leaning back in his chair,

"Take your pick, Julia," Tom waved his hand theatrically in a wide semi-circle, as if introducing a group of friends.

"Listen, Tom bloody Bright," Julia was furious now, "where is he?"

Tom casually looked at his watch. "By now? I reckon Poitiers, Toulouse maybe? Or even..." Julia smacked her hand on the desk and glared at Tom.

"Now look, if you've let that greasy dago pervert escape..." she didn't get chance to finish. The policemen, who till this point had remained impassive, exchanged a glance, colouring slightly. Tom slapped the table hard in return, which made everything go quiet. Danny jumped. Frances glanced at Rob, who drew his mouth into a tense scowl. Julia and the policemen all straightened up. The two police officers backed away involuntarily.

"Enough!" he said and rose slowly to his full height, leaning on clenched fists. Julia took a step back. "What is it with you vicious, mean-minded, petty little people?" he started, visibly trying to control his temper in his turn, speaking slowly and deliberately so that everyone could hear each word. "What right do you... or anyone else for that matter," and here he turned to survey the stage, his arms outstretched, "to judge another human being? What does the colour of their skin matter? Where they come from? Or who they choose to love?" He'd moved away from the desk now and was walking in a wide circle to get rid of some of the tension. "Do you know what it's like? Do you know in your heart, what it's like?" His eyes were intense and directed at the floor, his head slightly inclined, and his hands on his hips. "Having nowhere you can feel safe? Call home? Where your partner's not safe. Where you're not safe. Where you don't even think you can trust your own family? There's *family values* for you!" Again, Tom flicked his index and middle fingers to emphasise *family values.*

"And why?" He looked up now. "Not being able to be open about who you are? Frightened to get close to anyone. Not even wanting to tell someone you love them just in case. Constant fear of being exposed. Or being rejected. Worse, being shunned because they're not like that. Or hounded by morally repugnant do-gooders like the Julia Dulwiches of this world, bristling with expensive synthetic fabrics that don't even fit." He wiped the back of his hand across his mouth. Without thinking, Julia adjusted her jacket. Everyone seemed to be holding their breath.

"And yet, think about it." It was as if he was talking to himself now. "You're not doing anyone any harm? You're just getting on with your life. You're discreet. You don't want to show affection in public in case it offends anyone. And then, they kill the love of your life!" There was an audible gasp from somewhere. Everyone knew he was talking about José-Luis, but hadn't realised that anything like that had happened, even if this wasn't now entirely true. "You know what's worse even than that?"

"What...", Danny had started to say, but Frances clapped a hand over his mouth.

"What's worse isn't death. *That* you can deal with, and everyone is sympathetic and understands and just wants to help. No, what's worse is when you risk losing the one you love – the one you've always loved – for a second time. And you just don't know what to do about it." Tom looked down at the stage. "When you never get to be with that person, just to try. Because both of you are too scared to say anything. Too scared of what other people might think. It's not true you know," Tom looked up briefly at an astonished Julia, "it's not better to love and lose at all. It just hurts too much. I don't think I can bear it a second time." Olwena's eyes widened, and she turned for the safety of the darkness in the wings. Luisa held her breath, mentally going over what José-Luis had written in his last letter.

Paul gripped the guard rail, his knuckles white. He bit his lip. He left Terrence at the rail, he had something in his eye, he said. But he could still hear all the shouting. 'At last,' he said to himself. Everyone thought that Tom had been speaking about José-Luis to begin with. Now, though, Paul knew that he was speaking about him, Paul Armstrong. He'd come back to Weymouth to find him after all. To try again. After the sense of relief, finding where he fit, he was afraid he was going to lose it all again. That would just be too much.

Paul didn't know what to think let alone what to do. He'd wanted to take Tom's hand at the seawall on the way back from José-Luis and the beach hut. But he'd felt guilty. José-Luis was clearly upset, and it was up to them to help him get to Spain. For whatever reason. It didn't sit right to be so selfish. Though it meant he'd have to trust someone so that they could help their friend. And then again in the carpark when they got back from seeing José-Luis off. Just to walk back together to the stage door. Imagining an easy conversation about how José-Luis was free now and would find his happiness. About how maybe it was their turn. See how things went from there. Yet again, though, the adoring fans had got in the way. He wasn't brave enough to try anything else, he thought. But he had to try again, though. He had to do something. Tom's words clattered round in his head. He knew what he meant at last. To be scared to admit you loved someone. Not just because they might reject you, but because they may be repulsed by you and your sort. He suddenly gasped silently and opened his eyes wide in shock. Was that what Tom had thought all those years ago when he'd kissed Paul? Paul felt sick again.

"We're all God's creatures," Tom continued, pointing at Julia now, who took another step back as if he'd actually poked his finger in her shoulder, the policemen moving back in turn. "We all have the right to be happy and to be who we are. We're all given chances in life, and we need to take them. Take a leap of faith." The two policemen looked at each other, transfixed but aware that the whole stage crew could see them. Not wanting to show any emotion.

"Well, all I can say, Julia bloody Dulwich," it was all he could do to contain himself. "If you ever have children, in your tacky little *normal* life, I really hope you will find a way to love them as they are, not as you want them to be. Not as you think would make them acceptable to your Tory cronies." He was running out of steam now. More through his own heartache than a lack of passion about what he'd started here, and the moral justification of what he'd been saying. "I hope you can sleep at night. You and your fucking hollow family fucking values." There was a hush round the room. "Damn you and all of your fucking sort, Julia sodding Dulwich... go back to where you came from, crawl back under your Tory low-life stone, and leave decent people to live their lives." He slammed the palm of his hand flat on table. He looked at her again menacingly. Everyone held their breath, wondering if he would actually slap Julia. Instead, he turned, paused just briefly, pinching his bottom lip and trying to hold back the tears. For a moment, he thought he could smell that familiar and longed-for scent. Keeping his head low but desperately wanting to look up towards the stage loft, he walked quickly off stage.

Julia was stunned. She felt she should say something. Put these people right about good, solid Conservative values. This was a lost cause, though. Realising that all eyes were on her, hostile and menacing even, she turned on her heels and without looking at any of the people she used to work with, she stormed out. The two policemen smiled weakly and raised a hand in a brief, apologetic wave to the people staring back at them, and sheepishly, they backed up a few steps, then turned and followed her off the stage as quickly as they could and out of the theatre, a barely noticeable flex of the fingers from one of them. As if they'd wanted to offer each other a reassuring hand. Carlos, who'd been sitting quietly watching all of this, picked up his bandoneon and started playing *The Harry Lime Theme*. Suzie was the first one to laugh.

"Nasty blouse!" she said as she turned round and went to see if Tom needed anything.

"Alright, alright, ladies and gentlemen," Rob was trying to bring some order back into things, "Remember we've got a show to put on tonight."

"Bloody Hell!" said Frances. She turned to Rob. "Are you thinking what I'm thinking?" She wiped her hand on Danny's t-shirt and nudged him in the back to move away.

"I don't know what I'm thinking," Rob answered. "But I'll tell you something," he added, glancing briefly and without thinking up to where Paul's workspace was. Frances followed his gaze.

"What's that?" she asked.

"They better get a move on. It won't be long before Tom and the rest of them are off to Bristol." Rob turned and went back to his desk in the wings.

"This is it," Suzie whispered to Tom in the wings, "Go knock 'em dead!" The previous two nights were just a dress rehearsal compared to tonight, the big charity gala. If they were anything to go by, though, Tom's return to Weymouth was an out-and-out success.

As Tom walked onto the stage, he glanced briefly up to the stage loft hoping Paul would be there. He wasn't sure, but he thought he saw someone. He walked straight ahead centre stage before turning towards the audience, his arms stretched out in a large, virtual embrace. Taking the mic from the stand and waiting for Jason to get the feedback under control, he smiled broadly and cast his eyes around the packed theatre.

"Good evening, Weymouth!" he shouted, "It's been a long, long time."

There was a lot of cheering and shouting. "Too long!" came from the back of the stalls. "We love you, Tom! We love you, Tom!" chanted from a hen party sitting in the dress circle.

"Thank you! Thank you!" Tom said, confident now it seemed. In his element. "And thank you, Gwen Frampton!" he shouted towards where he knew his mother was sitting and blew her a kiss. What Tom had missed was that Bob had come with Gwen too and was sitting next to her. Since Tom had sent the car to collect his mother and arranged a night's stay in Weymouth, she'd told her husband to talk directly with the hotel. And that Bob should pay the difference. Bob shifted in his seat now. His wallet had taken a hit, but looking round before the lights had gone down, he was only too aware that this was not the type of crowd where he felt comfortable.

"God," he complained, "these seats are so bloody uncomfortable. My arse has gone to sleep!" Gwen poked him in the ribs and looked sternly at him through the dark, telling him to keep quiet.

Up in the circle above, Pauline sat gloomily next to her husband, Peter Tipler, who despite himself was leaning forward in his seat apparently mesmerised by the whole thing. He'd spotted Ed Aldridge when they'd come in and, slapping him on the back in an over familiar way, asked him if he remembered him and Pauline back at school. "Of course," Ed lied and rushed off to find Amelia Mobberley. Meanwhile, adding to Pauline's annoyance, Charlie Donaldson was locked in a passionate embrace with Vickie, his latest fiancée, he'd announced when they all met up at the pub across the road. So neither of them knew what was happening around them. Down closer towards the stage, there were camera flashes from all sides. Gwen blinked back at her son as Carlos and the ensemble took up their instruments and began to play. Everyone loved it. Towards the back of the stalls almost swallowed up by a coach party of pensioners from Poole, Ed and Amelia were completely carried away by it all. This wasn't Ed's kind of music, of course, but this was special, he said. He'd wanted to tell everyone around them that he was the one who'd given Tom his big break. Amelia took advantage of the darkness to slip her arm through Ed's and nestle into his shoulder. Tom didn't disappoint, though. It felt good to be home after all, he thought. Mostly, anyway. He hadn't lost all hope yet.

After two and a half hours which seemed to fly by, Tom took the mic from the stand and walked to the front of the stage.

"Ladies and Gentlemen," he began, "and even Tories," there was a pantomime hiss round the auditorium, "I've got some news for you." He went to the wings and Suzie handed him a drink and a sheet of paper. He took a swig and then came back, standing centre stage once more. Reading from the paper, he said: "Thanks to *your* generosity, ladies and gentlemen, we have collected £5,000 for Dorset cancer charities." There was loud applause and whistles. Tom held a hand up so he could continue. "£2,500 for Great Ormond Street Hospital for children..." more cheering, "and £1,000 for local schools." There was a lot of shouting and clapping again. In the upper circle, people were drumming their feet. Tom waited patiently for the noise to die down enough for him to carry on. "And, ladies and gentlemen... there's one more," he said and there was a general shushing around the auditorium. In the wings, Suzie searched her pad for what Tom was going to say. As far as she knew, that was it. There wasn't another charity they'd collected for as the audience came in to take their seats. "We have raised £1,500 for the Terrence Higgins Trust," applause and stamping of feet again, "which I will personally make up to £2,500." There were loud cheers and whistles. Frances raised her eyebrows towards Suzie from the wings on the other side of the stage. She hadn't seen the Terrence Higgins Trust on the list in the foyer. Suzie shrugged her shoulders. She trusted Tom would not say things in public if he didn't mean them. Whoever the beneficiaries, the Tom Bright charity gig in his hometown had been a great success after all. Rob was sitting relaxed on his stool in the wings, trying to remember where he'd heard the name Terrence Higgins.

"Well, Weymouth," Tom said through a smile now not quite so broad and relaxed. The dry ice machine was starting to send vapour across the stage, lapping round his feet, and obscuring the musicians and backing singers further upstage. He didn't want it all to be over. To be heading off towards Bristol with no José-Luis, and no lover either, no husband, no best friend of his own after all. He didn't want to admit it, but he couldn't bear the thought of no Paul either. He scanned the audience.

"Well, we must do this again sometime!" Cheers and applause. Whistling from the upper circle. Peter Tipler on his feet waving and shouting, the sweat pouring down his back making his shirt stick. Pauline looked on in disgust. More camera flashes. Little pockets of "We love you, Tom" and "Encore!"

"We've come to a part of the show I've never done before." The audience were still making a bit of a racket, but already there were people shushing others. "Not even the last two performances ended like this!" There was general appreciation in the audience, enjoying the special treatment for the charity gala. "Tonight...," Tom went on, "and maybe for one night only..." Some people to his right laughed. "Tonight, I'm going to show you a Latin American dance that's not too well known over here yet. But, trust me, it will be big." He stepped back and accepted a glass of water from Danny. His mouth was very dry. "And we're going to be dancing to a track from my Spanish album which I'm sure you'll all remember..." There was random shouting from the audience. After a while, Tom shook his head. "No, you're all miles off. It's *¿Me quieres?"* The audience exploded once more. "See," he almost laughed, "You *do* know it!"

There was something about the way Tom spoke and played the audience. Frances, Rob and the rest of the crew knew he could sing. They'd heard it all through rehearsals and were always surprised at how amazing and fresh it sounded each time. They knew he could dance too which they put down to the hard work he'd put in with the likable José-Luis, whom they all now missed. What they hadn't realised, though, was just how close and intimate he seemed to be with his audience. Paul understood this quality. Paul had always loved him for this. He was never jealous of other people and how they reacted to Tom. It was something which had brought him out of his shell. From that very first, accidental meeting, Paul had been smitten by it. These past few weeks had shown him just how precious that was. How much he'd missed it in this half life he'd thought was enough. Tonight, the end of the short run, was going to be special.

"Let me set the scene. Our hero – played by me, of course," he takes a small, theatrical bow to more clapping and whistling, "Our hero is sad and lonely." A general 'aah!' flits around the audience. "Thank you! Thank you! So... sad and lonely, he stands looking down over the sea... that's what all this mist's for," he adds, swirling some of the dry-ice vapours with his foot. There's some pockets of laughter around the audience which soon subside. "So, he stands looking down into the sea, ready to end it all." Everyone in the wings looks at one another. This wasn't what he'd said in rehearsals.

There's a solitary "No!" from somewhere in the dress circle. "Thank you, Madam," Tom replies. He's smiling, but there's something about him, thinks Olwena, standing in the wings, clutching her favourite white hankie to her face. She doesn't want to miss this performance. And she's worried about this change of wording. Luisa stands next to Olwena upstage left, clapping her hands excitedly and quietly up in front of her lips. Her eyes sparkle in the reflected light from the main spot centre stage. At last, this is the finale they'd all been working towards for the past weeks. Last minute changes mean everyone is under extra pressure, but also excited. Not everyone, though, is in on the secret. This is going to be spectacular, though, all thanks to José-Luis. He's there even from afar. This would almost be how the Argentine Tango used to be danced, she muses. She can't wait.

"But then..." Tom's now milking this for all he can get, Bob thinks shifting uncomfortably in his seat and trying to make out the fingers on his watch, "a mystery lover approaches through the gloom." He looks stage left and someone shouts up at the stage: "I'll be there, Tom!" Again, Tom smiles, but he looks very tired to his new colleagues standing captivated in the wings. "A mystery lover approaches." Tom's hand slowly sweeps across the stage at thigh height, tracing the imaginary path of the lover with his index finger as they come towards centre stage. The lights all dim leaving a single spot on Tom's face. "They take each other's hands and fold their arms gently around one another. And, Ladies and Gentlemen, for the first time on a British stage... well, this one anyway... the lovers consummate their love in a dance called the Argentine Tango." There's loud applause again, whilst Carlos plays a few bars to get the mood right.

"Now, I want to dedicate this to a dear friend, José-Luis Esperanza, who put this whole thing together. Made it at all possible." Bob shifts in his seat. "Get on with it!" he growls, but Gwen kicks his shin, and he sucks in his breath. "Unfortunately," Tom continues, "he isn't able to be here to see this, but we love you, José-Luis." The crowd clap their appreciation for whoever that is, joined by loud applause and whistles from the wings, and the musicians on their feet clapping and shouting in Spanish. Tom looks out across the audience wishing not just José-Luis could be there, with Donatello, but that Paul was here. By his side. On stage. "And I want to dedicate it to someone very special to me. I don't know where they are right now. I know... I just hope they're close." There's a hush backstage. "But wherever they are at this very moment, I just want them to know how much I love them. I always have and I always will." Frances and Rob exchange anxious looks. "I know that now." Tom bows his head for a moment. Gwen edges forwards in her seat. The single spot goes out and the stage is in complete darkness.

As Carlos begins to play a short Latin American folk song, Tom rushes into the wings stage right to change trousers and shoes for the dance. He walks back to centre stage, adjusting his sleeves and stretching the legs of his trousers to stop them from riding up quite so tight. And now, Carlos begins the introduction, solo. As it comes back up, the lighting is still very dim. Somewhere a solitary spotlight picks up the reflective strips down each seam of the trouser legs as they catch the light. Tom turns, dead centre now, and prepares himself. He moves his head from side to side to flex the muscles, rolls his arms from the shoulders twice, then shakes them whilst hanging loosely at his side. The audience is completely silent. Waiting. Tom lowers his head. The bandoneon is the only sound in the whole theatre. Olwena dabs at her eyes with the J.B.-monogrammed hankie.

Through the swirling dry ice vapour, a figure appears from the wings, upstage left. Moving slowly and deliberately, ball flat, in perfect time with Carlos's music, they progress downstage towards Tom as expected, switching back and forth with perfect *ochos*. No one can see who it is. Tom, meanwhile, is waiting in anticipation. He and Luisa have rehearsed this many times, to make it right. It must be slow and sensual. It must express longing and desire, so that when the two meet and take hold, it is obvious that this is just what they'd both longed for. That they are deeply in love and destined to be together. To take the audience to places where they'd never been before through their dance. To show them what they'd never seen before, or thought could be this beautiful. But to help them understand that this is how they want the story to be. Exactly like this. For the lovers to be happy. That's all.

Tom is still looking down at the stage as a red, Cuban-heel shoe appears in front of him. Puzzled – this is a man's shoe like his own – he looks up briefly but can see nothing in the gloom. He can't swish the ice mist away with his hand otherwise he'd break the mood. The mystery dancer comes closer, then stops. Just at that moment, Gwen gasps noiselessly, a single tear slowly making its way down her cheek. She doesn't know whether it's surprise, relief, sadness or happiness. She lets it drip into her lap. She can't move in case she attracts Bob's attention. It's going to be difficult for Tom, she knows that, especially now. More difficult than it has been up till then. But she also knows that this was meant to be all along. He won't be alone anymore. It will all work out no matter what. And that's all she wants.

The music changes as the mystery dancer bends slightly into their supporting leg, while tracing a wide rondée with their right foot, perfectly balanced. Drawing both feet together and straightening the legs, they step forward, barely an inch away from Tom now. The audience gasp ever so slightly. Tom still can't see who it is. He's looking down, as they'd rehearsed, to his own right hand. He can smell something familiar, though. A scent he'd thought he'd forgotten, but which he's fallen in love with so many times ever since he's been back. His heart is in his throat. He can barely breathe. Slowly, Paul takes Tom's right hand in his left and raises their hands just above shoulder height. Sliding his right hand and arm under Tom's left, Paul lets his hand move lower into the small of Tom's back. Paul draws Tom close and rests Tom's left cheek gently against his right as Carlos finishes the introduction and, at last, the dance proper begins.

Printed in Great Britain
by Amazon

13690602R00203